PLAYS CHILDREN LOVE

VOLUME II

A TREASURY OF
CONTEMPORARY &
CLASSIC
PLAYS FOR CHILDREN

PLAYS CHILDREN LOVE

VOLUME II

A TREASURY OF
CONTEMPORARY &
CLASSIC PLAYS
FOR CHILDREN

Edited by
COLEMAN A.
JENNINGS
& AURAND
HARRIS

Foreword by
CAROL
CHANNING

ST. MARTIN'S PRESS
NEW YORK

 For information, address St. Martin's Press, 175 Fifth Avenue, New York, N.Y. 10010.

Library of Congress Cataloging-in-Publication Data

Plays children love.

Summary: A collection of nineteen plays to be performed for young audiences or by child actors.
1. Children's plays, American. [1. Plays—Collections] I. Jennings, Coleman A., 1933—
II. Harris, Aurand.
PS625.5.P54 1988 812'.008'09282 87-28696
ISBN 978-0-312-07973-4
0-312-07973-7 (paperback)

D 20 19 18 17

Grateful acknowledgment is made to:

Anchorage Press, Inc., for permission to reprint *Treasure Island* by Aurand Harris, copyright © 1983 by Anchorage Press; *The Wind in the Willows* by Moses Goldberg, copyright © 1974 by Anchorage Press; *Jim Thorpe, All-American* by Saul Levitt, copyright © 1977 by Saul Levitt and Harrison Fisher, copyright © 1980 by Anchorage Press; *The Forgotten Door* adapted by Gregory A. Falls, copyright © 1981 by Gregory A. Falls, copyright © 1986 by Anchorage Press; *Ride a Blue Horse* by Aurand Harris, copyright © 1986 by Anchorage Press; "How the Camel Got His Hump" and "How the First Letter Was Written" from *Just So Stories* dramatized by Aurand Harris, copyright © 1971 by Anchorage Press.

Dramatic Publishing Company, for permission to reprint *Charlotte's Web* dramatized by Joseph Robinette, copyright © 1983 by Dramatic Publishing Company; *The Wizard of Oz* by Anne Coulter Martens, copyright © 1963 by Dramatic Publishing Company.

Samuel French, Inc. for permission to reprint "The Bremen Town Musicians" and "The Golden Goose" from *Story Theatre* by Paul Sills, copyright © 1971 by Samuel French; *The Best Christmas Pageant Ever* by Barbara Robinson, copyright © 1983 by Samuel French, based on the book copyright © 1972 by Barbara Robinson.

Nellie McCaslin, for permission to reprint "Who Laughs Last?" from *Legends in Action, Ten Plays of Ten Lands* by Nellie McCaslin, copyright © 1945 by Row, Peterson and Company, copyright © 1986 by Nellie McCaslin.

Scott Meredith Literary Agency Inc., for permission to reprint "Giants" by Syd Hoff from *Giants and Other Plays for Kids* by Syd Hoff, copyright © 1973 by Syd Hoff.

New Plays for Children, for permission to reprint *Golliwhoppers!* by Flora Atkin, copyright © 1972 by Flora B. Atkin, copyright © 1973 by New Plays for Children, Inc.

Plays Inc., Publishers, for permission to reprint "The Three Little Kittens" by June Barr from *Children's Plays from Favorite Stories*, copyright © 1959, 1970 by Plays, Inc.

Lowell Swortzell, for permission to reprint *The Chinese Cinderella*, copyright © 1962 by Lowell Swortzell.

CONTENTS

PART ONE
Plays for Adult Performers

PART TWO
Plays for Children to Perform

FOREWORD
Carol Channing

"Money, you should pardon the expression, is like manure. It's not worth a thing unless it's spread around, encouraging young things to grow." This is the declaration that Thornton Wilder had his "Dolly Gallagher Levi" make in his play *The Matchmaker,* later to become *Hello, Dolly.*

Well, to me, literature is the "money" of the theatre and "it's not worth a thing unless it's spread around, encouraging young things to grow." The earlier we, as children, start reading and performing the classics, the richer our lives will become. What a blessing it is for us to have available a second volume of *Plays Children Love.*

An experience I had in the fourth grade in school led me to discover "the play's the thing."

You see, someone in my class nominated me for secretary of the student body. The procedure was that the nominee was to get up on the school auditorium stage and accept the nomination. I, as this nominee, was to tell my fellow students the reasons why they should vote for me. I could not think of one reason. I just stood there, onstage for the first time, panic-stricken. Now, I was an only child, so my delight was to move around my room walking, talking, and thinking like whoever I wanted to be. So, at this moment, I whipped into playing Miss Berard, the principal of the school, telling the students to "Go to the polls and vote for Carol" and ended with her usual whistle to quiet the auditorium. I heard my first laugh!!! So naturally I went on to portray whoever fascinated me either on the faculty or among the students. Standing there, with everyone consumed with laughter, I realized that this is closer than touching one another. This is closer than affection. These classmates of mine are willing to lend their mentalities to what I see in all these people. I suddenly realized that we are all alike. We laugh at the same things, cry, fall in love, with all the same things. I was no longer an only child.

I ran off the stage (amid gales of laughter, of course), into the cloakroom and hid behind the coats so that no one could see and cried for joy: "Oh God, I'll do anything to get back on that stage again. To have that close warm feeling of everyone experiencing an emotion simultaneously. Laughing *together*. I'll crawl across a desert with no water, I'll go without sleep."

My father was my confidante. When he got home, I told him about this tremendous experience. He listened and said "Carol, there is an old French adage that says 'Be careful what you set your heart upon, for you shall surely get it.'" Well, needless to say, I won the election and got to read the minutes each Friday (finding that I was living for Fridays). Whoever made a motion, I read it in his character, exaggerating what happened a little for the sake of holding the audience, but no one seemed to mind.

Then I learned that there is such a thing as a play! In a play, it is not just laughter that we all share, but any and all of the emotions.

I could not wait to become a part of the school theatre, to perform with my classmates, to try the characters on for size—*and* in a story! The story was what held the audience . . . whether it was the Princess in *The Birthday of the Infanta* or Toad in *Toad of Toad Hall* or Pooh in *Winnie the Pooh*. It was the play that was "the thing." It was the story that we were telling that excited the audience.

Little did I know that some day I would be recording children's albums, everything from *Winnie the Pooh* to Ludwig Bemelmans' "Madeline" stories. My son at the age of three learned to read while listening to records and looking at the words in the book at the same time.

Then at Bennington College I was exposed to Shakespeare, Shaw, Ibsen and Strindberg. I harkened back to my earlier days in grade school where I first learned the value of "the spoken word."

Later in the Broadway theatre, I was again impressed with the power of the "spoken word." It is the custom, before a production goes "out of town" to break-in for a Broadway opening, to have a "run-through" for fellow theatre-folk. These so-called "run-throughs" are without costumes, scenery, lights, or any of the usual theatrical accoutrements, just the performers on stage delivering their lines. It is in these "work-light run-throughs" that many believe the production is the most moving. It is with simply the actors and their lines that the audience gets the clearest message of the playwright.

Again I was reminded of the value of what we did on the grade school stage with my fellow classmates in exciting an audience. Yes it is stunning to produce a five million dollar Broadway production, but never let us forget that "the play is the thing" and that without the play, no amount of money can make it theatre.

Anita Loos, the creator of *Gentlemen Prefer Blondes* had her heroine, Lorelei Lee, announce that "Fate keeps on happening." Yes, "Fate" does keep on happening through the spoken word and the earlier we, as children, learn this, the richer our lives will become. To me, the theatre is a human necessity.

When I had the honor of being asked to address you readers of *Plays Children Love,* Volume II, I felt quite at home, because everyone I know in the theatre is a child . . . in spirit at least. We enter a world of "make believe" and we are in a realm more believable than life itself.

Scripts and Royalty Fees

Any group that produces a play for an audience, whether for paid admission or not, is required by copyright law to purchase enough copies for the entire cast from the publisher and to pay a prescribed royalty fee for each performance in advance. An address for buying scripts and paying the royalty fee precedes each play in this anthology.

INTRODUCTION

The term, "children's theatre," causes many people to think of elementary-school children acting in simple, fifteen-minute skits or playlets performed for the monthly Parent-Teacher Association meetings. This is not children's theatre. "Children's Theatre" or "Theatre for Children and Youth" is a production of a high-quality script, written and acted for the age level and interest of an audience of elementary or junior high school children. The play is produced for the children by adults or advanced students, who give it the same thorough attention and preparation that is given any of their productions for adults. This type of theatre that is written, acted, directed and designed specifically for children is a manifestation of the twentieth century, particularly of the last twenty years. Not only are there now more plays to produce, there are increasing numbers of better productions.

The ten plays in Part One of this anthology are scripts primarily meant for adults to perform for children.

Parallel with this professional approach to staging plays for children and youth is the idea that under certain conditions and with suitable material children can perform for each other. The ten plays in Part Two are script that children can perform informally for each other, using an improvisational approach to acting. There will, of course, be some cross-over between the two sections. Some of the shorter plays in Part Two are from the literature of plays created for adult performers. In some instances the children might want to create interesting scenes from the longer plays in Part One.

The introduction to the earlier anthology, *Plays Children Love: A Treasury of Contemporary and Classic Plays for Children* (1981), details an approach to theatre for children and youth, including rehearsal and production techniques, characteristics of the child audience, an improvisational approach to play production, and standards for excellence in production. The introduction to this anthology is a continuation of the suggestions set forth in that volume.

Selecting the best plays for any particular situation is usually one of the most difficult tasks facing directors and producers. In comparison to adult theatre the number of plays written for children is very small. Fortunately, however, today there are many more good plays to choose from than were available even ten years ago. Selecting the plays for an anthology is equally difficult as one tries to achieve a balance of types and styles of plays, both classic and modern. The process is further complicated by the fact that some excellent plays are not available for reproduction in anthologies. In searching for the appropriate play for a particular situation, a director should consult not only children's theatre anthologies but the catalogues of the play publishers. Several publishers are represented in this collection.

Excluding the numerous anthologies of non-royalty classroom skits and playlets, there have been only twelve major collections of plays for children published in the United States since 1921. Although these plays are primarily for adults to present for children, there are also a number that could be performed by children. These twelve anthologies are listed in chronological order as a resource guide for parents, teachers and directors/producers of children's theatre.

A Treasury of Plays for Children. Edited by Montrose J. Moses. Boston: Little Brown & Company, 1921.

Another Treasury of Plays for Children. Edited by Montrose J. Moses. Boston: Little Brown & Company, 1926.

Twenty Plays for Young People. Edited by William B. Birner. New Orleans: Anchorage Press, 1967.

All the World's a Stage: Modern Plays for Young People. Edited by Lowell Swortzell. New York: Delacorte Press, 1972.

Contemporary Children's Theatre. Edited by Betty Jean Lifton. New York: Avon Books, 1974.

Six Plays for Children by Aurand Harris, Biography and Play Analyses. Edited by Coleman A. Jennings. Austin: University of Texas Press, 1977.

Dramatic Literature for Children: A Century in Review. Edited by Roger L. Bedard. New Orleans: Anchorage Press,1984.

Plays Children Love: A Treasury of Contemporary and Classic Plays for Children. Edited by Coleman A. Jennings and Aurand Harris. New York: Doubleday & Co., 1981.

Theatre for Youth: Twelve Plays with Mature Themes. Edited by Coleman A. Jennings and Gretta Berghammer. Austin: University of Texas Press, 1986.

Six Plays for Young People from the Federal Theatre Project (1936-39), An Introductory Background and Analysis. Edited by Lowell Swortzell. Westport, Connecticut: Greenwood Press, 1986.

Six Adventure Theatre Plays. Edited by Patricia Whitton. Rowayton, Connecticut: New Plays Incorporated, 1987.

Wish in One Hand, Spit in the other, A Collection of Plays by Susan Zeder. Edited by Susan Pearson-Davis. New Orleans, Louisiana, 1988.

Fourteen of one hundred and twenty-nine plays that appear in these anthologies are repeated in two or more of the volumes. Only one script in *Plays Children Love,* Volume II, has appeared in a previous anthology.

The original publication dates of the twenty plays in this anthology range from 1945 to 1986. Some tell an original story; others are based on literature, fairy tales, myths, and fables. They are comedies and dramas; some realistic, others fanciful. Part One begins with the classic children's story *Charlotte's Web* and ends with *The Forgotten Door,* a modern space-age story.

Charlotte's Web by E. B. White, author of *Stuart Little, Trumpet of the Swan,* and other fine books for children, has been dramatized by Joseph Robinette in two versions: one, seventy-five minutes long, and the other, sixty minutes long. The shorter version is the one that appears in this anthology, since it requires a smaller cast, has greater options for doubling actors, and its sixty-minute playing time is similar to that of the other plays in the collection.

The enchanting characters from White's classic are here: Wilbur, the irresistible young pig who desperately wants to avoid the butcher shop; Fern, a girl who understands what animals say to each other; Templeton, the gluttonous rat who can occasionally be talked into a good deed; the Zuckerman family; the Arables; and, most of all, the extraordinary spider, Charlotte, who gives her life to save Wilbur.

In this beautiful, perceptive story about friendship the Narrator ends the play with the following: "Wilbur kept good his promise. He never, ever forgot Charlotte. Even years later, he fondly remembered his 'true friend and good writer.' Mr. Zuckerman took fine care of Wilbur all the rest of his days. And the pig was often visited by friends and admirers, for nobody ever forgot the year of his triumph. And the miracle of Charlotte's Web."

The Best Christmas Pageant Ever, by children's writer Barbara Robinson, originally appeared as a short story in *McCall's Magazine,* and, in 1972, was expanded to a full-length children's book which has sold over 800,000 copies. The author dramatized her work in 1983. The hilarious story is a memorable acquaintance with the outrageous Herdman children who, in discovering the Christmas story, help everyone else rediscover its meaning.

The six Herdman children are horrible. In fact ". . . they were the worst kids in the whole history of the world. They lied and stole and smoked cigars, even the girls, and talked dirty and hit little kids and cussed their teachers and took the name of the Lord in vain and . . . they wrote this really really dirty word on the back of Naomi Waddell's favorite turtle . . . with fluorescent paint, so it glows in the dark. When you can't even see the turtle, you can still see the word."

The plot concerns the efforts of a woman and her husband to stage the annual Christmas pagent despite having to cast the Herdman children, who have never heard of the story. Their involvement creates mayhem, but out of the chaos comes one of the funniest interpretations of the Christmas story ever, a heartwarming play in which the Herdmans surprise even themselves.

This delightful comedy is an alternative to the traditional Christian nativity story and, in many instances, would have appeal beyond the specific religious group from which it comes.

Golliwhoppers! is a collection of four American "tall tales." Dramatized by Flora B. Atkin, the folktales are: "Big Jesse Febold Ebenezer Chopalong," a backwoods tall tale; "The Sun Snatchers," an Indian legend; "The Knee-High Man," a black fable; and "Goll-Gollee-Gee," a mountain ballad.

In Atkin's introduction to the acting version of the play she notes that the stories cover ". . . a wide range of American folklore and delve into this country's rich cultural background. The four tales emphasize the main currents running through our heritage: pitting of wits against nature, common sense, optimism, personification of animals as tricksters and heroes, progression of extravagance, and reluctance to give wickedness its due. Regional colloquialism, dialects, dance and music provide an atmosphere of authenticity."

The Wizard of Oz by L. Frank Baum is certainly one of the best-known stories in children's literature. It has been dramatized numerous times for both stage and film. The Anne Coulter Martens' version included herein was originally dramatized in 1963. Each dramatization varies in approach, but the basic story line remains of Dorothy's meeting the Scarecrow, the Cowardly Lion, the Tin Woodman, and the Wizard as she seeks a way out of Oz and back to Kansas. The theme of learning that one's inner strengths are what really matter in life makes this an especially appealing story.

Many of Baum's other stories have been dramatized, but none have gained the popularity of this story, made famous by the 1937 MGM film with Judy Garland, Ray Bolger, Bert Lahr, Jack Haley, Frank Morgan, and Margaret Hamilton.

Treasure Island, as adapted by Aurand Harris, is an exciting theatrical treatment of Robert Louis Stevenson's novel. As a child Stevenson had been an avid collector of the popular Toy Theatres, and later in an essay, "A Penny Plain and Twopence Coloured," he described in vivid detail his lifelong fascination with the miniature theatre books full of cardboard figures, elaborate scenic backdrops, and accompanying scripts of adventure with titles that fired his imagination to a peak that the stories themselves could never match. Harris has, therefore, included stage and scenic directions throughout his dramatization of *Treasure Island,* to suggest a live Toy Theatre in the production of the play.

Young Jim Hawkins joins an oddly mixed crew aboard the HMS *Hispañola* in a hazardous pursuit of lost treasure. Conflict between good and evil mount, and Jim courageously faces danger as he learns that evil may well masquerade as good. During his adventure Jim matures from boy to man, helped along by all the famous Stevenson characters: the good Doctor and Squire, the sinister Blind Pew, the marooned Ben Gunn, the infamous Long John Silver, and a colorful crew of buccaneers.

The Wind in the Willows, Kenneth Grahame's classic animal fantasy, has been freely adapted for the stage by Moses Goldberg. The appeal of this book, which has survived generations, is due in large part to the endearing cast of eccentric human-like animals: a bashful mole, a loyal rat, a toad attracted to any new fad, and a wise old badger.

Toad, the wealthy, self-indulgent owner of Toad Hall, has discovered the joy of having a motor car, and, much to the consternation of his animal friends, drives it without having bothered to learn how. After several near-misses, his friends, Rat, Mole, and Badger, insist that he stay home for his own safety. Not so easily stopped, Toad borrows a police car and ends up in jail. While he is gone, the weasels take over Toad Hall. Only with the help of his friends is the vandalized Toad Hall restored to Toad—Toad who has a new enthusiasm: airplanes.

Jim Thorpe, All-American by Saul Levitt, with music by Harrison Fisher, was commissioned by the Alliance for Arts Education of the John F. Kennedy Center, where it premiered in 1977.

This play is a dramatization of the life of Jim Thorpe, a Sac and Fox Indian, football, baseball, and track star, winner of two gold medals in the 1912 Olympics and cited by King Gustavus Adolphus of Sweden as "the greatest athlete in the world." His life itself was drama: a sudden rise to worldwide fame, cut short by a tragic fall when, through an innocent incident, his medals were forfeited and his honors stripped away. Written with vivid scenes of athletic triumph and tribal pageantry, the play unfolds as a vision of the late Chief Blackhawk, the old warrior of the Sac and Fox tribe. The music is available from Anchorage Press.

Ride a Blue Horse, commissioned for an Indianapolis, Indiana, arts festival, is a tribute to their native son, "Hoosier Poet" James Whitcomb Riley. This original script by Aurand Harris begins on Riley's seventy-fifth birthday, 1924, which was proclaimed a national day of celebration in his honor by President Woodrow Wilson.

In the play the poet recalls his youth—the merry-go-round at the country fair; the old swimming hole; the painful dunce cap at the cruel village school; the bonfires of Halloween; an unforgettable little Orphan Annie; the Underground Railroad and the horror of the Civil War; and the medicine show where his poems first won public applause.

In addition to illustrating how Riley's poems were created from his childhood memories of place, people and dreams, Harris shows the plight of a gifted child coping with a universal problem—that of being different.

Interspersed within the script are parts of Riley's most famous poems, such as "Little Orphant Annie," "Knee-Deep in June," "The Old Swimmin'-Hole," and "When the Frost Is on the Pumpkin." By the close of the play this "different" child, who was "knee-deep in poems," has grown up to create very appealing works that paint vivid pictures of rural and small-town life in the nineteenth-century Midwest.

Dandelion is a prize-winning revue of songs, scenes, and blackouts created by America's most outstanding original theatre company for children, The Paper Bag Players of New York City. Founded by Judith Martin in 1958, the Paper Bag Players have won numerous awards, including an Obie, the New York State Artist Award, and an American Theatre Association Award. The Paper Bag Players were the first children's theatre company to receive a grant from the National Endowment for the Arts and to perform at Lincoln Center. Although based in New York, the Paper Bag Players are a touring company and have performed in thirty-two states, as well as Canada, England, Scotland, Israel, Iran, Egypt, Manila, Hong Kong, and Taiwan.

Dandelion is a humorous fantasy that tells the history of the world in sixty minutes, interspersed with ideas on the life cycle, evolution, and culture. The music by Donald Ashwander is available from the publisher, Baker's Plays. Also, Baker's acting edition includes illustrations for making properties and costumes from boxes and paper bags.

The Forgotten Door was adapted for the stage by Gregory A. Falls from the popular book by Alexander Key, originally published in 1965. In this modern space-age story, Jon, a boy from outer space, accidentally falls to earth and loses his memory. He does, however, retain his ability to talk with animals and to know what people are thinking. These special powers quickly entangle him in a suspense-filled plot that culminates in his escape to the mountains.

Jon is a likable, gentle hero surrounded by a cast of interesting well-drawn characters who variously aid or thwart his desire to go home. As the conflict swirls about the boy, many scenes allow imaginative, theatrical staging. The play, enriched by its underlying theme of universal brotherhood, will certainly become one that children love.

In each of the ten scripts the playwrights have suggested certain ideas for the design of the scenic elements and the staging of the action. The actual interpretation of the script will, however, vary from producer to producer depending upon the concept for any particular production.

Whatever approach is chosen, the producer/director must remain true to the meaning of the playwright's script. For children the most important part of any play is the story, and it is the director's responsibility to bring the story to life honestly, without condescension or cuteness. The director helps the actors create the characterizations in truthful interpretations, whether the characters are human beings, animals, inanimate objects, or fantasy creatures. Exaggerated, dishonest acting has no place in theatre for children and youth. This interpretation pitfall and other problems can be avoided if one starts with a well-written script.

As noted earlier, directors seeking the best plays for children should consult not only the available anthologies but the catalogues of the major play publishers. To receive permission to produce the best plays one must pay a royalty fee to the publisher, part of which is shared with the playwright. Usually the plays that require royalty fees are of higher quality than those that do not. All of the plays in this anthology have required royalty fees except for the ones in the public domain. The individual copyright pages should be consulted for the particulars for each script.

In good theatre for children it is essential that both playwrights and directors *show* the story through dramatic action rather than *telling it* through talk and static stage pictures. The director, along with the actors, must plan for continual, motivated movement illustrating the dramatic situations of the characters. Children are uninterested in dull, motionless scenes and become bored with characters who wander about the stage aimlessly, moving just to keep the production lively. Initially children may respond vocally to such running about, but their attention soon wanes and they lose interest in the play. One of the keys to successful directing for youth is to evoke interesting, believable characterizations from the actors as they move in continually changing stage pictures that illustrate the characters' motivations and enhance the plot.

In addition to bringing the play to life with actors and designers, the director must be aware of extraneous factors that contribute to a truly satisfying theatre experience. Examples of these important factors are: preparing the children in advance through study guides and discussions; performing in a clean, attractive theatre space; providing well-designed interesting programs; having an organized, efficient method of getting the audience in and out of the theatre; and suggesting follow-up activities for both teachers and parents. To be successful producers of theatre for children and youth, adults must respect their audience and be guided by the belief that only the very best is good enough for children.

It is also important in most situations to avoid introductory curtain speeches, intermissions, and the meeting of the cast after the performance. Necessary information, from theatre etiquette to specifics about the particular production, should be shared with the children before they enter the theatre. Curtain speeches often turn into dull lectures. The children are in the theatre to see the play, not to hear a lecture by a director, principal, or theatre mascot. Furthermore, curtain speeches often make it harder for the actors to capture the audience's immediate attention as the play begins.

The *playing time* for most full-length children's plays is fifty to sixty minutes, without intermission, an ideal length for holding the attention of the child audience. Intermissions stop the action and require the actors to regain and rebuild the momentum after the break. Intermissions can also be overstimulating when children leave their seats for the restrooms and drinking fountains. The practice by some groups of using the intermission as a time to sell candy and soft drinks, which inevitably return with the children to the auditorium, only detracts from the total effect of the production.

In adult theatre the audience does not meet the cast after the production, nor should they in children's theatre. Meeting the cast emphasizes autograph-seeking rather than a thoughtful reflection of the script and production. Viewing the actors and costumes close at hand can destroy much of the magic of the theatre—the illusion created by stage lighting and an appropriate distance. In addition, for many actors, meeting audience members is an uncomfortable situation.

The only exception to the rule of no contact with cast in costume is for a group of blind children. For them, understanding a particular production can be greatly enhanced if they touch the actors' faces and costumes before becoming audience members. The meeting of children and cast should be arranged before the performance, by invitation and in the privacy of backstage.

If a group of students is especially interested in theatre, arrangements may be made for them to have a backstage tour after the performance. These tours can be exciting, educational, and much more meaningful to the particularly interested than just seeing the actors in the lobby.

A study guide for the play prepared for teachers, parents, and children will enhance the audience's understanding and enjoyment. A typical study guide will include the definition of theatre for children, especially noting that it consists of a play *for* children acted by adults for an audience *of* children; a detailed plot summary; specific ideas to be presented before seeing the play; the design approach for the production; special vocabulary used in the play; notes about the playwright; a selected bibliography of children's books related to the play; and post-production questions, assignments, and creative drama activities.

Part Two of this volume contains playlets, plays, or sections of scripts appropriate for children to perform. In contrast to the professional productions of adults performing for children is the improvisational, informal method of working with children. In this form of theatre, the process of producing the play is more important than the performance itself.

In creative drama, or the improvisational method, the children hear or read the story, play the characters in a variety of situations, and then create the entire story. This process is repeated several times, with the children taking turns playing the various roles. It is important that they thoroughly understand the story and all the characters. After each enactment, the leader and children discuss ways their work succeeds as well as possible improvements.

Through the use of imagination, pantomime, and sound effects, all of these plays can be staged without costumes or scenery. If such support is desired, it is better to use simple props, costumes, and set pieces—preferably of the children's own devising—rather than attempt to recreate the "real" clothing and locales. It is important to capitalize on the young participants' creative thinking. Children will willingly accept any idea that is presented honestly in an exciting and engaging manner. Simplicity and imagination are two keys to success in improvisational staging.

If the children share their interpretations of the play with other classmates or their families, they should retain the spontaneous, informal approach to the script and avoid a final staged production in which lines are exactly correct in word and delivery and movement is carefully directed. Throughout the process the leader should act as a guide, providing encouragement and an atmosphere in which the children can create their own interpretations of the plays.

The ten short plays or segments from longer plays included in Part Two are ideal for children to create improvisationally. The old favorites, *The Bremen Town Musicians* and *The Golden Goose,* are from the full-length adult play, *Story Theatre,* by Paul Sills. In this script Sills uses a technique that became known as the story theatre method of dramatization in which the actors alternate between being a narrator and a specific character.

How the Camel Got Its Hump and *How the First Letter Was Written* are Aurand Harris's adaptations of two of Rudyard Kipling's *Just So Stories.*

Kipling's imaginative view of primitive man is first seen when the Camel, with his grumbling "Hump," is chastened by severe punishment into lightening man's burden. In the second story a child uses a crude drawing to send a message, which is widely misinterpreted and nearly precipitates a war. Later, we realize that the first letter has been written and all ends happily.

Nellie McCaslin originally adapted the well-known Polish legend, *Who Laughs Last?*, for her book *Legends In Action—Ten Plays of Ten Lands*. This story tells of a jester, who was thought to be dull-witted; yet he played a merry prank that brought him a fortune and baffled a king.

More than three hundred versions of the Cinderella legend have been known throughout the world, for the rescue of a poor but beautiful girl by a charming prince has universal allure. Lowell Swortzell has dramatized versions from three different cultures. One is *The Chinese Cinderella*.

An effective way to introduce children to Shakespeare is through one of the most famous comic segments of all of his plays, the rehearsal scene from *A Midsummer Night's Dream* (circa 1595). Bottom the Weaver and his fellow "mechanicals" have come to the wood to rehearse the "lamentable comedy" (a play within the play) of Pyramus and Thisbe. The exaggerated and stereotyped acting of the rustics under the guidance of the inept director, Quince, makes for high hilarity.

In *Plays from African Folktales*, Carol Korty has collected four stories representative of various regions of Africa. Each contains lively characters and reflects a spirit of humor and humanity common to so many African folktales. The trickster Mr. Hare, from Nigeria, in *Mr. Hare Takes Mr. Leopard for a Ride* is an antecedent of the American Br'er Rabbit.

Giants, from Syd Hoff's *Giants and Other Plays for Kids*, is a short playlet that children especially enjoy creating because the child characters cleverly outwit an adult "giant." Syd Hoff, whose books include *Henrietta, Danny and the Dinosaur*, and *The Horse in Harry's Room*, understands children and what interests them.

June Barr's dramatization of *The Three Little Kittens* captures the charm of this simple poem. The repetition, rhyme, and story line is especially appealing to kindergarten-level children.

Children also like plays that they *make up*. Two playlets that were written by children are included here. The difference between writing a story, which they had done, and writing a play was explained to the group. In a story you tell it. In a play you show it—with characters, dialogue, and action. They were shown the correct form in which to write a play. Using their own ideas, dialogue, and stage directions, the children wrote an opening scene for *Little Red Riding Hood* to learn the correct form.

SCENE I

SCENE: Kitchen. Mother at table.

MOTHER: *(Calls)* Little Red Riding Hood.

RED RIDING HOOD: *(Offstage.)* Yes, Mother. *(Enters)*

MOTHER: Here is a basket full of cookies. *(Wolf peeks in window at back.)* I want you to take them to Grandmother. But be careful in the woods.

RED RIDING HOOD: I will.

MOTHER: Stay on the path.

RED RIDING HOOD: I will.

MOTHER: Don't talk to strangers.

RED RIDING HOOD: I won't.

MOTHER: And if you get tired—

RED RIDING HOOD: I'll eat a cookie. *(Wolf licks his chops, and disappears.)*

After they knew the form and had experimented with dialogue, the children decided what makes a good play. *A good play has one main character who wants something. In trying to achieve this the characters encounter trouble—conflict!—which builds to a climax, and which is followed by a satisfying ending.* With the adult's guidance and encouragement, each child wrote a dramatization of the nursery rhyme, "Little Miss Muffet."

Little Miss Muffet
Sat on her tuffet
Eating her curds and whey.
Along came a spider
And sat down beside her
And frightened Miss Muffet away.

Since this rhyme would be performed by younger children, Miss Muffet could be either a Miss or a Mr. as both boys and girls enjoy playing the part.

The first question the children had to decide was who was the main character—Muffet or Spider? Two versions, composites of several children's plays, are given here to show that either Muffet or Spider can be the main character, depending on how the playwright structures the plot.

In the first playlet the Spider is the main character. His problem is that he wants something to eat. This will cause a conflict that will build to a climax and provide a satisfying ending. In imagining the main character, the children decided that the spider was a parent and to make the problem more desperate, there would be three children—spiders who are also hungry!

THE SPIDER AND MUFFET

CHARACTERS

Spider
First Little Spider
Second Little Spider
Third Little Spider
Muffet

SETTING

Under a tree. Bushes and a tuffet.

Spider enters, peeks about cautiously to be sure all is safe, then motions to First Little Spider. First Little Spider enters, showing by his/her walk and action that he/she is hungry. Spider beckons again. Second Little Spider enters, also hungry. Spider beckons again. Third Little Spider enters, showing he/she is the hungriest.

FIRST LITTLE SPIDER: Mama [Papa], I'm hungry.

SECOND LITTLE SPIDER: I'm hungry, too.

THIRD LITTLE SPIDER: I'm hungry—three!

SPIDER: I know. Four days and not a fly to eat. But today I will get you some food. I promise! *(Little spiders jump up and down and squeal, "Goody, goody, goody." Spider "Sh's" them. They freeze.)* Listen. What do I hear? *(Loud footsteps are heard off left. Spider creeps to side, looks, listens, hurries back to children.)* Someone is coming. Quick! Hide! *(Spiders quickly hide at right.)*

MUFFET: *(Enters at left, with imaginary bowl and spoon; sits on tuffet-stool and "eats".)*

SPIDER: *(Peeks out, sees Muffet, whispers to children.)* I smell food. I see food. I will get food for all of us!

LITTLE SPIDERS: Goody, goody, goody.

SPIDER: Sh! *(Children freeze. Spider cautiously, with high steps and a slow rhythm, creeps toward Muffet.)*

MUFFET: Ah-ha-ah-ha. *(Coughs loudly.)*

SPIDER: *(Jumps, frightened, and runs back to children; whispers.)* I'll get it this time.

LITTLE SPIDERS: Goody, goody, goody.

SPIDER: Sh! *(Children freeze. Spider again, cautiously, with high steps, creeps behind Muffet. Spider puts hands out for bowl.)*

MUFFET: A-a-a-a-chew! *(Sneezes loudly.)*

SPIDER: *(Jumps and runs back to children; whispers.)* I'll get it—for sure—this time.

LITTLE SPIDERS: Goody, goody, goody.

SPIDER: Sh! *(Children freeze. Slower and with higher steps, Spider again creeps toward Muffet. When Spider is ready to pounce, he/she gives a frightening cry.)* Boo-oo-oo-oo-oo!

MUFFET: *(Frightened, screams.)* EE-ee-ee-ee-eeck! *(Drops bowl and runs off.)*

SPIDER: Come, children, come. Eat! *(Little Spiders shout, "Goody, goody, goody," and run to bowl. All eat hungrily and happily.)*

CURTAIN

The second playlet uses Muffet as the main character.

MUFFET AND THE SPIDER

CHARACTERS

Muffet
Mother/Father
Spider

SETTING

Scene 1. In the kitchen.
Scene 2. In the yard.

SCENE 1

In the kitchen. Mother/Father and Muffet.

MOTHER: Here is a bowl of curds and whey. I want you to sit on the tuffet and eat it all.

MUFFET: Do I have to?

MOTHER: Yes, you MUST.

MUFFET: Why?

MOTHER: It's good for you.

MUFFET: It tastes ickky!

MOTHER: *(Overly sweet.)* I like it.

MUFFET: Then you eat it!

MOTHER: *(Becoming annoyed.)* Muff—et!

MUFFET: I hate it!

MOTHER: YOU WILL EAT THIS.

MUFFET: No.

MOTHER: Or there will be no TV tonight.

MUFFET: No.

MOTHER: No money—no allowance for the next week.

MUFFET: Please—

MOTHER: And you will be grounded—stay in your room for the weekend.

MUFFET: *(Gives up.)* All right. Give me the bowl.

MOTHER: That's a good boy/girl.

(Mother gives "bowl" to Muffet. Mother exits. Muffet walks to new area.)

SCENE 2

In the yard. A stool is at side.

MUFFET: *(Sits, looks at "bowl" and makes a terrible face. His/her actions, reactions, facial expression, and dialogue shows how he/she dislikes the food; tries, but can't eat it. It is a comic scene that also gains the audience's sympathy for the main character.)*

SPIDER: *(A hungry spider enters, smells food, sees food.)* Food! And I haven't eaten for two days. *(Starts cautiously creeping toward Muffet.)*

MUFFET: Aw-aw-ugh. *(Coughs and gags loudly with food.)*

SPIDER: *(Frightened, runs back, gathers his/her courage and again creeps slowly toward Muffet.)*

MUFFET: Oh-oh-aw-aw-w-w! *(Again Muffet makes a noise, groans, and gags at food.)*

SPIDER: *(Frightened, runs back. With determination, he/she starts again, and creeps slowly, cautiously to Muffet. Puts out his/her hands for bowl, and gives a loud shout.)* Boo-oo-oo-oo-oo!

MUFFET: *(Jumps, frightened at the noise, but turns and sees it is a spider.)* Oh, it's a spider. I like crawly animals.

SPIDER: *(Rubbing his/her stomach and eyeing the food.)* Food! Food!

MUFFET: *(Looks at Spider.)* Are you hungry? *(Spider nods. Muffet beams with an idea.)* Oh-oh! Would *you* like some curds and whey?

SPIDER: Yes! yes, yes!

MUFFET: Take it. *(Spider takes "bowl".)* Eat some. Eat some more. Eat it all.

SPIDER: Thank you. *("Eats" loudly.)*

MOTHER: *(Voice, offstage.)* Muffet! *(Muffet and Spider freeze.)* Is the bowl empty? Are the curds and whey all gone? [NOTE: The playwrights chose NOT to have parent ask: "Have you finished the curds and whey?" because Muffet's natural answer would be: "Yes, Mother." This would be telling a lie, and the young playwrights did not want this.]

MUFFET: Oh, yes! *(Muffet sinks on tuffet. Spider peeks out, and licks his lips.)*

CURTAIN

After the playlets were written, they were rehearsed and then performed by the students in informal productions either without special costumes, scenery, and properties or with props the cast made themselves. During the rehearsals the young playwrights saw the need and the importance of re-writing, which they did willingly and effectively. Upon hearing the applause for one's own made-up play, each playwright experienced that rare and satisfying feeling of having created something that others liked.

These two playlets help show that by using nursery rhymes, fables, or original plots, children, with encouragement and guidance, can write and perform their *own* plays—more plays that children love.

PART ONE

PLAYS FOR ADULT PERFORMERS

CHART OF STAGE POSITIONS

The abbreviations commonly used in noting stage directions appear in many of the scripts in this collection. The following chart of stage positions is provided to help the reader visualize the action of the play.

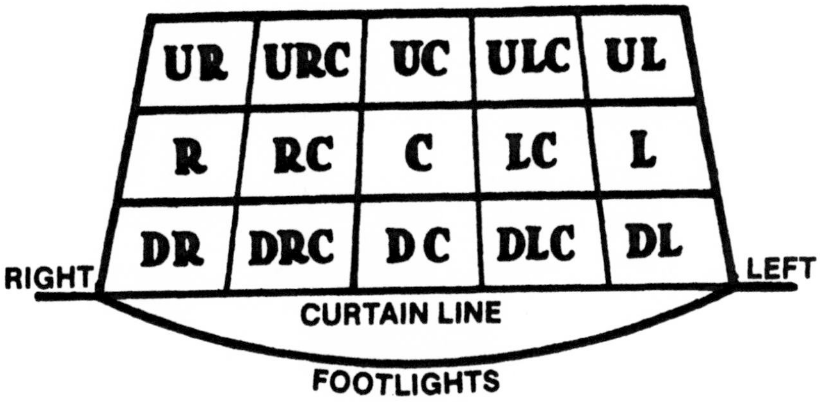

STAGE POSITIONS

Upstage means away from the footlights, *downstage* means toward the footlights, and *right* and *left* are used with reference to the actor as he faces the audience. R means *right*, L means *left*, U means *up*, D means *down*, C means *center*, and these abbreviations are used in combination, as: UR for *up right*, RC for *right center*, DLC for *down left center*, etc. A territory designated on the stage refers to a general area, rather than to a given point.

CHARLOTTE'S WEB

by

JOSEPH ROBINETTE

from the book by E. B. White

Adapted for small casts and touring groups

CHARLOTTE'S WEB

CHARACTERS

Fern Arable: A young girl
John Arable: Her father
Avery Arable: Her brother
Homer Zuckerman: Her uncle
Lurvy: A hired hand

Wilbur: A pig
Templeton: A rat
Charlotte: A spider
Goose
Gander
Sheep

Narrator

Extras: Reporter (Mr. Carter), Spectators, Judges, President of the Fair, Spider (off-stage voice), Mrs. Arable (off-stage voice), Uncle (a pig).

TIME

The Present.

SETTING

The Arable Farm; the Zuckerman Barn; the County Fair

AT RISE OF CURTAIN: *In darkness, the sounds of a farm just before daybreak are heard: crickets, hoot-owls, whippoorwills, etc. The sounds may be on tape or produced "live" offstage by the actors. The lights come up faintly as the Narrator enters.*

NARRATOR: *(To audience.)* Shhh! Listen to the sounds of the morning. Very, very early morning. So early, in fact, the sun isn't even up yet. Listen to the crickets . . . the hoot-owls . . . a frog down by the pond . . . a dog up at the next farm . . . And today there's another sound. It tells that something exciting happened during the night. *(Squealing of young pigs is heard offstage.)* Some brand-new pigs were born. *(Wilbur, a pig, enters in wide-eyed amazement.)* Here's one of them right now—exploring his new home. His name is—well, actually, he doesn't have a name yet. For the moment, he's still just a little pig. But as you'll see, he isn't just any ordinary pig.

WILBUR: Who am I? Where am I? I've never been here before. *(A beat.)* I've never been *anywhere* before. Everything seems so strange. But I like it . . . I think.

NARRATOR: The new pig has been born here at the Arables' farm. Before long, we'll meet the Arables. We'll also meet the others—the people *and* the animals—who will play an important part in the little pig's life. *(A beat.)* Now, where should we start? Wait a minute. We've already started. It's early morning. We're at the Arables' farm. Some pigs were born during the night. And the sun is just beginning to come up. For now, that's all you need to know. *(The Narrator exits as the lights come up full. A rooster crows. Delighted, Wilbur looks off in the direction of the sound. He excitedly explores his new environment until he hears offstage voices.)*

FERN'S VOICE: *(Offstage.)* Where's Papa going with that ax?

MRS. ARABLE'S VOICE: Out to the hoghouse. Some pigs were born last night.

FERN'S VOICE: I don't see why he needs an ax.

MRS. ARABLE'S VOICE: Well, one of the pigs is a runt. It's very small and weak. *(Wilbur looks about in alarm, then points to himself and mouths the word "me?".)* So your father has decided to do away with it. *(Wilbur runs to a downstage corner in fear.)*

FERN'S VOICE: I've got to stop him. *(Fern, a young girl, enters hurriedly.)*

FERN: Papa can't kill it just because it's smaller than the others. *(Fern sees Wilbur. She looks at him lovingly for a moment, then starts toward him. John Arable, Fern's father, enters from another direction carrying an ax.)*

FERN: *(Shielding Wilbur who cringes behind her)* Papa, please don't kill it. It's unfair. *(Wilbur nods vigorously.)*

ARABLE: Fern, I know more about raising a litter of pigs than you do. A weakling makes trouble. Now run along!

FERN: But it's unfair. The pig couldn't help being born small, could it? *(Wilbur shakes his head.)* This is the most terrible case of injustice I ever heard of. *(Wilbur nods. Fern and Wilbur fold their hands pleadingly.)*

ARABLE: Oh . . . All right. I'll let you take care of it for a little while. *(Wilbur collapses in relief.)*

FERN: *(Hugging Arable.)* Thank you, Papa. *(She runs to Wilbur and pets him.)*

ARABLE: You can start him on a bottle, like a baby. *(Avery, Fern's older brother, enters carrying an air rifle in one hand and a wooden dagger in the other.)*

AVERY: What's going on? What's Fern doing over there?

ARABLE: Your sister has a guest for breakfast, Avery. In fact, for a little while, she's going to be raising that pig.

AVERY: *(Taking a closer look at Wilbur.)* You call that miserable thing a pig? *(Wilbur turns his nose up at the remark.)* He's nothing but a runt. *(Wilbur tries to draw himself up in a "he-man" pose, but is not very successful. Avery laughs.)*

ARABLE: Come in the house and eat your breakfast, Avery. The school bus will be along in half-an-hour. *(He and Avery exit.)*

FERN: My very own pig. *(Wilbur smiles.)* Now, I have to name you. A perfect name for a perfect pig. *(She thinks for a moment.)* Fred. That's a good name . . . but not for you. Clarence . . . no, you don't look like a Clarence . . . Maximillion. Because you're worth a million to me . . . *(A pause. They both laugh and shake their heads.)* Maybe I'm trying too hard. Let's see . . . Barney, Herman, Lawrence, Newton, Morris, Warren, Willie, Wilbur, William— *(Wilbur nudges her.)* Wait a minute. Wilbur. *(Wilbur nods.) (Trying it out.)* Willll-bur. *(Wilbur smiles and nods vigorously.)* Wilbur. What a beautiful name!

MRS. ARABLE'S VOICE: *(From offstage.)* Breakfast, Fern!

FERN: I'm coming! I mean *we're* coming. Fern and *Wilbur*! *(She takes his hand, and they exit.) (The Narrator enters.)*

NARRATOR: Fern loved Wilbur more than anything. Every morning as soon as she got up, she warmed his milk, tied his bib on and warmed his bottle for him. *(Wilbur enters wearing a bib and sucking a bottle.)* Everyday was a happy day for Wilbur. He was very contented living with Fern and the Arable family.

WILBUR: I *love* it here.

NARRATOR: No longer was Wilbur a runt. *(Wilbur pulls himself up.)* He was growing each day. *(Somewhat cockily, he strikes a pose.)* In fact, he was becoming quite a specimen of a pig.

WILBUR: *(Flexing his muscle.)* I chalk it up to good, clean living.

ARABLE'S VOICE: *(Offstage.)* Suppertime, Wilbur.

WILBUR: And to good fattening food. *(Arable enters carrying a bucket.)*

ARABLE: Okay, pig, it's time you graduated from a bottle to slops. Skim milk, potato skins, leftover sandwiches and marmalade drippings. *(Wilbur repeats each item after Arable with growing enthusiasm. He fairly swoons as Arable hands him the bucket, takes the bottle, removes the bib and exits. Wilbur quickly "drinks" from the bucket, stopping occasionally to "chew.")*

NARRATOR: Before long Wilbur was five weeks old.

WILBUR: I'd say it's about time for a birthday party.

NARRATOR: He was big.

WILBUR: *Now* let them call me a runt.

NARRATOR: And strong.

WILBUR: Anyone for arm-wrestling?

NARRATOR: And healthy.

WILBUR: Check out the pink in these cheeks.

NARRATOR: *And* he was ready to be sold.

WILBUR: For a pretty fair price, I'm willing to— *(A beat, then with panic.)* Sold!? Oh, no! *(The Narrator exits as Wilbur drops his bucket and collapses.)*

FERN'S VOICE: *(Offstage.)* No, Papa, you can't sell him. You just can't. *(Arable enters, followed by Fern.)*

ARABLE: He's eating too much. I can't provide for him any longer. I've already sold Wilbur's ten brothers and sisters. *(Fern runs to the trembling Wilbur. She sobs and embraces him.)*

FERN: Oh, Wilbur. Wilbur!

ARABLE: *(After a beat.)* Oh, all right. Maybe we can call the Zuckermans. Your Uncle Homer sometimes raises pigs. And if Wilbur goes there to live, you can walk down the road and visit him anytime you like.

FERN: Oh, thank you, Papa. Thank you.

ARABLE: Come along. We'll call Uncle Homer. *(He picks up the bucket. Fern and Wilbur embrace in a great relief, then shake hands.)*

FERN: Can Wilbur come, too?

ARABLE: Why not? Maybe we'll let him make the call himself. *(He laughs as they start to leave.)*

FERN: It's not funny. He *can* talk, you know.

ARABLE: Oh, Fern. What an imagination! *(They exit.)* *(The scene changes to the Zuckerman barn. Homer Zuckerman enters carrying a trough and an armload of straw which he sets down.)*

HOMER: *(Looking about.)* Dirt, spider webs. That pig oughta feel right at home in this barn. *(Hammering is heard offstage.)* *(Calling off.)* Patch that fence up real good, Lurvy. We don't want the pig to get out of the barnyard! I'd better slide this door back so he can't get in there where the cows are either. *(He slides a sizable door at stage right across an opening. A large spider web is revealed behind the door as it is moved.)* I still can't believe we're going to have a new pig around here. But Fern seemed so desperate to find a home for it, I just couldn't say no. And she only asked six dollars for it. When that pig's big enough to kill and eat, he'll be worth a lot more than six dollars.

FERN'S VOICE: *(Offstage.)* Uncle Homer! Are you in there?

HOMER: Here they are. Come on in, Fern. *(Fern and Wilbur enter.)*

FERN: Hi, Uncle Homer. I'd like you to meet Wilbur.

HOMER: Oh, he has a name, does he? *(He laughs.)* Well, here's your new home, pig, uh, Wilbur. Hope you like it. Fern, your Aunt Edith just opened a big can of peaches. Let's go in and have a dish.

FERN: Okay. Thanks. But let me stay with Wilbur just for a minute . . . till he gets used to his surroundings.

HOMER: Sure thing. *(He laughs and exits. For a moment Fern and Wilbur look about.)*

FERN: It's very nice here, Wilbur. *(He smiles.)* And I can come down and visit you almost everyday. *(He nods.)* Now I'd better go. I'll see you tomorrow. *(They wave to each other as Fern exits.)*

WILBUR: *(After a beat.)* I know I'm going to miss living with the Arables, but this place doesn't seem too bad. It's a very large barn. And old, I'll bet. I like the smell. Hay and manure. Horses and cows. It has a peaceful smell . . . as though nothing bad could happen ever again in the world. *(A beat.)* Fern was right. It *is* very nice here. *(He yawns, lies down and closes his eyes. A moment later, Templeton, a rat, enters and regards the dozing Wilbur suspiciously.)*

TEMPLETON: *(Out of Wilbur's earshot.)* So, this is our new resident. That's right. Relax and enjoy yourself—while you can. Oh, yes. They'll treat you very well. And fatten you up very nicely. Then suddenly one day you wake up and— *(He makes a slitting sign across his neck with his finger.)* it's all over. Oh, well, I will admit it's nice to have a pig around the place again. That means leftover slops for me. I'm sure you'll find it in your charitable little heart to share your food with dear old Templeton. *(He chuckles with a sneer, then creeps away as he hears the Goose and the Gander entering. They circle Wilbur, studying him carefully.)*

GOOSE: Hello, hello, hello.

WILBUR: *(A bit startled.)* Who . . . who are you?

GOOSE: The Goose.

WILBUR: Oh. Hi, Goose.

GOOSE: And this is my friend, the Gander, Gander, Gander.

WILBUR: But I only see one Gander. You introduced me to three.

GOOSE: No, no, no.

GANDER: We tend to repeat, repeat, repeat ourselves.

GOOSE: Do you have a name . . . besides "pig"?

WILBUR: Yes. They call me Wilbur.

TEMPLETON'S VOICE: *(Offstage.)* Wilbur? That's a pretty tacky name, if you ask me.

GOOSE: Well, nobody, nobody, nobody asked you.

WILBUR: Who was that?

GANDER: Templeton, the rat. *(Templeton enters.)*

TEMPLETON: In person.

SHEEP'S VOICE: *(Offstage.)* What's all the commotion in here.

GOOSE: It's the old, old sheep. *(The Sheep enters.)*

GANDER: We have a new resident.

GOOSE: His name is Wilbur.

SHEEP: Oh, yeah. I overheard the Zuckermans discussing him.

WILBUR: *(Pleased.)* Discussing me?

SHEEP: They plan to keep you nice and comfortable. And fatten you up with delicious slops.

WILBUR: Oh, I *am* going to like it here.

SHEEP: Just the same, we don't envy you. You know why they want to make you fat and tender, don't you?

WILBUR: No, I don't.

GOOSE: Now, now, now, old sheep. He'll learn soon enough.

WILBUR: Learn what? *(A beat.)*

SHEEP: Oh, nothing. Nothing at all. Nice to meet you . . . Wilbur. *(He exits.)*

WILBUR: *(A bit concerned.)* My pleasure, I'm sure.

GOOSE: Well, I have eggs to hatch. *(She exits.)*

TEMPLETON: And I have trash piles to raid. *(He exits.)*

GANDER: Good—good—goodnight, Wilbur. Better get some rest after such a long day. *(He exits.)*

WILBUR: Yes, thank you, I will. The animals seem nice . . . I think. I'm not sure about Templeton. *(Another beat.)* And I'm a trifle concerned about the old sheep's remark. *(Slightly imitating Sheep's voice.)* "You know why they want to make you fat and tender, don't you?" . . . Well, I don't know. And the old sheep didn't tell me . . . Well, I'm not going to worry about it just now. I'm much too tired. *(He yawns, lies down and closes his eyes. As the lights slowly dim, Charlotte, a spider, comes out from behind the web. She carefully creeps over to Wilbur and smiles.)* [NOTE: If desired, Charlotte may remain offstage. If so, only her voice is heard.]

CHARLOTTE: *(Quietly.)* Go to sleep, Wilbur. Go to sleep, little pig. *(She crosses back upstage and disappears behind the web. The lights are low. Wilbur is sleeping.) (The Narrator enters, and noises of thunder, lightning and rain are heard. The lights come up slowly as Wilbur stirs.)*

WILBUR: Oh, no. Morning already. And it's raining. In my dreams I had made such grand plans for today. Let's see.

NARRATOR: Six thirty.

WILBUR: Breakfast.

NARRATOR: Seven o'clock.

WILBUR: A nap indoors.

NARRATOR: Eight o'clock.

WILBUR: A nap outdoors. *(Dejectedly.) In the sun.*

NARRATOR: Nine o'clock.

WILBUR: Dig a hole.

NARRATOR: Ten o'clock.

WILBUR: Fill up the hole.

NARRATOR: Eleven o'clock.

WILBUR: Just stand still and watch the flies. And the bees and the swallows.

NARRATOR: Twelve noon.

WILBUR: Lunch.

NARRATOR: One o'clock.

WILBUR: Sleep.

NARRATOR: Two o'clock.

WILBUR: Scratch itchy places by rubbing against the fence.

NARRATOR: Three o'clock.

WILBUR: A visit from Fern.

NARRATOR: Four o'clock.

WILBUR: Supper.

NARRATOR: And four thirty on—

WILBUR: Freetime! *(A pause.)* I get everything all beautifully planned out, and it has to go and rain. *(After a final outburst of thunder and lightning, the Narrator exits.)* I'm lonesome. And I know Fern won't come in such bad weather. Oh, *honestly*. I'm less than two months old and already I'm tired of living. *(Lurvy enters carrying a bucket. He wears a raincoat and hat.)*

LURVY: Morning, pig. My name's Lurvy. I'm Mr. Zuckerman's helper. I'm the one that feeds you. Time for breakfast now. Skim milk, bits of doughnuts, wheatcakes with maple syrup and custard pudding with raisins. *(He "pours" the slops into the trough.)* Yes sir, a meal fit for a pig! *(Wilbur sniffs it, then turns away.)* What's wrong with you? *(A beat.)* We must have a sick pig here. *(Calling offstage.)* Mr. Zuckerman! Come out to the barn. *(He exits.)*

WILBUR: It does look delicious. But I don't want food. I want love. I want a friend. Someone who will play with me.

CHARLOTTE'S VOICE: *(Offstage.)* Do you want a friend, Wilbur? I'll be a friend to you. I watched you all night and I like you.

WILBUR: Where are you? And *who* are you?

HOMER'S VOICE: *(Offstage.)* I think this will do the trick, Lurvy. *(Homer, carrying a container and a spoon, and Lurvy enter.)*

HOMER: Now he won't like this medicine, so you hold him and I'll feed it to him. *(Lurvy grabs Wilbur who protests.)* Come on, boy. This is sulphur and molasses. It'll cure what ails you.

LURVY: Okay, dose him up, Mr. Zuckerman. *(Homer gives Wilbur, who gags, a spoonful of medicine.)*

HOMER: There, that wasn't so bad, was it? *(Wilbur makes a face and nods vigorously.)* I think I'll give you a second dose just for good measure. *(He forces another spoonful down Wilbur who gags again.)* Good work, Lurvy. That pig will be well in no time. *(He and Lurvy exit. Wilbur catches his breath and clears his throat.)*

WILBUR: Attention, please! Will the party who just spoke to me make himself or herself known. *(A pause.)* Please tell me where you are if you are my friend.

CHARLOTTE: *(Entering.)* Salutations.

WILBUR: *(excitedly.)* Oh, hello. What are salutations?

CHARLOTTE: It's a fancy way of saying "hello."

WILBUR: Oh. And salutations to you, too. Very pleased to meet you. What is your name, please? May I have your name?

CHARLOTTE: My name is Charlotte.

WILBUR: Charlotte what?

CHARLOTTE: Charlotte A. Cavatica. I'm a spider.

WILBUR: I think you're beautiful.

CHARLOTTE: Thank you.

WILBUR: And your web is beautiful, too.

CHARLOTTE: It's my home. I know it looks fragile. But it's really very strong. It protects me. And I trap my food in it.

WILBUR: I'm so happy you'll be my friend. In fact, it restores my appetite. *(He begins to eat from the trough.)* Will you join me?

CHARLOTTE: No, thank you. My breakfast is waiting for me on the other side of my web.

WILBUR: Oh. What are you having?

CHARLOTTE: A fly. I caught it this morning.

WILBUR: *(Choking.)* You eat . . . flies?

CHARLOTTE: And bugs. Actually, I drink their blood.

WILBUR: Ugh!

CHARLOTTE: That's the way I'm made. I can't help it. Anyway, if I didn't catch insects and eat them, there would soon be so many, they'd destroy the earth, wipe out everything.

WILBUR: Really? I wouldn't want *that* to happen. Perhaps your web is a good thing after all.

CHARLOTTE: Now, if you'll excuse me. I'm going to have my breakfast. *(She exits behind the web.)*

WILBUR: *(With uncertainty.)* Well, I've got a new friend, all right. But Charlotte is . . . brutal, I think. And bloodthirsty. How can I learn to like her, even though she is pretty, and very clever, it seems. *(He glances back at the web, then slowly lies down. The Narrator enters.)*

NARRATOR: Wilbur was suffering the doubts and fears that often go with finding a new friend. But as the days passed by, he slowly discovered that Charlotte had a kind heart and that she was loyal and true. *(A beat.)* Spring soon became summer. The early summer days on a farm are the happiest and fairest of the year. Lilacs and apple blossoms bloom. The days grow warm and soft. And now that school was over, Fern could visit the barn almost everyday. *(He exits as Fern enters. The Sheep, Templeton and Charlotte enter and greet her with animal sounds which soon give way to clear voices.)*

FERN: Hi, everybody! *(She sits on a stool.)* Wilbur, here's a little piece of pineapple-upside-down cake for you. *(He applauds, takes it and begins to eat.)*

CHARLOTTE: *(On a perch near the web, looking offstage.)* Attention, everyone. I have an announcement. After four weeks of unremitting effort on the part of our friend, the Goose, the goslings have arrived. *(All applaud as the Goslings chirp offstage.)* We're very happy for the mother. And the father is to be congratulated, too.

GANDER'S VOICE: *(Offstage.)* Thank you. Thank you. Thank you. We're as pleased as can be, be, be.

WILBUR: What a wonderful day. Brand new goslings *and* pineapple-upside-down cake.

TEMPLETON: By the way, Wilbur, I overheard the Zuckermans talking about all the weight you're putting on. They're very happy.

WILBUR: Good.

SHEEP: You know why they're happy, don't you?

WILBUR: You asked me that once before, but you didn't tell me why.

CHARLOTTE: Now, now, old sheep.

SHEEP: He has to know sometime.

WILBUR: Know what?

SHEEP: Wilbur, I don't like to spread bad news. But they're fattening you up because they're going to kill you.

WILBUR: *(Dismayed.)* They're going to *what*? *(Fern is rigid on her stool.)*

SHEEP: Kill you. Turn you into smoked bacon and ham. It'll happen when the weather turns cold. It's a regular conspiracy.

WILBUR: Stop! I don't want to die. I want to stay with all my friends. I want to breathe the beautiful air and lie in the beautiful sun.

SHEEP: You're certainly making a beautiful noise. If you don't mind, I think I'll go outside where it's quieter. *(He exits.)*

WILBUR: But I don't want to die.

CHARLOTTE: Wilbur, quiet down. *(A beat as Wilbur tries to control himself.)* You shall not die.

WILBUR: What? Who's going to save me?

CHARLOTTE: I am.

WILBUR: How?

CHARLOTTE: That remains to be seen. *(The Gander enters.)*

GANDER: Excuse me, excuse me, excuse me. But all this noise is keeping the goslings awake.

CHARLOTTE: We'll try to keep it down. By the way, how many goslings are there?

GANDER: Seven.

TEMPLETON: I thought there were eight eggs. What happened to the other egg?

GANDER: It didn't hatch. It was a dud, I guess.

TEMPLETON: Can I have it?

GANDER: Certainly, -ertainly, -ertainly. Add it to your nasty collection. *(Templeton exits.)* Imagine wanting a junky, -unky, -unky old rotten egg.

CHARLOTTE: *(Laughing lightly.)* A rat is a rat. But, my friends, let's hope that egg never breaks. A rotten egg is a regular stink bomb. *(Templeton enters with the egg.)*

TEMPLETON: Don't worry. I won't break it. I handle stuff like this all the time.

AVERY'S VOICE: *(Offstage.)* Fern!

FERN: In here, Avery. *(Templeton sets the egg down by the trough and exits hurriedly.)*

AVERY: *(Entering.)* Mother sent me to get you. You're going to miss supper.

FERN: Coming. Bye, everybody. And thank you, Charlotte, for whatever it is you're going to do to save Wilbur.

AVERY: Who's Charlotte?

FERN: The spider over there.

AVERY: It's tremendous! *(He picks up a stick.)*

FERN: Leave it alone.

AVERY: That's a fine spider, and I'm going to capture it. *(He advances toward Charlotte.)*

FERN: You stop it, Avery.

AVERY: I want that spider. *(She grabs the stick, and they fight over it.)* Let go of my stick, Fern!

FERN: Stop it! Stop it, I say! *(Wilbur waves to Fern that he has an idea. He rushes behind Avery and kneels, then makes a "pushing" motion with his hands. Fern pushes Avery over Wilbur, and Avery falls into the trough. The Gander exits.)*

AVERY: Help!

FERN: I warned you, Avery.

AVERY: That's not fair. You and Wilbur ganged up on me.

FERN: *(Wrinkling her nose.)* What's that smell?

AVERY: I think we broke a rotten egg. Goodnight, what a stink! Let's get out of here. *(He and Fern quickly exit.)*

TEMPLETON: *(Emerging from his hiding place.)* My beloved egg. *(He gathers the pieces and exits crying.)*

CHARLOTTE: I'm glad that's over. I hope the smell will go away soon. *(A pause.)*

WILBUR: Charlotte?

CHARLOTTE: Yes.

WILBUR: Were you serious when you promised you would keep them from killing me?

CHARLOTTE: I've never been more serious in my life.

WILBUR: How are you going to save me?

CHARLOTTE: Well, I really don't know. But I want you to get plenty of sleep and stop worrying. And I want you in bed without delay. *(He stretches out on the straw as the lights begin to dim.)*

WILBUR: Okay. Goodnight, Charlotte.

CHARLOTTE: Goodnight, Wilbur. *(A pause.)*

WILBUR: Thank you, Charlotte.

CHARLOTTE: Goodnight. *(The barn is now in shadows. Wilbur falls asleep.)* What to do. What to do. I promised to save his life, and I am determined to keep that promise. But how? *(A pause.)* Wait a minute. The way to save Wilbur is to play a trick on Zuckerman. If I can fool a bug, I can surely fool a man. People are not as smart as bugs. *(A beat.)* Of course. That's it. This will not be easy, but it must be done. *(She turns her back to the audience.)*

First, I tear a section out of the web and leave an open space in the middle. Now, I shall weave new threads to take the place of the ones I removed. *(She chants slightly.)*

Swing spinnerets.
Let out the thread.
The longer it gets,
The better it's read.

(She begins to "write" with elaborate movements, though her actions are deliberately indistinguishable.) Attach, girl. Attach. Payout line. Descend. Complete the curve. Easy now. That's it. Back up. Take your time. Now tie it off. Good. *(She chants.)*

The message is spun.
I've come to the end.
The job that I've done,
Is all for my friend.

(She steps aside as a special light reveals the words "Some Pig" written in the web. [NOTE: The center part of the web may be affixed with velcro to the rest of the web. It can then be pulled off and discreetly discarded by Charlotte. Underneath would be the now-exposed writing which is similarly velcroed over the next writing, and so on.] *(Reading aloud.)* "Some Pig." *(She smiles.)* Not bad, old girl, for the first time around. But it *was* quite exhausting. I'd better catch a little nap before daybreak. *(She exits behind the web. The lights begin to brighten as a rooster crows. Wilbur begins to stir. He is having a bad dream.)*

WILBUR: No, no. Please don't. Stop! *(He wakes up.)* Oh, my goodness. That was a terrible dream. There were men with guns and knives coming out here to take me away. *(Lurvy enters carrying a bucket. Wilbur retreats slightly.)*

LURVY: Here you go, pig. Breakfast. Lots of good leftovers today. *(He sets down the bucket.)* Absolutely de—de— *(He sees the writing in the web.)* What's that? I'm seeing things. *(Calling offstage.)* Mr. Zuckerman! Mr. Zuckerman! I think you'd better come out to the pig pen quick! *(He exits hurriedly.)*

WILBUR: *(Unaware of the writing in the web.)* What did he see? There's nothing here but me. *(He feels himself.)* That's it. He saw me! He saw that I'm big and healthy and—and ready to be made into . . . ham. They're coming out here right now with guns and knives. I just know it. What can I do! *(A beat.)* Wait! The fence that Lurvy patched up. Maybe it's loose again. I have to get out. I have no choice. It's either freedom . . . or the frying pan. *(He sees the bucket.)* But first, a little sustenance. *(He drinks from the bucket.)* Now, I'm ready. I'm breaking out of this prison. They'll never take me alive! *(A beat.)* They'll never take me dead, either. *(Another beat.)* What am I saying? I've got to get out of here. *(He starts to rush offstage.)* Chaaarrrge! *(He exits running. A crash is heard offstage.)*

CHARLOTTE: *(Entering, yawning.)* What was that? Wilbur, where are you?

WILBUR'S VOICE: *(Offstage.)* I'm free.

HOMER'S VOICE: *(Offstage.)* Now, Lurvy, what could be so important that you had to drag me out here before I've finished—

LURVY'S VOICE: *(Offstage.)* You'll see, Mr. Zuckerman. You'll see. *(They enter.)*

HOMER: All I can see is—the pig's not here!

LURVY: What?

HOMER: Look out there in the chicken yard. *(He points offstage.)* He's escaped. Let's go!

LURVY: But . . . look at the spider web, Mr. Zuckerman.

HOMER: No time right now. Gotta catch that pig. *(They exit.)*

HOMER'S VOICE: *(Offstage.)* Head him into the corner, Lurvy. Run him back this way!

CHARLOTTE: Oh, no. *(The Goose and Gander enter.)*

GANDER: What—what—what's all the fuss?

GOOSE: There's so much noise, noise, noise—

GANDER: The goslings can't sleep. *(Offstage noises are heard. Wilbur enters being chased by Homer and Lurvy.)*

GOOSE AND GANDER: *(Cheering Wilbur.)* Go, go, go, Wilbur! Don't let them catch you! Run, run, run! *(Wilbur does a U-turn and exits again, eluding his chasers who also exit. The chase is heard offstage.)*

CHARLOTTE: Now stop this! Don't encourage him. If Wilbur does escape, he'll never stand a chance in the outside world. So, if he runs through here again, we've got to stop him. *(The chase is heard coming closer.)* Get set! Here he comes.

WILBUR: *(As he enters running.)* I'll make it this time! I saw an open gate that leads to the woods. Thank you, everybody, for all your— *(The Goose and Gander tackle him and hold him down.)* What is this? Even my friends have turned against me! *(Homer and Lurvy are heard offstage. Wilbur squirms as he is held down.)* I'll not go down without a fight! I'll struggle all the way to the butcher block! I won't be bacon for anybody! *(Homer and Lurvy enter breathlessly. The Goose and Gander quickly let go of Wilbur whose bravado quickly disappears as he cowers.)*

HOMER: Well, you certainly gave us a run for our—

LURVY: Mr. Zuckerman. Mr. Zuckerman. Look! This is what I wanted to show you. *(He points to the web. They ALL stare at it for a moment. Wilbur, the Goose and Gander see it, too.)*

HOMER: *(Amazed.)* A miracle has happened on this farm.

LURVY: A miracle.

HOMER: "SOME PIG." I don't believe it. *(Wilbur begins to regain his confidence.)* You'd better hurry and take care of the chores, Lurvy.

LURVY: Sure thing, Mr. Zuckerman. *(He exits.)*

HOMER: I'm sure we'll have lots of visitors today when word of this leaks out. I've got to call the minister right away and tell him about this miracle. Then I'll call the Arables. But first, I've got to tell Edith. She'll never believe this. Edith! Edith! *(He exits. Wilbur, the Goose and Gander applaud and congratulate Charlotte.)*

WILBUR: *(Himself again.)* Oh, Charlotte. Thank you, thank you, thank you.

CHARLOTTE: It seems to have worked. At least for the present. But if we are to save Wilbur's life, I will have to write more words in the web. And I need new ideas. Any suggestions?

GANDER: How, how, how about "PIG SUPREME"?

CHARLOTTE: No good. It sounds like a rich dessert.

GOOSE: How about "terrific, terrific, terrific"?

CHARLOTTE: Cut that down to one terrific and it will do very nicely. I think it might impress Zuckerman. How do you spell "terrific"?

GANDER: I think it's tee, double ee, double rr, double eye, double ff, double eye, double see, see, see, see, see.

CHARLOTTE: What kind of acrobat do you think I am?

GANDER: Sorry, sorry, sorry.

CHARLOTTE: I'll spell the word the best way I can. *(The Goslings are heard chirping offstage.)*

GANDER: The goslings are hungry. I have to go find some worms, worms, worms, to feed them. *(He exits.)*

GOOSE: He's such a good provider. *(She exits.)*

WILBUR: *(Looking at the web.)* "Some Pig." That may just save my life.

CHARLOTTE: For a while, I hope. But I need more words. Maybe Templeton can help. Where is he?

WILBUR: Probably sleeping next door. *(Calling out.)* Templeton, are you asleep in there?

TEMPLETON: *(Entering.)* How can anybody sleep with all this racket?

WILBUR: Did you see the message in the web?

TEMPLETON: It was there when I went out this morning. It's no big deal.

CHARLOTTE: It was a big deal to Zuckerman. Now I need new ideas. When you go to the dump, bring back a clipping from a magazine. It will help save Wilbur's life.

TEMPLETON: Let him die. I should worry.

SHEEP: You'll worry next winter when Wilbur is dead and nobody comes down here with a nice pail of slops.

TEMPLETON: *(After a beat.)* I'll bring back a magazine clipping.

CHARLOTTE: Thank you. *(A beat.)* Tonight, I will tear my web apart and write "Terrific." Now go out into the yard and lie in the sun, Wilbur. I need a little rest. I was up all night.

WILBUR: *(Leaving.)* Thank you, Charlotte. You're the best friend a pig ever had. *(He exits.)*

CHARLOTTE: *(Smiling to herself.)* Some pig. *Some pig. (She lies down for a nap as the lights fade.) (The Narrator enters.)*

NARRATOR: As the day went on, the news about the words in Charlotte's web began to spread throughout the county. People came from miles around to see the words on the web. News of the wonderful pig spread clear up into the hills where the farmers talked about the miraculous animal on Zuckerman's farm. Charlotte knew there would be even more visitors the next day. So that night, while the other creatures slept, she began to work on her web. *(Charlotte rises and begins to work.)*

CHARLOTTE:

Swing spinnerets.
Let out the thread.
The longer it gets.
The better it's read.

(She begins to "write.")

NARRATOR: Spinning and weaving, she began to form the new letters. Again, she talked to herself as though to cheer herself on.

CHARLOTTE: Descend. Payout line. Whoa, girl. Steady. Now for the R.

NARRATOR: On through the night the spider worked at her difficult task. It was nearly morning when she finished.

CHARLOTTE:

The message is spun.
I've come to the end.
The job that I've done,
Is all for my friend.

NARRATOR: She then ate a small bug she was saving. *(Charlotte mimes eating a bug.)* After that, she crawled behind the web and fell asleep. *(Charlotte exits behind the web as the Narrator exits. A light comes up on the web to reveal the word "Terrific." A moment later, Wilbur enters yawning.)*

WILBUR: I can't believe I spent the entire day *and* night outside sleeping. Oh, well. It's very refreshing. Especially in the summer.

LURVY: *(Entering with a bucket.)* I'm afraid to look. I know it can't happen again. *(He looks at the web.)* But it did! "TERRIFIC." Another miracle! Mr. Zuckerman! Come quick. It's another miracle. *(He exits.)*

WILBUR: *(Looking at the web.)* It's beautiful. *(Fern enters.)*

FERN: Good morning, Wilbur. *(He motions toward the web.)*

FERN: "TERRIFIC." Hooray for Charlotte! She did it again! *(Wilbur shushes her.)* Oh, she's still sleeping. It must have been a long night for her. *(Wilbur nods.)*

HOMER'S VOICE: *(Offstage.)* Edith, phone the reporter on the Weekly Chronicle and tell him what happened! *(He enters, followed by Lurvy.)*

HOMER: *(Looking at the web.)* Well, what do you know. There it is as plain as day. "TERRIFIC." What do you know!

LURVY: *(Pointing to the web.)* Another miracle!

HOMER: We're going to have visitors all over the place today.

LURVY: I don't know where we'll put them. Yesterday, the driveway was practically full of cars and trucks.

HOMER: We can park the vehicles in the open field. John Arable said he and Avery will direct traffic.

LURVY: I'll go make up a couple of parking signs.

HOMER: Good idea, Lurvy. *(Lurvy exits.)*

FERN: Does this mean you're not going to kill Wilbur, Uncle Homer?

HOMER: Wilbur's safe for now. As long as he's attracting all this attention. Anyway, who said anything about killing him?

FERN: But that's what happens to pigs. In the cold weather. The old sheep said— Uh, never mind.

HOMER: Fern, honey, your daddy thinks you spend a little too much time with these animals. Maybe you should play with children your own age. Like Tommy Watson or Henry Fussy.

FERN: Tommy Watson? Ugh! Henry Fussy? Yuk!

HOMER: Well, it was just a thought. Let's go help your Aunt Edith. She'll be doing lots of baking for the visitors today.

FERN: Okay, Uncle Homer. 'Bye, Wilbur. See you later. *(They exit.) (A moment later, Charlotte enters, stretching and yawning.)*

WILBUR: Oh, Charlotte. They're so excited about the new word. And they're expecting more visitors today.

CHARLOTTE: That's wonderful. But we still have to worry about the future. Your life is not secure yet.

WILBUR: I know. But I can face anything with a friend like you. Friendship is one of the most satisfying things in the world. *(Templeton enters holding the lid of a soapflake box.)*

TEMPLETON: You'd better believe it, buster. And you'd better not forget the friendship of old Templeton who just happened to be at the dump all night looking for words to save you. *(Homer enters carrying a bucket. Templeton ducks out of sight.)*

HOMER: Sorry, pig. Lurvy got so excited he forgot to leave your breakfast this morning. *(He pours the food into the trough as Wilbur begins to eat.)* Mrs. Zuckerman threw in a whole fresh piece of apple strudel she's baking for the visitors. That's what you get for being a terrific pig. And I'll let you in on a little secret. If all this excitement continues, I might even think about taking you to the County Fair. *(He exits. Templeton comes out of hiding.)*

WILBUR: Did you hear that? The County Fair. That means I would get to live for at least another month.

CHARLOTTE: And maybe longer if you win a blue ribbon. *(The Goose enters and sees the web.)*

GOOSE: Look, look, look at that! "Terrific." My word, I do believe that was my word.

CHARLOTTE: Indeed it was.

WILBUR: Charlotte, will you go to the Fair with me?

CHARLOTTE: I don't know. The Fair comes at a bad time for me. That's when I'll be making my egg sac and filling it with eggs. But right now I have to think about writing new words. What did you bring, Templeton?

TEMPLETON: It's from an empty package of soapflakes. And I'm not going back for any more. *(He hands her the box lid.)*

CHARLOTTE: *(Reading it.)* "With new radiant action." *(Wilbur and the Goose repeat the words approvingly.)* Wilbur, let's see if you're radiant. *(He responds to each command.)* Run about . . . jump into the air . . . roll over . . . and do a split. *(The others applaud.)* It may not be radiant, but it's interesting.

WILBUR: I feel radiant. I really do.

CHARLOTTE: Then radiant you shall be. *(Wilbur and the Goose cheer.)* I'd better start writing at once.

WILBUR: Poor Charlotte. This is so much work for you.

CHARLOTTE: I don't mind. You're a good little pig, Wilbur, and you deserve to live. Now, everybody stand in front of me, so the others won't notice that I'm writing if they come back before I finish. *(All make a line in front of her, standing on boxes, bales of hay, etc., if necessary. Charlotte is now partially hidden.)*

Swing spinnerets.
Let out the thread.
The longer it gets,
The better it's read.

(She begins to write.)

GOOSE: Templeton would need to go to the Fair, too. Somebody, somebody, somebody has to run errands and do general work.

TEMPLETON: I'm staying right here. I haven't the slightest interest in Fairs.

GOOSE: That's because you've never, never, never been to one. You'd love it. Every-every-everybody spills food at a fair. Popcorn, frozen custard, candy apples—

TEMPLETON: Stop! That's enough! You've twisted my whiskers. I'll go. *(Wilbur and the Goose applaud.)*

CHARLOTTE: Attach, ascend, repeat.

GOOSE: *(Looking back at Charlotte.)* Charlotte's working fast, fast, fast.

CHARLOTTE: I've pretty well got the hang of it now.

WILBUR: *(Glancing offstage.)* Look, someone's coming. *Two* people.

GOOSE: I'll go see who it is, is, is. *(She exits.)*

WILBUR: Hurry, Charlotte.

CHARLOTTE: I'm almost finished. Just have to cross the final T. Over to the right, payout line, attach.

WILBUR: *(Calling to the Goose.)* Who is it?

GOOSE'S VOICE: *(Offstage.)* Looks, looks, looks like Mr. Zuckerman and a newspaper reporter. He's carrying a camera.

WILBUR: A camera? Do you think he's going to take my picture?

TEMPLETON: I doubt he's here to take *my* picture. Though he could do worse. *(Striking a pose.)* Look at that profile.

WILBUR: Quiet, Templeton. They're nearly here. Quickly, Charlotte, quickly!

CHARLOTTE: Repeat, attach . . . and finished. *(Wilbur and Templeton quickly disassemble their "coverage." Templeton and Charlotte hide behind crates or boxes. In the web is the word "RADIANT.")*

HOMER'S VOICE: *(Offstage.)* Right this way, Mr. Carter. Here we are. *(He and Carter, a reporter, enter.)* We're mighty honored to have the chief reporter of the Weekly Chronicle out here to cover this story.

CARTER: I'm mighty honored to cover it, Mr. Zuckerman. Why don't I get a picture of you and the pig together? *(He readies the camera.)*

HOMER: Sure thing. Come here, boy. *(He poses next to Wilbur.)*

CARTER: Say cheese. *(Templeton appears, unseen by Homer and Carter.)*

TEMPLETON: *(Licking his lips.)* Cheese? *(Wilbur frantically shushes Templeton, who exits disgustedly.)*

HOMER: Cheese! *(Carter takes the picture.)*

CARTER: That'll make the front page for sure.

HOMER: Good. I want everybody to see this *terrific* pig. Just like it says in the web.

CARTER: But Mr. Zuckerman. That's not what it says in the web.

HOMER: *(Looking at the web.)* Glory be! There's a new word. *(Fern enters.)*

FERN: Uncle Homer, Aunt Edith wants you to— *(She sees the web.)* Radiant.

HOMER: Radiant.

CARTER: Radiant.

HOMER: Well, sir. That does it. I have an announcement you can print in your newspaper, Mr. Carter. I'm going to enter this pig in the County Fair. *(Wilbur and Fern, who cheers, dance around. Charlotte, unseen by the others, appears and waves to Wilbur, then hides again.)* And if he can win a blue ribbon, I guarantee we'll never make bacon and ham out of him. *(Fern and Carter applaud.)*

FERN: Can I go to the Fair, Uncle Homer? After all, Wilbur used to be my pig.

HOMER: We'll *all* go. We'll all need to help Wilbur win that blue ribbon.

CARTER: There'll be lots of competition. Lots of fine pigs.

FERN: But none as terrific as Wilbur.

CARTER: *(Pointing to the web.)* Or as radiant.

HOMER: Yep, he's some pig, all right. *(All laugh.)* Come on. Let's go to the kitchen for some fresh apple strudel and iced tea.

CARTER: Sounds good, Mr. Zuckerman. *(Homer, Carter and Fern exit. Charlotte emerges from her hiding place.)*

WILBUR: Charlotte, you did it. Thank you, thank you.

CHARLOTTE: Well, we got you *to* the Fair. But that's only half the battle.

WILBUR: Will you come with me Charlotte? *Please.*

CHARLOTTE: I'm not sure. I need to think about it. *(A beat.)* But first, I need some rest. This day has been particularly exhausting.

WILBUR: Of course, Charlotte. You've earned some peace and quiet. I'll be out in the sun taking a nap. *(He exits.)*

CHARLOTTE: I'm suddenly very tired. I know I won't be able to help Wilbur much longer. I'll have to lay my eggs soon. I do want them to hatch right here in the barn where it's warm and safe. *(A pause.)* But I'll take the chance anyway. I *will* go to the Fair with Wilbur. People will be expecting to see a word in the web. It may help him win. And he just has to win that blue ribbon. His whole future—if he's to have a future at all—totally depends on what happens at the Fair. *(She goes behind the web. For a moment the stage is empty.)* [NOTE: An optional INTERMISSION may be used at this point.]

The Narrator enters, and, as he speaks, he rearranges the "furnishings" from the barn to suggest an area in the livestock locale at the Fair—especially Wilbur's pen and ample passage room around it. The upstage right web is removed, and another web is "hung" up left. [NOTE: The setting may be changed during the Intermission, if used, and at the beginning of Act Two, the Narrator is revealed on stage.]

NARRATOR: The days of summer drifted on. Before long the crickets sang in the gardens. They sang the song of summer's ending. *(A beat.)* The end of summer brings many things. Late harvesting. Thoughts of school. *And* the County Fair. *(Carnival music is heard.)* Now the County Fair is a very special occasion. The sights—the smells—the sounds. Especially the sounds. *(He assumes a "pitchman's" role, or the following speeches may be made by off-stage voices.)* Step right up, ladies and gentlemen. Ride the giant ferris wheel. Only ten cents. One thin dime. You can see the whole county from the top of the giant ferris wheel. *(Changing voices as he moves to another part of the stage.)* Get your footlong hot dogs, giant hamburgers, french fried potatoes. It's all here, and more, at the Lion's Club Barbecue Pavilion. *(Again moving and changing voices.)* Harness racing, livestock judging, 4-H exhibits, rides, balloons, prizes. Come one, come all to the County Fair. *(Assuming his normal voice.)* Everybody at the Zuckermans and the Arables got up early the day of the Fair. They fed Wilbur an extra special breakfast, gave him a warm bath, then loaded him into a crate filled with straw. They brought him to the Fair in the Zuckermans' truck. Of course, there were two other creatures in Wilbur's crate, too. Nobody but Wilbur—and maybe Fern—knew that Charlotte and Templeton had come along for the ride. Yes, it promised to be a couple of pretty exciting days at the County Fair. *(He exits. A moment later Fern enters leading Wilbur who is attached to a rope.)*

FERN: *(Calling out.)* We're back from our walk! *(Homer enters with a bucket.)*

HOMER: Did you see most of the Fair?

FERN: Just where they keep all the animals. I can't wait to go to the midway and ride everything. *(Arable enters carrying a sign reading "Zuckerman's Famous Pig.")*

HOMER: Bring the sign over here, John. Let me help you. *(He gives Arable a hand.)* Thanks for filling in for Lurvy.

ARABLE: My pleasure. It was good of Lurvy to stay at the farm and run things while we're here.

HOMER: Yes it was. I know how much he'd have enjoyed the Fair.

HOMER: *(They lean the sign on a box or crate.)* "Zuckerman's Famous Pig." That oughtta do the trick.

VOICE ON A LOUDSPEAKER: Attention please! Will the owner of a Pontiac car, license number H-2439, please move your car away from the fireworks shed!

FERN: Papa, can I have some money so I can go to the midway? Avery's already there.

ARABLE: That's because Aunt Edith agreed to take him. I'm not sure you should go by yourself.

FERN: Please, Papa.

ARABLE: *(After a pause.)* Oh, all right. The Fair only comes once a year. *(He gives her some money.)*

FERN: Thank you, Papa. 'Bye, Uncle Homer. *(She exits.)*

ARABLE: Now hurry back. We'll be leaving in a little while. *Tomorrow's* the big day.

HOMER: Yep. That's the day when this little pig's gonna win that blue ribbon. *(Wilbur smiles.)* Let's look around a little while, John—while we're waiting for the others.

ARABLE: Good idea.

HOMER: Let's wander over to the cattlebarn and see the Holsteins and the Guernseys.

ARABLE: Sure thing, Homer. *(They exit. Wilbur yawns and goes to sleep.) (Charlotte appears from behind a box or crate and looks about cautiously.)*

CHARLOTTE: I thought they'd never leave. It's easier to hide in a barn than out in the open like this. I don't want anyone to see me until I've written in my web tonight. *(Somewhat sadly.)* It may be the last time I ever write. *(A pause.)* Templeton's out exploring. He promised to bring me back a word. I hope he cooperates. If I don't write a word, I'm sure Wilbur will have a difficult time winning that blue ribbon. *(She looks at the sleeping Wilbur.)* He's a cute little pig, and smart. But I'm sure there will be bigger pigs here. And even better looking ones. *(Uncle, a large pig, enters sniffing around. A moment later he sees Charlotte.)*

UNCLE: Hi, there.

CHARLOTTE: May I have your name?

UNCLE: No name. Just call me Uncle.

CHARLOTTE: Very well . . . Uncle. You're rather large. Are you a spring pig?

UNCLE: Sure, I'm a spring pig. What did you think I was, a spring chicken? Haw, haw, that was a good one. Eh, sister?

CHARLOTTE: Mildly funny. I've heard funnier ones, though. What are you doing over here?

UNCLE: They're still working on my pen. I just walked away. They'll come after me when they see I'm gone. But I thought I'd wander around and look at the competition. *(He looks down at Wilbur.)* Well, no problem here. From what I've seen so far, I've got that blue ribbon all sewed up. But I won't *needle* you about it.

VOICE: *(Offstage.)* Uncle! Where are you, Uncle?

UNCLE: Well, better be getting back. I've got to get spiffy for the crowds that will be coming to admire me. So long, sister. *(He exits. Wilbur wakes up.)*

WILBUR: *(Drowsily.)* Oh, hi Charlotte. Where is everybody?

CHARLOTTE: Off to see the Fair.

WILBUR: Did I hear you talking to someone?

CHARLOTTE: A pig that's staying next door.

WILBUR: Is he better than me? I mean . . . bigger?

CHARLOTTE: I'm afraid he is much bigger.

WILBUR: Oh, no.

CHARLOTTE: He also has a most unattractive personality. He's going to be hard to beat. But with me helping you, it can be done.

WILBUR: When will you be writing the new word?

CHARLOTTE: Later on, if I'm not too tired. Just spinning this new web earlier today took a lot of my strength. *(Two Spectators enter. Charlotte eases to the background.)*

1ST SPECTATOR: Well, here's a good-looking fellow. *(Reading the sign.)* "Zuckerman's Famous Pig." *(Wilbur smiles.)*

2ND SPECTATOR: Look at his silky white coat. And his nice curly tail.

1ST SPECTATOR: I think he's the finest pig we've seen today.

2ND SPECTATOR: *(Looking offstage.)* Let's go look at that pig over there. *(He exits.)*

1ST SPECTATOR: *(To Wilbur.)* I think I've heard of you. Aren't you that "radiant" pig who's supposed to be "terrific"? *(Wilbur smiles and nods.)*

2ND SPECTATOR: *(Offstage.)* Look over here at *this* pig. *(1st Spectator exits.)* He's gigantic.

1ST SPECTATOR'S VOICE: *(Offstage.)* And he seems to be *very* confident.

2ND SPECTATOR'S VOICE: He may get the blue ribbon after all.

1ST SPECTATOR'S VOICE: Well, let's go look at the horses and see if we can pick the winner over there.

WILBUR: Oh, dear. Did you hear that, Charlotte?

CHARLOTTE: Chin up, young friend. Those weren't the judges. They were merely the spectators. The judges are the ones who count. *(Templeton enters carrying an article torn from a newspaper.)*

TEMPLETON: *(Handing it over to Charlotte.)* Well, here's your order.

CHARLOTTE: I hope you brought a good one. It is the last word I shall ever write.

WILBUR: *(Alarmed.)* Charlotte, what do you mean?

CHARLOTTE: *(Studying the article.)* Templeton, my eyes seem to be going. I'm having trouble reading this. What's that word?

TEMPLETON: Humble. *(Spelling it out.)* H—u—m—b—l—e.

CHARLOTTE: Humble has two meanings—"not proud" and "close to the ground." That's Wilbur all right.

TEMPLETON: Well, I hope you're satisfied. I'm not going to spend all my time delivering papers. I came to this Fair to enjoy myself.

CHARLOTTE: You've been very helpful, Templeton. You may run along now.

TEMPLETON: I'm going to make a night of it. The Goose was right. This Fair is a rat's paradise. What eating! What drinking! 'Bye, 'bye, my humble Wilbur. Fare thee well, Charlotte, you old schemer! This will be a night to remember in a rat's life. *(He exits.)*

WILBUR: Charlotte, what did you mean when you said this would be the last word?

CHARLOTTE: Shhh!

WILBUR: But, Charlotte . . . *(Homer enters. Charlotte hides.)*

HOMER: Fern! Fern! *(He stops and looks around.)* Where on earth could that young lady be? *(Seeing Wilbur.)* Well, boy, I see you're awake. Hope you're all set for the big day tomorrow. *(Fern enters.)*

FERN: Hi, Uncle Homer. Where is everybody?

HOMER: Waiting for you. We all met at the midway and decided to go back to the truck so we can be heading home. I told your daddy I'd look for you here while I was checking on Wilbur. Where were you?

FERN: Riding the Ferris wheel with Henry Fussy.

HOMER: Henry Fussy?

FERN: I met him at the midway. He even bought a ticket for me.

HOMER: Well, well. Your daddy will certainly be interested to hear that. Let's be going now.

FERN: Is Wilbur going to be safe here all alone?

HOMER: Sure. They have night watchmen to look after the animals after the people leave.

FERN: *(Petting Wilbur.)* I'll be thinking about you tonight, Wilbur.

HOMER: Get lots of sleep, boy. The judges come around first thing in the morning. They may even get here before we do. *(He and Fern begin to exit.)*

FERN: I can't wait to tell Papa about my Ferris wheel ride with Henry. One time we stopped at the very top, and you could really see the whole county. Or at least I guess it was the whole county. *(Homer laughs as they exit. Wilbur waves wistfully as the lights fade slightly.)*

CHARLOTTE: Well, I'd better be getting to work.

WILBUR: Is this really going to be your last word, Charlotte?

CHARLOTTE: I think so. I don't have much strength left. And tonight I have *another* job to do.

WILBUR: Is it something for me?

CHARLOTTE: No. It's something for *me* for a change.

WILBUR: What is it?

CHARLOTTE: *(As the lights fade even more.)* I'll tell you in the morning. *(Fireworks are heard in the background. Special lighting effects may accompany the sounds.)*

WILBUR: Listen.

CHARLOTTE: It's the fireworks. *(They listen for a moment. The sounds and lighting effects, if used, begin to fade.)*

WILBUR: This is the first night I've ever spent away from home. *(A pause.)* I'm glad you're with me, Charlotte. I never feel lonely when you're near.

CHARLOTTE: Thank you. That's what a friend likes to hear.

WILBUR: Charlotte?

CHARLOTTE: Yes?

WILBUR: Even if I don't win the blue ribbon . . . and the worst happens . . . I will never forget you.

CHARLOTTE: That's very nice of you to say. Now, go to sleep.

WILBUR: Goodnight. *(Wilbur stretches out and goes to sleep.) (The Narrator enters.)*

NARRATOR: Before long, Wilbur was asleep. Charlotte could tell by the sound of his breathing that he was sleeping peacefully in the straw. *(Charlotte goes to her web, and, with her back turned, she begins to work.)* By now, the Fair was quiet, and the people were gone. It was a good time for Charlotte to work. Though she was very tired, she worked quickly, for she had yet another job to do. *(A pause.)* Before long, she finished writing in the web.

CHARLOTTE: *(Slowly.)*

The message is spun.
I've come to the end.

(A beat, as she catches her breath.

The job that I've done,
Is all for my friend.

NARRATOR: After she had written the new word in the web, she moved on to another project. *(Charlotte moves away from the web slightly. Though she is largely obscured by the dim lights, her movements are now very elaborate and mysterious.)* It carried her far into the night. *(She climbs up and sticks an egg sac—a ball-like object—high up on the wall, then collapses and crawls into hiding.)* When she was finally finished, she was exhausted, and she fell into a deep, deep sleep. *(A pause.)* The first light of the next morning revealed the word in Charlotte's web. *(A light illuminates the word "HUMBLE.")* It was very early when the judges came around to determine the winners of the blue ribbon. *(The other lights slowly begin to come up as two Judges silently enter. They observe the sleeping Wilbur, write on a scoresheet, then exit in the direction of Uncle's pen.)* [NOTE: The Judges' appearance is optional. If they do not appear, they will merely be referred to by the Narrator.] The blazing orange sun slowly began to rise on the most important day of Wilbur's life. *(The Narrator exits. Wilbur awakens and yawns, then notices the web.)*

WILBUR: Oh, look! There's the new word. Charlotte! *(Charlotte enters.)* Thank you, Charlotte.

CHARLOTTE: "HUMBLE." It fits you perfectly.

WILBUR: *(Looking at the egg sac.)* And what's that object up there? It looks like cotton candy. Did you make it?

CHARLOTTE: I did indeed. It's my egg sac. The finest thing I've ever made.

WILBUR: What's inside it? Eggs?

CHARLOTTE: Five hundred and fourteen of them.

WILBUR: You're kidding. Are you really going to have five hundred and fourteen children?

CHARLOTTE: *(With a touch of sadness.)* If nothing happens, yes. Of course, they won't show up till next spring. I won't ever see my children.

WILBUR: Of *course* you will. We'll *all* see them.

CHARLOTTE: Wilbur, I don't feel good at all. My eggs and I may not make it back to the barn.

WILBUR: Charlotte, don't say that.

CHARLOTTE: Now stop worrying about me. This is your big day today. I'm sure you'll win.

TEMPLETON'S VOICE: *(Offstage.)* What a night! *(He enters. His stomach is bloated.)* What a night! What feasting and carousing. I must have eaten the remains of thirty lunches. Oh, it was rich, my friends, rich!

CHARLOTTE: You ought to be ashamed of yourself. You'll probably have an attack of acute indigestion.

TEMPLETON: Don't worry about me. I can handle anything. Wilbur's the one you should be worrying about.

CHARLOTTE: What do you mean?

TEMPLETON: I've got some bad news for you. As I came past that pig next door—the one that calls himself Uncle—I noticed a blue ribbon on the front of his pen. That means he won first prize. *(A pause.)*

CHARLOTTE: *(Softly.)* Oh, no. *(Wilbur sits down slowly. Charlotte goes to him and puts her arm around him.)*

TEMPLETON: Wait till Zuckerman gets hankering for some fresh pork and smoked ham. He'll take the knife to you, my boy. *(Wilbur stares straight ahead.)*

CHARLOTTE: Be still, Templeton. Don't pay any attention to him, Wilbur!

WILBUR: *(After a beat, still looking ahead.)* It's all right. *(Another beat.)* Whatever will happen, will happen. *(Gaining courage.)* I may not live as long as I'd like, but I've lived very well. A good life is much more important than just having a *long* life. So starting now I'm going to stop worrying about myself. There are more important things than just thinking about yourself all the time. Like *you*, Templeton. You didn't even notice that Charlotte has made an egg sac.

TEMPLETON: Egg sac?

WILBUR: *(Pointing to it.)* Up there. She is going to become a mother. For your information, there are five hundred and fourteen eggs in that peachy little sac.

TEMPLETON: Well, congratulations! This *has* been a night! *(He finds an out-of-the-way spot, covers himself with some straw or an old blanket and goes to sleep.)*

CHARLOTTE: I'm sorry about the blue ribbon, Wilbur. But you're being very brave about it.

WILBUR: Bravery is just one of the many things I've learned from you, Charlotte . . . my friend. *(Homer enters carrying a bucket.)*

HOMER: Good morning, pig. Here's a big, fresh breakfast for you. *(He empties the bucket into the trough, then sees the web.)* Well, what do you know about that—"Humble." Yet another miracle! You're sure to win that blue ribbon now. *(Wilbur turns away sadly.)* What's the matter, boy? And why aren't you eating anything?

FERN'S VOICE: *(Offstage.)* Oh, no!

HOMER: What is it, Fern?

FERN'S VOICE: I can't believe it.

HOMER: Can't believe what?

FERN: *(Entering, near tears.)* That pig over there has already won the blue ribbon.

HOMER: What? Have the judges been by already?

FERN: It's not fair. He won just because he's fat. I'll bet the judges are fat, too.

HOMER: There, there. *(He gives her a handkerchief and she blows her nose.)*

FERN: I'm just glad the others decided to come later.

HOMER: They'll be disappointed, too, when they get here. But at least the new word in the web might cheer everybody up.

FERN: *(Seeing the web.)* "Humble." Oh, Charlotte, you did it again.

HOMER: Charlotte? Who's Charlotte?

VOICE: *(Offstage.)* Zuckerman? Who's Zuckerman?

HOMER: Why, that's me. I'm Zuckerman. *(The President of the Fair enters.)*

PRESIDENT: I'm the president of the Fair. Pleased to meet you. *(They shake hands.)*

HOMER: What can I do for you, Mr.—President?

PRESIDENT: You can get that pig of yours up to the grandstand as soon as possible.

HOMER: What for?

PRESIDENT: Didn't the judges tell you?

HOMER: They were already gone when we got here.

PRESIDENT: That pig of yours is getting a special award.

HOMER: What?

PRESIDENT: A special award. It's even more important than the blue ribbon.

FERN: Oh, Uncle Homer! *(They embrace.)*

PRESIDENT: And I'm going to make the presentation! If you don't mind, I'd like to practice my speech before I have to do it in front of the crowd.

HOMER: Sure, go right ahead.

PRESIDENT: *(Taking out some note cards.)* Ladeez and gentlemen, we now present Mr. Homer L. Zuckerman's distinguished pig. *(A beat.)* You can applaud. *(Fern and Homer do so vigorously.)* Many of you recall when the writing first appeared mysteriously on the spider web in Mr. Zuckerman's barn, calling the attention of all to the fact that this was some pig. Then came the word "terrific." Next, the word "radiant" appeared in the web. And now, this very morning—the word "humble." Whence came this mysterious writing? Not from the spider. Needless to say, spiders can't write. *(Fern and Wilbur clear their throats.)* No, ladeez and gentlemen, this miracle has never been fully explained. We simply know that we are dealing with supernatural forces here, and we should all feel proud and grateful. *(He motions for Fern and Homer to applaud, and they do so.)* Now, on behalf of the governors of the Fair, I take the honor of awarding a special prize of twenty-five dollars to Mr. Zuckerman. *And* a handsome bronze medal, which far outshines any blue ribbon, to this radiant, this terrific, this humble pig. *(Fern and Homer applaud and cheer.)* I'll give you the money and medal at the real ceremony. Come along now. The crowds are already gathering at the grandstand. *(Straightening his tie.)* Do I look okay?

HOMER: Fine, Mr. President.

PRESIDENT: Gotta look better than fine today. Gotta look as good as him. *(Pointing to Wilbur.)*

HOMER: Oh, you do, Mr. President. You look—perfect as a pig.

PRESIDENT: A *prize-winning* pig. Follow me.

HOMER: We'll be right there. *(The President exits.)*

FERN: *(Embracing Homer.)* Uncle Homer, isn't this wonderful!

HOMER: We'll load Wilbur in the truck right now and take him to the grandstand. Then we'll go home directly from there. *(He gathers up the trough, the bucket, and the sign, then hands Fern a coin.)* Go call your daddy. Tell him to pick up your Aunt Edith and the others and get on out here. They've got to be present for this ceremony.

FERN: Sure thing, Uncle Homer. By the way, after the ceremony do you think I'll have time to ride the Ferris wheel with Henry Fussy?

HOMER: Henry Fussy? I think so. In fact, we'll make the time, if necessary. *(He laughs and exits.)*

FERN: *(Hugging Wilbur.)* I'm so proud of you, Wilbur. I knew from the very first day you were—some pig. *(She exits.)*

WILBUR: Charlotte. Charlotte? Did you hear? Isn't it wonderful? *(A beat.)* Charlotte? Are you all right?

CHARLOTTE: *(Appearing.)* Yes. A little tired perhaps. But, I feel peaceful now that I know you will live safe and secure.

WILBUR: Oh, Charlotte. Why did you do all this for me? I've never done anything for you.

CHARLOTTE: You have been my friend. That in itself is a tremendous thing. After all, what's a life anyway? We're born, we live a little, we die. By helping you, perhaps I was lifting up my life a trifle. Heaven knows anyone's life can stand a little of that.

WILBUR: Charlotte, I would gladly give my life for you . . . I really would.

CHARLOTTE: I'm sure you would.

WILBUR: Charlotte, we're all going home today. Won't it be wonderful to be back in the barn again?

CHARLOTTE: I will not be going back to the barn.

WILBUR: *(Alarmed.)* Not going back? What are you talking about?

CHARLOTTE: I'm done for. In a day or two I'll be dead. I'm so tired I can't even crawl up to my egg sac.

WILBUR: Charlotte, Charlotte! My true friend.

CHARLOTTE: Come now, Wilbur, let's not make a scene.

WILBUR: I won't leave you alone to die. I shall stay, too.

CHARLOTTE: You can't. They won't let you. Besides, even if you did stay, there would be no one to feed you. The Fair Grounds will soon be empty and deserted. *(Wilbur goes to the side of the pen and looks offstage.)*

WILBUR: I have an idea. But we have to do it quickly. *(He rushes to where Templeton is hiding and awakens him.)* Templeton, Templeton! Wake up! Pay attention!

TEMPLETON: Can't a rat catch a wink of sleep?

WILBUR: Listen to me! Charlotte is very ill. She won't be coming home with us. I must take her egg sac with me. I can't reach it, and I can't climb. Please, *please*, Templeton, climb up and get the egg sac.

TEMPLETON: *(Yawning.)* So, it's old Templeton to the rescue again, is it? Nothing doing.

WILBUR: *(Glancing offstage.)* I will make you a promise. Get Charlotte's egg sac for me and from now on I will let you eat first when Lurvy slops me. You get first choice of everything in the trough.

TEMPLETON: You mean that?

WILBUR: I promise. I cross my heart.

TEMPLETON: *(After a beat.)* All right, it's a deal. *(He climbs up to get the egg sac.)*

WILBUR: Use extreme care. I don't want a single one of those eggs harmed. *(Templeton brings the egg sac to Wilbur.)* Charlotte, I will protect it with all my might. Thank you, Templeton. Now you'd better go and hide in the crate if you want a ride back home.

TEMPLETON: You bet I'm going back home, now that I get first choice of everything in the trough. *(He exits.)*

HOMER'S VOICE: *(Offstage.)* Okay, boy, time to go to get your award!

WILBUR: Oh, Charlotte! *(Wilbur crosses quickly to Charlotte and em-*

braces her. Homer enters carrying a rope. Charlotte hides in the shadows.)

HOMER: *(Tying the rope around Wilbur.)* Well, sir, it turned out to be a mighty fine Fair, after all. Mighty fine. Let's go, Wilbur. This will be a day you can tell your grandchildren about. *(Wilbur looks back and sees Charlotte, who has appeared.)*

WILBUR: *(Sotto voce.)* Goodbye, Charlotte. Goodbye. *(He waves to her as he and Homer exit.)*

CHARLOTTE: Goodbye, Wilbur. Thank you for saving my egg sac. *(Faintly.)* Thank you . . . and goodbye . . . my friend. *(The lights fade, leaving a special on Charlotte who slowly waves. The Narrator enters.)*

NARRATOR: Charlotte summoned all her strength and waved to Wilbur. She went back to her web and wrapped herself in it. *(Charlotte detaches the web, wraps it around herself and slowly exits.)* And never moved again. *(The faint sound of carnival music is heard.)* Next day, as the Ferris wheel was being taken apart and the race horses were being loaded into their vans and the entertainers were packing up their belongings and driving away in their trailers, Charlotte died. *(A pause.)* The Fair Grounds were soon deserted. The sheds and buildings were empty and forlorn. The fields were littered with bottles and trash. Of the hundreds of people that had visited the Fair, nobody knew that a gray spider had played the most important part of all. *(A beat.)* No one was with her when she died. *(A pause. He begins to "reset" the Zuckerman's barn. He gets the trough from just offstage and places it at center.)* Wilbur returned to his beloved barn. The animals were delighted with his success at the Fair. But everyone missed Charlotte very much. For the rest of the fall and all through the winter, Wilbur watched over Charlotte's egg sac as though he were guarding his own children. Patiently he awaited the end of winter and the coming of little spiders. *(The Narrator exits. A moment later Templeton enters and goes to the trough.)*

TEMPLETON: Oh, good. Wilbur hasn't eaten his breakfast yet. *(He begins to eat. The Sheep enters.)*

SHEEP: Wilbur hasn't eaten anything these past few days. He keeps waiting out in the yard for the eggs to hatch. *(A beat, as he watches Templeton eat.)* Templeton, you would live longer if you ate less.

TEMPLETON: Who wants to live forever?

GOOSE'S VOICE: *(Offstage.)* You, you, you tell them.

GANDER'S VOICE: *(Offstage.)* No, no, no. You do the honors.

GOOSE: Very, -ery, -ery well. *(She enters.)* I am pleased to announce that the Gander and I are expecting goslings.

TEMPLETON: Again? It must be spring. Everything's sprouting.

SHEEP: Including your stomach. *(Wilbur, wearing a medal, enters hurriedly. He carries the open egg sac.)*

WILBUR: They're here! They're here!

TEMPLETON: Who's here?

WILBUR: The spiders. They hatched. All five hundred and fourteen. Look! *(He points offstage.)*

GOOSE: They seem to be climbing up, up, up the rafters.

WILBUR: Yes. They're going up to where the breezes are blowing. Oh, look. They're floating away on little clouds of silk. Wait! Won't you please stay? *(Dejectedly.)* They're all leaving.

SHEEP: Happens every time.

WILBUR: Wait . . . please! *(Waving sadly.)* Goodbye! *(A beat.)* I'm glad they hatched. But I wish they would stay. Some of them anyway. I'm being deserted by Charlotte's children.

SHEEP: They have to live their own lives, you know.

WILBUR: Yes, I know. But I was just hoping . . . oh, never mind. *(A Spider's Voice is heard offstage.)*

SPIDER'S VOICE: Salutations!

WILBUR: Who said that?

SPIDER'S VOICE: Me. I'm up *(over)* here. Three of us are staying.

WILBUR: *(Ecstatic.)* This is wonderful! Wonderful!

SPIDER'S VOICE: We like this barn. And we like you.

WILBUR: *(To the Others.)* Did you hear that, everybody? Three of Charlotte's children are staying.

SPIDER'S VOICE: Where did you get that handsome medal you're wearing?

WILBUR: Well, it's a long story. And I'll tell you all about it. But right now, I'm going to take the medal off. *(He removes it from his neck.)*

ALL: What? Did you hear that? What does he mean?

WILBUR: To celebrate this very special day, I'm putting the medal where it rightfully belongs. Templeton, please hang it on that nail where Charlotte's web used to be.

TEMPLETON: Another favor?

WILBUR: This is the last one, I promise.

TEMPLETON: *(Taking the medal.)* I know—till the next one. *(He climbs up and hangs the medal on the nail.)* Like this?

WILBUR: Perfect. *(Templeton climbs down.)* I hereby dedicate my medal to the memory of dear Charlotte whom I will never forget. *(All nod in agreement.)*

SHEEP: Very thoughtful of you, Wilbur.

GOOSE: *None* of us will ever, ever, ever forget her.

WILBUR: I will love her children and her grandchildren dearly, but none of them will ever take her place in my heart. She was in a class by herself. *(A beat.)* It is not often that someone comes along who is a true friend and a good writer. Charlotte was both. *(All turn and form a tableau, looking at the medal which is now lit by a special. All lights, except the one on the medal, dim. The Narrator enters.)*

NARRATOR: Wilbur kept good his promise. He never, ever forgot Charlotte. Even years later, he fondly remembered his "true friend and good writer." Mr. Zuckerman took fine care of Wilbur all the rest of his days. And the pig was often visited by friends and admirers, for nobody ever forgot the year of his triumph. And the miracle of Charlotte's web. *(The lights fade to: Blackout)*

CURTAIN

THE BEST CHRISTMAS PAGEANT EVER

by

BARBARA ROBINSON

THE BEST CHRISTMAS PAGEANT EVER

CHARACTERS

Father (Bob Bradley: A solid family man, 35-38
Mother (Grace Bradley): Trim, attractive, 35ish
Beth Bradley: The narrator, strong voice and presence, 10-11
Charlie Bradley: Traditional kid brother, 8-9
Ralph Herdman: Ragged, scroungy, slouching manner, touch of adolescent cool, 12-13
Imogene Herdman: Loud, bossy, crafty, 11-12
Leroy Herdman: Tough, sure of himself, 10-11
Claude Herdman: Tough, combative, 9-10
Ollie Herdman: Looking for trouble, Claude's usual partner in crime, 8-9
Gladys Herdman: Small, wiry, feisty, 7-8
Alice Wendleken: Prim, proper, pain in the neck, 10-11
Mrs. Armstrong: Largish woman, managerial in voice and manner, 50ish
Mrs. Slocum: Pleasant, motherly woman, 35-60
Mrs. Clark: 35-60
Mrs. Clausing: 35-60
Mrs. McCarthy: A younger, less imperious version of Mrs. Armstrong, middle 40s
Maxine: 10-11
Elmer Hopkins: 12-13
Hobie: 9-10
David: 8-9
Beverly: 7-8
Fireman: 25-30
Fireman: 25-30
Shirley: 5-6

Juanita: 5-6
Doris: 9-10
Reverend Hopkins: Middle to late 40s

Extra angel choir members, baby angels, shepherds.

Total: 4 males, 6 females, 8 boys, and 9 girls

Much of the action takes place on the forestage in front of the curtain, in short spotlighted scenes. The two interiors—living room-dining room, and church—can be full or partial sets, with minimal furnishing and set decoration. The set piece that serves as a focal point for the Herdmans, stage left, is a simple climbing structure like a jungle gym. Mrs. Armstrong's hospital bed can be a single bed on casters, or a rollaway cot. It is especially effective for Mrs. Armstrong to be elevated above stage level on a movable platform.

Staging and lighting directions given here are for a traditional proscenium stage with usable apron space and reasonably broad light facilities (spotlights, dimming capacity, etc.). The set piece and elevated platform are devices used in the first professional production at the Poncho Theatre in Seattle, and are included here as suggested staging. The play has also been mounted successfully in limited space and less formal settings. In such productions the absence of full sets and sophisticated lighting will seem appropriate to the nature of the play.

The play has no intermission.

NOTE: In the first production of *The Best Christmas Pageant Ever*, a different opening scene was used. It is included at the end of this script as a suitable alternate for certain audiences.

As the play opens the curtain is down. House lights down. Spotlight up on Beth, sitting DSR.

BETH: The Herdmans were the worst kids in the whole history of the world. They lied and stole and smoked cigars, even the girls, and they talked dirty and cussed their teachers and took the name of the Lord in vain and set fire to Fred Shoemaker's old broken down tool house.

(Spotlight up on set piece, SL. During Beth's speech the Herdmans come on from the wings left and position themselves on and around the set piece, with Gladys at the top level, in a pose reminiscent of the first illustration in the book, The Best Christmas Pageant Ever.)

BETH: There were six of them—Ralph, Imogene, Leroy, Claude, Ollie and Gladys—and they went through the Woodrow Wilson school like those South American fish that strip your bones clean. They went around town the same way—stealing things and tearing things up and whamming kids . . . so it was hard to get away from them. There was only one safe place.

CHARLIE: *(Offstage, singing.)*

Sweet hour of prayer, sweet hour of prayer,
Because there are no Herdmans there.
And Jesus loves us, as they say,
Because he keeps them miles away.

BETH: That's my little brother, Charlie. That's what he said when the Sunday school teacher asked what was his favorite thing about church. Charlie said, "No Herdmans." That made the teacher mad because all the other kids said nice things about God and Jesus and good feelings. But old Charlie told the real truth—*No Herdmans!*

(Spotlight off Beth. Herdmans exit SL. Curtain rises on the living room-dining room set. There is a table and four chairs SR.: A door URC.: A sofa, lounge chair, end tables, one with telephone, SL. As curtain rises, Mother, Father, and Charlie enter through the door. Beth moves back to join them. They are returning from church, and all except Beth wear coats. Father has a newspaper under his arm. Charlie speaks as he enters.)

CHARLIE: I don't care what everybody else said, that's what they really thought. All that other stuff is okay but the main good thing about church is that the Herdmans aren't there, ever. *(Charlie drops his coat on the sofa.)*

FATHER: *(Taking his coat off.)* That's not a very Christian sentiment, it seems to me.

MOTHER: *(Collecting the coats.)* It's a very practical sentiment. Charlie was black and blue all last year because he had to sit next to Leroy Herdman in school. *(She exits to hang up the coats.)*

FATHER: Is he the worst one? Leroy?

CHARLIE: They're all the worst one.

BETH: Ralph's the biggest, so if Ralph gets you . . .

CHARLIE: That doesn't make any difference. Gladys isn't big, but she's fast, and she's mean, and she bites.

FATHER: I'm sorry I asked. Just stay away from all of them.

CHARLIE: That's what I said. Stay away from them. Go to church.

MOTHER: *(As she enters.)* I'm glad to hear you feel that way.

CHARLIE: *(Suspicious.)* Why?

MOTHER: No arguments this year about the Christmas pageant.

CHARLIE: I don't want to be a shepherd again!

MOTHER: Tell Mrs. Armstrong you want to be a Wise Man.

CHARLIE: I don't want to be *in* it!

MOTHER: Everybody's in it. Think how I'd feel sitting there on Christmas Eve, if my own children weren't in the pageant. Think how your father would feel. *(There is a moment of silence, as everyone looks at Father, knowing exactly how he feels on this subject.)*

MOTHER: You'd feel terrible, wouldn't you, Bob?

FATHER: Well . . . actually, I didn't plan to go. *(Mother starts to protest.)* You know how crowded it always is, they can use my seat. I'll just stay home, put on my bathrobe, relax . . . there's never anything different about the Christmas pageant.

MOTHER: There's going to be something different this year.

FATHER: What?

MOTHER: Charlie's going to wear your bathrobe. *(She exits into kitchen.)*

FATHER: *(Calls after her.)* You just thought that up, Grace!

BETH: *(To Charlie.)* Why don't you be Joseph? Elmer Hopkins'll pay you a dollar to be Joseph. *(To Father.)* Elmer's sick of being Joseph all the time just because his father's the minister. Nobody wants to be Joseph.

CHARLIE: Nobody wants to be *in* it!

FATHER: *(To Beth.)* What are you going to be this year?

BETH: I'm always in the angel choir.

FATHER: Well, why can't Charlie be in the angel choir?

CHARLIE: Because I can't sing!

FATHER: From what I've heard in the past, that's not a serious drawback. *Away In A Manger* always sounds to me like a closetful of mice.

CHARLIE: *(To Beth.)* What do you wear in the angel choir?

BETH: Bedsheets.

CHARLIE: Oh, boy, some choice . . . a bathrobe or a bedsheet. Come on, let's go watch TV. *(They start out.)*

MOTHER: *(Entering from kitchen with coffee cup.)* You know, Mrs. Armstrong works very hard to give everyone a lovely experience.

BETH: Oh, Mom, Mrs. Armstrong just likes to run things. *(They exit.)*

MOTHER: They're right, of course. She directs the pageant, she runs the potluck supper, she's chairman of the Bazaar . . . I think Helen Armstrong would preach the sermon if anyone would let her.

FATHER: Is that George Armstrong's wife?

MOTHER: Yes.

FATHER: Well, maybe she'll try to manage the hospital, because that's where she is. I saw George at the drug store and he told me his wife broke her leg this morning . . . she'll be in traction for two weeks and laid up till the first of the year.

MOTHER: The first of the year! . . . Why, they'll have to cancel Christmas.

FATHER: She's in charge of Christmas?

MOTHER: Well, she's in charge of the pageant, and she's in charge of the bazaar. . . . I feel sorry for Helen, but who's going to do all those things?

(Lights offstage: Spotlight up DSL on Mrs. Slocum, telephoning.)

MRS. SLOCUM: Yes, I'll take over the bazaar, Edna, if you'll do the potluck supper. I don't know what in the world we'll do about the pageant, unless. . . . How about Grace?

(Spot off Mrs. Slocum; Spot up DSR on Mrs. Clark, telephoning.)

MRS. CLARK: I just can't, Edna. I've got company all Christmas week. . . . How about Grace?

(Spot off Mrs. Clark; spot up DSL on Mrs. Clausing, telephoning.)

MRS. CLAUSING: . . . How about Grace?

(Spot off Mrs. Clausing; up on Mrs. McCarthy, DSR telephoning.)

MRS. MCCARTHY: Hello. . . . Grace . . . ?

(Spot off Mrs. McCarthy: Stage lights up on living room-dining room set. Mother hanging up phone with stunned expression.)

MOTHER: Bob . . .

FATHER: What?

MOTHER: I have to direct the Christmas pageant.

FATHER: Does that mean I have to go?

(Stage lights down; spot on Beth, DSR.)

BETH: Our Christmas pageant isn't what you'd call four-star entertainment. Mrs. Armstrong breaking her leg was the only unexpected thing that ever happened to it. It's always the same old Christmas story, and the same old carols, and the same old Mary and Joseph . . . and that's what my mother was stuck with . . . that, and Mrs. Armstrong.

(Spot out on Beth; up on Mrs. Armstrong in hospital bed SL. She is in the middle of phone conversation. The phone conversation and the family conversation are to be simultaneous, with the phone conversation to be background. Key parts of Mrs. Armstrong's conversation are italicized and should be heard. This dialogue can be blocked, just as movement is blocked, and Mrs. Armstrong's speeches are deliberately lengthy and full so the audience can be aware of her droning on in the background.)

MRS. ARMSTRONG: . . . tell you again, Grace, how important it is to give everyone a chance. Here's what I do—I always start with Mary and I tell them we must choose our Mary carefully because Mary was the mother of Jesus . . .

(Spotlight up on dinner table scene DSR. Father and Charlie seated: Beth setting the table, pouring water, etc. Mother on telephone.)

MOTHER: I know that, Helen.

MRS. ARMSTRONG: Yes, and then I tell them about Joseph, that he was God's choice to be Jesus' father. That's how I explain that. Frankly, I don't ever spend much time on Joseph because it's always Elmer Hopkins, and he knows all about Mary and Joseph . . .

CHARLIE: I thought Mrs. Armstrong was in traction. How can she talk on the phone if she's in traction?

BETH: What do you think traction is?

CHARLIE: Like when they put you to sleep?

FATHER: No such luck. . . . Beth, we need salt and pepper . . . and napkins . . . *(Beth exits to kitchen.)*

MRS. ARMSTRONG: . . . but I do explain about the Wise Men and the shepherds and how important they are. And I tell them, there are no small parts, only small actors. Remind the angel choir not to stare at the audience, and don't let them wear ear-rings and things like that. And don't let them wear clunky shoes or high heels. I just hope you don't have too many baby angels, Grace, because they'll be your biggest problem . . .

(Father takes slice of bread, hands the plate to Charlie, who takes five or six slices, and reaches for butter.)

FATHER: You will leave some for the rest of us, won't you, Charlie?

CHARLIE: I'm hungry. Leroy Herdman stole my lunch again.

FATHER: How can you let him do that to you, day after day?

CHARLIE: How can I stop him? . . . Where's the chicken?

FATHER: *(To Mother.)* Grace, where's the chicken?

MOTHER: *(Hands over phone.)* It's still in the oven.

CHARLIE: I'll get it. *(He exits.)*

(This leaves Father alone at the table, as Mrs. Armstrong drones on in the background. He is obviously disgruntled about this situation and after a moment he gets up, takes hat and coat from rack at the door, and exits out the door.)

MRS. ARMSTRONG: You'll have to get someone to push the baby angels on, otherwise they get in each other's way and bend their wings. Bob could do that, and he could keep an eye on the shepherds too. Oh, another thing about the angel choir. Don't let them wear lipstick. They think because it's a play . . . *(Doorbell buzz or chime.)*

MOTHER: Helen, I have to go. There's someone at my door.

MRS. ARMSTRONG: . . . that they have to wear lipstick, and it looks terrible. So tell them . . . *(Doorbell again.)*

MOTHER: Someone at my door, Helen. I'll talk to you later. *(Hangs up; doorbell again; starts toward door, calling.)* Yes . . . yes, I'm coming . . .

FATHER: *(In doorway.)* Lady, can you give me some supper? I haven't had a square meal in three days.

MOTHER: Oh, for heaven's sake, it's you!

FATHER: *(Coming in.)* I was very lonely at the table.

MOTHER: *(As they move down to the table.)* Well, I guess Helen feels lonely at the hospital.

FATHER: Not as long as the telephones are working. *(Beth and Charlie enter with food.)*

CHARLIE: I'll bet she told you about no small parts, only small actors.

BETH: And getting someone to shove the baby angels on, and make the shepherds shut up.

MOTHER: Yes. She suggested your father.

FATHER: Does that mean I have to go?

(Spot off family; up on Mrs. Armstrong, in mid-sentence of yet another telephone directive.)

MRS. ARMSTRONG: And, Grace, don't use just anybody's baby for Jesus . . . get a quiet one. Better yet, get two if you can . . . then if one turns out to be fussy, you can always switch them . . .

(Curtain comes down during this speech. Spot on Beth, DSR.)

BETH: My mother didn't pay much attention to Mrs. Armstrong. She said Mrs. Armstrong was stuck in the hospital with nothing to do but think up problems, and there weren't going to be any problems. Of course, Mother didn't count on the Herdmans. That was Charlie's fault.

(Spot off Beth; up on Leroy Herdman and Charlie, entering SL.)

CHARLIE: Hey, Leroy, you give me back my lunch!

LEROY: Sure, kid, here. *(Hands him a lunch bag.)*

CHARLIE: *(Looks inside.)* You stole my dessert again!

LEROY: How do you know?

CHARLIE: Because it isn't here.

LEROY: What was it?

CHARLIE: Two Twinkies.

LEROY: That's right. That's what it was. *(Starts to leave.)*

CHARLIE: Hey, Leroy! You think it's so great to steal my dessert every day and you know what? I don't care if you steal my dessert. I'll even give you my dessert. I get all the dessert I want in Sunday school.

LEROY: *(Interested in this.)* Oh, yeah? What kind of dessert?

CHARLIE: All kinds. Chocolate cake and candy bars and cookies . . . and Twinkies and Big Wheels. We get refreshments all the time, all we want.

LEROY: You're a liar.

CHARLIE: . . . and ice cream, and doughnuts and cupcakes and . . .

LEROY: Who gives it to you?

CHARLIE: *(Momentarily stumped.)* Uh . . . the minister.

LEROY: Why? Is he crazy?

CHARLIE: No. . . . I think he's rich.

LEROY: *(Pause.)* . . . Sunday school, huh?

(Spot off boys; spot up on Beth, DSR.)

BETH: That was the wrong thing to tell Herdmans . . . and, sure enough, the very next Sunday there they were in Sunday school, just in time to hear about the Christmas pageant . . .

(Spot off Beth; spot up on Alice and Imogene, DSL.)

IMOGENE: What's a pageant?

ALICE: It's a play.

IMOGENE: Like on TV? What's it about?

ALICE: It's about Jesus.

IMOGENE: *(Visibly disenchanted about Sunday school.)* Everything here is.

ALICE: And it's about Mary. Mostly, it's about Mary.

IMOGENE: Who's Mary?

ALICE: I am. . . . Well, *probably* I am. I know the part.

(Alice walks off SL.: Imogene watches her go, then looks out at the audience, wearing a cheshire cat smile. Spot off Imogene. Curtain opens on church setting with risers in place. As curtain opens, kids are straggling in, with Mother herding them along.)

MOTHER: Come on, Beth. . . . Charlie, you and David come. *(She leads the reluctant Charlie to a seat.)* Now, this won't take very long if you all settle down. . . . Today we're going to decide who will play the main roles in our Christmas pageant, but of course everyone will have an important part to play. You know what Mrs. Armstrong always tells you—there are no small parts, only small actors. Isn't that what Mrs. Armstrong always says?

ELMER: That's what she always says, but she never says what it means.

MOTHER: Don't you know what it means?

MAXINE: I know what it means. It means that the short kids have to be in the front row of the angel choir or else nobody can see them.

MOTHER: Well . . . not exactly. It really means that the littlest baby angel is just as important as Mary.

ALICE: *(Full of herself.)* I don't think anyone is as important as Mary.

BETH: Well, naturally, that's what *you* think, Alice. I think Jesus is more important.

MAXINE: I still think it means short kids have to be in the front row . . .

MOTHER: Girls, girls! . . . *Everyone* is important . . . Mary, Jesus, *and* the short kids. Now, is everyone here? Beverly, will you just step out in the hall and see if anyone else is coming? *(Beverly exits.)* Now you little children will be our angels, so please remind your mothers that you'll need bedsheets. . . . *(As she talks, the Herdmans enter, with Gladys bringing up the rear, having dispatched Beverly. Other children begin to murmur, wiggle around, poke each other, point at the Herdmans.)* People in the angel choir will need bedsheets too, and if any of you have old bathrobes at home. . . . *(Aware of the rising clamor, she stops.)*

. . . Now, what's the matter? *(As Mother turns and sees the Herdmans, they move in. Ralph and Leroy shove their way onto a bench, causing a ripple of movement there: Gladys does the same on another bench: Imogene, Claude and Ollie start across the stage to do likewise. To forestall any mayhem.)* Well, let's make some room there, for the Herdmans. *(A lot of room is made, like the parting of the Red Sea, and the Herdmans occupy their space.)* Now what happened to Beverly?

GLADYS: I think she went home. I think she got sick.

MOTHER: Did she say she was sick?

GLADYS: She just left. All I did was, I just said "Hi, Beverly" . . . and she just left.

MOTHER: I see. Well, will someone please tell Beverly about the rehearsals? . . . the next four Wednesdays, after school. Plan to be here for every one.

ELMER: What if we get sick?

MOTHER: You won't get sick. Of course, Mary and Joseph must *absolutely* come to every rehearsal . . .

ELMER: What if they get sick?

MOTHER: They won't get sick either, Elmer.

ELMER: Well, Beverly got sick and we didn't even start yet.

MOTHER: We don't *know* that Beverly got sick. Now, I want you to think about Mary. . . . We all know what kind of person Mary was. She was quiet and gentle and kind, and the girl who plays Mary should try to be that kind of person. Who would like to volunteer for that part? *(Everyone looks at Alice, but it is Imogene who raises her hand.)*

MOTHER: Did you have a question, Imogene?

IMOGENE: No, I want to be Mary . . . and Ralph, over there, he wants to be Joseph.

RALPH: Yeh, right.

MOTHER: Oh. Well . . . Well, I'll just make a list of volunteers for these parts and then we'll all decide who it should be. *(Writes on her clipboard.)* Ralph Herdman. Now, who else would like to be Joseph? . . . Did you raise your hand, Elmer?

ELMER: No.

MOTHER: Just raise your hands, please, any volunteers. . . . Any of you shepherds? *(Her eye falls on Charlie, who makes every effort to seem invisible.)* Very well . . . Ralph Herdman will be our Joseph. Now, Imogene has volunteered to be . . . *(Tiny break here, as if she can hardly bear to connect Imogene with Mary.)* . . . Mary. I'll just write that down. . . . What other names can I put on my list? . . . Janet? . . . Roberta? . . . Alice, don't you want to volunteer?

ALICE: *(Choking it out.)* No, I don't want to.

GLADYS: I'll be Mary!

IMOGENE: Shut up, Gladys. I'm already Mary. You be a Wise Man.

MOTHER: Well, the Wise Men are usually boys. Of course, they don't *have* to be, and we could . . .

LEROY: I'll be a Wise Man!

OLLIE: Me, too. Claude, you wanta be a Wise Man? Raise your hand.

CLAUDE: What's a Wise Man?

RALPH: Just raise your hand! *(Claude raises his hand.)*

GLADYS: What's left to be?

IMOGENE: Some angel.

GLADYS: I'll be that. What is it?

MOTHER: It's the Angel of the Lord, who brought the good news to the shepherds. *(There is a flurry of raised hands among the shepherds.)*

MOTHER: There, we do have some volunteers after all! Yes, Hobie, would you like to be a Wise Man?

HOBIE: No, I just wanted to say I can't be a shepherd. We're going to Philadelphia.

MOTHER: Why didn't you say so before?

HOBIE: I just remembered.

DAVID: My mother doesn't want me to be a shepherd.

MOTHER: Why not?

DAVID: I don't know. She just said, don't be a shepherd.

CHARLIE: I'm not going to be a shepherd!

MOTHER: *(Reverting from pageant director to exasperated parent.)* Oh, yes, you are! . . . . What's the matter with all of you?

ELMER: I don't want to be a shepherd . . . Gladys Herdman hits too hard!

MOTHER: Why, Gladys isn't going to hit anybody! The Angel of the Lord just visits the shepherds in the fields and tells them Jesus is born.

ELMER: And hits them!

MOTHER: Elmer, that's ridiculous, and I don't want to hear another word about it, from anyone. No shepherds may quit . . . or get sick. Now that's all for today, boys and girls, and you can go. . . . *(There is a scramble for the door. Beth and Alice move DS calling after them.)* . . . but I expect to see everyone here on Wednesday at 6:30! *(Mother moves DS and takes Alice's arm.)* Alice, what's wrong with you? Why in the world didn't you raise your hand?

ALICE: *(Miserably.)* I don't know.

MOTHER: You don't know! Alice, I expected you . . .

(Sounds of a scuffle offstage; yells—ouch! . . . Cut it out! . . . Let go. . . . Let me go!)

VOICE: Mrs. Bradley! Get Gladys offa me!

MOTHER: . . . to volunteer. Don't you want to be Mary?

VOICE: Mrs. Bradley!! *(Mother exits, with an exasperated look at Alice.)*

BETH: Oh, come on, Alice! *(Mimicking her.)* I don't know . . . !

ALICE: I didn't dare raise my hand. Imogene would have killed me! She said, "I'm going to be Mary in this play, and if you open your mouth or raise your hand you'll wish you didn't." And I said, "I'm always Mary in the Christmas pageant." And she said, "Go ahead then, and next spring when the pussywillows come out I'll stick a pussywillow so far down your ear that nobody can reach it . . . and it'll sprout there and grow and grow, and you'll spend the rest of your life with a pussywillow bush growing out of your ear!"

BETH: You know she wouldn't do that!

ALICE: She would too! Herdmans will do anything. You just watch, they'll do something terrible and ruin the whole pageant . . . and it's all your mother's fault!

(During the Alice–Beth conversation the curtain closes behind them. At the end of the conversation they move off. The phone conversations are spotlighted in different areas of the forestage. Spot up on Mrs. McCarthy, telephoning.)

MRS. MCCARTHY: Jane? . . . Edna McCarthy. Did you hear about the . . . Well, it must be Grace's fault somehow! How else would the six of them end up in a Christmas pageant, when they ought to be in jail!

(Spot off Mrs. McCarthy; up on Irma Slocum, telephoning.)

IRMA: Vera? . . . Irma Slocum. I just heard that Imogene Herdman is going to be Mary in the Christmas pageant, and I . . . Is that a fact? All six of them? Vera, I live next door to that outfit and I'd rather live next door to a zoo. Has Grace gone crazy?

(Spot off Mrs. Slocum; up on Mrs. Armstrong in hospital bed, or in wheelchair, with leg in a cast, propped out in front of her.)

MRS. ARMSTRONG: Where did they come from? Who let them in? Imogene Herdman! . . . What kind of a child is that, to be Mary the Mother of Jesus? Where was Reverend Hopkins, I'd like to know. . . . He was what? . . . visiting shut-ins! Well, I'm shut-in, and he wasn't visiting me!

(Spots up on all ladies. Following speeches are simultaneous, till Mrs. Armstrong's last line.)

MRS. MCCARTHY: I said, why don't you let them hand out programs at the door? Grace said we never have programs for the pageant, but I said . . .

MRS. SLOCUM: . . . better nail down the church and lock up the silver service and hide the collection plates before they clean them out . . .

MRS. ARMSTRONG: What was the matter with Grace? Couldn't she have sent them away? Tell them to go home? Oh, I feel responsible . . . if I'd been up and around this never would have happened!

(Spots off all three ladies; up on Mother and Father as they enter from the wings SR. Each is carrying a grocery bag, and we can assume that some good friend in the supermarket has relayed Mrs. Armstrong's message.)

MOTHER: *(In high dudgeon, mimicking Mrs. A.)* . . . if I'd been up and around, this never would have happened! Well, let me tell you . . .

FATHER: Don't tell me, I'm on your side . . . the car's over there.

MOTHER: Helen Armstrong is not the only woman alive who can run a Christmas pageant! I made up my mind just to do the best I could under the circumstances, but now I'm going to make this the best Christmas pageant ever, and I'm going to do it with the Herdmans! After all, they raised their hands and nobody else did, and I don't care. . . .

FATHER: Good for you, Grace. *(Trying to move her along.)* The car's over there . . .

MOTHER: And you're going to help me!

FATHER: *(Stopped by this.)* Does that mean . . .

MOTHER: You have to go!

(Curtain up on church setting with kids sitting on the risers and on the floor. Mother, SL, is setting up the scene.)

MOTHER: The inn is back here, offstage . . . and the shepherds come in and gather around the manger . . .

LEROY: Where'd all the shepherds come from, anyway?

CLAUDE: What's an inn?

ELMER: It's like a motel, where people go to spend the night.

CLAUDE: What people? Jesus?

ALICE: Oh, honestly! Jesus wasn't even born yet. Mary and Joseph went there.

RALPH: Why?

ELMER: To pay their taxes.

OLLIE: At a motel?!?

IMOGENE: Shut up, Ollie! Everybody shut up! I want to hear *her*. *(To Mother.)* Begin at the beginning.

MOTHER: The beginning . . . ?

IMOGENE: The beginning of the play. What happens first?

MOTHER: Imogene, this is the Christmas story from the Bible. . . . Haven't you ever heard the Christmas story from the Bible? *(Pause, as she realizes that they have not.)* . . . Well, that's what this Christmas pageant is, so I'd better read it to you. *(There is a chorus of groans and grumbles from all the kids as Mother looks for a Bible on the benches and finds one.)*

BETH: I don't believe that, do you? That they never heard the Christmas story?

ALICE: Why not? They don't even know what a Bible is, and they never went to church in their whole life, till your dumb brother told them we got refreshments. Now we have to waste all this time for nothing.

MOTHER: All right now. *(Finds the place and starts to read.)* There went out a decree from Caesar Augustus, that all the world should be taxed . . . *(All the kids are visibly bored and itchy, except the Herdmans, who listen with the puzzled but determined concentration of people trying to make sense of a foreign language.)* . . . and Joseph went up from Galilee with Mary his wife, being great with child . . .

RALPH: *(Not so much trying to shock, as he is pleased to understand something.)* Pregnant! She was pregnant! *(There is much giggling and tittering.)*

MOTHER: All right now, that's enough. We all know that Mary was pregnant. *(Mother continues reading, under the Beth–Alice dialogue.)* . . . And it came to pass, while they were there, that the days were accomplished that she should be delivered, and she brought forth her firstborn son . . .

ALICE: *(To Beth.)* I don't think it's very nice to say Mary was pregnant.

BETH: Well, she was.

ALICE: I don't think *your mother* should say Mary was pregnant. It's better to say 'great with child.' I'm not supposed to talk about people being pregnant, especially in church.

MOTHER: *(Reading.)* . . . and wrapped him in swaddling clothes and laid him in a manger, because there was no room for them in the inn.

IMOGENE: My God! They didn't have room for Jesus?

MOTHER: Well, nobody knew the baby was going to be Jesus.

IMOGENE: Didn't Mary know? *(Points to Ralph.)* Didn't he know? What was the matter with Joseph, that he didn't tell them? Her pregnant and everything . . .

LEROY: What's a manger? Some kind of a bed?

MOTHER: Well, they didn't have a bed in the barn, so Mary had to use whatever there was. What would you do if you had a new baby and no bed to put the baby in?

IMOGENE: We put Gladys in a bureau drawer.

MOTHER: *(Slightly taken aback.)* Well, there you are. You didn't have a bed for Gladys, so you had to use . . . something else.

RALPH: Oh, we had a bed . . . only Ollie was still in it and he wouldn't get out. He didn't like Gladys. *(Yells at Ollie.)* Remember how you didn't like Gladys?

BETH: *(To Alice.)* That was pretty smart of Ollie, not to like Gladys right off the bat.

MOTHER: *Anyway* . . . a manger is a large wooden feeding trough for animals.

CLAUDE: What were the wadded up clothes?

MOTHER: The what?

CLAUDE: *(Pointing in the Bible.)* It said in there . . . she wrapped him in wadded up clothes.

MOTHER: *Swaddling* clothes. People used to wrap babies up very tightly in big pieces of material, to make them feel cozy . . .

IMOGENE: You mean they tied him up and put him in a feedbox? Where was the Child Welfare?

GLADYS: The Child Welfare's at our house every five minutes!

ALICE: There wasn't any child welfare in Bethlehem!

IMOGENE: I'll say there wasn't!

MOTHER: *(Raising her voice.)* . . . And there were shepherds, keeping watch over their flocks by night. And lo, the Angel of the Lord came upon them, and the Glory of . . .

GLADYS: *(Leaps up, flinging her arms out.)* Shazam!

MOTHER: What?

GLADYS: Out of the black night, with horrible vengeance, the Mighty Marvo . . .

MOTHER: I don't know what you're talking about, Gladys.

GLADYS: The Mighty Marvo, in Amazing Comics . . . out of the black night, with horrible vengeance . . .

MOTHER: This is the angel of the Lord, who comes to the shepherds . . .

GLADYS: Out of nowhere, right? In the black night, right?

MOTHER: Well . . . in a way . . . *(Gladys repeats her big line, almost to herself, as she sits down, looking pleased.)*

GLADYS: Shazam . . . !

MOTHER: *(Reading.)* Now when Jesus was born, there came Wise Men from the East, bearing gifts of gold and frankincense . . .

CLAUDE: *(To Ollie.)* What's that?

MOTHER: . . . and myrrh . . .

OLLIE: What's that?

MOTHER: They were . . . special things. Spices, and precious oils . . .

IMOGENE: Oil! What kind of a present is oil? We get better presents from the welfare!

LEROY: Were they the welfare? The Wise Men?

MOTHER: They were kings and they were sent . . .

IMOGENE: Well, it's about time somebody important showed up! If they're kings, they can get the baby out of the barn, and tell the innkeeper where to get off!

MOTHER: *(Ignoring this turn of plot.)* . . . They were sent by Herod, who was . . . well, he was the *main* king, and he wanted to find Jesus and have him put to death.

IMOGENE: My God! He just got born! They're gonna kill a baby?

RALPH: Who's Herod in this play?

MOTHER: Herod isn't in the play.

LEROY: He's out to kill the baby, and he isn't even in the play?

IMOGENE: Well, somebody better be Herod. *(Singles out a victim.)* Let Charlie be Herod, and he says, go get me that baby. And they say okay, because he's a king and all . . .

OLLIE: *(Warming to this scenario.)* But then they don't do it! They go back and get Herod! *(He makes a throttling gesture.)*

CHARLIE: I'm not going to be Herod!

MOTHER: No one is going to be Herod! *(The Herdmans, caught up in the spirit of things, are ranging over the stage, arguing, shoving other kids out of the way. Charlie scrambles over the choir risers, other kids, and his own feet to get to his Mother.)*

CLAUDE: No . . . Joseph gets the shepherds together and they go wipe out Herod! *(He makes a machine gun gesture.)*

CHARLIE: See? They're going to put one in, and it's going to be me, and I'll get killed!

MOTHER: *(Desperate.)* Forget about Herod! There's no Herod!

IMOGENE: And I run away with the baby till the fight's over!

RALPH: *(Collaring a stray shepherd by the front of his shirt.)* Somebody ought to fix the innkeeper . . . Gladys, you wipe out the innkeeper!

GLADYS: I can't! . . . I'm an angel!

(Curtain falls. Spotlight on the Herdmans as they enter from the wings SL and gather on and around the set piece. They are arguing about the pageant.)

IMOGENE: Well, I wouldn't just hang around out in the barn. I'd go get a room.

CLAUDE: She said there wasn't any room.

IMOGENE: Then I'd throw somebody out. I'd tell them I've got this baby and it's the middle of winter . . . so either get out or move over.

RALPH: I'd go after ol' Herod.

LEROY: I'd send the angel after him. She could just point her electric finger and turn him into a pile of ashes.

GLADYS: *(Happily.)* Yeh! . . . Zap!

OLLIE: What's the name of this play? She never said.

CLAUDE: Christmas pageant.

OLLIE: That's no name. That's what it *is*.

GLADYS: I know a name! . . . I know a name! I'd call it . . . Revenge at Bethlehem!

(Spotlight off Herdmans; up on Beth, SR.)

BETH: Revenge at Bethlehem! The Herdmans thought the Christmas story came right out of the F.B.I. files! At least they picked out the right villain—it was Herod they wanted to gang up on and not the baby Jesus. But the baby Jesus quit the pageant anyway. It was supposed to be Eugene Slocum, but Mrs. Slocum said she wasn't going to let Imogene Herdman get her hands on him. So we didn't have a baby Jesus, and that bothered my mother. She kept trying to scratch up a baby . . . even at the last rehearsal.

(Spotlight off Beth. Curtain up on church scene. Children are assembling for the rehearsal, in a motley assortment of costumes. Mother is counting noses, so to speak. Beth and Alice meet DS. Alice is writing in a small notebook. They are, by this time, on somewhat testy terms—Alice constantly on the attack, Beth on the defense.)

BETH: What do you keep writing in that book?

ALICE: It's . . . like a diary.

BETH: *(Snatches the book and reads.)* It is not. It's all about the Herdmans. *(Reads aloud.)* Imogene curses and swears all the time. Ralph talks about sexy things. Mrs. Bradley . . . *(Gives Alice a fierce look.)* . . . Mrs. Bradley called Mary pregnant . . . *(If looks could kill.)* . . . Gladys Herdman drinks communion wine . . . It isn't wine, it's grape juice.

ALICE: I don't care what it is, she drinks it. I've seen her three times with her mouth all purple. They steal, too—if you shake the birthday bank it doesn't make a sound, because they stole all the pennies out of it. And every time you go in the ladies' room the whole air is blue, and Imogene Herdman is sitting there in the Mary costume, smoking cigars!

BETH: *(Angry.)* And you wrote all this down? What for?

ALICE: *(Nose to nose with Beth.)* For my mother and Reverend Hopkins and the Ladies Aid Society and anybody else who wants to know what happened when the whole Christmas pageant turns out to be a big mess!

MOTHER: All right, everyone, let's get quiet. Beth, will you and Alice please come up here so we can get started. Now, this is our last rehearsal, and we're going to . . . *(Mrs. McCarthy enters in apron, carrying a baking pan.)*

MRS. MCCARTHY: Grace, I just wanted to tell you that we're all back in the kitchen making applesauce cake. We'll try not to bother you . . . I guess this is your dress rehearsal.

MOTHER: *(Glances at the uncostumed crowd.)* It's supposed to be. . . . Oh, Edna . . . didn't I hear that your niece had a baby a month or so ago? . . . A little girl?

MRS. MCCARTHY: *(Pleased and proud.)* Yes! She's five weeks old, and . . .

MOTHER: Well, I wonder how it would be if I were to call your niece and ask if we could borrow . . . *(Mrs. McCarthy, seeing the lay of the land and not liking it, leaps in.)*

MRS. MCCARTHY: Grace . . . no! I could make up some lie and tell you the baby's sick or cranky or something, but the truth is that she's perfectly healthy and happy and beautiful, and we all want her to stay that way. So we're certainly not going to hand her over to Imogene Herdman. Sorry, Grace. *(Mrs. McCarthy leaves.)*

DAVID: Mrs. Bradley, you can have my little brother for Jesus.

MOTHER: *(Newly hopeful.)* I didn't know you had a new baby, David.

DAVID: He's not new. He's four years old, but he's double-jointed and he could probably scrunch up.

MOTHER: Well, I don't think . . .

IMOGENE: I'll get us a baby.

MOTHER: How can you do that?

IMOGENE: There's always two or three babies in carriages outside the supermarket. I'll get one of them.

MOTHER: Imogene! You can't just walk off with somebody's baby! . . . I guess we'll forget about a baby. We'll just use the doll.

IMOGENE: Yeh. That's better, anyway . . . a doll can't bite you.

MOTHER: And, Imogene . . . you know Mary didn't wear earrings.

IMOGENE: I have to wear these. I got my ears pierced and if I don't keep something in them, they'll grow together.

MOTHER: Well, they won't grow together in an hour and a half. What did the doctor tell you to do?

IMOGENE: What doctor?

MOTHER: Well, who pierced your ears?

IMOGENE: Gladys.

ALICE: *(To Beth.)* She probably did it with an ice pick. I'll bet Imogene's ears turn black and fall off.

MOTHER: Well, we'll find something smaller. . . . Now, is that your costume? Is *that* what you're going to wear? *(To the whole group.)* You're all supposed to have your costumes on today.

BABY ANGEL SHIRLEY: I can't find my halo.

BABY ANGEL JUANITA: My wings got all bent.

ANGEL CHOIR MEMBER DORIS: Janet's got my robe.

BABY ANGEL SHIRLEY: My mother doesn't have any white sheets. Can I wear a sheet with balloons on it?

HOBIE: I haven't got any costume. I was never a shepherd before.

CHARLIE: You have to wear your father's bathrobe. That's what I have to do.

HOBIE: He hasn't got a bathrobe.

CHARLIE: What does he hang around the house in?

HOBIE: His underwear.

MOTHER: All right . . . pretend you're wearing costumes.

DAVID: Are we going through the whole thing?

MOTHER: Yes, of course . . . *(Mutters and groans.)* . . . but first we're going to practice just the entrances, so all of you go where you're supposed to be, and we'll start with the shepherds. *(Angels and Shepherds scramble offstage. Angel Choir stand around waiting for the full run-through. Ralph and Imogene slouch over to the manger and sit down. Mother comes down off the stage and stands in the aisle, or sits in the first row of seats.)* Just read the last few words, Maxine.

MAXINE: . . . shepherds keeping watch over their flocks by night . . .

MOTHER: Music . . . shepherds! *(Shepherds straggle in, pushing and shoving each other, and assemble around the manger.)*

MAXINE: And an Angel of the Lord appeared to them and . . .

GLADYS: *(Bursting out from behind the choir.)* Shazam!

MOTHER: No, Gladys!

GLADYS: *(Swooping at the Shepherds.)* Out of the black night . . .

MOTHER: No! *(Takes Gladys by the arm and heads her back to the choir risers.)* Go on, Maxine. *(As Mother returns to her seat, Gladys makes another threatening swoop toward the Shepherds.)*

MAXINE: . . . a multitude of the heavenly host . . .

MOTHER: Music . . . angels!

(The Baby Angels come on and are corraled into position.)

MOTHER: Music . . . Wise Men! *(Leroy, Claude, and Ollie enter, slouching aimlessly down the aisle and up to the manger. As they approach, Imogene holds up the doll by the back of the neck, waving it in the air.)*

IMOGENE: I've got the baby here . . . don't touch him! I named him Jesus!

MOTHER: *(Hurrying on stage.)* No, no, no! You don't say . . .

(Ralph grabs the doll. He and Imogene tussle over it as the shepherds scramble out of the way, creating a tangle of bodies and voices.)

MOTHER: *(Nerves fraying away.)* . . . anything! Mary doesn't say anything. No one says anything! Mary and Joseph . . .

IMOGENE: *(To Ralph.)* Let go! . . . Give it back! . . . *(Ralph and Imogene are pounding each other, till Mother gets in the middle and separates them.)*

MOTHER: *(Total exasperation.)* . . . make a lovely picture for us to look at while we think about Christmas and what it means! . . . Now, put the doll back.

IMOGENE: *(Disgruntled.)* I don't get to say anything . . . some angel tells me what to call the baby. . . . I would have named him Bill.

ALICE: Oh, what a terrible thing to say! *(Scribbles in her note book.)*

RALPH: What angel was that? There's angels all over the place. Was that Gladys?

MOTHER: No, Gladys brought the good news to the shepherds.

GLADYS: Yeh . . . *(Yells at the Shepherds.)* Unto you a child is born!

IMOGENE: Unto *me!* Not them, me! I'm the one that had the baby!

MOTHER: No, no, no. That just means that Jesus belongs to everybody. Unto *all* of us a child is born. *(Big sigh.)*

IMOGENE: Why didn't they let Mary name her own baby? What did that angel do, just walk up and say "Name him Jesus?"

MOTHER: *(Fed up with this.)* Yes.

ALICE: *(Piety personified: We can almost hear the harps and violins.)* I know what the angel said. She said . . . "His name shall be called Wonderful, Counselor, Mighty God, Everlasting Father, the Prince of Peace." *(There is a moment of amazed silence at this performance, so Imogene's response is loud and clear.)*

IMOGENE: My God! He'd never get out of the first grade if he had to write all that!

(This throws the rehearsal into confusion. There is a babble of voices—shock, laughter, grumbling at Alice, who marches offstage with her nose in the air, followed by Angel Choir members arguing with her ["Why did you have to say all that?" "We'll never get out of here!" "Nobody asked you, Alice"]. *The Shepherds, seeing a chance to escape, also scramble offstage, pushing and shoving and calling excuses* ["Gonna get a drink of water," "Have to go to the bathroom," "Be back in a minute."] *Ralph grabs the doll and throws it to Leroy who runs offstage, pursued by Imogene and the other Herdmans. All this is simultaneous.)*

MAXINE: *(Above the clamor.)* Mrs. Bradley, what should I do? Should I start over?

MOTHER: *(Sinking wearily on angel choir riser.)* Five minutes, Maxine. *(Calls to the others.)* Five minutes! *(Maxine leaves.)*

(Spotlight on Beth, DSR.)

BETH: We never did start over. And we never did go through the whole thing. *(Mrs. McCarthy enters SR and crosses, sniffing the air, to exit SL, as Beth speaks.)* The five minutes turned into fifteen minutes, and Imogene Herdman spent the whole time smoking cigars in the ladies' room. Then Mrs. McCarthy went to the ladies' room and saw all the smoke and called the fire department. And they came . . . right away.

MRS. MCCARTHY: *(Running on stage.)* Fire! There's a fire!

(She is followed by children running in from both directions. Sound of fire siren. Two firemen hurry up center aisle, carrying fire extinguishers and coiled hoses, shouting . . . ["Take the big hose in the side," "The place is full of kids," "Get the kids out," "Get everybody out," "Somewhere on the first floor"] *All the children, the firemen, Mrs. McCarthy and Mother mill around the stage, herding children off SR and L. The Herdmans are square in the middle of all this, grabbing at hoses, jumping on a fireman's back, etc. Lights down on set: Spotlight on Beth, DSR.)*

BETH: They cleared everybody out of the building and dragged a fire hose through the church looking for a fire to put out . . . but the only one they found was in the kitchen . . . and the applesauce cake burned up. Of course all the ladies were mad about that, and Mrs. McCarthy was mad, and my mother was mad.

(Spot off Beth; spot up on Mother and Mrs. McCarthy DSL.)

MOTHER: Why in the world did you call the fire department about a little smoke?

MRS. MCCARTHY: It was a lot of smoke. The ladies' room was full of thick smoke.

MOTHER: It couldn't have been. You just got excited. And now look—the church is full of firemen and the street is full of baby angels crying and shepherds climbing all over the fire truck and half the neighborhood. . . ! Didn't you know it was cigar smoke?

MRS. MCCARTHY: No, I didn't know it was cigar smoke! I don't expect to find cigar smoke in the ladies' room of the church!

(Spot off ladies; spot up on Beth.)

BETH: Alice Wendleken's mother was mad, too, and the whole Ladies' Aid Society was mad . . . and Reverend Hopkins said he didn't know what to think.

(Spot off Beth; spot up on Reverend Hopkins and Mother, SLC)

REVEREND HOPKINS: I've been on the telephone all day, and I can't make head or tails of it. Some people say they set fire to the ladies' room. Some people say they set fire to the kitchen. Vera Wendleken says all they do is talk about sex and underwear.

MOTHER: That was Hobie Clark talking about underwear. And they didn't set fire to anything. The only fire was in the kitchen, where the applesauce cake burned up.

REV. HOPKINS: Well, the whole church is in an uproar. I don't know . . . Jesus said, "Suffer the little children to come unto me," but I'm not sure he meant the Herdmans. . . . Grace, don't you think we should cancel the pageant?

MOTHER: I'll bet that was Helen Armstrong's idea.

REV. HOPKINS: We could blame it on the fire . . . makes a good excuse.

MOTHER: I'll bet that was Edna McCarthy's idea.

REV. HOPKINS: Everyone seems to think it's going to be a . . . a . . .

MOTHER: Disaster? *(Obviously, that's the word he had in mind.)* Well, they're wrong! . . . It's going to be the best Christmas pageant we ever had!

REV. HOPKINS: But, Grace. . . . I don't think anyone will come to see it!

(Spot out on them; up on Beth, DSR)

BETH: I didn't think so, either, and neither did Charlie . . . but we were wrong. On Christmas Eve the church was jammed full. Everybody came . . . to see what the Herdmans would do.

(Spot out on Beth, leaving stage area dark. Mother and Father enter from back of theatre and walk down center aisle to the stage. She is carrying tote bags, extra sheets, paper cups, etc. He is carrying a very large tree-type potted plant.)

MOTHER: Wait till I turn the lights on. *(House lights up.)* Now, watch your step.

FATHER: I can't even see where I'm going. I don't know what in the world you expect to do with this thing . . .

(Mother puts her various burdens on the floor and rummages through the tote bag, looking for an extra script. She pulls out one or two extra halos, rolls of scotch tape, box of tissues and a big white first aid kit with a red cross on the side of it.)

MOTHER: I thought it might look like a palm tree. *(Looks at the plant.)* I see now that it doesn't. . . . Oh, I don't have any idea what's going to happen tonight! We've never once gone through the whole thing, and the Herdmans still think it's some kind of spy story. It may be the first Christmas pageant in history where Joseph and the Wise Men get in a fight and Mary runs away with the baby.

(They are setting up the tree, the manger, counting the shepherds' crooks, etc. during their dialogue. House lights remain up, so that when the pageant begins, the lights can go down, and we will see it as a play within a play.)

MOTHER: Where are the kids?

FATHER: All the kids in the world are down in the basement, putting on bedsheets.

MOTHER: I mean our kids.

BETH: *(As they enter from SL)* We're here.

MOTHER: Well, go get your costumes on. It's getting late.

BETH: It's just going to be awful, you know. They look like trick or treat—all dirty and fastened together with safety pins and wearing their mouldy old sneakers . . . Mary and Joseph, I mean. They look like refugees or something.

FATHER: Well . . . that's what they were . . . Mary and Joseph. They *were* refugees, in a way. They were a long way from home, didn't have any place to stay, didn't know anybody. They were probably cold and hungry and tired . . . and messy. *(Beth is struck by the sense of this new idea: Charlie is not.)*

CHARLIE: I don't know about cold and hungry, but they're sure messy. *(They leave.)*

MOTHER: Oh, dear. . . . Do you think I should . . .

FATHER: I think you worry too much. Now . . . *(Briskly, to get her mind off the Herdmans)* . . . I'm going to push baby angels onstage, and I'm going to hand out shepherds' crooks and then push *them* onstage. . . . When do I do all that?

MOTHER: *(Hands him script.)* Just follow this script.

FATHER: *(Flips through script.)* Baby angels . . . shepherds . . . Wise men . . . It doesn't seem to say here where the fire engines come in.

MOTHER: *(In no mood for jokes.)* Oh-h-h!

FATHER: Just kidding. *(He pats her shoulder, collects the crooks, and exits.)*

(During preceding dialogue Angel Choir members, Shepherds, two or three Herdmans, Baby Angels drift on and offstage and are now more or less in place.)

MOTHER: Is everyone here? . . . Beth, I want you and Alice down front where you can help the baby angels. *(Goes to wings and calls.)* Will you all come on stage please? *(With a predictable amount of shoving and jostling, everyone assembles on stage.)* I just want to see how you look. *(Brief pause while she sees, and the audience sees, that they do indeed look like trick or treat.)* Gladys, where's your halo?

GLADYS: Our cat buried it. . . . Listen, I think I ought to say something besides the baby came. Why would they all get up and tear off after some baby they don't even know? I ought to tell them it's Jesus, and I ought to tell them where he is.

MOTHER: No, Gladys. You tell them, "Unto you a child is born" . . . and that's *all* you tell them. Now, let's all go backstage, and try to be quiet while people are coming. And good luck!

ALICE: Mrs. Bradley, actors don't say good luck, actors say break a leg.

MOTHER: Yes, I know that, Alice, but in this case I don't think . . . *(Claude, Leroy, Ollie and Gladys attack each other in response to "break a leg." Mother separates them.)* For those of you who don't know what that means, it's just a theatrical saying. It doesn't really mean break a leg . . . your own or anyone else's! *(They all exit, Imogene last, dangling the doll upside down, by one leg.)* And, Imogene, try to remember that that's a baby. *(Starts to exit, and adds.)* And, for tonight anyway, it's the baby Jesus.

(She exits, leaving Imogene alone. House lights down half. In this scene Imogene, surrounded for the first time with the simple, traditional trappings of Christmas—the stillness, the dim light, the words "The Baby Jesus" in her mind—reflects the sense of wonder and mystery evoked in everyone on Christmas Eve. She cradles the doll awkwardly in her arms, takes a cloth from the manger and wraps the doll in it . . . straightens her veil, smooths her costume . . . becomes Mary. She looks out toward the audience, and we sense that she is a little shy about her own emotional reaction: That she hopes there is no one there to see her in this uncharacteristic moment. She exits SL. House lights down. Stage lights up half. Maxine enters SL and lights candles across the back of the stage. (Note: can be light-cued, but more effective if battery operated candles are used.) As Maxine crosses to her place on the risers, Angel Choir starts "O Little Town of Bethlehem" offstage, and then enters, single file, singing. They take their places on risers, SR. Alice and Beth should be DS so we can hear their conversation. Maxine on the US end of top riser. When the carol is finished, Maxine speaks.)

MAXINE: In the days of Caesar Augustus a decree went out that all the world should be taxed, and Joseph went into Bethlehem with Mary his wife, who was great with child. And while they were there she brought forth her first born son, and wrapped him in swaddling clothes and laid him in a manger because there was no room for them in the inn.

(Angel Choir sings "Away in a Manger," as Ralph and Imogene enter SL. They are hesitant, awkward, visibly sobered by this Christmas Eve service and by all the people watching them. Imogene handles the doll with a kind of motherliness, puts it up on her shoulder, as if to burp it. It may be necessary or useful for the choir to continue, humming, as Beth and Alice talk.)

ALICE: Look at them, aren't they awful! What's she doing with the baby? Oh! . . . I don't think it's very nice to burp the baby Jesus, as if he had colic.

BETH: Well, he could have had colic, just like any other baby.

ALICE: I don't care. It looks awful. And *they* look awful.

BETH: So what? They just came a long way and now they don't have any place to sleep, and they've got a new baby to worry about.

ALICE: Who, Ralph and Imogene?

BETH: No. Mary and Joseph. *(Ralph and Imogene take their places at the manger.)*

MAXINE: And in that region there were shepherds in the field, keeping watch over their flocks by night.

(Choir sings "While Shepherds Watched Their Flocks by Night" [One verse of this, and all carols.] During this carol the shepherds enter down center aisle, collecting their crooks one by one from Father. They cluster in front of the stage, sitting and standing.)

MAXINE: And an angel of the Lord appeared to them. . . . *(No Gladys.)* . . . An angel of the Lord appeared to them. . . . *(Still no Gladys.)* The glory of the Lord shone round about and they were sore afraid *when the angel of the Lord* appeared to them and said, Be not. . . . *(Gladys, having chosen her moment, now roars up the aisle, around the shepherds, and up on stage with her message.)*

GLADYS: Hey! . . . Hey! . . . Unto you a child is born! . . . It's Jesus, and he's in the barn. . . . Go see him! *(When the Shepherds hesitate, she grabs one to move him along, and then another one.)* Go on, he's over there. . . . Go on! *(Shepherds move on stage and gather around the manger.)*

MAXINE: *(Though flustered, recovers.)* And suddenly there was a multitude of the heavenly host, saying Glory to God in the highest, and on earth peace among men.

(Choir sings "Angels We Have Heard on High" while Baby Angels enter SL, steered along by Father. We see him doing this because one angel comes on, turns around and goes back, and must be redirected. Another angel comes on, stops cold, and must be moved along. They join the crowd on stage, lining up in front of the angel choir. The first "Gloria" of the chorus is sung with a blast.)

NE: When Jesus was born, there came Wise Men from the East to worship him, bringing gifts of gold and frankincense and myrrh.

(Choir sings "We Three Kings of Orient Are" as Leroy, Ollie and Claude enter down center aisle, with Leroy carrying a ham, wrapped with a merry Christmas ribbon.)

ALICE: They look awful, too. And what's that Leroy's got?

BETH: *(Craning her neck to see.)* It's . . . it's a ham!

ALICE: A ham! I'll bet they stole it!

BETH: No . . . I think it's the ham from their welfare basket.

ALICE: You mean it's their own ham? . . . Then they must hate ham.

BETH: Well, even if they hate ham, Alice, it's the only thing they ever gave away in their whole life. *(Choir hums "We Three Kings" as Wise Men kneel at the manger.)*

MAXINE: Being warned in a dream that they should not return to their own country, the Wise Men departed another way. The shepherds also departed, praising God for all that they had seen and heard. But Mary kept all these things and pondered them in her heart.

(Choir sings "Silent Night." It is assumed that the congregation would join in this carol, and as Father steps just inside the wings we see that he, too, is singing. Mother steps just inside the wings, SR, and she too is singing. Imogene takes the doll from the manger and holds it. She is crying. Choir continues, humming.)

ALICE: Beth . . . Look . . . Mary's crying. *(She turns and leans back toward the wings where Mother is standing.)* Mrs. Bradley . . . Mary's crying.

(Curtain falls as the choir is humming. Mrs. McCarthy and Mrs. Slocum come up from the audience and meet at the stage.)

MRS. MCCARTHY: Could you believe that was Imogene Herdman? And all the rest of them? Irma, this was the best Christmas pageant we ever had, and I'm not sure why, but I think it was them. Could that be?

MRS. SLOCUM: Oh, I always get weepy about the pageant. I guess it's the children and the carols and all. . . . But you're right, this was the best one . . . and it should have been the worst.

MRS. MCCARTHY: There was just something . . . different.

MRS. SLOCUM: Well, the angel of the Lord was different!

MRS. MCCARTHY: Yes, but you know, I liked that! Had lots of spirit. Sometimes you can't even hear the angel of the Lord. *(Starts off SL.)* I must find Grace, and tell her . . .

MRS. SLOCUM: *(Following.)* I just wish now that I'd let her have Eugene to be the baby Jesus.

MRS. MCCARTHY: *(Stops.)* Who was the baby Jesus?

MRS. SLOCUM: Why, it was a doll.

MRS. MCCARTHY: Oh, I don't think so, Irma. That was no doll.

MRS. SLOCUM: Well . . . it did seem real. *(They exit.)*

(Spot up on Beth DSR.)

BETH: It did seem real, as if it might have happened just that way. We all thought the pageant was about Jesus, but that was only part of it. It was about a new baby, and his mother and father who were in a whole lot of trouble—no money, no place to go, no doctor, nobody they knew. And then, arriving from the East—like my uncle from New Jersey—some rich friends.

(The curtain opens behind her. Father looks out, as if he's the one who pulled the curtain, and crosses to meet Mother, who enters from the opposite side. She is smiling and is obviously pleased with the pageant, the Herdmans, and herself. He hugs her and they have a conversation which we don't hear, but can surmise—they are talking about the surprise success of the whole thing, about Gladys, about the balky baby angels, about the ham. As they talk they gather up shepherds' crooks, hymn books, abandoned pieces of costumes, and then leave together. Beth's speech is simultaneous with this action.)

BETH: Because of the Herdmans, it was a whole new story—Imogene, burping the baby, and the Wise Men bringing such a sensible present. After all, they couldn't eat frankincense! And even Gladys—"He's in the barn. Go see him" . . . so the shepherds didn't have to stumble around all over the countryside. *(Behind her, Imogene enters, looks around the empty stage, then lays the doll in the manger and leaves.)* But I guess it wasn't like that for Imogene. For her, the Christmas pageant turned out to be all wonder and mystery, as if she just caught on to what Christmas was all about. When it was over we had a party in the basement, but the Herdmans didn't stay. They didn't have any cocoa and they didn't walk off with all the cookies, and they wouldn't even take their candy canes. *(Behind her Mother and Father and Charlie enter. About to close up and go home. Father is wearing his bathrobe. Beth moves back to join them.)*

FATHER: I guess that's about it. Any kids left downstairs?

MOTHER: No, everyone's gone. . . . You know you have your bathrobe on. You aren't going to wear it, are you?

FATHER: Why not? Maybe people will think I was a shepherd. I wouldn't mind being taken for a shepherd in this Christmas pageant.

CHARLIE: Yes, you would! When it was over some lady came up and hugged me because I was a shepherd. . . . Should I bring this ham?

MOTHER: It's the Herdmans' ham from their welfare basket . . . but they wouldn't take it back. Leroy said, "It's a present. You don't take back a present."

CHARLIE: Leroy said that? They must hate ham.

BETH: You and Alice Wendleken!

FATHER: . . . What about the lights?

MOTHER: They're on a timer. They go off at midnight.

FATHER: That's not far away. *(Looks at his watch, and then at the others)* . . . It's almost Christmas. *(We hear, offstage, the sound of carillon bells.)*

MOTHER: . . . almost Christmas, kids.

BETH: . . . almost Christmas, Charlie.

(Lights dim: Candles still on, as they reach out to each other, to touch hands, to draw together. We hear (with the bells and rising above them) a reprise of lines from the pageant, spoken by different people, so there is a mix of voices and pace. The lines should flow together.)

"And it came to pass in the days of . . .
"And there were shepherds abiding. . . .
"A multitude, praising God. . . .
"I bring you good tidings of great joy . . ."

GLADYS: *(Offstage.)* Hey! . . . *(She runs on to CS [spotlight on her], and points at the audience.)* . . . Hey, unto you a child is born!

(All lights down for slow count of 4-5. Lights up. Entire company on stage, to sing "Joy to the World." We should hear the first phrase in a strong burst.)

CURTAIN

THE BEST CHRISTMAS PAGEANT EVER—ALTERNATE OPENING SCENE

(As the play opens, the curtain is down. Beth is sitting SR. Alice and Maxine are sitting SL. Spotlight on Beth.)

BETH: The Herdmans were the worst kids in the whole history of the world. They lied and stole and smoked cigars, even the girls, and talked dirty and hit little kids and cussed their teachers and took the name of the Lord in vain and set fire to Fred Shoemaker's old broken down tool house.

(Spot up on Maxine and Alice.)

ALICE: And that's not all! Somebody sent five dozen doughnuts for the firemen and the Herdmans ate them all, and what they couldn't eat they stuffed in their pockets and down the front of their shirts.

MAXINE: And they wrote this really really dirty word on the back of Naomi Waddell's favorite turtle, so now Naomi can't take it to the Y.M.C.A. pet show . . . her mother won't let her.

ALICE: What was the word? *(Maxine whispers it.)*

ALICE: *(Horrified.)* Oh-h-h!

MAXINE: And that's not all! They did it with fluorescent paint, so it glows in the dark. When you can't even see the turtle, you can still see the word.

ALICE: And they put a whole bunch of tadpoles in the school drinking fountain, and Miss Barnes swallowed two or three by mistake. Somebody yelled, "Mildred, stop! You're drinking tadpoles! . . . but it was too late.

MAXINE: Did she get sick?

ALICE: Not right away.

(Spotlight on Beth, as Alice and Maxine move off.)

BETH: And *that's* not all! *(Change of tone and delivery here, to say to the audience* . . . Now I'm going to tell you about the Christmas Pageant and what they did to that.) . . . There were six of them . . . *(During Beth's speech the Herdmans come on from the wings left and position themselves on and around the set piece, with Gladys at the top level, in a pose reminiscent of the first illustration in the book,* The Best Christmas Pageant Ever.) . . . Ralph, Imogene, Leroy, Claude, Ollie and Gladys . . . and they went through the Woodrow Wilson school like those South American fish that strip your bones clean. And they went around town the same way—stealing things and tearing things up and whamming kids. So it was hard to get away from them. There was only one safe place.

CHARLIE: *(Offstage, singing.)*
Sweet hour of prayer, sweet hour of prayer,
Because there are no Herdmans there.
But Jesus loves us, as they say,
Because he keeps them miles away.

BETH: That's my little brother, Charlie. That's what he said when the Sunday school teacher asked what was his favorite thing about church. Charlie said, "no Herdmans." That made the teacher mad because all the other kids said nice things about God and Jesus and good feeling. But old Charlie told the real truth—*No Herdmans!*

GOLLIWHOPPERS!

by

FLORA B. ATKIN

A dramatization motivated by the themes and traditions of American folklore

---

GOLLIWHOPPERS!

CHARACTERS

A troupe of seven to nine traveling players who converge upon the scene to share their tales of America's earlier days with young and old.

Players act, sing, narrate, mime, chant, dance, work puppets, and play simple music instruments interchangeably. [NOTE: Music to be used in the performance of this script may be purchased from the publisher, New Plays for Children.]

SETTING

A bit of space, indoor or out, flat or raised, and children to watch and participate.

PROLOGUE AND EPILOGUE

(The present)

THE TALES

(America's earlier days)

Big Jesse Febold Ebenezer Chopalong: Backwoods tall tale
The Sun Snatchers: Indian legend
The Knee-High Man: Negro cante-fable
Goll-Gollee-Gee: Mountain ballad

PROLOGUE

Curtains open, full daylight; ladder, stage center; standard, upstage right.

Players enter from as many different doors into auditorium as possible. Player One carries fiddle-type instrument; Player Two carries signboard map; Player Three carries stool; other players carry knapsacks and hobo bundles containing properties and sound effects; all players wear kazoos as pendants around necks; four players carry map insignia attachments in pockets.

(Player One enters, looks around, tests ladder, climbs up, tunes fiddle, plays introduction to Greeting Song [music A], continues to accompany throughout Prologue.)

(Player Two enters, places map on standard.)

PLAYER TWO: *(Sings.)* Hi—Huzza—Hello!

(Other players enter from different doors of auditorium, travel through audience greeting everyone.)

OTHER PLAYERS: *(Sing.)* Hi—Huzza—Hello!

ALL: *(Sing in barber-shop type harmony.)*

Hello to you, greetings all
G'morning how 'ja doo!
Hi ya,
  Howdy,
    Peace,
      —and how!
Top of the morning to you!
(daytime)
(evening)

(Greeting Song repeated as all reach stage, put props down, gather together downstage.) (Music B.)

In the not so long ago
  America's earlier days
Folks would get together
  in mighty curious ways
without the flicks and radio

FIRST PLAYER: —No television screen?

SECOND PLAYER: Before bedtime

THIRD PLAYER: —But after chow

FOURTH PLAYER: —at twilight, in between

ALL: Told tales about their blunders and sang their country's wonders.

(Momentary silence and freeze.)

(Loud whisper.) GOLLIWHOPPERS!

(SING.)

Let us get together *(All do grand right-and-left.)*
In mighty curious ways
From the not so long ago
Of America's earlier days.

TRANSITION AND INTRODUCTION TO FIRST TALE

All hum "America's Earlier Days" on kazoos, place knapsacks and props for tales 2, 3, and 4 far upstage left; Caller takes knapsack with props for first tale, crosses to down right. Percussionist carries knapsack with sound effects down left; ladder moved upstage and turned on diagonal.

Map brought downstage. Fade out of melody. All freeze, focus on map. One player puts "tree" insignia in Illinois region of map.

CALLER: Rarrapin' Tarrapin' backwood boasters
Lally-gaggin' on old settlers' day
Story swappers! Golliwhoppers!
They danced a galumping sashay!

Golliwhopper one!
Big Jesse Febold Ebenezer Chopalong!

("Band" [fiddler and washboard player] plays introduction to Backwoods Polka, [music 1] as six players choose partners and take places for polka. Map replaced on standard.)

Golliwhop in! Story begin!

BIG JESSE FEBOLD EBENEZER CHOPALONG

(To be played broadly with exaggerated pantomime; stoneboat, hollow log, deerskin tugs, and axe all pantomimed; "dead" animals move along together, with upper bodies rigid to suggest riding on stoneboat; hand props procured from caller's knapsack as needed.)

CALLER: *(Sings.) (Six players do vigorous polka.)*

Hitched his mule and went to the lake
Tossed a pebble and killed a snake
Big Jesse Febold Ebenezer Chopalong

Caught him a trout fish by the snout
When he turned his overalls inside out
Big Jesse Febold Ebenezer Chopalong

(Dance changes to waltz rhythm, ends with spin of partner, plopping down, feet sprawled.)

When he swung his trusty ax
All the beasts they sure made tracks
　　With nary a gun
　　He was never outdone
Big Jesse Febold Ebenezer Chopalong

(Melody fade-out, laughter by players as they cross up left to observe and react until needed as characters in tale.)

(Narrates): Big Jesse Febold Ebenezer Chopalong! A "genuine" American folk hero from the pioneer days of our country. He swung his ax and he cut a path through the wilderness from Maine to Illinois in two days. Folks tell all kinds of tales about him . . . funny stories . . . tall tales!

("Big Jesse" player crosses to caller, gets cap and bandanna-kerchief from caller's knapsack and begins to "grow" in size, as he dons costume pieces.)

JESSE: *(Jesse strides to center, pantomimes chopping and building, [sound effects with wood blocks and sticks]; caller fades out up right.)*

Now when Big Jesse Febold Ebenezer Chopalong was eighteen, he cleared a place in the woods . . . Built a log cabin . . .

(Wife-player crosses to Jesse; Grant Wood pose; [brief music interlude].)

And took him a wife.

(Wife fades out [turns, goes up right], dons dust cap and apron. Jesse down right.)

One spring morning, as usual, Big Jesse was chopping away with his trusty ax . . .

(Jesse makes grandiose swing through air, with "ax," starts to chop, stops in mid-air.)

AMELIA: When his wife, Amelia, came out a-lookin' for him. *(Amelia crosses to Jesse.)* "Big Jesse Febold Ebenezer Chopalong, lay off that everlasting chopping and go hunting! You know right well we have had nothing to eat but hominy mush for almost six weeks."

JESSE: "No use in going hunting until the barge comes up the river, Amelia . . . Don't even have one load for my gun."

AMELIA: "Our salt gourd is rattlin' hollow. I cooked the last ground of coffee for your breakfast. Well, at least go on down to the lake and cut a section from that old hollow chestnut log . . . If I don't have a new hominy barrel we won't even have hominy mush to eat."

JESSE: *(Sighs resignedly.)* So Big Jesse sharpened his ax, tied some new deerskin tugs he had just fashioned to his stoneboat, his trusty stoneboat that could glide over the bumpy trail like a sled over snow. *(Jesse sharpens "ax," crosses up right, ties "tugs" to "stoneboat.")* Then he hitched up Old Skidmore, the mule. *(Caller dons ears, becomes mule.)*

MULE: *(Brays.)*

JESSE: And they headed down the steep winding trail.

(Jesse "rides stoneboat," pulled by mule. Amelia waves goodbye, turns upstage, fades out of scene.)

Skid-a-long, Skidmore!

(Zig-zag ride down left [music I], [clip-clop with coconut shells].)

Gee around there, you skiddy old mule—gee—gee.
Whoa, Skidmore!

SKIDMORE: *(Brays.)* When they got down to the lake, Big Jesse unhitched Old Skidmore so he could wander around and eat all the grass he wanted.

(Skidmore establishes lake down left by taking a drink, then wanders around stage, actively reacting to action that follows. Jesse moves "stoneboat" out of way.)

JESSE: Jesse strode over to the hollow log and began to chop a section for the new hominy barrel . . .

(Jesse crosses down right to establish "hollow log," makes grandiose swings to chop, stops short in mid-air.)

GEESE: "Honk, Honk, Honk."

(Geese players swoop into lake down left and "swim" in circles continuing to "honk" under dialogue.)

SKIDMORE: Jesse had hardly swung his ax when a terrific honking noise made him look around.

JESSE: "Well, I'll be jiggered! The lake is covered with wild geese!" He put his ax down and eased into that water. He swam around underneath all those geese *(Jesse crosses to lake, swims in amongst geese.)* and tied their feet up with a rope from around his waist. Poked his head up amongst them— *(Slaps hands, hollers.)* "Whoosh!"

GEESE: "Honk, Honk, Honk." *(Geese, flustered, begin to flap wings, honk loudly, stretch necks.)*

SKIDMORE: Those geese got lined up somehow and pulled Big Jesse Febold Ebenezer Chopalong out of the water and took off with him a-hanging on.

(Geese grab one another in chain, Jesse hanging on behind, fly all over stage in circles.)

GEESE: "Honk, Honk, Honk."

SKIDMORE: Right on around the lake in circles they flew.

JESSE: When they were about to light, Jesse snubbed the line so tight those geese fell down—

GEESE: Dead!

(Jesse jerks "line," causing geese to pivot and fall down. Geese are motionless for a second. Geese raise heads on "dead" and down again. [Thud sound on drum].)

JESSE: Then Jesse went back to his chopping. *(Jesse strides over to hollow log, starts grandiose swing to chop. [Rustling sound]. Deer player peers out from around ladder.)*

SKIDMORE: He had hardly swung his ax when a big rustling in the woods made him look around. *(Jesse stops short in mid-air, spies deer.)*

JESSE: "As fine a big buck deer as I've ever seen peering out at me." *(To deer.)* "Grin, grin." *(Jesse grins.)*

SKIDMORE: *(To audience.)* "Anybody knows a deer can't stand grinning. *(Jesse continues to say "Grin" until deer is dead.)*

DEER: *(Frightened.)* Seeing Big Jesse Febold Ebenezer Chopalong grinning so wide, from ear to ear, the big buck deer, from sheer fright, fell over *(Pause.)* Dead. *(Deer freezes, falls over, is motionless for a second, then raises head to say "dead" and down again. [Thud.])*

JESSE: Then Jesse went back to his chopping. *(Jesse to log, starts to chop again.)*

SNAKE: Hiss! *(Snake [dead goose player] rises, slithers toward Jesse.)*

SKIDMORE: He had hardly swung his ax when a hissing sound made him look around.

(Jesse stops in mid air, spies snake coming toward him. Snake continues hissing.)

JESSE: "As quick-slithering a snake as I've ever seen, coming after me."

(Rabbit [second dead goose player] rises, hops forward, squats between Jesse and snake.)

RABBIT: And a little rabbit just sitting there innocently watching.

SNAKE: *(Hisses.)* Seeing Big Jesse stoop to seek a little pebble *(Jesse picks up pebble),* the snake opened his mouth wide to strike.

JESSE: *(Tosses pebble high into air. Skidmore follows pebble's flight through air.)* But Jesse tossed that little pebble up into the air and it landed straight down the snake's throat.

SNAKE: The snake choked, fell over and landed on . . .

(Snake makes choking noises, slithers down on rabbit.)

RABBIT: Little rabbit just sitting there innocently watching.

SNAKE AND RABBIT: And they both fell down—*(Pause.)* dead. *(Snake and rabbit down, raise heads for "dead," and down again. [Thud.])*

JESSE: Then Big Jesse went back to his chopping. *(Jesse to log, starts to chop again.)*

SKIDMORE: He had hardly swung his ax when a scritching-scratching sound *(Scratching sound.)* made him look around. Looking up he saw a big shaggy black bear lumbering his way. *(Bear [dead deer player] appears stage left.)*

JESSE: Now Jesse was not one to run away.

SKIDMORE: Besides, bears are short-sighted.

JESSE: But the wind was in the wrong direction and that bear gave out a grunt like a saw going through an oak tree.

(Bear starts long low grunt crescendoing to a growl after Jesse's comment, starts lumbering stage right. Jesse begins to back away.)

JESSE: In one galumptuous spring, Jesse reached the nearest tree and climbed up lickety-split. His feet slipped and he sank down, into the hollow heart of the tree, into something soft and sticky. Just when he thought he was disappearing altogether, his feet touched bottom and there he stood up to his chin in wild honey.

(Jesse leaps to ladder, climbs 2 or 3 rungs, sidles around to supports on back, and by bending knees, appears to sink down inside.)

BEAR: Black bear climbed the tree *(Sniff, sniff.)*, smelled the sweet honey, and started to back down inside the tree trunk to get to the honey.

(Bear goes up 2 or 3 rungs, turns around as he sidles to side of ladder and begins to let rear down "inside," so rear faces Jesse.)

JESSE: The instant the bear's tail was within reach, Jesse clamped his fist in the bear's fur and bellowed *"Scat!" (Jesse grabs bear in back.)*

BEAR: *(Roars.)* The terrified bear tore out of the tree trunk.

(Bear pulls self up, Jesse hanging on till he is on top of ladder, and then lets go of bear who jumps off ladder, falls down, raises head for "dead" and down again. [Thud.])

JESSE: Dragging Jesse up with him.

BEAR: The bear plunged to the ground below *(Pause.)*, dead.

JESSE: Jesse climbed down the trunk. He was that sticky with honey it took him a long time. *(Jesse slowly comes down ladder, very sticky action.)* When he got down, he went to the shore to wash. He was so stuck with the honey, he lost his balance, and kersplashed into the lake. *(Jesse down left, into "lake," treads water, waves.)*

SKIDMORE: *(Brays.)* Big Jesse just stayed out there a-treading water, enjoying it.

JESSE: *(Action pantomimed as narrated.)* After a while Jesse climbed out of the lake and felt something flapping around inside his overalls. He shook himself and pulled out a big trout fish from his pants leg, and a snapping turtle out of the back of his shirt. By then it was getting late. With one big chop, Jesse cut off a section of that big hollow log, and made a hominy barrel. *(Jesse crosses to "log," down right, one galumptuous swing and chop [loud chop sound]. "Dead" animals reverberate.)* Then with one little thwack, he made a hole in the tree for the honey to drain out into his barrel. *(Jesse takes "barrel" to "tree" [ladder]. Little chop on "tree" [thwack sound].)*

SKIDMORE: *(Sniffs, brays in disgust.)* The honey had hardly started to drip when a powerful smell, and it wasn't honey, made Big Jesse look around.

(Skunks [geese players] up on knees into row.)

JESSE: *(Smells.)* "Skunks! As pretty a family of skunks sitting on a log as I ever seen!"

SKIDMORE: *(Action pantomimed as narrated.)* As quick as a jagged flash of lightning Big Jesse chipped a few shavings from the edge of the log and tossed them into the air.

SKUNKS: The skunks took those shavings for snow flakes and began to shiver and shake from the cold, till they froze stiff. *(Shivering sounds with spoons.)*

JESSE: Big Jesse banged the log . . . wham! *(Jesse kicks "log," [beater on woodblock].)*

SKUNKS: Those skunks toppled over . . . dead! *(Skunks fall over, pause, raise heads for "dead" and down again. [Thud.])*

JESSE: Jesse picked up the new hominy barrel full of honey, put it on the stoneboat and hitched up Old Skidmore.

(Jesse brings "barrel" and "stoneboat" down right. Skidmore crosses down right, faces left to be "hitched.")

SKIDMORE: Then Big Jesse loaded all those dead animals on the stoneboat.

(Jesse stands up the "dead" animals and places them on stoneboat. Bear is rolled into place, then lifted. Animals assume grotesque poses, with frozen stares and leers [music A while animals loaded]. Jesse pulls Skidmore. Stoneboat full of animals follows. [Music continues slowly, clip-clops start; both increase in tempo as they near home.])

And they started up the path for home.

JESSE: It was dark, pitch dark, and Jesse could not see where he was going. He had to grope each step of the way back up the steep trail.

(Jesse and Skidmore with stoneboat and animals behind reverse zig-zag trip. Stoneboat gets further and further behind and stops far over on stage left.)

SKIDMORE: Skidmore *(Grunt.)* knew the way. But it was a heavy load. And those deerskin tugs began to stretch.

(Jesse and Skidmore continue up right.)

JESSE: Rain began to fall. Jesse started going triple-double time in a frolic gait to keep warm.

([Music tempo fast.] Amelia, holding imaginary lantern, appears down right looking for Jesse. [Music out.] Jesse stops up right, pats Skidmore, but does not look stage left.)

"Whoa, Skidmore, we're home!"

AMELIA: "Big Jesse Febold Ebenezer Chopalong! Where have you been all day and out in this rain at night?"

JESSE: "Been chopping your hominy barrel."

AMELIA: "Choppin' a hominy barrel? All day? Well where is it, and where is the stoneboat?" *(Amelia looks behind Skidmore.)*

JESSE: "Right behind me."

AMELIA: "No stoneboat here."

JESSE: "I declare! Who absquatulated with my stoneboat?" *(Jesse looks behind Skidmore.)*

AMELIA: "The deerskin tugs probably stretched so much in the rain that the stoneboat got left behind in the woods."

JESSE: "Well it's too dark tonight to go find it, and besides I'm boliterated and exflunctitated and I'm so hungry that my stomach thinks my mouth's gone on vacation."

AMELIA: So they went in to their supper . . .

AMELIA AND JESSE: Of cold hominy mush. *(Amelia and Jesse turn upstage, Skidmore goes to sleep.*

[Brief music interlude.]
[Rooster crows—percussionist.])

SKIDMORE: *(Awakens.)* The next morning the sun shone bright and hot.

MUSICIAN: "It's so hot today, the corn is probably popping in the field."

("Dead" animals move up slowly to Skidmore.)

PERCUSSIONIST: "It's so hot today, if I were to go fishing I'd meet the fish swimming up the dry trail."

(Amelia and Jesse appear, cross down right fanning and mopping themselves from heat, are not aware of stoneboat.)

AMELIA: "Big Jesse, you go get that stoneboat."

JESSE: "Too hot today, Amelia, even if your tongue were coated with bear grease, you couldn't make me go."

AMELIA: *(With nagging persistence.)* "Big Jesse Febold Ebenezer Chopalong!"

JESSE: *(Sighs.)* So Big Jesse sharpened his ax, and got ready to start down the path for the stoneboat.

SKIDMORE: *(Brays.)*

(Skidmore senses something behind him, tries to call attention to it.)

AMELIA: "Well, pickle my turnips, the stoneboat is here! Right to the cabin door."

(One after the other, all three look up, surprised, notice stoneboat.)

JESSE: "Well, paddle my gullywhump! *(Looks up surprised.)* The sun was that hot it dried the deerskin tugs till they shrank and drew the stoneboat whippety-cut up to the door."

SKIDMORE: "Well, pull my ears! Three brays for the sun!"

AMELIA: *(Amelia pokes in amongst dead animals, lifting limbs, discovering all the loot.)* "Oh, oh! I'll smoke the bear meats, salt the fish, make hats from the skunk skins, a belt from the snake skins; I'll dry the deerskins, I'll make turtle soup, and bake the rabbit in honey for Sunday dinner, and we'll have feather beds out of the goose feathers. *(To Jesse.)* Big Jesse Febold Ebenezer Chopalong, you told a tarradiddle. You said you didn't have any powder for your gun."

JESSE: "Not an acorn's worth, Amelia. But I can swing an ax! Or my name ain't Big Jesse Febold Ebenezer Chopalong." *(Jesse makes one big final swing and chop [chop sound] and holds pose.)*

(Skidmore removes ears, stands up-right.)

SKIDMORE-CALLER: Golliwhop. Story stop!

TRANSITION AND INTRODUCTION TO SECOND TALE

All hum "America's Earlier Days" on kazoos. Properties replaced in knapsack. Ladder placed stage center, with stool immediately downstage of it. Narrator-Drummer dons vest, gets drum and beater. Sun-holder player hands out props for new tale.

Map brought forward. Fade out of melody. All freeze, focus on map. One player puts "sun" insignia on map in south-west region.

(Narrator-drummer crosses downstage, drumming very rhythmically.)

NARRATOR: *(Setting an epic mood.)*

Harvest ceremonials
Indian medicine show
Fiestas, round-ups
Pow-wows long ago!

Golliwhopper two!
The sun snatchers!

(Narrator crosses to stage left, continues drumming as map replaced on standard. Villagers assemble stage left. Medicine men to center; all don costume pieces. [Drum stops for a moment.])

Golliwhop in! Story begin!

The Sun Snatchers

(Land of Darkness action is on stage right; Land of Sun on stage left; a stylized, dance-like movement throughout, suggesting a long-time-ago legend.)

In the early days of the world, in the time of the very long ago, there was no sun on this side of the world.

(Narrator resumes drumming, punctuating and accenting action and dialogue as needed.)

From the Eskimos of Alaska down to the Indian tribes of California and Oklahoma, the people were in darkness.

(Narrator crosses down left.)

MEDICINE MAN-WHO-CHANTS: *(Chants.)* O Great Spirit, bring back the warm sun for us!

(Medicine Man-Who-Chants sits on stool, shakes rattles to rhythm of spoken lines.)

MEDICINE MAN WHO-CHANTS: Brighten our dark cold sky. Bring us the warm sun so that our people may live.

NARRATOR: The tribal medicine men made their strongest charms and performed ritual dances to try to bring light.

(Medicine Man-Who-Chants hums softly in high falsetto under narrator. [Drum out.])

MEDICINE MAN WHO-CHANTS:

Yo mah-ah nah, sah ooo-nahd
wo-ah-kah, gah-ah-nahn
    Hah-wah
    Kah-wah
    Gwee—chud
Wah-chah been-ah-nehm
Hah-ah zay-dah dem
    Hah-wah
    Kah-wah
    Gwee—chud

(Medicine Man-Who-Chants recites in deep low voice to rhythm of music II, as Medicine Man-Who-Dances shakes rattles and dances.)

NARRATOR: But the darkness continued. There was much sorrow among the people. They stumbled around trying to find their way.

(Narrator resumes drumming.)

(Medicine Men fade out upstage removing stool, as Villagers of Land of Darkness grope their way downstage.)

LONG RUNNER: It is as dark as midnight inside the earth. *(Runners grope around down right, bumping into each other, expressing cold and darkness through posture, shivering.)*

SHORT-LONG RUNNER: It is as cold as the ice on the frozen river.

SHORT RUNNER: I'm as hungry as a bear after his long winter sleep. Ugh!

(Long Runner collides with Short Runner.)

LONG RUNNER: Sorry, little brother, I did not mean to bump into you. I did not see you.

SHORT-LONG RUNNER: It is so dark. How shall we get along?

(Runners freeze momentarily.)

NARRATOR: The world grew colder and colder. The night showed no sign of ending.

LONG RUNNER: I don't like the darkness.

SHORT-LONG RUNNER: I'm cold.

(All huddle, to keep warm.)

SHORT RUNNER: Without the sun, the plants are dying.

(Each turns downstage, looks out on his line.)

LONG RUNNER: Without the sun, there is no food to eat.

SHORT-LONG RUNNER: Without the sun, we cannot live.

LONG RUNNER: There used to be a sun.

SHORT RUNNER: Where has it gone?

SHORT-LONG RUNNER: Who could have taken it?

LONG RUNNER: Someone must have stolen it. Wake me when you find it. I'm going to try to sleep.

(Long Runner breaks away from group, lies down, others turn upstage. Coyote stalks downstage, observes villagers, goes into audience; characterizes all his action and lines with cunning.)

SHORT-LONG RUNNER: Brr! I'm cold.

NARRATOR: Coyote was coming along and saw how unhappy the people were.

COYOTE: *(To audience.)* I guess we'd better do something about this.
(Coyote returns to stage to villagers down right.)
(To villagers.) There is a sun.

VILLAGERS: *(Seeing coyote for the first time, turn downstage.) (Ad lib, disbelieving.)* There is? . . . Where? . . . Where is it?

COYOTE: It's on the other side of the world . . . to the east.

SHORT RUNNER: What's it doing there?

COYOTE: The people who have it won't let it go. They keep it close by, so no one will take it away from them.

SHORT-LONG RUNNER: What good is it to us then?

COYOTE: Not any—right now. But we could go and borrow that sun . . . for a while.

SHORT RUNNER: Borrow it?

LONG RUNNER: Yes. Let's borrow it. *(Long Runner gets up, rejoins group.)*

SHORT-LONG RUNNER: It wouldn't really be stealing. *(With hope and growing enthusiasm.)*

LONG RUNNER: No, because we don't want to keep it for always.

SHORT RUNNER: We could give it back to them . . . sometimes.

SHORT-LONG RUNNER: Sort of take turns.

LONG RUNNER: But how do we get it?

COYOTE: *(To Long Runner.)* How far can you run?

LONG RUNNER: *(A bit pompously.)* A long way. I have won for my village many times in the racing festivals.

COYOTE: *(To Short-Long Runner.)* How far can *you* run?

SHORT-LONG RUNNER: *(Modestly.)* A *short* long way. We are a small village. We have only one *long* runner here.

COYOTE: *(To Short Runner.)* How far can *you* run?

SHORT RUNNER: *(Embarrassed.)* A short way.

COYOTE: I don't run far myself *(Aside.)* If I can avoid it *(To villagers.)* But I have a plan. Come close.

(Short huddle and buzz. Coyote comes out of huddle.)

Now let's go fetch the sun back.

NARRATOR: So Long Runner—
Short-Long Runner—
and Short Runner,
with Coyote close behind, started forth, groping their way in the darkness.

(Villagers line up one at a time, as narrator calls each name and drums his individual rhythm (1 heavy beat for Long Runner, 2 or 3 irregular beats for Short-Long Runner, pattery sound for Short Runner.)

COYOTE: *(Spurring Villagers on, a long piercing call.)* Light Hayolkal-al-al.

(Villagers start forth groping their way. Coyote surreptitiously places mountains [ladder] in the path.)

NARRATOR: Over the mountains they traveled.

(Coyote continues to repeat call softly under narration.)

VILLAGERS: *(Chant.)*

To the east to find light
Through the darkness of night
To the land of the light.

(Villagers chant as they climb mountain; Coyote running around, spurring them on.)

COYOTE: Light Hayolkal-al-al.

(Villagers continue groping along. Coyote places trees [ladder turned sideways] in path.)

NARRATOR: Through the forests of tall trees they traveled.

(Coyote's call continues softly under narration as Villagers repeat chant.)

COYOTE: Light Hayolkal-al-al.

(Villagers crawl under ladder, spurred on by Coyote's action and call.)

NARRATOR: Down through the canyons they traveled.

(Long Runner and Short-Long Runner start down into the auditorium, as though letting themselves down into a canyon.)

SHORT RUNNER: *(Hesitating.)* Night stretches as far as I can see. How will we find our way across the wide plains?

(Short Runner pauses at edge of stage. Others stop to listen.)

COYOTE: The wind will pick up my call as it blows across the plains, and lead you in the right direction.

SHORT RUNNER: But it's a far journey. One voice is not enough to carry.

(Short Runner remains on edge of stage.)

COYOTE: Other coyotes out there will hear me. Coyotes have sharp ears. Some of them will surely answer my call.

(Coyote indicates audience, goes down into audience taking them into the plan as he did on his entrance.)

SHORT RUNNER: And their voices will be carried along by the wind to guide us. *(Ad libs.)* Oh I hope they will help us *(or)* I think I hear one now.

(Ad lib reaction to audience response as Short Runner climbs down canyon.)

COYOTE: Light Hayolkal-al-al.

(Coyote remains near stage, calling; listening for and encouraging audience coyote response. Narrator crosses down right, continuing drumming.)

VILLAGERS: *(Chant.)* To the east to find light through the darkness of night to the land full of light.

(Villagers grope along audience left aisle toward rear of auditorium; Short Runner stopping mid-way in aisle; Short-Long Runner eventually stopping in rear of auditorium.)

LONG RUNNER: Long Runner ran ahead of the others.

(Long Runner starts across rear of auditorium to audience right aisle. Sun Holder, on stage, gradually raises sun.)

After a while Long Runner saw a little rim of light ahead like the sun coming up in the winter time.

COYOTE: Light Hayolkal-al-al.

(Sun Players position themselves stage left for stick-ball game.)

VILLAGERS: *(Chant.)*

To the east there *is* light
On the trail marked by light
To the land full of light!

NARRATOR: The light grew stronger and stronger, till the sky was a whole blaze of light ahead of Long Runner. Finally Long Runner came to the village of the people who had the sun.

(Short-Long Runner remains in rear of auditorium, as Long Runner continues to stare down audience right aisle. Focus is on Long Runner and stage. Other runners and Coyote fade out in audience [squat].)

SUN PEOPLE: *(Ad lib.)* You missed it . . . my turn next . . . watch this swing . . .

(Long Runner watches game, unseen by players. Sun Players, with imaginary long sticks, are swatting at the sun-ball, running and jumping all around.)

NARRATOR: They were playing a stickball game, using the sun as a ball.

LONG RUNNER: *(Long Runner enters land of Sun People.) (To Sun People.)* Hah oo! Greetings!

SUN PLAYERS: *(Ad lib.)* Hah oo! Enter and be welcome, stranger.

(Sun Players continue game with only a glance at Long Runner, who watches for a moment or two.)

LONG RUNNER: Friends, may I play your game too?

SUN PEOPLE: *(Ad lib.)* You may, stranger, if you think you know how. Choose a stick . . . take your place in line.

(Long Runner joins in game, watching carefully.)

NARRATOR: Long Runner joined in the game. He played for a long time. All the while he was playing, he was making his plan.

SUN PLAYER ONE: Hold the pole higher. The sun is falling.

(Sun Holder begins to tire, fidgets, switches sun pole from one position to another.)

SUN HOLDER: It is tiresome to hold it. Why do I always have to be the one to hold the sun?

SUN PLAYER TWO: Watch what you are doing. We'll lose the sun.

SUN HOLDER: Well, someone else could hold it for a while.

SUN PLAYER ONE: Hold still and don't ruin the game.

SUN HOLDER: I too would like to play in the game.

SUN PLAYER TWO: If that sun falls against the Earth, everything will burn up.

LONG RUNNER: I will hold it for you for a while.

(Game stops abruptly.)

SUN HOLDER: *(Surprised.)* You will? Well, er, uh, thanks!

SUN PLAYER ONE: *(Sun Players move in to Long Runner, a bit suspiciously.)* Wait a minute. Do you know how to hold the great sun?

SUN PLAYER TWO: You have to be very careful and hold it tightly and never let it go.

LONG RUNNER: Do not worry. I shall not let it go.

NARRATOR: Long Runner took the pole and put it in the position he had seen the sun people do so many times, but instead of swinging it out to be hit, he swung it over his shoulder and started running with it.

(Sun Holder gives pole to Long Runner, who momentarily blinds Sun People by swinging sun in their eyes, as he runs off stage, starts up audience aisle, retracing his steps.)

SUN PLAYER ONE: *(Aghast.)* Our sun is being stolen.

(Sun Players, after initial shock, start into audience, but cannot catch up with Long Runner.)

SUN HOLDER: —The stranger is a thief.

SUN PLAYER TWO: Follow him.

SUN PLAYER ONE: Without the sun we cannot see.

(Sun People slow down.)

SUN PLAYER TWO: It has grown dark and cold.

NARRATOR: So they turned back.

(Sun People return to stage, fade out up left, after which Narrator crosses down left.)

LONG RUNNER: Long Runner ran a long way. He ran and ran, but *(Voice gasping, slowing down.)* when he started to give out, he met up with . . .

(Long Runner runs up aisle with sun, meets Short-Long Runner in rear. Each runner continues slowly to stage after handing over the sun to next.)

SHORT-LONG RUNNER: Short-Long Runner, who grabbed the sun and ran and ran. Just when his breath was about to give out he met up with . . .

(Short-Long Runner takes sun and runs, meets Short Runner midway in audience left aisle.)

SHORT RUNNER: Short Runner who grabbed the sun and ran. When he couldn't run any farther . . .

(Short Runner takes sun and runs toward stage, tires quickly.)

COYOTE: *(Very near stage.)* Coyote came along. Coyote just walked along so easy that . . .

(Coyote "appears," takes sun from Short Runner.)

LONG RUNNER: Long Runner . . .

(Narrator accompanies each runner's name with his individual drum rhythm.)

SHORT-LONG RUNNER: Short-Long Runner . . .

SHORT RUNNER: And Short Runner . . .

THREE RUNNERS: All caught up and together . . .

NARRATOR: They climbed the canyon walls, traveled through the forests of tall trees, and over the mountains, till they reached their own village.

(Coyote and runners on to stage, through ladder, over the ladder, return to village stage right.)

COYOTE: Well, now you have the sun.

(Coyote hands sun to Short Runner, then fades out repositioning ladder.)

SHORT RUNNER: Yes, now we have light and the plants will grow.

SHORT-LONG RUNNER: Now we have light. We can see what we are doing.

(Villagers cavort, exuberant, passing sun from one to the other, then begin to tire, become irritable.)

LONG RUNNER: Now we have light, we can see where we're going.

SHORT RUNNER: That sun is as hot as a forest fire.

SHORT-LONG RUNNER: That sun is just too hot.

SHORT RUNNER: Don't give it to me. That bright sun can put your eyes out.

LONG RUNNER: There's too much light.

SHORT-LONG RUNNER: Yes, we don't need so much light.

(Short-Long Runner is stuck holding sun.)

RAVEN: *(Raven on ladder rung, observing.)* Awk! Awk!

NARRATOR: Raven had come to live near the village. He saw how unhappy the people were, and felt sorry for them.

RAVEN: Awk! Aawk! I must help the poor people who have too much sunshine.

NARRATOR: So Raven flew around the village gathering the people together.

(Raven descends ladder, flies around villagers; one by one, they see him, and gather round.)

SHORT-LONG RUNNER: Raven has come.

SHORT RUNNER: It is Raven, who sets things right.

NARRATOR: They gathered round to see what he would do.

RAVEN: Why don't you place the sun where it will shine on you without its being too hot?

LONG RUNNER: Where?

SHORT RUNNER: How could we?

RAVEN: Take it to the top of the tallest mountain peak.

SHORT RUNNER: How could we get it there? I can't climb that high.

SHORT-LONG RUNNER: Nor can I.

LONG RUNNER: And I'm too tired.

RAVEN: Give me the sun. I do not tire so easily. I will fly the sun to the tallest mountain, and up into the sky.

(Raven takes sun, flies around.)

NARRATOR: And Raven flew the sun up into the sky.

(Raven "flies" up ladder, moves sun around.)

SHORT RUNNER: That's a good place for it.

LONG RUNNER: It's far enough away not to burn anything.

SHORT-LONG RUNNER: It has plenty of room to move around.

(Sun People turn forward, see sun.)

SHORT RUNNER: It can travel from one side of the sky to the other.

SUN PLAYER ONE: The sun is up in the sky.

SUN HOLDER: We shall have light again.

SUN PLAYER TWO: But we shall have to find something else to use when we play our stickball game.

SHORT RUNNER: Now all the people on both sides of the world can divide the light evenly.

RUNNERS AND SUN PEOPLE: *(Chanting.)*
From the east comes the light
To the west goes the light.

(Raven slowly moves sun from side to side in an arc above ladder.)

(Villager unobtrusively climbs ladder from upstage, takes sun pole, releasing raven's wings which are free to spread out.)

NARRATOR: And that's the way it was. And that's the way it is to this very day. Some people believed it was the coyote who brought the sun.

(Coyote appears downstage.)

COYOTE: Light Hayolkal.

NARRATOR: Some said it was the Raven.

(Raven spreads wings.)

RAVEN: Awk! Awk!

NARRATOR: But one tribe in the northwest made a totem story pole in honor of both the animals that helped bring the sun to all the people.

(Sun Player hands large totem masks to Raven and Coyote, who don them, and with sun above them, Raven on ladder, and Coyote immediately below him, form totem pole and hold pose.) (Drum flourish.)

Golliwhop! Story stop!

TRANSITION AND INTRODUCTION TO THIRD TALE

All hum "America's Earlier Days" on kazoos. Properties replaced in knapsack. Ladder brought downstage left, stool to stage center. Narrator for third tale hands out props.

Map brought forward. Fade out of melody. All freeze, focus on map. One player puts "boot" insignia on map in southeast region.

NARRATOR: *(Recites.)*

They kick their feet and stomp
In the Alabama swamp
Don't need no bands
Just slap their hands

Golliwhopper three!
The Knee-High Man

(All clap in rhythm set by Narrator's recitation as map replaced on standard. Puppeteer sits on stool, and other players gather in tight semicircle around stool, sit on floor.)

Golliwhop in! Story begin!

THE KNEE-HIGH MAN

(To be played in a spirit of conviviality, intimacy and spontaneity.)

ALL: *(Chant.)*

When the sun—goes down—
Time to gath—'er round—
When the moon—comes out—
We begin—to *shout*!

(Pattin' Juba slapping and stomping [music III] as puppeteer assembles Knee-High Man puppet, and Narrator dances and assists Puppeteer.)

We kick our feet and stomp
In the cool wet swamp
Don't need—no bands—
Just slap—our hands—

When the sun—goes down—
Time to gath—'er round—
When the moon—comes out—
We begin—to *shout*!

(Puppeteer with finished puppet crosses down center.)

NARRATOR: The Knee-High Man! He lived down by the swamp. No bigger than a kidney bean when he was born, full grown he was still only knee-high to a man . . . He was always wanting to be big instead of little.

(Knee-High Man scrunches in boot, then stretches up.)

(Narrator moves to right of center to comment and assist. Stool moved downstage.)

KNEE-HIGH MAN: I'm gonna ask the biggest thing in this neighborhood how I can get sizable.

(Knee-High Man joins players in slapping hands. Audience joins in spontaneously.)

ALL: *(Chant.)*

When the sun—goes down—
Time to gath—'er round—
When the moon—comes out—
We begin—to *shout*!

(One player becomes boar, pulls sleeves over hands to make hooves, starts a loud "grunt" under last line of refrain, gets up, crosses toward Knee-High Man.)

BOAR: *(Grunts.)* Mr. Wild Boar was coming along.

KNEE-HIGH MAN: Good evening, brother Wild Boar.

BOAR: Why hello there, Mr. Knee-High Man.

KNEE-HIGH MAN: Brother Wild Boar, can you tell me how I can get sizable like you?

BOAR: You want to be big like me?

KNEE-HIGH MAN: Um-mm.

BOAR: First you eats lots of corn cobs, rotten fruit skins, and slop. Then you snorts and snorts and squeals and squeals.

Next you runs around and around and around.

(Boar demonstrates each action with gusto, and onomatopoetic sounds [snorts, snuffles, squeals] as he crosses stage.)

And after that, you wallows in the swamp mud.
And first thing you know, you gets big like me.

(Boar fades out, joins players.)

KNEE-HIGH MAN: *(Calling after Boar.)* Oh, thank you, brother Wild Boar. I'm sure gonna do all the things you told me to do. *(To audience or narrator.)* And I'm gonna be sizable like brother Wild Boar.

(Narrator, down on knee, sympathizes and assists.)

First I eats lots of corn cobs . . . can't chew them. Rotten fruit skins . . . tastes awful . . . and slop.
Ooh those corn cobs made my stomach hurt.

(Narrator gently pats puppet's stomach [boot].)

Now I'm gonna snort and squeal.

(Puppet-size noises.)

Ooh, snorting and squealing make my neck hurt. Hurts my throat and my ears too.
Next I runs around and around.

(Puppeteer runs Knee-High Man in a small circle and back to stool.)

Running sure makes my body tired, and trying so hard hurts my mind, but I'm gonna be sizable. *(To audience.)* What else did brother Wild Boar tell me to do? . . . Oh yes, wallow in the swamp mud. Now how am I gonna do that?

(Narrator scoops up imaginary mud and Knee-High Man "wallows" in narrator's arms.)

Ugh. I'm cold, wet and dizzy. Well I done did all brother Wild Boar told me . . . *(To audience.)* Now am I sizable?

(Players react amusedly, shake heads.)

(Disappointed.) How come brother Wild Boar ain't helped me none?

(Players shrug shoulders.)

ALL: *(Chant.)*

When the sun—goes down—
Time to gath—'er round—
When the moon—comes out—
We begin—to *shout*!

ALLIGATOR: *(Bellows.)*

(Knee-High Man and players slap hands. Alligator player pulls on long green socks, begins loud "bellow" under last line of refrain.)

KNEE-HIGH MAN: Good evening, Sister Alligator.

ALLIGATOR: Why hello there, Mr. Knee-High Man.

KNEE-HIGH MAN: Sister Alligator, can you tell me how I can get sizable like you?

ALLIGATOR: First you eats lots of snakes, turtles and frogs.

(Alligator eats each with relish; crunching and squishing sounds. Loud bellows.)

Then you bellows and bellows. Next you takes your tail and thrash it and swish it all around.

(Thrashes "tail," [legs together], players dodge "tail."*)*

After that, you buries yourself deep in the swamp mud, and first thing you knows, you is big like me.

(Alligator fades out, joins players.)

KNEE-HIGH MAN: *(Calling after her.)* Oh, thank you, sister Alligator. *(To audience. Narrator and players "catch" food animals and hand them to Knee-High Man.)* First, I eats lots of snakes . . . tastes tough; turtles . . . they stick in my throat; and frogs . . . can't get that frog down.

Ooh! Those turtles made my stomach hurt. *(Narrator sympathizes.)* Now I'm gonna open my jaws wide and bellow. Bellowing sure hurts my jaws.

(Puppet-size bellows.)

Next I'm gonna thrash and swish my tail around. How'm I gonna do that?

(Narrator takes boot foot and "swishes" it.)

Ooh, thrashing sure hurts my body. And trying so hard hurts my mind. But I'm gonna be sizable. *(To audience.)* Now, what was the other thing I'm s'posed to do? . . . Oh yes, bury myself in the swamp mud . . . could hardly breathe. Ugh! I'm all muddy and cold. *(To audience.)* Now am I sizable?

(Players shake heads.)

(Sighs.) All those things just made me littler.

Now how come sister Alligator ain't helped me none?

(Players shrug, amusedly.)

ALL: *(Chant.)*

When the sun—goes down—
Time to gath—'er round—
When the moon—comes out—
We begin—to *shout*!

(All slap to rhythm. Owl Player dons eye-glasses, appears up in "tree" [ladder], starts hooting under last line of refrain. Players rise, cross to stage right, form new grouping, facing owl.)

OWL:

Hoot, hoot, hoot, hoot.
Swamp people wanting to be what
They ain't have bad luck.
Swamp people wanting to be what
They ain't have bad luck.
Hoot, hoot, hoot, hoot-aaahh!

KNEE-HIGH MAN: Good evening, Mr. Hoot Owl.

OWL: Hello-o-o-o-o, Mr. Knee-High Man.

KNEE-HIGH MAN: Mr. Hoot Owl, you're so wise, can you tell me how I can get sizable?

OWL: How come you wants to be big, Mr. Knee-High Man?

KNEE-HIGH MAN: I wants to be sizable so when I gits into a fight I can whup.

OWL: Anybody ever try to pick a scrap with you?

(Puppet tries to fight with Players, who pet him, amusedly.)

KNEE-HIGH MAN: I guess I ain't got no cause to fight.

OWL: And you ain't got no cause to be bigger than you is.

KNEE-HIGH MAN: But, Mr. Hoot Owl, I wants to be sizable so when I get chased, I can git away fast.

OWL: Can anybody see you when you scrunch down inside your boot in the swamp grass?

KNEE-HIGH MAN: Anybody see me?

(Puppet scrunches down.)

PLAYERS: No!

KNEE-HIGH MAN: Then I guess I ain't got no cause to run.

OWL: And you ain't got no cause to be bigger than you is.

KNEE-HIGH MAN: But, Mr. Hoot Owl, I wants to be sizable so I can see a far ways.

OWL: Well, can't you climb a tree?

(Puppet climbs ladder.)

KNEE-HIGH MAN: Yes, and I can see a far ways from up here.

OWL: Mr. Knee-High Man, you ain't got no cause to be bigger in de body, but you sure got cause to be bigger in de brain. Hoot!

KNEE-HIGH MAN: Um-hmm.

(Knee-High Man finally comprehends, expresses contentment by "dancing" around on top of ladder and nodding head. Owl continues to hoot softly under narration.)

OWL:

Swamp people proud of who they
  Is has good luck.
Swamp people proud of who they
  Is has good luck.
Hoot, hoot, hoot, hoot-aaahh!

NARRATOR: So from that day on, Mr. Knee-High Man was satisfied, and he was never wanting to be big again.

Golliwhop. Story stop!

TRANSITION AND INTRODUCTION TO FOURTH TALE

All hum "America's Earlier Days" on kazoos. Properties placed in knapsack. Ladder placed sideways up center. Caller for fourth tale gives out props, crosses down right, fiddler down left. Players don costume pieces.

Map brought forward. Fade out of melody. All freeze, focus on map. One player puts "apple" insignia on map in Appalachian region.

CALLER:

Roof-raising parties
With seven course meals
From apple pie to apple jack
They danced the mountain reels

Golliwhopper four!
Goll-Gollee-gee

(Fiddler tunes up [music IV] as other players in contra formation to dance a modified Virginia Reel, with Caller and Old Woman as head couple.)

Golliwhop in! Story begin!

Goll-Gollee-Gee

(Outdoor sequences stylized and rhythmic, with music accompaniment, suggesting a dance ballad—and extension of the introductory reel. Action in Old Woman's house played somewhat more realistically.)

CALLER: *(Sings.)*

Have you seen my hired maid
Come by here in a promenade?
Wears her hair in a pigtail
braid
Swiped my gold, but didn't get
paid.

(All forward and back. All do si do.)

ALL: *(Sing.)*

A toe and a heel, everybody reel
A toe and a heel, everybody reel
A toe and a heel, everybody reel
Find my money that gal did steal!

(Head couple reels alternately with each other, and with other dancers in turn down the line. Other couples toe and heel and clap.)

CALLER: *(Sings.)*

Have you seen my hired girl
Come by here with a swish and a
swirl?
Wears her hair in a fancy curl
Swiped my gold, and away she whirl.

(Head couple promenades back to place as others swing their partners.)

Take her arm and down the middle
With your foot, keep time to the
fiddle
On to the gate, don't be late
Keep it going lickety spate.

(Head couple forms arch, slides down line as other couples go under and follow suit until all return to original positions.)

ALL: *(Sing.)*

A toe and a heel, everybody reel
A toe and a heel, everybody reel . . .

(Couples promenade, fade out. [Music out].)

CALLER: Down in the Appalachian Mountains of Virginia and the Carolinas they tell a story about a stingy old woman who kept a big fat purse with all her money in it, a' hanging up in the chimney. She was so stingy it hurt to spend a penny. All she ate was ashcakes and water.

(Old Woman establishes ladder area as fireplace; pokes purse up chimney [hangs it on hook inside ladder].)

Time came, she was getting so old, she couldn't see very well . . .

(Old Woman starts to sweep with broom upside down, discovers her mistake, reverses broom.)

OLD WOMAN: I have to have someone to help with the housework and all.

CALLER: So she sent way over to the other side of Dog Hobble Ridge for a hired girl. Now this girl, Lazey Lou, was mighty lazy.

(Lazey Lou, lazily and slovenly, strolls down center.)

LAZEY LOU: *(To audience.)* I have no intentions of working very hard.

OLD WOMAN: *(To caller.)* I have no intentions of paying her very much. *(Old Woman hands broom to Lazey Lou.)*

LAZEY LOU: I'll mess around just enough to get around Old Woman. *(Lazey Lou pushes broom near chimney).*

OLD WOMAN: Get away from that chimney, and sweep the dust puddles from under the bed.

LAZEY LOU: Yes Ma'am.

CALLER: One day, Old Woman wanted to go out visitin'.

(Old Woman adjusts bonnet.)

OLD WOMAN: While I'm gone, Lazey Lou, you're to make the bed, wash the dishes, and darn the socks. And mind you, don't you dare look up the chimney. *(Exits down right.)*

(Lazey Lou watches Old Woman leave, looks up chimney, pulls down purse, hands broom to caller.)

CALLER: Lazey Lou watched till Old Woman was good and gone. Then she went and looked straight up the chimney. Got to pokin' around with her broom stick, and directly a big fat purse fell down.

(Lazey Lou looks inside purse.)

LAZEY LOU: Jumpin' Jiminies! Gold! Scads of gold pieces!

CALLER: That girl, she took that purse and run!

(Lazey Lou closes purse, raises leg to sprint—holds stylized pose for split second.)

Ran down the road a piece.
And then she took out across the pasture field.

(Music in. Lazey Lou runs into audience and back onto stage as Cow crosses into place down right, Horse down left; Tree up on third rung of ladder, with arm holding branch over top of ladder and part way down other side.)

COW: *(Moos.)* There was Brimful, the milk cow, a'hurtin' so bad. Nobody had milked her all day.

(Ballad; half sung—half spoken; rhythmically, but in character; action in stylized reel dance steps; music IV-a.)

COW: *(Mooing.)*

Lazey-Lou, la-zy girl.
Where you running with a whirl?

LAZEY LOU: I'm running from that stingy hag.

COW: Please stay and milk my brimful bag.

LAZEY LOU:

Got no time to fool with you.
I'm wealthy now, with work I'm through.

COW: Please stay and milk my brimful bag.

LAZEY LOU: I'm off with a jig and gone with a jag.

CALLER: *(Narrates.)* And off she went, over the fence, and down to Bear-Wallow Hollow.

(Lazey Lou continues run-around to horse. Caller holds out broom handle as fence, for Lazey Lou to go over. Cow fades out.)

HORSE: *(Neighs.)* There was Old Roany, the plough horse, a hurtin' bad from having been beaten so hard the day before.

(Ballad: half sung—half spoken; with action in stylized reel.)

HORSE: *(Neighs.)*

Lazey Lou, la-zy girl.
Where you running with a whirl?

LAZEY LOU: I'm running from Old Woman's shack.

HORSE: Please stay and rub my old sore back.

LAZEY LOU: Got no time to fool with you.
I'm wealthy now, with work I'm through.

HORSE: Please stay and rub my aching back.

LAZEY LOU: I'm off with a tick and gone with a tack.

CALLER: *(Narrates.)* On she went, across to old Wine Sappy Orchard.

(Lazey Lou continues run-around to ladder. Horse fades out.)

TREE: *(Groans.)* There was old Apple Tree with its branches all loaded down to the ground with apples nobody had picked.

(Ballad: half sung—half spoken.)

TREE: Lazey Lou, la-zy girl.
Where you running with a whirl?

LAZEY LOU: *(Short of breath.)* I'm running from Old Woman's farm.

TREE: Please pick my apples, and rest my arm.

LAZEY LOU: *(Panting.)* Got no time to fool with you. I'm wealthy now, with work I'm through. *(Hesitates.)* But I think I'll hide up in your arm while I catch my breath all safe from harm. *(Climbs on struts of ladder, hides head behind branch.)*

CALLER: *(Narrates.)* Old Woman, she got back late that evenin'.

(Lazey Lou and tree fade out [turn upstage, descend ladder and cross up left.] Music out.)

Went in the house and hollered for that girl.

(Old Woman enters from down right.)

OLD WOMAN: Lazey Lou, where are you, girl? Lazey Lou-u-u.

CALLER: When nobody answered, Old Woman looked up the chimney, saw her money purse gone.

(Old Woman crosses to ladder, looks for purse.)

OLD WOMAN: Goll-Gollee-Gee! *(Old Woman continues to holler and squawk Goll-Gollee-Gee under caller's lines as she follows same pattern as Lazey Lou. Music in. Animals, Tree, and Lazey Lou in place.)*

CALLER: She took off down the road with a loop loop dee dee a hollerin' and a squawkin'.

OLD WOMAN: Goll-Gollee-Gee, my money's gone from me.

CALLER: *(Narrates.)* Took out across the pasture field.

(Ballad: sung, Old Woman and Cow "reel" together in character.)

OLD WOMAN: *(To cow.)*

Have you seen my hired maid
Come by here in a promenade?
Wears her hair in a pigtail braid.
Took my gold, but didn't get paid.

COW:

With a toe and heel she did reel.
With a toe and heel she did reel.
Run right past a skootin' fast
With a purse of money, that gal did steal.

OLD WOMAN: Goll-Gollee-Gee, my money's gone from me.

(Old Woman continues to holler and squawk "Goll-Gollee-Gee" under caller's lines as she heads for horse.)

CALLER: *(Narrates.)* Come to the fence, Old Woman skooted under, and down to Bear-Wallow Hollow.

(Caller holds out broom handle for Old Woman to go under. Ballad: sung as Old Woman and Horse "reel" together in character.)

OLD WOMAN: *(To horse.)*

Have you seen my hired maid
Come by here in a promenade?
Wears her hair in a pigtail braid.
Took my gold but didn't get paid.

HORSE: *(Neighs.)*

With a toe and a heel she did reel.
Run right past, a skootin' fast
With a purse of money that gal did steal.

OLD WOMAN: Goll-Gollee-Gee, my money's gone from me.

(Old Woman continues on to tree, hollering and squawking.)

CALLER: Ran right across to Wine-Sappy Orchard.

OLD WOMAN: *(Sung, to Tree.)*

Have you seen my hired maid
Come by here in a promenade?

TREE: *(Spoken.)* Yes Ma'am. She's up here right now fast asleep. You want her?

OLD WOMAN: *(Spoken.)* Yes, I want her.

(Tree raises branch. Lazey Lou falls out, dropping purse. Old Woman grabs purse, chases Lazey Lou, Old Woman heeling and toeing and kicking, Lazey Lou spinning and reeling. Lazey Lou fades out. Tree fades out. Music out.)

CALLER: *(Sung.)*

With a toe and a heel she did reel
With a toe and a heel she did reel
She run her back to Dog Hobble Ridge.
Without the purse that girl did steal.

CALLER: *(Spoken.)* Then Old Woman took her purse and went back home. But she couldn't get her work done up by herself, and her eyesight kept getting worse.

(Caller places stool stage center. Old Woman to ladder, hangs purse in chimney, loosens bonnet, gropes for broom. Caller gives broom to her.)

OLD WOMAN: I have to have someone to help with the housework and all.

CALLER: So she sent way over to the other side of Mad Sheep
Mountain for another hired girl.
Right mean this girl, Rudey Rue.
A good hard worker, but mean plumb through.

(Rudey Rue crosses to Old Woman, grabs broom, starts vigorous sweeping near chimney.)

RUDEY RUE: When do I get my wages?

OLD WOMAN: You just get on with your work, and don't you go pokin' 'bout that chimney.

RUDEY RUE: *(Grumbles behind Old Woman's back.)*

CALLER: Old Woman she just stayed there and watched that girl. She wouldn't go out visitin'. She sat rockin' in her chair. A' watchin' Rudey Rue work. But after a while Old Woman fell asleep. *(Old Woman sits on stool, rocks, watches, nods, finally falls asleep, snores.)* Rudey Rue watched till Old Woman was good and asleep. Then she went and looked straight up the chimney and got to pokin' around with her broom stick. Directly a big fat purse fell down.

(Rudey Rue finds purse, runs into audience with it to look into it as Old Woman and stool fade out.)

RUDEY RUE: *(Loud whisper.)* Jumpin' Jiminy! Gold! Scads of gold pieces! Real gold!

CALLER: That girl, she took that purse and run . . . ran down the road a piece, and then she took out across the pasture field.

(Music in. Cow, Horse and Tree in place. Rudey Rue follows pattern of previous girl. All action much quicker this time.)

COW: Moo, moo, moo.

(Rudey Rue approaches Cow who begs to be milked.)

(Ballad: sung and danced.)

RUDEY RUE:

Got no time for the likes of you.
I'm wealthy now, with work I'm through.

COW: Please stay and milk my brimful bag.

RUDEY RUE: I'm off with a jig and gone with a jag.

CALLER: *(Spoken.)* And on she went. Over the fence, and down to Bear-Wallow Hollow.

(Rudey Rue continues runaround over broom stick to Horse.)

HORSE: Neigh, neigh.

(Horse begs to have back rubbed.)

(Ballad: sung and danced.)

RUDEY RUE:

Got no time for the likes of you.
I'm wealthy now, with work I'm through.

HORSE: Please stay and rub my aching back.

RUDEY RUE: I'm off with a tick and gone with a tack.

CALLER: *(Spoken.)* On she went across to Wine-Sappy Orchard.

(Rudey Rue to Tree.)

TREE: *(Groans.)*

RUDEY RUE: *(Sung.)*

Shake your own apples from your arm.
I'm just gonna climb up to hide from harm.

(Quick fade out of tree and Rudey Rue—as Old Woman appears on stool.)

CALLER: *(Spoken.)* Pretty soon Old Woman woke up.

OLD WOMAN: Rudey Rue, where are you, girl? Rudey Rue-ue-ue!

CALLER: When nobody answered, Old Woman looked up the chimney, saw her money purse gone, and started down the road a hollerin' and a squawkin'.

(Old Woman looks up chimney, starts her chase. Music in. Caller picks up stool.)

OLD WOMAN: Goll-Gollee-Gee, my money's gone from me.

CALLER: Came to Brimful.

(Ballad: sung and danced.)

OLD WOMAN: *(To Cow.)*

Oh, have you seen my hired maid?
She came by here in a promenade.

(Cow fades out.)

CALLER: *(Spoken.)* On she run.

OLD WOMAN: Goll-Gollee-Gee, my money's gone from me.

CALLER: Came to the fence. Old Woman skooted under and down to Bear-Wallow Hollow.

(Old Woman under broom stick, hollering and squawking, to Horse.)

HORSE: *(Neighs.)*

(Ballad: sung and danced.)

OLD WOMAN: *(To Horse.)* Oh, have you seen my hired girl?

HORSE: She come by here with a swish and a swirl.

(Horse fades out.)

CALLER: On she run . . .

OLD WOMAN: Goll-Gollee-Gee, my money's gone from me.

CALLER: Across to Wine-Sappy Orchard.

(Old Woman to Tree.)

OLD WOMAN: *(Sung.)* Have you seen my hired girl?

TREE: *(Spoken.)* Yes Ma'am. She's up here right now fast asleep. You want her?

OLD WOMAN: Yes, I want her.

(Tree raises branch, Rudey Rue drops purse, falls down.)

CALLER: *(Sung.)*

A toe and a heel she did reel
A toe and a heel she did reel.
She run her back to Mad Sheep Mountain
Without the purse that girl did steal.

(Old Woman picks up purse, "reels" Rudey Rue down left. Music out. Rudey Rue fades out, becomes percussionist. Tree fades out. Caller puts stool into place.)

CALLER: *(Spoken.)* Old Woman took her purse and went back home.

(Old Woman gropes to ladder, finally hangs up purse, loosens bonnet, tries to do work.)

OLD WOMAN: I'll stay by myself 'fore I'll bother with another hired girl.

CALLER: But Old Woman was getting real old, and she couldn't see worth a darn.

OLD WOMAN: I just can't seem to get my work done up at all.

CALLER: So she sent way across Tickle Creek Canyon into the next county for another girl. Now this girl, Sukey Sue, was all right. Done the best she could. Never said nothin'. Just worked right on. *(Sukey Sue crosses to Old Woman. Sukey Sue works hard and quietly as Old Woman follows her around.)* Old Woman treated Sukey Sue awful bad. She watched her all the time. Didn't let her out of her sight. Just kept pilin' more and more work on her.

(Sukey Sue on knees, scrubbing.)

OLD WOMAN: Can't go a visitin'. Can't even go to sleep.

CALLER: But one day Old Woman's eyes got so bad she mistook Sukey Sue for her rocking chair and she just had to go to the store and buy some spectacles.

(Old Woman sits on Sukey Sue. Sukey Sue jumps up. Old Woman falls down. Old Woman adjusts bonnet.)

OLD WOMAN: While I'm gone, Sukey Sue, you're to dust the cobwebs, make the bed, churn the butter, and wash the clothes. Then you can rake the yard, split the firewood, feed the chickens, pump the water, and darn the socks. *(Sound effects: each chore plucked off on fiddle up the octave, and down in a soft glissando on "darn the socks.")* But mind you, don't you dare look up the chimney, you hear?

SUKEY SUE: Yes Ma'am.

(Old Woman exits down right.)

CALLER: Well that girl went on about her work.

(Sukey Sue pantomimes chores. Sound effect for chores; fiddle plucking off each chore up the octave, along with individual sounds for each chore, all crescendoing.)

She dusted the cobwebs,
Made the bed, *(Washboard with crinkly paper.)*
Churned the butter, *(Guiara.)*
Washed the clothes, *(Washboard.)*
Raked the yard, *(Spoons on washboard.)*
Split the firewood, *(Woodblocks.)*
Fed the chickens, *(Oral clucking.)*
Pumped the water. *(Kazoos.)*
And then she sat down in front of the fireplace to darn the socks.

(Sukey Sue sits on stool, exhausted. Long descending glissando on fiddle and kazoos. Sounds out. Sukey Sue begins to darn socks, rocks in rocking chair, stops rocking, looks toward chimney.)

She tried hard not to think about looking up the chimney, but she just couldn't keep it off her mind.

SUKEY SUE: Ain't a goin' to do it. I ain't a gonna do it. *(Resumes rocking, fast.)*
Now what in the world do you reckon she's got hidden up in that chimney? *(Slows down, looks toward chimney.)*
No, I ain't gonna look. Ain't gonna do it. *(Resumes rocking. Hesitates, rocks again.)*
Now I reckon there ain't no harm in jest looking. *(Stops rocking. Puts darning down, crosses to ladder, looks up inside.)*
What in the world is that thing? *(Sukey Sue takes broom, pokes purse. It falls down, she looks inside.)*
What pretty shiny money! Mighty shiny money!
Guess I better be gettin' back to my darning. *(Sukey Sue tries to put purse back two or three times, but it won't stay up on hook.)*
Old Woman won't be liking I took down her purse. What will she do to me? What shall I do? I'd better run. *(To audience.)* But what should I do with the purse?

(Audience will make several suggestions such as "take it," "leave it," "hide it.")

(Ad libs according to audience response.) Oh I couldn't do that *(Or.)* That's a good idea. I'll leave it.

(Sukey Sue places purse on floor at stage right of ladder.)

CALLER: That girl she run. Ran down the road a piece and then took out across the pasture field.

(Sukey Sue starts out on same circuit as previous hired girls. Horse, Cow, and Tree into places. Caller removes stool and broom. Music in.)

COW: Moo Moo Moo. *(Begs to be milked.)*

SUKEY SUE: Well, I'm in a hurry, but I reckon I can take time to help you. *(Sukey Sue "milks" fingers of Cow player.)*

CALLER: So she milked Brimful into a bucket there by the fence, and stripped her good and dry.

COW: *(Moos.)* Thank you. Have some milk to drink.

(Sukey Sue over the broom stick, to Horse. Cow fades out.)

CALLER: Had her a drink of milk and on she went, over the fence, down into Bear-Wallow Hollow.

HORSE: Neigh. *(Begs to have back rubbed.)*

SUKEY SUE: Well, I'm sort of in a hurry, but I reckon I can take time to help you. *(Sukey Sue rubs Horse's back.)*

HORSE: *(Neighs.)* Oh, that feels so good. Thank you. Now get on my back and I'll ride you down to Wine-Sappy Orchard.

CALLER: So she jumped on his back and they rode plumb to the edge of the field.

(Sukey Sue makes a little jump into side-saddle position; both "trot" to stage right, and Sukey Sue jumps off.)

SUKEY SUE: Thank you, Old Roany.

CALLER: Pretty soon she came to old Apple Tree.

(Sukey Sue to Tree.)

TREE: *(Groans and moans, begs to be picked.)*

SUKEY SUE: Well, I'm in a hurry, but I reckon I can take time to help you, too.

CALLER: So she picked and picked and picked . . .

(Sukey Sue "picks"; tree branch rises on each "pick"; "picking" sound on fiddle.)

TREE: Oh, thank you. That feels so good. Now you climb up here and eat all the ripe apples you want. If that Old Woman comes by here, don't you worry none, she won't find you.

(Sukey Sue up ladder, tree lowers branch to hide Sukey Sue's face. Music out.)

(Tree and Sukey Sue fade out up stage. Old Woman enters from down right wearing spectacles, adjusting them constantly.)

CALLER: Well, Old Woman, she got back late that evening, all tuckered out. Old Woman went into the house and hollered for that girl.

OLD WOMAN: Sukey Sue, where are you, girl? Sukey Sue-ue-ue.

CALLER: She looked up the chimney and didn't see her money purse.

(Old Woman looks up chimney, heads for pasture, continuing to holler and squawk all the way. Animals, Tree and Sukey Sue in place. Music in.)

OLD WOMAN: Goll-Gollee-Gee, my money's gone from me. *(To Cow.)* Where is she?

COW: *(Moos.)* I been eating. I ain't noticed hardly nobody come past here at all. *(Cow fades out.)*

OLD WOMAN: Goll-Gollee-Gee *(Beginning to get out of breath.)* My gold is gone from me. *(To Horse.)* Where is she?

HORSE: *(Neighs.)* I ain't seen hardly nobody come by here at all, Ma'am.

(Horse fades out.)

OLD WOMAN: Goll-Gollee-Gee, my gold is gone from me. *(To Tree.)* Did she go by here?

TREE: No Ma'am. Nobody's gone *by* here. *(Tree and Sukey Sue fade out.)*

CALLER: But Old Woman went right on.

OLD WOMAN: *(Slowing down, mumbles.)* Goll-Gollee-Gee, Goll-Gollee-Gee, where could that girl, Sukey Sue, be? Goll-Gollee-Gee, Goll-Gollee-Gee.

(Old Woman continues clockwise, petering out, to down right, collapses. [Fiddle and kazoo groan to a halt].)

CALLER: She ran till she give plumb out.
Man came along and found her by the side of the road. Got her up, and dragged her back home.

(Caller assumes role of "man," helps Old Woman back home. Old Woman mumbles all the way. Other players, except for Sukey Sue, discard their characterizations. All watch with interest as Old Woman finds purse.)

OLD WOMAN: *(Shouts.)* Found my money, Sukey Sue did not steal!

(Music in. Other players, including Sukey Sue, clapping softly, gather together stage left to start the Mountain Reel. Caller and Old Woman do not dance.)

CALLER: *(Sings.)*

Have you seen her hired maid
Come by here in a promenade?
Wears her hair in a pigtail braid . . .

(Dancers forward and back, do si do, right hand turn, etc., on each stanza [simple movements that can stop easily on each spoken fourth line].)

OLD WOMAN: *(Spoken rhythmically.)* Where is that girl who didn't get paid?

(Players and music stop abruptly on Old Woman's line, point to Sukey Sue.)

CALLER AND DANCERS: *(Sing.)*

Toe and a heel, everybody reel
Toe and a heel, everybody reel
Toe and a heel, everybody reel . . .

(Sukey Sue shyly crosses to Old Woman as others dance.)

OLD WOMAN: *(Spoken rhythmically.)* Paid that girl who did *not* steal.

(Old Woman pays Sukey Sue.)

ALL: *(Sing.)*

Toe and a heel, everybody reel
Toe and a heel, everybody reel
Toe and a heel, everybody reel

(Caller and fiddler remain on stage as other players "reel" into audience, invite participation.)

CALLER: *(To audience, sings.)* Will you join us in our reel?

(Continues to sing chorus several more times, with appropriate changes of last line.)

Take a partner and do the reel.
Hope you like our mountain reel.
Keep on going with the reel.
Thanks for joining in the reel.
Now it's time to end the reel.

(Players return to stage. Music out.)

Golliwhop! Story stop!

EPILOGUE

ALL: *(With occasional solo line.)*

From the not so long ago—
America's earlier days
What fun we've had pretending—
In mighty curious ways.

(Fiddler plays music B as players sing, gather their props, don their knapsacks.)

With simple props, and ladder too,
  (To audience.) And help from all of you,
We've gathered round, in mime and sound,
  (To audience.) And you can do it, too.

We've told about the blunders
And sung this country's wonders.

(Loud whisper.) Golliwhoppers!

We've Golliwhopped together
  In song and dance and play
We thank you for inviting us
  And now we're on our way.

(All converge down stage.)

INDIVIDUALLY: *(Each gives his name, "I'm Johnny," "Elaine," etc.)*

ALL:

G'bye, so long, farewell *(Two times.)*
Farewell to you, goodbye to all
Adios and toodle-oo
Adieu,
  Be seein' ya
    Peace,
      And how!
Top of the morning to you.

(Exit through audience, shaking hands, gathering at rear door for last word; music A.)

Golliwoppers!

(All exeunt.)

CURTAIN

THE WIZARD OF OZ

by

ANNE COULTER MARTENS

from the book by L. Frank Baum

COPYRIGHT NOTICE

THE WIZARD OF OZ

CHARACTERS

Dorothy: who lives in Kansas
The Scarecrow: who wants brains
The Tin Woodman: who wants a heart
The Cowardly Lion: who wants courage
Melinda: the Good Witch of the North
Boq, Zog: Munchkin people
The Poppies: deadly flowers
Verdo: who guards the Wizard
Jade: the Wizard's maid
Belinda: the Wicked Witch of the West
Inky, Blinky, Slinky: Belinda's cats
Amber, Topaz: Winkie girls
Winkle, Wonkle: Winkie boys
Glinda: The Good Witch of the South
Ruby, Garnet: Glinda's soldiers
The Wizard of Oz: The terrible

TIME

A little while ago.

SETTING

The Land of Oz

Scenes: The Land of the Munchkins.
The Throne Room of the Wizard in the Emerald City.
The kitchen of the Bad Witch Belinda.
The Throne Room of the Wizard.

ACT ONE

SCENE ONE

THE LAND OF THE MUNCHKINS

The color theme for this scene might be blue, except for the Yellow Brick Road, which begins offstage DR and meanders in a curve toward UL and offstage again, narrowing a bit as it goes. This road may be painted on some material such as oilcloth, and rolled up for removal at the end of the scene. A small clump of trees is UR, their trunks partly hidden by shrubbery. Just upstage of the road, near UL, is a portion of a rail fence which supposedly partly encloses a cornfield. All we see are a few tall cornstalks. There may be other bits of shrubbery here and there about the stage. Entrances are at L and R stage, and of course the road leads off UL.

Before rise of curtain there is a blackout. Then the lights come up dimly. Against sound effects of rising wind, Dorothy hurries in DR, in front of the curtain, carrying Toto (a stuffed dog) in her arms.

DOROTHY: *(Calling in alarm.)* Aunt Em! Uncle Henry! Where are you? A big black storm's coming! *(Wind sounds increase.)* Oh, Toto, what are we going to do? You shouldn't have run away from me. *(Pauses DC and calls.)* Aunt Em! *(Starts toward DL.)* I'm sorry I ran outside, but I had to find Toto! *(Pauses again and calls.)* Where are you—in the storm cellar? *(To Toto.)* But I'll never be able to open the storm door—the wind's too strong. *(If possible, large fans, off DL and DR, may blow her hair and clothes.)* Let's run for the house, Toto. *(Lights dim on Dorothy as wind sounds increase. Lights now flick off and on, indicating lightning. Dorothy becomes frightened.)* Hurry, hurry! Houses don't blow away, do they—even in Kansas? *(Storm sounds grow louder, lightning flickers, and Dorothy runs out DL. There is a blackout with storm sounds continuing. During blackout, after Dorothy has left stage, there is a loud crashing sound off L.)*

At rise of curtain the stage is very dimly lighted. Boq and Zoq come in R and scurry around, looking up at the sky in fright. Whirling wind sounds are still heard.

BOQ: *(Pointing upward.)* A big black wind up high—see!

ZOQ: *(Looking up, then letting her gaze travel down and over to L stage.)* A house came flying down—whee! *(Points L.)*

(Boq and Zoq give little cries of alarm and run to hide behind the shrubbery upstage. A door and a doorstep, with the protruding legs and feet of a witch sticking out underneath, can be seen at the entrance L. On the "feet" are silver shoes. The wind sounds die away: the stage gradually lightens to full daytime brightness. Dorothy enters through the door and pauses on the step with Toto in her arms.)

DOROTHY: I thought our house would never stop flying! *(Looks around.)* But where have we landed? *(Steps down to look around.)* The most beautiful place I've ever seen! *(Toto barks.)* But it doesn't look a bit like Kansas. *(Boq and Zoq peek out, then hide again.)*

(Melinda enters R and moves C.)

DOROTHY: *(Politely.)* Excuse me, but I am a little confused. Where am I?

MELINDA: Welcome, noble Sorceress, to the country of the Munchkins. This is the Land of Oz.

DOROTHY: *(Surprised.)* The Land of Oz? I've never heard of it before.

MELINDA: Fancy that! *(Approaching Dorothy.)* The Munchkin people are grateful to you for killing Lucinda, the Wicked Witch of the East, and setting them free from bondage. *(Boq and Zoq peek out, smiling, then hide again. Toto barks in their direction.)*

DOROTHY: Hush, Toto. *(To Melinda.)* But there must be some mistake. My name is Dorothy, and I haven't killed anything.

MELINDA: Your house did, when it landed. See? *(Points to doorstep.)* There are her feet in the silver shoes, sticking out from your doorstep.

DOROTHY: *(Upset.)* Oh, dear! What ever shall we do?

MELINDA: Don't distress yourself, my dear. Lucinda was a very wicked witch indeed, and now you have set the good little Munchkins free. *(During this speech Boq and Zoq come out of hiding timidly, smiling at Dorothy. They come C.)*

BOQ: I'm Boq.

ZOQ: And I'm Zog.

BOQ: We thank you muchly. *(Bows.)*

ZOQ: For doing thusly. *(Curtsies.)*

DOROTHY: I didn't do anything, really. But you're most welcome.

MELINDA: I'm Melinda, the Witch of the North, and a friend of the Munchkins.

DOROTHY: Oh, my! Are you a real witch?

MELINDA: Of course. *(Taking step toward her.)* And a good one, too.

DOROTHY: But I thought all witches were wicked. *(Steps back, a little frightened, and Toto barks. Dorothy shushes him.)*

MELINDA: Gracious, but you *are* misinformed. Your schooling must have been most inadequate.

DOROTHY: *(A little indignant.)* I went to a very good school. And what's more, I got fine grades on my report card!

MELINDA: Fancy that! Yet you had never heard of the Land of Oz. And you're very mixed up about witches.

DOROTHY: *(Meekly now.)* I'm afraid so. *(Sits on doorstep.)*

MELINDA: In the Land of Oz there have always been four witches, two of them good, two of them bad. Now Lucinda, the Wicked Witch of the East, is dead. But in the West lives an even wickeder witch, Belinda. *(As if from far away, sound of crazy laughter is heard. Boq and Zoq quickly dash over and cower behind Melinda. Toto barks.)* Ah! Belinda has found out about this and is angry. *(Crazed laughter is heard again.)* But don't be afraid. She lives far away, in the Land of the Winkies.

DOROTHY: *(Relieved.)* I don't ever want to meet *her*!

MELINDA: Let's hope you never do. Now, of the two good witches, I am one. Melinda of the North. The other one is

Glinda the Good, Witch of the South. *(As if from far away, happy sound of tinkling bells is heard.)*

DOROTHY: *(Looking around.)* What was that?

MELINDA: The gentle sound of Glinda the Good. It means that she, too, knows now that Lucinda is dead.

DOROTHY: *(Gaining confidence, rising.)* You really are a good witch? *(Following patter may be half sung, half chanted. Boq and Zoq join hands and slowly circle Melinda as they chant.)*

BOQ: She's a good witch,
A do-as-she-should witch.

MELINDA: A do-as-I-should witch.

ZOQ: A very sweet witch,
A happy-to-meet witch.

MELINDA: A happy-to-meet witch.

BOQ AND ZOQ: A gentle-and-kind witch,
A lucky-to-find witch.

MELINDA: A lucky-to-find witch.

DOROTHY: Then I'm certainly glad you found *me*. Funny, my Aunt Em and Uncle Henry told me there were no witches any more.

MELINDA: Who are Aunt Em and Uncle Henry?

DOROTHY: *(Now moving toward RC and glancing about.)* I live with them in Kansas. *(Quickly, turning to her.)* That is, I did live with them until the big black wind blew Toto and me and our house here.

MELINDA: *(Thoughtfully.)* Kansas . . . h'm. I don't recall any mention of it in our geography books. *(Moves C.)* Tell me, is it a civilized country?

DOROTHY: Oh, my, yes! *(During this conversation, Boq and Zoq sit down near doorstep, shielding it. At this time, witch's "legs" are removed, leaving only the silver shoes.)*

MELINDA: Then that accounts for it. In the civilized countries I don't believe there are any witches left. But here in Oz we still have witches—*(Pauses, then speaks with some awe.)*—and even a very great Wizard.

DOROTHY: *(Impressed.)* A Wizard?

MELINDA: He lives in the Emerald City, and he's more powerful than all the rest of us put together.

BOQ: *(Getting up with a cry of surprise.)* How strange! *(Points to silver shoes.)*

ZOQ: *(Rising, too.)* A change! *(Points to shoes.)*

MELINDA: *(Crossing L, as Dorothy follows.)* Gracious me! The wicked Lucinda has disappeared completely, leaving nothing but her silver shoes. *(Picks up shoes.)*

DOROTHY: How very odd!

MELINDA: She was so old—she dried up quickly. Now the shoes are yours, my dear.

DOROTHY: *(Taking them slowly.)* Such pretty silver shoes!

MELINDA: Why don't you put them on?

DOROTHY: Do you think I should?

MELINDA: Yes, I think you should put them on. Who knows—they may be magic shoes. *(Dorothy sits on step, takes off her old shoes and puts on silver ones. Then she stands up, dancing around, to C stage.)*

DOROTHY: *(Delightedly.)* They're a perfect fit!

MELINDA: Naturally.

DOROTHY: Thank you so much for your kindness. But now will you please tell me which direction I must go to find Kansas? *(Melinda and Boq and Zoq look at each other, then at Dorothy, and shake their heads.)*

MELINDA: That's impossible. The Land of Oz is completely surrounded by a deadly desert, and no one can cross it.

DOROTHY: *(With a little sob, moving DR.)* Oh, dear! I simply must go back to Aunt Em and Uncle Henry.

MELINDA: *(Crossing toward her.)* Don't you like it here?

DOROTHY: *(Politely.)* The country's very beautiful.

MELINDA: You mean that Kansas is even lovelier?

DOROTHY: Oh, no, no! The part where I live isn't really beautiful at all. But it's my *home.*

MELINDA: *(Gently.)* I understand. Home is always the most beautiful place in the world.

DOROTHY: *(Eagerly.)* Then you'll help me?

MELINDA: Such knowledge is beyond my own power. *(Turns and moves toward DLC.)* But there may be a way. *(Boq and Zoq move down to Melinda and stand behind her, rather shyly.)*

DOROTHY: *(Coming DC.)* Oh, I do hope so!

MELINDA: Go to the Emerald City and ask the Great Wizard of Oz to help you.

DOROTHY: *(Timidly.)* Is he a good man?

MELINDA: He's a good Wizard. Whether he's a man or not, I don't know. No one has ever seen him face to face.

DOROTHY: How can I get to this Emerald City?

MELINDA: *(Crossing to her, as Boq and Zoq follow behind her.)* You must walk. It's a long journey and perhaps a dangerous one.

DOROTHY: D-dangerous?

MELINDA: Because you've killed the Witch of the East, the Wicked Witch Belinda of the West may try to cast a spell upon you.

DOROTHY: A magic spell?

MELINDA: *(Nodding.)* Belinda's very clever, and she probably hates you now.

DOROTHY: *(Worried.)* Oh, dear!

MELINDA: Just be very careful, my dear.

DOROTHY: Oh, I will! Thank you for warning me. You're a very nice Witch.

BOQ AND ZOQ: *(Peeking out from behind Melinda, on either side.)* A give-good-advice Witch.

MELINDA: *(Smiling.)* Yes, a give-good-advice Witch. Just follow the Yellow Brick Road to the Emerald City. And good luck, my dear! *(Boq and Zoq bow and curtsy as Melinda crosses R, pauses to wave back at Dorothy, and then goes out R.)*

BOQ AND ZOQ: A cannot-delay Witch,
A go-on-her-way Witch. *(They bow and curtsy to Dorothy and then run quickly out R.)*

DOROTHY: *(Still DC.)* A go-on-her-way Witch. But which way is my way? *(Looks around in bewilderment.)*

SCARECROW: Straight ahead, of course. *(Surprised, Dorothy looks around to see who has spoken.)*

DOROTHY: Did somebody speak to me? *(Moves up to fence, leans over fence and parts some cornstalks. There is the scarecrow, supposedly perched on a long pole. He is standing on a small box, which is hidden by cornstalks, so he towers somewhat over Dorothy.)*

SCARECROW: Certainly. How do you do?

DOROTHY: I'm pretty well, thank you. How do you do?

SCARECROW: Not too well. It's very boring to be perched up here night and day to scare away the crows.

DOROTHY: Can't you get down?

SCARECROW: No. The pole is stuck up my back. *(Wiggles a bit uncomfortably.)* I'd be much obliged if you'd lift me off it. *(Toto barks.)*

DOROTHY: Now, Toto! He seems a very friendly Scarecrow. *(Climbs over fence, puts Toto down and, standing in front of scarecrow, apparently lifts Scarecrow down from pole. She does it quite easily, as if he is very light in weight.)*

SCARECROW: *(Now down off box.)* Thank you very much. *(As Dorothy picks up Toto and climbs back over fence and returns to road, he climbs over, too, but loses his balance and falls down.)* Oops! Sorry, I'm not too steady on my feet yet. But I feel like a new man.

DOROTHY: *(Helping him up.)* Really?

SCARECROW: I practically am a new man. A Munchkin farmer made me just last week. *(Brushes himself off a bit.)* Do you think he did a good job? *(Picks off a few straws.)*

DOROTHY: *(Politely.)* Just lovely.

SCARECROW: You don't have to be *too* complimentary. I'm well aware that one of my eyes is painted a little crooked.

DOROTHY: *(Diplomatically.)* Well—as long as you can see out of it.

SCARECROW: May I ask who you are and where you're going?

DOROTHY: My name is Dorothy, and I'm going to the Emerald City to ask the Great Wizard of Oz to send me back to Kansas.

SCARECROW: Where's the Emerald City?

DOROTHY: *(Surprised.)* Don't you know?

SCARECROW: *(Shaking his head.)* I don't know anything. *(Sadly, moving C.)* I'm stuffed with straw, so I have no brains at all.

DOROTHY: Oh, I'm sorry.

SCARECROW: *(Sudden idea.)* Do you think if I go to the Emerald City with you, the Great Wizard would give me some brains?

DOROTHY: I really can't say for sure—*(Moving to him.)*—but come with me if you like, and ask him.

SCARECROW: That sounds like a good idea. *(Quickly.)* Not that I *know* a good idea when I hear one. You can't do any real thinking with straw.

DOROTHY: *(Nodding.)* I see.

SCARECROW: *(Worried.)* Some of it shows? *(Hastily stuffs a few wisps of straw back into seams of his head.)* The Munchkin farmer wasn't very good at sewing up seams.

DOROTHY: *(Staunchly.)* I *like* the way he made you. It gives you a sort of—of—*(Struggles for right words.)*—happy-go-lucky look.

SCARECROW: *(Sadly.)* Thank you. But I'd really prefer to be the intellectual type, with a very high I.Q.

DOROTHY: What does that mean?

SCARECROW: You should know better than to ask *me* what *anything* means. *(Taps his head, steps backward, almost trips and goes sprawling again.)*

DOROTHY: *(Helping him up.)* I think you could be quite intelligent if you had a few brains.

SCARECROW: It's so nice of you to say so. *(From direction of trees UR a faint groan is heard. He stops, listening.)* Did you hear a groan?

DOROTHY: *(Glancing UR.)* Yes! Someone must be hurt! *(Hurries toward trees, parts shrubbery and looks down. Scarecrow follows.)*

SCARECROW: Great cornstalks! It's a man, made out of tin!

DOROTHY: Look how rusty he is! *(They bend down and help the Tin Woodman to his feet. He stands stiffly, as if unable to move, and holds his ax high.)* Did you groan just now?

TIN WOODMAN: I've been groaning off and on for a long time, but no one has ever heard me before. *(Toto barks and Dorothy holds him tighter.)* Don't worry, he can't hurt me. *(Proudly.)* I'm made entirely out of tin, as you can see.

DOROTHY: Can we do something to help you?

TIN WOODMAN: *(With a "stiff" jerk of his head, indicating behind him.)* Would you be kind enough to look for my oil can? My joints are rusted so badly, I can't move them at all.

DOROTHY: *(Looking in shrubbery and under trees.)* You think it's here somewhere?

TIN WOODMAN: I lost it one rainy day when I was cutting wood.

DOROTHY: *(Holding up an oil can.)* Oh, here it is! *(Goes to him.)* Where do I start?

TIN WOODMAN: Oil my neck first. I do hate a stiff neck. *(Dorothy oils his neck and he turns his head this way and that.)* Ah, much better than old-fashioned rubbing liniment! *(Sighs in relief.)*

SCARECROW: Now the joints on his arms. He needs elbow grease. *(Dorothy oils arm joints, and Tin Woodman flexes his arms, then lowers his ax and leans on handle.)*

TIN WOODMAN: How good it feels. *(To Scarecrow.)* How did you know I wanted to let go of my ax?

SCARECROW: I didn't really *know*, because I haven't any brains. But I just thought it might be a good idea. *(To Dorothy.)* I'll oil his leg joints. *(Takes oil can and does so. Tin Woodman tries out his arm and leg joints, stiffly at first, then with greater ease. He walks around shrubbery, onto road, to C stage.)*

TIN WOODMAN: *(Gratefully.)* I thank you from the very bottom of my tin feet. I'd thank you from the bottom of my heart, but unfortunately I don't have a heart. *(Sighs. Dorothy and Scarecrow have joined him at C.)*

DOROTHY: No heart at all?

TIN WOODMAN: I'm a woodman, you know, and I've had so many accidents when my ax slipped. So I asked a tinsmith to make me nice shiny new parts that couldn't be hurt when my ax slipped.

DOROTHY: *(Polishing him vigorously with her handkerchief.)* You'll soon be bright and shiny again.

TIN WOODMAN: But the tinsmith wasn't clever enough to make me a heart. *(Sadly.)* So I've been heartbroken ever since.

DOROTHY: Oh, that's too bad!

TIN WOODMAN: Just thinking about it makes me so sad that I sometimes cry. *(Turning his face to her.)* Please wipe my eyes quickly! *(Dorothy dabs at his eyes.)* Thank you. I must keep my oil can with me or the tears will rust my parts again. *(Bends stiffly and picks up oil can, left on ground by Scarecrow.)*

SCARECROW: We're on our way to the Emerald City to see the Great Wizard of Oz.

DOROTHY: I want him to send me back to Kansas, and the Scarecrow wants the Wizard to give him some brains.

TIN WOODMAN: *(Hopefully.)* Do you suppose the Great Wizard could give me a heart?

DOROTHY: I should think so.

TIN WOODMAN: Then will you allow me to join you on the journey?

DOROTHY: *(Taking his arm.)* We'll be glad of your company.

SCARECROW: *(Crossing L, to doorstep.)* I myself think brains are better, for a fool wouldn't know what to do with a heart if he had one. *(Perches lightly on doorstep.)*

TIN WOODMAN: *(Crossing LC.)* I'll take the heart. Brains don't make a person happy, and happiness is the best thing in the world.

DOROTHY: *(Joining Tin Woodman.)* And home is the very best place.

TIN WOODMAN: Will it take us long to get to the Emerald City?

SCARECROW: Having no brains, I haven't the faintest notion. But there's still one Wicked Witch left in this land, and in my foolish way I suggest that we all be on guard against her.

DOROTHY: That's what the Good Witch Melinda said. *(They hear a deep growl from UR, behind trees. Scarecrow jumps up and all retreat DL, in alarm. Toto begins to bark.)*

SCARECROW: Watch out! *(The Cowardly Lion comes bounding toward them from behind trees. With one blow of his paw he sends Scarecrow sprawling. Then he knocks down Tin Woodman.)*

TIN WOODMAN: Run, Dorothy, run! He can't hurt *me*! *(Undecided, Dorothy just stands still. Toto growls. As Lion growls back and opens his big mouth, as if to bite, Dorothy slaps him on the nose.)*

DOROTHY: Don't you dare bite Toto! You ought to be ashamed of yourself, a big beast like you trying to bite a poor little dog!

LION: *(Retreating a few steps.)* I didn't bite him. *(Rubs his nose.)*

DOROTHY: *(Marching directly to him.)* But you tried to. You're nothing but a big coward.

LION: *(Hanging his head in shame.)* I know it. I've always known it. But how can I help it?

DOROTHY: *(Reproachfully.)* Striking a stuffed man like the poor Scarecrow! *(Helps Scarecrow to his feet.)*

LION: Is he really stuffed? *(Watches as Dorothy rearranges some of Scarecrow's outfit.)*

DOROTHY: Of course he is!

LION: *(Looking down at Tin Woodman.)* Is this one stuffed, too?

DOROTHY: He's made of tin. *(She and Scarecrow help Tin Woodman to his feet.)*

LION: *(Looking at his paws.)* No wonder he blunted my claws. And I wasn't going to bite your dog—I'm really just a coward at heart. *(Sighs deeply.)*

DOROTHY: How can you possibly be a coward when you're so strong and big?

LION: *(Sadly.)* I suppose I was born that way.

DOROTHY: But the lion is the King of Beasts!

LION: *(Moving C.)* I know. That's why all the other animals in the forest are afraid of me. They *think* I'm brave. *(Sits down on ground, on road, and dabs at his eyes with fluffy end of his tail. Now Dorothy, Scarecrow and Tin Woodman come C and stand around Lion.)*

TIN WOODMAN: That's very sad. If I had a heart, I'd be sorry for you.

LION: Thank you just the same. *(Sniffs sadly.)*

SCARECROW: *(Bending over him.)* Do you have any brains?

LION: I guess so—but I've never tried to use them.

DOROTHY: All of us are going to the Emerald City to ask the Great Wizard of Oz to help us. Maybe you'd like to come along?

LION: *(Hopefully.)* Do you think he could give me courage? *(Starts to rise.)*

SCARECROW: Just as easily as he could give me brains.

TIN WOODMAN: Or give me a heart.

DOROTHY: Or send me back to Kansas.

LION: *(Worried.)* I might be afraid on the journey. *(Sinks back again.)*

TIN WOODMAN: We'll all stick together and help each other. Please say you'll come!

LION: That's a very kindhearted offer.

TIN WOODMAN: Oh, not at all! It's because I have no heart to guide me that I have to be so considerate of other people's feelings.

LION: *(Getting up.)* All right. Let's go!

DOROTHY: Exactly what I said to myself before. But which way? *(Looks R and L.)*

SCARECROW: On the Yellow Brick Road.

DOROTHY: How are we going to find it? *(Scarecrow looks down and points.)*

SCARECROW: We're already on it, see?

DOROTHY: *(Delightedly.)* Why, so we are! *(Gives him a grateful hug.)*

SCARECROW: *(Modestly and in some embarrassment.)* It didn't take any brains to figure that one out.

(The Poppies dance in from R, humming softly and waving their bright red petals.)

DOROTHY: *(With a happy cry.)* Oh, look! Beautiful dancing flowers!

TIN WOODMAN: Now where could they have come from?

DOROTHY: They're just lovely. *(Stands C, with Toto in her arms.)*

SCARECROW: Very nice, but let's get started. *(Starts along road, toward UL, followed by Tin Woodman and Lion.)*

DOROTHY: No, wait! They're going to dance.

LION: *(Joining her.)* They're singing, too.

SCARECROW: Dorothy, let's go!

DOROTHY: *(Entranced.)* Not yet. *(Poppies dance in a circle around Dorothy, Toto and Lion at C, and sing softly. Following lyrics to music of Brahms' "Lullaby" are suggested, but any other "sleep-type" music may be sung or hummed by Poppies.)*

POPPIES: Go to sleep, go to sleep,
As the poppies are creeping,
Close your sleepy eyes awhile
As the poppy flowers beguile.

Go to sleep, don't delay,
You will dream of the daybreak,
Go to sleep, drift away,
You will never more awake.

(Effect of Poppies is soon evident. Dorothy rubs her eyes and begins to yawn. Lion gives an enormous yawn and starts to slump. Only Scarecrow and Tin Woodman are unaffected as they stand on road, away from others. Scarecrow beckons to Tin Woodman, and they move DL.)

TIN WOODMAN: What's the matter?

SCARECROW: These are *deadly* Poppy Flowers! They put people to sleep.

TIN WOODMAN: I'm not sleepy.

SCARECROW: Nor I. But look at the others! *(As Poppies continue their lullaby and circling, Dorothy lies down, Toto in her lap, her head down, almost asleep.)*

TIN WOODMAN: But who would want them to go to sleep?

SCARECROW: Since I don't have brains, I don't really know. But it *might* be Belinda, the Wicked Witch of the West.

TIN WOODMAN: You're right! *(Goes toward circle and tries to attract Lion's attention.)* Lion! Come here!

LION: *(Sleepily, straightening up.)* Did someone call me? *(Yawns prodigiously and starts to slump again. Poppies keep on singing their song. Lion stretches and seems about to lie down. Scarecrow and Tin Woodman grab him by tail and pull him DL. Now only Dorothy and Toto are in deadly circle of sleep.)*

SCARECROW: *(To Lion.)* You've got to frighten those Poppies away!

LION: Huh? *(Pats a yawn.)* After I take a little nap. *(Starts to slump.)*

TIN WOODMAN: *(Pulling at him.)* No, no! You've got to do it now.

LION: Why all the hurry? *(Starts to lie down.)*

SCARECROW: *(Holding him up.)* Listen to the words of their song, and you'll know. *(They listen until they hear clearly the words: "You will never more awake." Lion shakes his head to clear it of sleep. Scarecrow gives Lion a little push.)* Hurry, before it's too late to save Dorothy and Toto!

LION: *(Nervously, holding back.)* I'm afraid. Oh, if only I wasn't such a coward! *(Finally pulls himself together; with a tremendous roar, he bounds toward Poppies, threatening them with his paws. Poppies scream in sudden fright and run out R. Lion is equally frightened by Poppies' screams and hides behind cornstalks UL. Dorothy remains almost asleep at C. Scarecrow and Tin Woodman pull Dorothy to her feet, shaking her awake.)*

TIN WOODMAN: Wake up! Dorothy, open your eyes!

SCARECROW: The Wicked Belinda sent the Poppies to put you to sleep forever! *(Dorothy rubs her eyes, trying to come fully awake. Lion peeks out from behind cornstalks, then comes toward others.)*

DOROTHY: I—I don't know what happened. All of a sudden I felt so very sleepy. But I'm all right now.

SCARECROW: Then let's be off for the Emerald City, and fast!

DOROTHY: All right. *(Looks L and then R.)* But I still don't know which way.

SCARECROW: You want to go in the right direction. Correct?

DOROTHY: Yes, of course.

SCARECROW: *(Frowning.)* The right way . . . h'm. *(Then triumphantly.)* Then go *right*, naturally! *(Points UL, which is right to them as they face that way.)*

DOROTHY: If I didn't know better, I'd say you had brains!

SCARECROW: *(Laughing.)* What a silly notion! *(Dorothy, between Scarecrow and Tin Woodman, starts UL with them, arm in arm. Lion brings up the rear. They start along Yellow Brick Road. As they go, soft, faraway tinkling of bells is heard.)*

DOROTHY: *(Stopping a moment to listen.)* Glinda the Good! She's glad we're on our way. *(They continue toward UL. Now sound of faraway crazy laughter is heard and they again stop short.)*

SCARECROW: Belinda the Bad! She's angry that the Poppies didn't stop us. *(Lion looks frightened, and turns, as if to run.)*

DOROTHY: *(Pulling him back.)* We won't let *anything* stop us now. On to the Emerald City, and the Great Wizard of Oz! *(With her arm around Lion, they all skip out UL.)*

CURTAIN

ACT ONE

SCENE TWO

THE THRONE ROOM OF THE WIZARD OF OZ IN THE EMERALD CITY.

The color scheme here may be green. Near the UL corner of the room is a tall screen decorated with stars, moons, sun and signs of the Zodiac. (These may be made of aluminum foil.) In front of the screen is the Wizard's throne, a high-backed chair. There are two straight chairs URC. Against the wall DL is a table or cupboard on which are green bottles, jars and boxes. There is a large door R, a smaller door, or entrance, L.

At rise of curtain a soft green light may pervade the room. Verdo, the Soldier with the Green Whiskers, paces back and forth importantly, his old-fashioned gun over his shoulder. He paces from UC to DL and back again. Jade is dusting the chairs R with a feather duster.

JADE: *(Pausing.)* Captain Verdo . . . *(Verdo ignores her, continues pacing.)* Don't you ever get tired, just marching back and forth?

VERDO: *(As he paces.)* I obey the orders of the Great Wizard of Oz.

JADE: So do I. *(Half dancing as she dusts.)* I dust, I dust, I dust, I dust because I must.

VERDO: *(Stiffly.)* The matter's been discussed. Just dust. *(Playfully, Jade crosses and flicks his beard with the feather duster.)* Not my whiskers! *(Jade dances away from him, and he keeps on marching.)*

JADE: *(Pausing RC.)* It wouldn't surprise me if a little green bird had a nest in there. *(Laughs.)*

VERDO: *(Pausing DL.)* Let's have no more of this silly chatter. Guarding the Throne of the Great Wizard is no laughing matter. *(Continues pacing.)*

JADE: Yes, sir. *(Continues to dust, then turns back to him.)* Verdo . . .

VERDO: *(Impatiently, pausing.)* What now?

JADE: Have you ever actually *seen* the Great Wizard?

VERDO: *(Stiffly.)* No.

JADE: Neither have I. I wonder what he looks like.

VERDO: That's of no concern to us.

JADE: *(Moving to him.)* Do you think it's true, what people say about him?

VERDO: I never listen to gossip. *(Starts to pace, then stops and turns to her.)* What do they say?

JADE: *(In a low voice, full of awe.)* That he can take any form he wishes—a fierce animal, a bird, a mouse, or sometimes just nothing at all.

VERDO: Quite true, I believe.

JADE: But what he looks like—no one really knows?

VERDO: Correct. Get on with your dusting. *(Continues pacing.)*

JADE: *(Flitting about, waving her feather duster in air.)* I dust, I dust, I dust—*(There is a knock, door R. She stops in surprise and Verdo stands still.)* Someone's knocking!

VERDO: I have ears. *(Marches to door R and calls.)* Who stands without?

JADE: *(Standing behind him, giggling.)* Without what?

VERDO: *(Turning on her fiercely.)* Quiet! *(Calling.)* Who seeks admittance to the Throne Room of the Great Wizard of Oz?

DOROTHY: *(Offstage R.)* My name is Dorothy, and I've come with my friends to see the Wizard.

VERDO: The Great Wizard sees no one on Tuesdays.

DOROTHY: *(Offstage R.)* Today is Wednesday.

JADE: *(Poking Verdo.)* She's right.

VERDO: He sees no one on Wednesday without an appointment.

DOROTHY: *(Offstage R.)* I've come to make an appointment now. *(Verdo opens door stealthily a slit and looks out, then closes it quickly.)*

JADE: What's the matter?

VERDO: One of her friends is a huge lion! *(There are more knocks on door and Lion roars. Verdo and Jade jump quickly and back away from the door.)*

DOROTHY: *(Offstage R.)* Please let us in! The Lion won't hurt anyone, I promise.

JADE: Well, brave Captain of the Guard? . . .

VERDO: You know I'm the *only* guard. *(Looks unhappily at his gun.)* And my gun is *never* loaded.

DOROTHY: *(Knocking offstage R.)* Please! It's very important.

VERDO: *(Squaring his shoulders.)* Never let it be said that I'm afraid of anything! *(Crosses and opens door. Jade has moved to LC.)*

(Dorothy, Toto, the Scarecrow, the Tin Woodman and the Cowardly Lion come into the room. The Lion bounds forward to stand in front of the group. Verdo has backed to C after opening the door.)

LION: *(To his friends, holding up both front paws.)* Keep behind me. If there's danger here, I'll fight as long as I remain alive. *(Jade gives a little scream and runs DL. Verdo drops his gun and joins her. They all stand looking at each other for a moment. Jade nudges Verdo, indicating his gun, and he finally summons enough courage to pick it up and put it on his shoulder.)*

VERDO: Why have you come here?

DOROTHY: *(Pushing Lion gently to one side and coming C.)* To ask for help from the Wizard.

VERDO: Don't you know that the Wizard is powerful and terrible?

DOROTHY: Of course.

VERDO: And if your errand's a foolish one, he may get angry and destroy you?

SCARECROW: But our errand's not a foolish one.

TIN WOODMAN: We've been told that he's a good Wizard.

VERDO: He rules the Emerald City wisely.

LION: Then why didn't you want to let us in?

DOROTHY: *(Placatingly.)* Please excuse my friend for roaring so loudly. He didn't mean to frighten anyone.

LION: *(With spirit.)* Yes, I did, really. *(Then sadly.)* But I couldn't—because I'm such a coward. When I roar like that, all I get is a sore throat. *(Rubs his throat with a paw, then dabs at his eyes with tip of his tail.)*

DOROTHY: *(Crossing, putting an arm about Lion's shoulders.)* You see? He's very sweet, really.

LION: *(Almost in tears again.)* She says that of me, the King of Beasts!

DOROTHY: Do you think the Great Wizard will see us?

VERDO: *(To Jade.)* Go knock on his study door and ask permission.

JADE: Yes, Captain. *(Goes out L.)*

VERDO: You may be seated if you wish.

DOROTHY: Thank you. *(Sits on chair URC, with Toto on her lap. Scarecrow sits in other chair, while Tin Woodman stands near Dorothy. Lion starts to circle Verdo, who is standing at LC.)*

SCARECROW: *(Politely.)* Nice palace you have here.

VERDO: *(Stiffly, one eye on Lion.)* Thank you.

TIN WOODMAN: It was kind of you to let us in.

VERDO: Yes, it was.

LION: *(As he circles him.)* Do I make you nervous?

VERDO: Certainly not! *(But he does. After a pause.)* The Great Wizard very seldom receives visitors.

LION: He'd better see us! *(Gives a mild roar, and Verdo steps back hurriedly.)*

DOROTHY: *(Reprovingly.)* Stop roaring at the nice Captain!

LION: *(Meekly.)* I'm sorry. *(Moves DR.)*

VERDO: *(Clearing his throat.)* Where have you and your friends come from?

DOROTHY: Oh, very far away, especially me. I used to live in Kansas, and I didn't even know there *was* a Land of Oz.

VERDO: *(Shocked.)* I suppose they call that modern education?

DOROTHY: They call it being realistic, I think.

VERDO: *(Considering.)* Oh. Well, that's a problem for the educators to worry about. *I* know *I'm* real.

DOROTHY: *(Rising, moving to him.)* I know it's not polite to ask personal questions, but is your beard real, too? *(Looks closely at it.)*

VERDO: *(Stiffly.)* It most certainly is! *(Still smarting from Jade's remark.)* And there isn't a little green bird nesting in it! *(Dorothy steps back at this outburst.)*

(Jade comes in L and pauses there.)

DOROTHY: *(Crossing quickly to her, as Lion, Scarecrow and Tin Woodman follow.)* What did he say?

SCARECROW: Did you see him face to face?

TIN WOODMAN: Is he good and kind?

LION: Or fierce and terrible?

JADE: I heard his voice, and he has consented to receive you.

DOROTHY: Oh, good! *(Others ad lib their pleasure.)*

JADE: You're to be admitted to his presence one at a time.

DOROTHY: *(Uneasily.)* I'd feel better if we could all be together.

VERDO: You have heard the order of the Wizard. Who wants to be first? *(They look at one another. For a moment, no one speaks.)*

LION: *(In a small voice.)* In case he's fierce, maybe I, coward though I am.

SCARECROW: No, no! Only a very foolish person without a brain takes chances like this. So I'll be first.

JADE: The rest of you are to come with me and wait until he summons you. *(Rather nervously, Dorothy, carrying Toto, Tin Woodman and Lion start to follow Jade out L. In his nervousness Scarecrow trips over Lion and falls. Dorothy picks him up and straightens his hat.)*

DOROTHY: You're a true friend. *(Pats him on the back.)*

TIN WOODMAN: If I had a heart, it would tremble for you.

LION: Try to be brave, even though I'm not.

SCARECROW: I can only be my own foolish self.

DOROTHY: We wish you well. *(She and others go out L with Jade. Scarecrow is left alone with Verdo, who marches to door R and stands at attention facing it, his back to room.)*

SCARECROW: *(Coming C.)* Why do you turn your back?

VERDO: It is forbidden that I make any attempt to see the Wizard.

SCARECROW: Great cornstalks! He must be quite unusual.

VERDO: He is.

SCARECROW: Well, come to think of it, I'm a little unusual myself. *(Straightens up with an air of importance.)*

VERDO: No comment.

SCARECROW: *(After a pause, as he looks around.)* What do I do now?

VERDO: Wait for the Wizard to make his presence known. *(Lights begin to flash off and on in rapid succession. There is a brief period of complete darkness.)*

SCARECROW: *(After pause, in darkness.)* Is he here yet? *(To Scarecrow, the Wizard appears as a small green light which bounces around like a child's ball. This effect may be attained by using several green-bulb flashlights from different positions offstage. Green-light ball bounces on throne chair, on zodiac signs, on floor, and high on walls. Finally, Wizard speaks in a deep and awe-inspiring voice. If this is not practical, his voice comes from general direction of offstage UC.)*

WIZARD: The Great and Terrible Wizard of Oz is here!

SCARECROW: *(Surprised.)* That bouncing green light?

WIZARD: Who are you?

SCARECROW: Only a Scarecrow stuffed with straw.

WIZARD: That much I can easily see.

SCARECROW: *(Feeling about his person.)* Oh, shucks, I must be coming apart at the seams again!

WIZARD: Why do you seek me? *(Green-light ball bounces to L and Scarecrow runs after it.)*

SCARECROW: I come to ask if you will please put brains in my head instead of straw.

WIZARD: Ah, so you'd like to have brains? *(Green-light ball bounces to C and Scarecrow follows it.)*

SCARECROW: Yes, O Great Green Light!

WIZARD: Why should I do this for you? *(Light bounces DR and Scarecrow follows.)*

SCARECROW: Because you're wise and powerful, and no one else can help me.

WIZARD: I will consider your request after I've talked to the others. *(Light bounces UL.)*

SCARECROW: *(Disappointed, following.)* But, your Great Green Light—

WIZARD: *(Commandingly.)* You are dismissed. *(Green-light ball bounces all around room quickly and then disappears. Regular room lights go on and Verdo turns around.)*

VERDO: Did you see him?

SCARECROW: *(Coming C.)* Why, he's only a dancing green ball of light!

(Jade comes in L and pauses.)

JADE: Come with me, and wait. The Great Wizard is ready for the next visitor.

(The Scarecrow goes L as the Tin Woodman comes in L. They shake hands solemnly, then the Scarecrow goes out L with Jade.)

TIN WOODMAN: *(Looking around.)* Where's the Wizard?

VERDO: He will make his presence known. *(Faces door R again. Lights flash off and on rapidly, then slow to dimness with only occasional flashes. A deep gong sounds offstage. To get effect later of this gong sound coming from different parts of room, several gongs may be used offstage.)*

TIN WOODMAN: What was that?

WIZARD: *(Offstage UC.)* I am Oz, the Great and Terrible.

TIN WOODMAN: *(Moving C.)* You're a loud-sounding gong?

WIZARD: I am whatever I choose to be. Who are you?

TIN WOODMAN: I'm a woodman made of tin.

WIZARD: Why do you seek me? *(Gong sounds at L and Tin Woodman whirls to face it, startled.)*

TIN WOODMAN: *(Moving toward L.)* Because I have no heart, so I can't feel tenderness and love. I pray you to give me a heart so I may be like other men.

WIZARD: Why should I do this? *(Gong sounds UC and Tin Woodman follows sound.)*

TIN WOODMAN: Because you alone can help me.

WIZARD: I will consider your request after I have talked to the others. *(Gong sounds at R and Tin Woodman again follows sound.)*

TIN WOODMAN: Please, O Great Deep Gong—

WIZARD: *(Commandingly.)* You are dismissed. *(Room lights flash rapidly again, gong sounds several times, as if from different parts of room, and then is still. Tin Woodman has darted here and there, trying to follow various sounds. Regular room lights come on and Verdo turns around. Tin Woodman is now at LC.)*

VERDO: You heard him.

TIN WOODMAN: Why, he's only a deep-sounding gong!

VERDO: You think that because you have no heart to beat faster at his presence.

(Jade comes in L.)

JADE: Come with me. The Wizard is ready for the next visitor.

(As the Tin Woodman goes L, the Cowardly Lion comes in L. Jade gives him a friendly pat on the head and goes out L with the Tin Woodman.)

LION: *(Looking around.)* Is he afraid to face me?

VERDO: Prepare yourself. *(Faces door R. Lights flash off and on and then there is a blackout.)*

LION: *(In blackout.)* For what?

VERDO: Only the Wizard knows what form he will take this time.

LION: *(Moving toward Verdo in darkness, pleadingly.)* Can't you give me a little hint?

VERDO: Impossible.

LION: Will he be large or small?

VERDO: He could be either.

LION: I'm not so much afraid of small things. *(Sighs.)* Of course, that's because I'm such a coward.

VERDO: I knew that the minute you came in the door.

LION: *(Sadly.)* Everyone knows it.

VERDO: I hope you don't think that just because I happened to drop my gun—

LION: *(Quickly.)* Oh, no! I could see that you're a very brave soldier.

VERDO: Naturally.

LION: When is the Wizard coming?

WIZARD: Oz, the Great and Terrible, is already here. *(Room lights go on, but not to full brightness. Seated on throne (apparently) is a tall figure. He wears a dark green robe which falls to floor, and a very high turban decorated with glittering stones. A green mask hides his face. Green hands with long fingers protrude from folds of his robe.)* [NOTE: During blackout, a high step stool is brought in and Wizard stands on this, his long robe falling to floor to hide stool. His green mask and fingers are made of green foil, which glitter in the light. Lion has whirled about and now stares at him in awe. Lion growls a little, tentatively, then backs away from throne hurriedly.]

LION: You—you really *are* a Wizard!

WIZARD: *(In an awesome voice.)* Who dared to say otherwise?

LION: *(Stepping back some more.)* Not I, your Tall Wizardry.

WIZARD: Who are you?

LION: *(In a meek tone.)* I'm a Cowardly Lion, afraid of everything.

WIZARD: Why do you seek me?

LION: I come to beg that you give me courage, so that I may become the real King of Beasts.

WIZARD: Why should I give you courage?

LION: Because only you have the power to do so.

WIZARD: I will consider your request after I've talked to the little girl, Dorothy.

LION: *(Now moving toward him, but not too close.)* Please, your Tall Wizardry, don't frighten her.

WIZARD: What I must do, I must do. You are dismissed. *(Room lights flash rapidly and there is a brief blackout. During this blackout, step stool and Wizard go behind screen.)*

LION: *(Impressed.)* He's as tall as a tower!

VERDO: *(Turning.)* That very well may be.

LION: Where did he come from?

VERDO: You may as well ask, where has he gone?

(The room lights come on again, showing no sign of the Wizard. Jade comes in L.)

JADE: Come with me and wait. The Wizard is ready for Dorothy now. *(Lion goes L.)*

(Dorothy and Toto come in L.)

DOROTHY: Oh, dear, I'm getting very nervous!

LION: I know just how you feel.

DOROTHY: The Scarecrow says the Wizard's a bouncing green light, and the Tin Woodman says he's a deep-sounding gong.

LION: They're both wrong. The Wizard of Oz is a magician as tall as a tower! *(Quickly.)* But try not to be afraid. I'll be right outside the door in case you need me. *(Gives Dorothy an encouraging pat with his paw as he follows Jade out L.)*

DOROTHY: *(Moving C slowly, as Toto barks.)* Hush, Toto! This is no time to bark! *(To Verdo.)* I understand the Wizard is ready to see me.

VERDO: He is. *(Turns his face to door again. Room lights flash off and on rapidly, then there is a blackout.)*

DOROTHY: How can I see him when the room's so dark?

VERDO: Darkness makes no difference to him.

DOROTHY: But it does to me.

VERDO: Why?

DOROTHY: Because in the dark I don't know what's going on.

VERDO: You'll soon find out. *(Suddenly, as if suspended in air above throne chair, a large glittering ball appears. Dorothy gives a little cry of fright as she sees it.)*

DOROTHY: *(Awed.)* Why, he—he's a huge ball of fire! [NOTE: A large foil-covered ball, attached to a black rod and swinging on a heavy black cord, is manipulated by black-covered hands from over top of tall screen by Wizard, standing behind it. As Dorothy watches, a red spotlight plays on ball, making it glow like fire.]

WIZARD: I am Oz the Great and Terrible. Who are you?

DOROTHY: *(In a small voice.)* I am Dorothy, the small and meek.

WIZARD: Why have you come?

DOROTHY: To seek your help.

WIZARD: Who told you about me?

DOROTHY: Melinda, the Good Witch of the North. *(Ball swings slowly back and forth during scene.)*

WIZARD: Where did you get those silver shoes?

DOROTHY: From the Wicked Witch of the East, when my house fell on her and killed her.

WIZARD: Ah, yes. What do you wish of me?

DOROTHY: *(Stepping closer.)* Please send me back to Kansas where my Aunt Em and Uncle Henry are.

WIZARD: *(Reprovingly.)* You don't like the Land of Oz?

DOROTHY: Oh, yes, I do! But I miss my own people and I know they're worried about me.

WIZARD: Why should I do this for you?

DOROTHY: Because you're strong and I'm weak. Because you're a Great Wizard and I'm only a helpless little girl.

WIZARD: But you were strong enough to kill the Wicked Witch of the East.

DOROTHY: That just happened. I couldn't help it.

WIZARD: You have no right to expect me to send you back to Kansas unless you do something for me in return.

DOROTHY: But what can *I* possibly do?

WIZARD: If you wish me to use my magic power for you and your friends, you must help me first. Then I will help you.

DOROTHY: Tell me what to do. I'll try.

WIZARD: In the West there lives a wicked Witch named Belinda, who rules the Winkie country.

DOROTHY: *(Nervously.)* I've heard of her.

WIZARD: Belinda gained all her power by stealing a magic golden cap. Go there, get that cap, and bring it to me.

DOROTHY: Did she steal it from you?

WIZARD: *(Sharply.)* Don't ask questions. I want that magic cap.

DOROTHY: But how can *I* possibly get it away from her?

WIZARD: You destroyed the Wicked Witch of the East.

DOROTHY: Just by accident.

WIZARD: And you wear the silver shoes which bear a powerful charm.

DOROTHY: *(Looking down at her shoes.)* But I don't know what the charm is.

WIZARD: When you bring me the magic cap, I'll send you back to Kansas.

DOROTHY: If you, who are Great and Terrible, can't get it yourself, how do you expect me to do it?

WIZARD: That problem is for you to solve.

DOROTHY: But if she's such a terrible witch, I'm afraid!

WIZARD: Then your friends will never get the things they want. And you will never return to Kansas. *(To heighten effect of magic, a spotlight might throw colors of spectrum on ball, causing it to change from one color to another. Dorothy moves away in awe. There is a brief blackout. When lights go on full, there is no sign of Wizard.)*

DOROTHY: *(Crossing RC.)* Truly, the Wizard is Great and Terrible!

VERDO: *(Turning.)* Of course he is.

(Jade comes in L with the Scarecrow, the Tin Woodman and the Cowardly Lion.)

SCARECROW: *(Eagerly, moving C.)* Is he going to grant our requests? *(Tin Woodman and Lion follow.)*

DOROTHY: *(Unhappily.)* Not until we go to the land of the Winkies and take the magic golden cap from Belinda, the Wicked Witch of the West. *(They all look dejected, and shake their heads in despair.)*

SCARECROW: If she guesses what we're up to, she'll enchant us all. *(After a pause.)* But that's the chance we have to take. *(Straightens up.)* What are we waiting for?

DOROTHY: *(Sighing, crossing to them at C.)* I do so want to go back to Kansas, and to see my Aunt Em and Uncle Henry.

TIN WOODMAN: If I had a heart, it would ache for you. But I'll go along and keep you company.

LION: I'm too much of a coward to be much help, but I'll go, too.

SCARECROW: I'll be no help at all, because I'm such a fool. *(Crosses to Verdo.)* Which road leads to the Wicked Witch of the West?

VERDO: There *is* no road because no one ever wants to go that way.

SCARECROW: But Dorothy *must* get the magic cap.

VERDO: Belinda won't take very kindly to the idea.

DOROTHY: *(Wistfully.)* I keep thinking of Aunt Em worrying about me and trying not to cry. And Uncle Henry will blow his nose loudly and pretend he has a cold. I know they both miss me.

TIN WOODMAN: Naturally. People with hearts love each other very much.

DOROTHY: I must try not to be afraid of this witch. *(More firmly.)* Because I *have* to get back to Kansas!

SCARECROW: *(Crossing C again.)* Now you're talking sense, the way I'd talk if I had a brain.

LION: We're your friends. We'll all go with you.

DOROTHY: *(Turning to Verdo.)* Which way do we start?

VERDO: Keep to the West where the sun sets, and you can't fail to find the witch. *(Crosses L and opens door.)*

LION: *(Leading the way.)* Whatever happens, we'll stick together! *(Goes out L, head held high, followed by Scarecrow and Tin Woodman. Dorothy remains at C.)*

VERDO: *(Sadly, waving to them.)* Good-by.

JADE: *(Sadly, waving to them.)* We may never see you again. *(Gives a little sob and puts her hands over her face.)*

DOROTHY: *(Running to Jade.)* Please don't cry. We'll come back. I just *know* we'll come back! *(Runs out L with Toto in her arms. As Verdo is closing door after them, wicked laughter of Witch Belinda is heard, continuing as curtain falls.)*

CURTAIN

ACT TWO

SCENE ONE

THE KITCHEN OF BELINDA, THE WICKED WITCH OF THE WEST.

The color scheme here may be yellow. At UC stage stands what appears to be a cage. (A few wooden slats nailed to a framework will do.) There is a door, also with slats, attached to the front of the cage. A bench is LC, facing the audience. At RC is a table, with a chair left of it. On the table are a telescopelike object and a pretty golden cap. On the bench is a clothesbasket, filled with large pieces of cloth (yellow). There are entrances at R and L stage.

At rise of curtain, Winkle and Wonkle are hammering at the door to the cage, presumably finishing their work on it. Belinda, broom in hand, attended by her three yellow-faced black cats, Inky, Blinky and Slinky, is dancing about, rather grotesquely, half chanting, half singing as the Winkies work.

BELINDA: I'm the wickedest witch in all the land,
And ev'ryone trembles at my command.

CATS: *(Prancing happily after her.)* At her command!

BELINDA:

I'm very smart
With magic art;
I scream and yell
And cast a spell.

(Makes "spell" motions toward UC.)

CATS: *(Imitating motions.)* She casts a spell!

BELINDA:

I kick and fight,
I scratch and bite;
I stamp and shout,
I hit and clout.

(Hits Winkle and Wonkle with her broom, and they hammer faster.)

CATS: She hits and clouts!

BELINDA: *(Continuing to dance about.)*

I capture all
Who come to call,
And laugh with glee
At misery.

CATS: At misery. *(As Belinda laughs, they double over with glee.)*

BELINDA:

I'm the wickedest witch there ever was,
And I brag and brag about this because
I'm glad I'm bad!

CATS: She's glad she's bad!

BELINDA: I like to be bad!

CATS: She likes to be bad!

BELINDA: *(In a normal witch voice, not chanting, directly to audience.)* In fact, I'm very good at it!

CATS: *(Also directly to audience.)* She's very good at it!

BELINDA: *(Suddenly hitting Winkle with her broom again.)* Hurry and finish that cage, lazy Winkle.

WINKLE: *(Afraid.)* Yes, your Witchiness. *(Hammers faster.)*

BELINDA: *(Hitting Wonkle.)* Lazy Wonkle! I want it all ready when our visitors get here.

WONKLE: Yes, your Witchiness. *(Hammers faster.)*

BELINDA: *(To cats, coming LC with them.)* And you, my sweet kitty cats. *(Pets them.)* Be quiet and gentle when Dorothy comes in. I'm going to fool her into thinking I'm a good witch! *(Laughs, and Cats laugh.)* No hissing or scratching until I say so. Promise, Inky?

INKY: Not even one little hiss? *(Pause; Belinda shakes her head.)* I promise.

BELINDA: Blinky?

BLINKY: Not even one little scratch? *(Pause; Belinda shakes her head.)* I promise.

BELINDA: Slinky?

SLINKY: But I just had my claws sharpened yesterday. *(Pause; Belinda shakes her head. Slinky sighs.)* It won't be easy, but I promise.

BELINDA: *(Picking up telescope from table.)* Make sure that cage is good and strong while I check once more through my magic telescope. *(Goes to door R.)*

WINKLE AND WONKLE: Yes, your Witchiness. *(They "test" door. Belinda opens door R and peers out through her telescope. Cats follow her to door.)*

BELINDA: Hah! They're entering our courtyard now!

CATS: Our courtyard now! *(Give a drawn-out "miaow!")*

BELINDA: Ah, what fine slaves they'll make!

CATS: What fine slaves! *(They miaow.)*

BELINDA: But I wish I knew *why* they're coming here. Quick! Cover the door! *(Closes door R and puts telescope back on table.)*

WINKLE: *(Pleadingly.)* Please, your Witchiness—

WONKLE: —she's only a child.

WINKLE: If you let her go—

WONKLE: —we'll work harder than ever for you.

BELINDA: I never let *anybody* go! *(Laughs shrilly. Cats and Winkle and Wonkle take folds of yellow material from basket on bench and drape them over cage so that much of it is hidden and only door shows. There is a knock on door R. Belinda is by table.)*

She's here,
The little dear!

CATS: *(As they help drape cage.)* The little dear!

BELINDA: And she's wearing the silver shoes
That she doesn't know how to use!

CATS: Doesn't know how to use! *(Belinda and Cats laugh. Another knock on door R. Belinda crosses and opens door R, smiling. Winkle and Wonkle stand on either side of cage door, while Cats scamper over by bench and stand.)*

BELINDA: Come in, my dear. It's such a nice surprise to have company.

(Dorothy, surprised at this smiling welcome, enters R, carrying Toto.)

DOROTHY: Then you didn't expect me?

BELINDA: *(Taking her arm, bringing her in front of table.)* How could I possibly expect you when I don't even know your name?

DOROTHY: It's Dorothy, and I've been traveling all night. This is my dog, Toto. *(Toto growls at Belinda, then barks at Cats. Cats hiss at him.)*

BELINDA: *(Reprovingly, moving C.)* Now be good little kitty cats! *(To Dorothy.)* You must be very tired, my sweet. Sit down and rest. *(Indicates chair left of table.)*

DOROTHY: *(Hesitating.)* You *are* Belinda, the Witch of the West?

BELINDA: *(Sweetly.)* Of course. Do sit down, dearie, and take off those *clumsy* silver shoes which must surely *hurt* your feet.

DOROTHY: Thank you, but they really don't hurt at all. *(Sits left of table.)*

BELINDA: *(Crossing to her.)* Take them off anyway, and I'll get you a nice pair of comfy slippers to wear.

DOROTHY: *(Perplexed and confused.)* You're not one bit like what I expected.

BELINDA: Really?

DOROTHY: People said—

BELINDA: *(With a "hurt" tone.)* So they've been talking about me again! *(Moves DR and turns.)* People are forever making up stories about me. Jealous, you know.

DOROTHY: Jealous?

BELINDA: Because I rule the Winkie Country so well, and all the Winkies *love* me. *(Raising her broom threateningly as she looks to-*

ward Winkle and Wonkle.) Isn't that so? *(Brings broom down quickly and pretends to sweep as Dorothy looks at her.)*

WINKLE AND WONKLE: *(Afraid of her.)* Yes, your Witchiness.

BELINDA: *(Smiling.)* You see? All lies, the things people say.

CATS: All lies!

BELINDA: *(Moving over to Cats.)* Why, some of them actually think I'm a *bad* witch!

DOROTHY: *(Puzzled.)* And you're not?

BELINDA: *(As Cats snuggle around her lovingly.)* You can see for yourself how nice I am. *(Pets Cats, who purr loudly.)*

CATS: How nice she is! *(Toto barks at them again, but at a signal from Belinda, Cats remain quiet.)*

DOROTHY: Then maybe I was wrong to come here. *(Rising.)* Oh, now I don't know *what* to do!

BELINDA: *(Crossing to her.)* Just take off those silly-looking shoes, dearie. *(Pushes her back in chair.)*

DOROTHY: But I have friends waiting outside and I'll have to tell them we've made a big mistake. *(Rising.)* I'm sure a nice witch like you wouldn't steal anything.

BELINDA: *(Laughing shrilly.)* What a ridiculous notion! Invite your friends to come in, dearie.

DOROTHY: *(Going to door R.)* I hope you'll excuse my thinking wrong things about you.

BELINDA: *(Who has quickly followed her R.)* Everyone makes mistakes. *(Opens door and Dorothy goes out R.)* And you're making the biggest one of your life right now! *(She and Cats laugh as Belinda crosses back to Cats.)*

CATS: The biggest one of her life right now!

(After a moment, Dorothy comes in R with the Scarecrow, the Tin Woodman and the Cowardly Lion. They look about uneasily.)

TIN WOODMAN: *(To Dorothy, as they all come in front of table.)* We've been worried about you.

LION: Afraid you might be in trouble.

DOROTHY: Nonsense! Belinda is really a very nice witch.

SCARECROW: *(Scratching his head.)* If I had brains, I might be able to understand this.

BELINDA: Welcome, strangers. Why have you come to see me?

TIN WOODMAN: *(Embarrassed.)* Well, it's a little hard to explain.

LION: Maybe we'll tell you after a while. *(Scarecrow just scratches his head, perplexed.)*

BELINDA: Does your friend have something the matter with his head?

DOROTHY: Nothing serious.

SCARECROW: Just that there aren't any brains in it.

BELINDA: *(Coming C now.)* Don't let that worry you. Lots of my friends are a little short on brains.

DOROTHY: And you like them just the same?

BELINDA: I like them even better!

SCARECROW: *(Scratching head again.)* This really puzzles me.

BELINDA: Now, you must be tired. I have a very special room where visitors may rest when they're tired. *(Moves UC and indicates door of cage.)* Please step inside. *(Winkle opens door when Belinda prods him with her broom. Wonkle bows.)*

TIN WOODMAN: *(Crossing UC.)* I never get tired, because I'm made out of tin.

SCARECROW: *(Crossing UC.)* Nor I, because I'm stuffed with straw.

LION: *(Crossing UC.)* I do. And my throat hurts again, from roaring. *(Rubs his throat.)*

BELINDA: Oh, too bad! *(Indicates open door.)*

TIN WOODMAN: This is most kind of you. *(Goes inside cage.)*

LION: Surprisingly kind. *(Goes inside.)*

SCARECROW: If only I could think! *(Gives his head a slap, shakes it, then gives up effort and enters cage. Belinda closes door quickly and, taking a huge lock and key from her pocket, snaps it fast. At the same time Cats pull covering from cage and they all realize what has happened. Lion roars; Scarecrow and Tin Woodman groan in dismay. Toto barks and Cats hiss at him. Belinda goes into gales of Wicked Witch laughter.)*

DOROTHY: *(Indignantly, rushing UC.)* You *are* bad! You've locked my friends up in a cage!

BELINDA: *(Chanting happily.)*

I'm bad as can be, can be, can be.
I've locked them up and I have the key!

(Puts key in her pocket.)

CATS: She has the key!

DOROTHY: *(Frightened.)* What are you going to do to them?

BELINDA: I'll think about that after a while. *(Chants again.)*

But you are my slave, my slave, my slave,
And I know how to make my slaves behave!

(Raises her broom, and Winkle and Wonkle scurry DL.)

CATS: Her slaves behave! *(Lion roars.)*

BELINDA: *(Raising her broom.)* Stop that, you ugly beast, or I'll rub your sore throat with my own special vanishing cream!

LION: *(Subsiding.)* If only I wasn't such a coward!

TIN WOODMAN: If I had a heart, it would be breaking.

SCARECROW: If I had brains, we wouldn't have walked into this trap.

DOROTHY: Don't blame yourself. *(Defiantly, to Belinda.)* I *won't* be your slave!

BELINDA: Do you want to see the Lion starve? Or the Tin Woodman rust away? Or the Scarecrow used as kindling for my fire?

DOROTHY: *(Frightened.)* Oh, no! I—I'll do anything you say.

BELINDA: *(To Winkle and Wonkle.)* Go fetch my serving maids, Amber and Topaz!

WINKLE AND WONKLE: Yes, your Witchiness. *(They hurry out L.)*

DOROTHY: *(Unhappily.)* I've caused so much trouble for my friends, when all I really want is to go back to Kansas.

BELINDA: Do you think *I* care? *(Chants.)*

I laugh and laugh when I make folks sad,
Because I'm bad. *(Laughs.)*

CATS: Because she's bad! *(They laugh.)*

(Winkle and Wonkle enter L with Amber and Topaz, who look frightened.)

WINKLE: Here they are, your Witchiness—

WONKLE: —Amber and Topaz. *(Winkle and Wonkle bow and go out L. Amber and Topaz come in front of bench.)*

AMBER: Whatever you ask—

TOPAZ: —we're ready to do.

BELINDA: This is Dorothy, my new slave. She'll help you scrub and clean.

DOROTHY: *(Crossing down to them, trying to be friendly.)* Hello. *(They just look at her.)* Are you afraid to talk to me?

BELINDA: Of course they're afraid. *(To maids.)* Bring a pail of water and a mop.

AMBER: I'll get the pail—

TOPAZ: —and I, the mop. *(She and Amber scurry out L. Belinda and her Cats come down in front of table now.)*

BELINDA: *(Chanting.)*
Whatever I ask, they're ready to do,
They learned to obey and so will you.

CATS: And so will you.

BELINDA: Or else! . . . *(Points to cage.)* Are you good at mopping floors?

DOROTHY: I've never tried.

BELINDA: You look strong. Yes, I think I'll get a lot of work out of you.

(Amber comes in L with a pail partly filled with water, or perhaps sand. Topaz enters with mop. They pause at L.)

AMBER: The pail—

TOPAZ: —and the mop.

BELINDA: *(Crossing L, taking pail and mop and giving them to Dorothy.)* Get busy!

DOROTHY: I'll do my best.

BELINDA: *(Crossing RC, to Cats.)* Come, my precious ones, and sit outside in the sun with me. *(Cats follow her R. She pauses to take off her black hat and put on golden cap from table.)* How do you like my golden cap?

DOROTHY: *(Realizing that this is it.)* Oh! *(Quickly.)* Where did you get it?

BELINDA: *(Proudly.)* I stole it, naturally.

DOROTHY: It's very pretty.

BELINDA: Much more than just pretty, my pretty. But *you'll* never get your hands on it. *(Laughs, turning toward door R.)* If the sky clouds over, we'll come in. I hate the rain.

DOROTHY: Why do you hate rain?

BELINDA: *(Tauntingly.)* Wouldn't you like to know? *(Pauses again.)* But wait. Surely you don't want to get those silver shoes wet mopping the floor?

DOROTHY: *(Discouraged.)* Nothing matters to me but going back to Kansas.

BELINDA: *(Crossing back to C.)* How would you like to change shoes with me?

DOROTHY: No, thank you.

BELINDA: Then your silver ones would stay nice and dry.

DOROTHY: No!

BELINDA: *(Muttering, moving R angrily.)* Stubborn child! *(Goes out R with her Cats.)*

DOROTHY: *(Putting Toto down in corner UL.)* Now, you stay there and be good, Toto. *(Comes down in front of bench, starting to mop.)* Why do you suppose she doesn't like rain?

AMBER: We haven't—

TOPAZ: —the slightest idea.

DOROTHY: Do you *have* to work for her?

AMBER: All the Winkies have to because—

TOPAZ: —she came to our country and made us into slaves.

AMBER: We hoped you might destroy her the way—

TOPAZ: —you destroyed the Wicked Witch of the East.

DOROTHY: That just happened, when my house landed on her.

AMBER: *(Sadly.)* Oh—

TOPAZ: —dear!

DOROTHY: Do you have to work all the time?

AMBER: Yes, and if we don't hurry—

TOPAZ: —she'll get after us with her broom! *(She and Amber hurry out L.)*

DOROTHY: *(Dropping mop, going to cage.)* I'll never, never be able to get the golden cap—she's wearing it.

SCARECROW: Don't give up so soon.

DOROTHY: I blame myself for what's happened to all of you. Are you very uncomfortable in there?

SCARECROW: It *is* a little crowded.

TIN WOODMAN: I hope I don't cry and begin to rust.

LION: I should have torn that witch to pieces!

DOROTHY: She'd have stopped you with a magic spell. Why do you suppose she hates me so?

TIN WOODMAN: She hates everybody.

DOROTHY: But why me, especially?

SCARECROW: Maybe she thinks you have more magic than she has.

DOROTHY: But that's silly. They don't teach any magic in Kansas.

SCARECROW: Too bad. *(Sighs.)* There *must* be a way to get that golden cap.

DOROTHY: How?

SCARECROW: If only I could *think*! Then I'd tell you.

DOROTHY: Thank you. I know you would.

SCARECROW: It occurs to me that she's very anxious to get hold of those silver shoes of yours.

DOROTHY: *(Looking down, holding one foot up.)* I wonder why?

SCARECROW: Without a brain, how would I know? *(Lion gives a little sob, then dries his eyes with his tail.)*

DOROTHY: I feel like crying, too, when I think about Aunt Em in Kansas. *(Takes handkerchief from her pocket and dabs at her eyes.)*

TIN WOODMAN: *(Tearfully.)* Please stop! Now you've got me doing it! *(Lion uses tip of his tail to wipe tears from Tin Woodman's eyes.)* Thank you so much.

SCARECROW: This is no time for tears. If we don't get that cap very soon, there's no hope for any of us.

DOROTHY: I know that. *(They hear Belinda laughing offstage R, and Dorothy runs LC and starts mopping again.)* She's coming!

(Belinda comes in R. She leaves the door open.)

BELINDA: You're a very slow worker.

DOROTHY: *(Working faster, moving DL with mop.)* I haven't had much experience.

BELINDA: *(Coming C.)* Perhaps you're still tired from your long journey?

DOROTHY: I guess so.

BELINDA: *(Slyly.)* Now, then, my little dear, I'm not all bad. Sit down on the bench and rest a bit. *(Moves clothesbasket from bench and pats it.)*

DOROTHY: I really *am* very tired.

BELINDA: *(Soothingly.)* Of course you are, pet. *(Leads Dorothy to bench and makes her sit down.)* That's better, isn't it? *(Stands left of bench.)*

SCARECROW: Dorothy, be careful!

BELINDA: Quiet, you straw-stuffed creature! *(To Dorothy.)* Hmm . . . those silver shoes don't fit you very well, do they?

DOROTHY: Oh, yes, they do!

BELINDA: They have very peculiar toes.

DOROTHY: *(Pulling her feet together.)* *I* like them.

BELINDA: Not *my* type of shoe at all. But do you mind if I try one on? *(Reaches down toward a shoe.)*

DOROTHY: *(Pulling her feet away.)* No!

BELINDA: *(Quickly snatching a shoe from Dorothy's foot.)* Yes! *(Hurries R, standing on one foot while she tries to take off her old black shoe and put on silver one.)*

DOROTHY: *(Angrily, running after her.)* Give me back my silver shoe!

BELINDA: Never! It's mine, now.

DOROTHY: You had no right to take it away from me!

BELINDA: Some day I'll get the other one, too! *(Continues her efforts to remove her own shoe.)*

DOROTHY: I said, give it back to me! *(Runs back, picks up pail of "water" and runs R, dashing it over Belinda, who now loses her balance and falls to floor in front of open door.)*

BELINDA: *(Yelling.)* No—no! Don't put *water* on me! Oh, evil day! It's too late. Now see what you've done!

DOROTHY: *(Puzzled.)* What *have* I done?

BELINDA: *(Wailing.)* I'm melting away!

TIN WOODMAN: *(Excitedly, as they peer from cage.)* Look! She *is* melting away.

BELINDA: *(Wailing.)* How did you know that water would be the death of me?

DOROTHY: *(Bending over her.)* But I really didn't know! So that is why you don't like the rain. *(As Dorothy partly hides Belinda, she pulls her hands and feet under extra fullness of her robe.)* Mercy, her hands and feet have already disappeared! Soon there won't be much of her left.

(The Cats come in R and stand around, howling softly. During this time, Cats and Dorothy shield Belinda completely from audience. She

slips out of her black robe, leaving it and her black shoes on floor. She also leaves silver shoe and her golden cap, and crawls out R, either under drapes or through partly open and shielded door. As she goes, her voice can still be heard.)

BELINDA: To think that a little slip of a girl like you would be the end of me! *(Her voice begins to fade.)* I'm melt-ing—melt—ing—melt . . . *(She has presumably finished the job.)*

DOROTHY: Oh, dear me! She really *has* melted away! *(Steps to one side. Cats, moaning softly, now huddle DR. On floor can be seen black robe, old black shoes, golden cap and silver shoe. Dorothy picks up golden cap; triumphantly.)* The golden cap!

SCARECROW: *(Happily.)* You've got it! *(Dorothy puts cap on her own head, then picks up robe and black shoes and goes to cage.)*

DOROTHY: *(Holding them up.)* This is all that's left of her.

SCARECROW: Get the key out of her pocket and open the cage! *(Dorothy takes key from pocket of robe and presumably unlocks cage door.)*

(Winkle, Wonkle, Amber, and Topaz, and any extras, as desired, come timidly in at L now, to see what is going on. They stand in a group at L stage.)

AMBER: *(Happily.)* The Wicked Witch—

TOPAZ: —has melted.

OTHERS: She melted! *(They cheer as Scarecrow, Tin Woodman and Lion come out of cage.)*

DOROTHY: *(Coming C with her friends.)* Now we can go back to the Emerald City and claim our reward!

WINKLE: Can't you stay here—

WONKLE: —and be our ruler?

DOROTHY: Thank you, but we must be on our way. *(Sits at table and puts on her silver shoe, then stands up.)* There! *(Runs UL, picks up Toto, then comes C again.)*

WINKLE: You look very pretty—

WONKLE: —in the golden cap.

DOROTHY: Thank you.

AMBER: We think there's—

TOPAZ: —magic in it.

DOROTHY: So do I, or the Wizard wouldn't want it so much.

LION: *(Crossing R.)* Come, come, let's get started. *(Growls at Cats. Cats go to Dorothy in a close group and chant.)*

CATS:

We're not *very* bad,
And we would be glad
To learn if we could
How to be good.

(Pleadingly.) How to be good? How to be good? How to be good?

AMBER: We'll—

TOPAZ: —teach you! *(They join hands with Cats, bringing them LC, in a little dance step.)*

DOROTHY: Good-by, and may your land always be free and happy. *(They all cheer and wave as she crosses R now with Scarecrow and Tin Woodman.)*

TIN WOODMAN: Now I'll get my heart!

SCARECROW: And I'll get brains!

LION: I'll be filled with courage!

SCARECROW: Because Dorothy has the golden cap! *(Goes out R with Lion and Tin Woodman.)*

DOROTHY: And the Great Wizard will have to send me back to Kansas! *(Waves. Toto gives a happy bark, and they go out R. Others on stage run to door R and cheer and wave.)*

CURTAIN

ACT TWO

SCENE TWO

THE THRONE ROOM OF THE WIZARD.

At rise of curtain, Verdo is again pacing back and forth with his gun over his shoulder. As he walks toward R, Jade enters L with her feather duster, puts it over her shoulder like a gun, and paces behind him. When he squares the corner and returns to march toward L, she moves nimbly out of his sight. This is kept up for a moment or two, with Verdo unaware that Jade is mimicking him. Finally, he sees her, when she isn't quick enough to side-step, and he stops short in wounded dignity.

VERDO: Just what is going on here?

JADE: *(Innocently.)* I'm just helping you with guard duty.

VERDO: *(Disgustedly.)* Girls!

JADE: *(Teasingly.)*

The Captain has whiskers so long and green,
The fanciest whiskers I ever have seen.

VERDO: *(Stroking his beard, pleased.)* Thank you. *(Jade picks up a pair of scissors from table DL, leaving her duster on table.)*

JADE:

But you look rather weird.
With so fancy a beard.

VERDO: *(Stiffly.)* That's your opinion.

JADE:

Do you mind if I clip
Just a bit at the tip?

(Comes toward him with scissors.)

VERDO: *(Backing UC.)* Keep away from me!

JADE:

I feel an urge to snip,
And clip, and clip, and clip.

VERDO:

Just dare—
And I'll clip your hair! *(Offstage R, Toto barks.)*

JADE: *(Turning toward door R.)* What was that? *(Toto barks again.)* That's Toto—Dorothy's dog!

VERDO: *(Alertly.)* But it couldn't possibly be! No one ever returns from the country of the Wicked Witch of the West. *(There is a knock on door R.)*

DOROTHY: *(Offstage R.)* May we come in, please?

JADE: It *is* Dorothy! *(Runs quickly R and opens door.)*

(Dorothy comes in R with Toto, the Scarecrow, the Tin Woodman and the Cowardly Lion. Dorothy is wearing the golden cap.)

DOROTHY: Hello! We're back.

VERDO: *(Who has come down to C.)* But how did you do it?

JADE: *(Happily.)* She gave you the cap?

DOROTHY: She couldn't help it; she's melted. *(Comes RC with others.)*

JADE: Melted?

TIN WOODMAN: Completely.

VERDO: Who melted her?

LION: *(Proudly.)* Dorothy.

VERDO: Great guns!

JADE: You must have wonderful magic indeed. *(Curtsies.)*

DOROTHY: Dear me, no.

VERDO: How extremely odd.

DOROTHY: What seems odd to me is anyone should *think* I have. *(Politely.)* Will you please let the Great Wizard of Oz know we're here?

SCARECROW: Tell him we've come to claim the rewards he promised us. *(Lights suddenly flash off and on and voice of Wizard is heard.)*

WIZARD: *(From general direction of offstage UL.)* Just leave the cap and go away. Come back tomorrow or the next day!

DOROTHY: *(Looking around.)* That was the Wizard speaking.

VERDO: He doesn't want to see you today.

DOROTHY: But we've done what he asked us to do.

WIZARD: *(Offstage UL.)* Come back next week.

DOROTHY: We don't want to wait that long.

WIZARD: *(Offstage UL.)* Then come next month. Or never!

DOROTHY: *(Uneasily.)* He sounds angry with us.

TIN WOODMAN: I thought he'd be pleased.

LION: So did I. *(Toto barks.)* [NOTE: If convenient, Wizard's voice, as scene continues, comes from various positions offstage—as he moves about offstage from UL to UC, to DL, then UR, DR, etc.]

DOROTHY: Why are you angry with us, Mr. Wizard?

WIZARD: *(Offstage.)* Because I'm in a bad mood.

DOROTHY: When will you be in a good mood?

WIZARD: *(Offstage.)* As soon as you go away.

DOROTHY: *(To her friends.)* Oh, dear, what shall we do now?

SCARECROW: I wish I knew.

DOROTHY: Please, Mr. Wizard, let us stay! We have something to tell you.

WIZARD: *(Offstage.)* I don't feel like listening.

DOROTHY: But this is important.

WIZARD: *(Offstage.)* So am I!

DOROTHY: *(Looking around.)* Where are you?

WIZARD: *(Offstage.)* I am everywhere. But to the eyes of common mortals I am now invisible.

DOROTHY: But you don't have to let us *see* you. All we ask is a chance to *talk* to you.

SCARECROW: *(Getting down on his knees.)* Please, O Great Green Light!

TIN WOODMAN: *(Likewise, but stiffly, awkwardly.)* Please, O Sounding Gong!

LION: *(On his knees.)* Please, O Tower-high Magician!

DOROTHY: *(Kneeling, too.)* Please, O Mighty Wizard of Oz! Because you promised.

WIZARD: *(Offstage, with a sigh.)* Very well. I will seat myself upon my throne. *(With happy cries, Dorothy and her friends jump up from their kneeling positions. Lights flash off and on again, but when flashing is over, throne still appears empty. His voice now comes directly from behind screen.)* I am here. *(Sternly.)* Jade and Verdo—depart! *(Jade and Verdo look nervously toward throne, then go out L. Dorothy and her friends walk to throne and speak to what they think is the invisible Wizard.)*

DOROTHY: We've come to claim our rewards.

WIZARD: What rewards?

DOROTHY: The ones you promised, O Great Invisible Wizard.

WIZARD: What promises did I make?

SCARECROW: You promised to give me brains.

TIN WOODMAN: You promised to give me a heart.

LION: And courage to me.

DOROTHY: You promised to send me back to Kansas if I brought you the golden cap.

WIZARD: Ah, yes. I remember now. How did you manage to get it from Belinda?

DOROTHY: I didn't know that water would make her melt away. But it did.

WIZARD: Completely?

DOROTHY: Absolutely and completely. She's gone.

WIZARD: *(After a pause.)* I must have time to think this over.

SCARECROW: *(Annoyed.)* But you've had plenty of time already.

TIN WOODMAN: I don't see why we should have to wait.

LION: You must keep your promises to us.

DOROTHY: *(Indignantly.)* Yes, you certainly must!

LION: *(Helpfully.)* Because if you don't— *(Lets out a mighty roar. His roar is so loud and fierce that Dorothy, who is nearest screen, jumps in alarm, knocks against screen, and it tips over with a crash. Now at last they see the Wizard standing there as he really is—a plump little man with an almost bald head. He is as surprised as they are.)*

WIZARD: Oh, goodness, gracious, mercy me!

TIN WOODMAN: *(Raising his axe.)* Who are you?

WIZARD: *(In a trembling voice.)* I am—Oz—the Great and Terrible.

ALL: *(In chorus, moving slightly closer.) You?*

WIZARD: *(Backing slightly.)* Don't hurt me, please don't!

SCARECROW: But I thought the Wizard was a bouncing green ball of light!

TIN WOODMAN: I thought he was a loud-sounding gong!

LION: I thought he was a mighty magician as tall as a tower!

DOROTHY: *(Dismayed.)* I thought he was able to turn himself into all these things, even into a ball of fire.

WIZARD: *(Meekly.)* No, you're all wrong. *(Makes a wide circle around them as he moves C.)* I've been making believe.

DOROTHY: *(As she and her friends follow right after him.)* Aren't you really a great Wizard at all?

WIZARD: *(Warningly, his finger to his lips, glancing L and R.)* Sh! I'm supposed to be very great.

DOROTHY: But not really?

WIZARD: *(Sadly, shaking his head.)* Not a bit of it, my dear. I'm just a common man.

SCARECROW: But this is awful! How will I ever get my brains?

TIN WOODMAN: Or I my heart?

LION: *(On verge of tears.)* Or I my courage?

DOROTHY: And how will I get back to Kansas?

WIZARD: *(Pleadingly.)* My dear friends, I beg of you to keep my secret. Think of all the trouble I'd be in if everyone knew the truth about me! *(Paces DR.)*

DOROTHY: Doesn't anyone else know?

WIZARD: Just you four, and myself. That's why I never let any of my people see me.

DOROTHY: *(Moving toward him.)* But you appeared in so many strange ways . . .

WIZARD: Just simple tricks, my dear. I used to work with a circus in Omaha, Nebraska. One day I went up in a balloon and it broke loose and floated all the way here, to the Land of Oz.

DOROTHY: *(Depressed.)* Just tricks. *(Sits in a chair URC, with Toto on her lap. She takes off golden cap and holds it.)*

WIZARD: *(Moving up to her.)* When the people of Oz saw me come down out of the sky, they naturally thought I must be a very powerful Wizard, so they made me their ruler.

DOROTHY: I think you're a very bad man.

WIZARD: Oh, no, I'm really a very good man! But I'm a very bad Wizard.

DOROTHY: Don't you know any magic at all?

WIZARD: *(Stalling.)* Well, now . . . *(Clears his throat.)*

SCARECROW: *(Wistfully.)* I'd be so proud if only you could give me some brains.

WIZARD: Experience is the only thing that brings knowledge. *(Crosses C and studies Scarecrow.)* It seems to me you're doing pretty well with just straw in your head. *(Scarecrow turns away sorrowfully.)* Wait! *(Scarecrow turns back.)* It so happens that I *do* have enough magic to help you out. *(Goes to table DL and gets a large box labeled Bran, which he holds behind his back.)*

DOROTHY: *(Rising, crossing C.)* I've always liked you the way you are, Scarecrow.

SCARECROW: But wait till you hear the splendid thoughts my new brain will turn out!

WIZARD: *(Moving to throne.)* Over here, please. Kneel down. *(Scarecrow kneels down, putting his head on throne seat.)* Now, then, a little opening in one of the seams . . .

DOROTHY: *(As she and her other friends move UC to watch.)* I'm afraid he wasn't stitched very well.

WIZARD: That doesn't matter. *(Holds up box so that audience may see it, then bends over Scarecrow, presumably putting some bran into his head.)* H'm—there seems to be room for quite a lot.

SCARECROW: Then make me very, very brainy.

WIZARD: *(Working.)* That's exactly what I'm doing. *(Finally stands back.)* There! You should be extremely intelligent. *(Puts box back on table and picks up a safety pin, holding it aloft.)*

DOROTHY: What's the safety pin for?

WIZARD: To pin the seams back together again. *(Presumably does this.)* You may get up now.

SCARECROW: *(Getting up.)* The operation is over?

WIZARD: Now you have "bran" new brains!

DOROTHY: How do you feel?

SCARECROW: *(Happily.)* Very wise! *(Moves confidently to DL, then back to UC.)* When I get used to my brains, I'm sure I'll know everything.

TIN WOODMAN: *(Tapping Wizard on shoulder.)* How about me? I'd so like to have a heart!

WIZARD: Some people seem to get along better without one.

TIN WOODMAN: Not me.

WIZARD: Hearts can be sad as well as glad.

TIN WOODMAN: That's exactly the kind of heart I want.

WIZARD: Then I'll be glad to oblige. *(Crossing DL.)* It just happens that I have a box full of hearts of all sizes. *(Opens a box on table and takes out a red pincushion heart.)* Isn't this a beauty? *(Holds it up as he moves to throne.)*

TIN WOODMAN: Just perfect. But is it a kind heart?

WIZARD: One of the very kindest. *(Stands in front of tin woodman.)* Hold still while I slip this heart inside. *(Presumably does so, then steps back.)* Do you feel it beating?

TIN WOODMAN: *(Listening for several seconds before speaking.)* I think so. *(Triumphantly.)* Yes, I'm sure I can feel it! Such a kind heart. *(Pats his "heart.")*

DOROTHY: *(Staunchly.)* I've always thought you were very kind-hearted.

TIN WOODMAN: I tried to be. But now it will come naturally.

LION: *(Tapping Wizard's shoulder lightly.)* I'm still here.

WIZARD: *(Studying him.)* M'm. So you are.

LION: *(Sadly.)* As cowardly as ever.

WIZARD: But you want to be brave?

LION: More than anything else, yes. Do you happen to have some courage for me?

WIZARD: *(Bustling to table.)* As a matter of fact, I do have a big bottle of courage on hand. *(Picks up a large green bottle, showing label Courage on back, and fills a glass with some green liquid.)*

LION: *(Half afraid.)* Will I need an operation?

WIZARD: Not at all. Just drink this. *(Crosses back and holds out glass.)*

LION: *(Afraid, stepping back.)* What is it?

WIZARD: You know, of course, that courage is always inside people. So when you drink this, it will be courage. *(Lion hesitates, looks at others, who are watching him, then drinks quickly, in one gulp.)*

DOROTHY: *(After moment of complete silence.)* How do you feel?

LION: *(Another moment of silence, then bounding around happily.)* I'm the bravest lion in all of Oz!

DOROTHY: *(As she and other friends clap and cheer.)* You've always been brave when I needed you.

LION: That's because you're my friend.

WIZARD: So there you are. *(Pleased with himself now.)* I guess I'm quite a Wizard after all.

DOROTHY: *(Going to him.)* Have you forgotten about me?

WIZARD: You? *(In a meek voice.)* Oh, yes, you.

DOROTHY: You promised to send me back home to Kansas. *(They all wait while Wizard walks back and forth, from throne to DR and back, his hands behind his back, thinking. Finally he stops at throne.)*

WIZARD: I'm truly sorry. *(Sighs.)* There's a deadly desert all the way around the Land of Oz, and I don't know any way to get you across it.

DOROTHY: *(With a sob.)* Then I'll never see Aunt Em and Uncle Henry again?

WIZARD: I'm afraid not. *(Sighs. Dorothy holds Toto tightly and turns away, moving RC.)*

SCARECROW: Poor Dorothy! Even my great brains can't help you.

TIN WOODMAN: My new heart aches in sympathy.

LION: I'd gladly face the fiercest beasts, but the deadly desert would kill us both.

WIZARD: *(More cheerfully, crossing to her.)* I'm sure you'll learn to like living here with us. Put on the golden cap, child, and let's see how pretty it looks on you.

DOROTHY: *(Reluctantly putting on golden cap.)* How can I be happy when I'm so far away from my real home? Oh, how I wish *someone* could tell me how to get back to Kansas! *(As she makes this wish, there is sound of tinkling bells offstage L.)*

(Jade and Verdo hurry in L. Verdo moves toward the door R. Jade pauses at LC.)

JADE: I hear the gentle bells of Glinda the Good!

(There is a knock on the door R and Verdo opens it. Two girl soldiers, Ruby and Garnet, come in R, carrying red-plumed rods on their shoulders like guns.)

RUBY: Make way—make way for Glinda the Good!

GARNET: She heard your wish and understood.

(Ruby and Garnet stand on either side of the door R and Glinda enters R. Everyone moves toward L stage, except Dorothy.)

JADE: *(Curtsying.)* Glinda the Good!

VERDO: *(Bowing.)* Sorceress of the South!

GLINDA: *(Coming RC.)* What can I do for you, Dorothy? *(As she talks, little tinkling bells are heard.)*

DOROTHY: *(Awed.)* How did you know I needed help?

GLINDA: I know all things that go on in the Land of Oz. And I came because you made a wish when wearing the magic golden cap.

DOROTHY: *(Feeling cap on her head.)* So that is the secret of the golden cap.

WIZARD: *(Pleased.)* Ah! *(Holds out his hand as he takes step toward her.)* Let me have it now.

DOROTHY: *(Stepping back.)* But you didn't keep your promise to me! And I don't think it belongs to you at all.

GLINDA: The Wicked Witch Belinda stole it from *me.*

DOROTHY: Then you're the one I must give it to. *(Gives cap to Glinda.)*

GLINDA: Thank you, my dear.

DOROTHY: Can you use it to send a message to my Aunt Em in Kansas?

GLINDA: *(Shaking her head.)* Its magic won't work outside the Land of Oz.

DOROTHY: *(Sadly.)* Then even you don't know a way to send me back to Kansas?

GLINDA: But I *do* know a way.

DOROTHY: Oh, tell me, please!

GLINDA: Your silver shoes will take you anywhere in the whole wide world!

DOROTHY: *(Surprised, looking down at them.)* These silver shoes will do that?

GLINDA: If you had known their power, you could have gone back to your Aunt Em the very first day you came to our country.

SCARECROW: *(Coming C.)* But then I wouldn't have my wonderful brains. *(Pats his head.)*

TIN WOODMAN: *(As he and Lion come C.)* And I wouldn't have my kind and tender heart. *(Places hand lovingly on heart.)*

LION: And I'd have been a coward forever.

SCARECROW: Oh, Dorothy, won't you stay with us?

DOROTHY: I dearly love you all. *(Hugs Scarecrow and Tin Woodman, and pats Lion on head.)* But Toto and I would like to go home now. *(To Glinda.)* If you please.

GLINDA: Any time you're ready, I'll tell you the secret of the silver shoes.

WIZARD: We'll miss you. Perhaps some day you'll come back for a visit?

DOROTHY: *(To Wizard.)* Oh, yes, some day! Do you know enough magic for that?

WIZARD: I'm afraid not.

GLINDA: But I do. *(Takes a ring from her finger.)* I'll make you a present of my Ruby-Star ring. *(Gives ring to Dorothy, who slips it on her finger.)*

DOROTHY: Thank you. But—

GLINDA: Any time you want to pay us a visit:

Turn the ring once,
Turn the ring twice,
Turn the ring three times 'round and then
Back to the Land of Oz again!

ALL: Back to the Land of Oz again!

DOROTHY: *(One arm outstretched, to all of them.)* I *will* come back and visit. Please don't forget me. *(To Glinda.)* And now, please? I'm so anxious to see my Aunt Em.

GLINDA: The silver shoes will carry you home in three steps, each made in the wink of an eye. All you have to do is click the heels together three times and command them to take you wherever you wish to go. *(Standing C, eyes closed, Dorothy clicks heels of her shoes together once, turning as she does so.)*

DOROTHY: Good-by, everyone, good-by! *(Clicks heels a second time.)* Thank you all for being so good to me. *(Clicks heels a third time.)* Silver shoes, carry Toto and me back to Kansas! *(Lights of many colors flash on and off, and then there is a blackout. Voices of all her friends are heard calling good-by, and tinkling bells of Glinda are heard, too. As blackout is complete, leaving stage in darkness, Dorothy's voice is heard calling joyfully, offstage.)* Aunt Em, Uncle Henry! I'm home again!

CURTAIN

TREASURE ISLAND

by

AURAND HARRIS

from the book by Robert Louis Stevenson

TREASURE ISLAND

CHARACTERS

Mrs. Hawkins
Jim Hawkins
Billy Bones*
Dogger*
Blind Pew*
Dirk
Black Dog
Doctor Livesey
Squire Trelawney
Johnny*
Morgan*
Long John Silver
Ben Gunn*

*The same actor may double in two parts.

TIME

The year 1750.

SETTING

England, at the Admiral Benbow Inn, on the dock at Bristol; at sea aboard the *Hispañiola;* and ashore on Treasure Island.

(Music by Kevin Dunn for this dramatization is available from Anchorage Press. Music is indicated in the italicized stage directions.)

Overture: a medley of "A Sailor-oh," "Sailing, Sailing," ending with a repeat of "A Sailor-oh."

Opening Song. Doctor Livesey, Mrs. Hawkins and Squire Trelawney enter in front of the main curtain and sing.

CHORUS:

We are going on
going on
going on
an—adventure.
We'll take you along
you along
you along
on—adventure!
So-o come along
come along
come along
come along,
You! And you! And you! And you!

JIM: *(A boy in the front row of the audience.)* Me?

CHORUS:

You will meet a pirate,
You will greet a pirate,
Hear a pirate sing with zest,
"Fifteen men on a dead man's chest."

JIM: *(Standing.)* Pirates? Pirates!

CHORUS:

Search for treasures, but take care!
Bones and skulls are buried there!

JIM: Buried treasures!

CHORUS:

Sail with pirates in disguise,
Crouch and catch you by surprise!

JIM: A pirate ship!

CHORUS: Dare you share the danger?
Draw a knife to save your life?
Come on board, man and boy!
Gun and sword, ship ahoy!

JIM: *(On the stage.)* I will. I will go with you!

CHORUS:

A great adventure it will be!
A treasure island in the sea!
Blow the bugle! Beat the drums!
Young Jim Hawkins, our hero, comes!

JIM: Me? Me?

CHORUS:

You're the hero in our story,
Who fights for right and glory;
Back to days of pirates bold,
Back to days of buried gold,
Back in time our story spins,
And our adventure, adventure, adventure,
adventure, adventure begins!

(Chorus exits. Jim remains, looking about in wonder. The main curtain opens, revealing the proscenium of an intimate theatre, resembling a life size Toy Theatre—like one with which Robert Louis Stevenson played when he was a boy. The main curtain of the Toy Theatre is closed, and on it suddenly is projected "TREASURE ISLAND."*)*

JIM: Treasure Island!

SCENE 1

The curtain of the Toy Theatre rises. See production notes for a simpler staging. The scene is the interior of the Admiral Benbow Inn, England, 1750. This is a painted backdrop, as were all the drops in a Toy Theatre, with furniture, windows, sky, trees, etc. painted on in perspective. The drop serves only as a background. All the action is played downstage in front of the Toy proscenium and close to the audience.)

MRS. HAWKINS: *(Enters UL inside the Toy Theatre. Music dims out.)* Jim? Jim Hawkins! There's much to do. Bring up another keg of ale—Jim? *(Comes downstage, outside "house.")* Here you are. Always outside looking at the sea. I heard the stage coach go by. We'll hope it brings a traveler. We could use another lodger at the Admiral Benbow Inn. Here, put on your apron.

JIM: *(Takes apron, puzzled.)* Apron?

MRS. HAWKINS: Now be about your work. Draw some water and come into the dining room and lay the table for tea. *(Exits into "house.")*

JIM: Wear an apron? Set the table for tea? Where are the pirates? The buried treasure? I thought I'd meet a fierce, fighting buccaneer. A terrifying robber of the sea! *(Billy Bones enters L, fulfilling Jim's description of him.)* With a pistol at his belt, and a cutlass at his side, a patch over his eye, and a voice like a clap of thunder.

BONES: *(Shouts.)* BOY! *(Jim jumps in fright.)* Be this the Admiral Benbow Inn? *(Jim nods.)* Aye, it's a handy cove, and has a good view of the sea. Be there many lodgers inside? *(Louder.)* I asked you, mate, if the rooms be filled with lodgers? *(Jim shakes his head.)* Then this is the place for me. *(Calls off L.)* Here you, bring up alongside the chest. *(Dogger, a villager, enter L, carrying a small sea chest.)* I'll be lodging here. Put it down inside.

DOGGER: Yes, Sir. *(Carrying the chest into "house," he stumbles. Bones holds him by the collar.)*

BONES: Easy, matey! That sea chest is all I have. Give it a care!

DOGGER: Safe it will be, sir, inside. *(Exits UL.)*

BONES: You, lad, can you not speak? *(Jim nods.)* Then pipe up. Give us a wag of your tongue.

JIM: Yes, sir.

BONES: You can call me "Captain."

JIM: Yes, sir. Captain.

BONES: The great thing with boys is discipline. If you be the serving boy, wear your apron.

JIM: But I . . .

BONES: Your apron—on! Before I raise my voice and my cutlass! Discipline, that's what you learn on my ship! *(Jim quickly puts on apron.)* I'll have a sit inside and a bottle of rum.

JIM: Rum?

BONES: Aye, lad, I'll tell you rum is my best mate. I been places hot as pitch, men dropping dead with Yellow Jack, and I lived on rum.

JIM: You've sailed in ships?

BONES: Aye, the stories I could tell. But I'm not talking. *(Tosses a coin in the air.)* See that? A silver fourpenny. It's yours—

JIM: *(Grabs for it.)* Mine?

BONES: —if—you keep your eyes open and tell me if any seafaring men be coming along. And mark ye, be on the lookout for the worst one. He's only got one leg.

JIM: One leg?

BONES: One leg—and a peg one. *(Exits into "house," UL, calling.)* Rum! I'm wanting a bottle of rum!

JIM: *(Excited, speaks to audience.)* He looks like a pirate.

BONES: *(Offstage, sings. No music, but see Music IV.)* "Fifteen men on a dead man's chest, Yo-ho-ho, and a bottle of rum—"

JIM: He sounds like a pirate!

BONES: *(Offstage, sings.)* "Drink and the Devil has done for the rest, Yo-ho-ho, and a bottle of rum."

JIM: I think he is a pirate! *(Music of "Yo-ho-ho" plays loudly, as Jim happily pantomimes dueling, excitedly slashing with imaginary cutlass. He gives a final happy "yo-ho-ho!" and exits DR. Music IV reaches a climax for the end of the scene.)*

SCENE 2

(The same. Mrs. Hawkins enters DL. She wears a hat and shawl. She enters "house," talking toward L, where she thinks Jim is, and hangs her hat and shawl in the closet which is at R.)

MRS. HAWKINS: I'm back, Jim. All the village is talking about the Captain. And after last night. Falling on the floor like he did!

Heart attack. Yes, and too much rum. Rum will be the death of him, all right. Well, I've sent for Dr. Livesey. I am not going to let the Captain die before he pays me for his lodging. Jim? Where are you?

JIM: *(Offstage.)* Up here.

MRS. HAWKINS: Every day he sits, watches every ship in the cove, every man that goes by. He's done something wicked, I'll wager, and his evil deeds are about to catch up with him. Jim! Where are you?

JIM: *(Offstage.)* Coming down.

MRS. HAWKINS: Down? Where?

JIM: *(Jumps to floor and crawls out of fireplace.)* In the fireplace.

MRS. HAWKINS: Jim, what have you been up to?

JIM: I've been up to the top! Climbed the pegs in the chimney and saved a bird's nest.

MRS. HAWKINS: *(Takes bird's nest.)* Let me have it. Now, Jim, you must keep the Captain quiet until the doctor comes. I want no more heart attacks. And no more rum. Listen. Someone is coming up the road. See who it is. *(She exits UR. Jim comes out of "house," looks DL.)*

JIM: It's a blind man.

PEW: *(Blind Pew is heard tapping his cane off DL. He enters, a dreadful looking figure, tapping his way toward the inn.)* Will any kind friend inform a poor blind man who lost the sight of his eyes defending England, where or in what part of this country he may now be?

JIM: You are in front of the Admiral Benbow Inn.

PEW: I hear a voice, a young voice. Come. Stand closer. Is this the inn where Billy Bones lives?

JIM: There is one here who calls himself "Captain."

PEW: Would he have a cut on his right cheek and a patch on his left eye?

JIM: Yes.

PEW: He's the same! *(Cackles with a laugh.)* We're going to give Bill a little surprise. Now lend me your hand and lead me in.

JIM: *(Pew feels for Jim's hand, then suddenly grips it, twisting Jim's arm behind him.)* Oh!

PEW: *(With menace and cruelty.)* Now, boy, take me in to the captain. Or I'll break your arm. March. *(Raises his cane to strike.)* Which way? *(Jim, in pain, leads Pew into "house.")* Call him to come out.

JIM: Captain. Captain, sir.

BONES: *(Offstage.)* Aye! Who calls?

PEW: When he come in the room, you cry out, "Here's a friend for you, Billy Bones."

BONES: *(Enters UL, dazed with rum.)* Who calls?

JIM: Here's a friend for you, Billy Bones. *(Pew pushes Jim aside.)*

BONES: Be it—aye, it is Blind Pew! *(Reaches for his cutlass.)*

PEW: Put your hand down, Bill. *(Raises his cane.)* I cannot see you, but I can hear a finger stirring. You know why I'm here. Boy, take his hand and bring it near me. Quick! His hand! *(Jim does as he was ordered. Pew dramatically puts a piece of paper into the palm of Bones.)* There. It's done. You've been warned, Billy Bones. You've been warned. *(Laughs.)* Boy, the door? Which way be the door! *(Jim frightened, starts Pew in the right direction.)* And now—I'm off. *(Pew quickly taps out and exits DR.)*

JIM: Shall I stop him?

BONES: Nay, it's too late. They give me the Black Spot.

JIM: What is—the Black Spot?

BONES: It's a summons. *(Reads.)* "Six o'clock." They'll come to kill me at six o'clock.

JIM: Who?

BONES: All of Flint's crew. I was Flint's first mate, and I'm the only one that knows—knows where the treasure is buried.

JIM: A buried treasure?

BONES: Aye, chests of gold and silver and jewels. A king's fortune, it is! And I have the map that shows where the money's buried.

JIM: A map?

BONES: It's the treasure map they want. It's the map they'll kill for. *(Choking.)* Rum! Get me some rum! So I can swallow! The map is in the chest. *(Starts L.)* We must get the chest! Aye! Get the chest. *(Talks as he exits L, and continues to speak while he is off stage.)* Rum! Fetch me some rum, lad!

JIM: I daren't, sir. You're sick and I promised that I wouldn't.

BONES: *(Offstage.)* Get the Constable! Call the Squire! Tell 'em all to lay on quick at the Admiral Benbow! Flint's gang is coming for the map. *(Enters, dragging the chest.)* Lend me a hand, boy. I'll shake them off.

JIM: How?

BONES: I'll ship to another reef. Aye, I'll give them the slip. *(Sits on chest, breathing heavily.)* A drink of rum, Jim. I'm begging you. A swallow of rum, boy. Look at me. I'm a poor old hulk on a lee shore. And I warn you, lad, if you don't give me a drink and I die a-choking, my blood will drip on you. *(Holds up hand which shakes.)* Aye, look! My fingers are a-fighting. I've got the shakes, I have. Look. I can see Old Flint. He's there in the corner. Do you see him?

JIM: No. No one is there.

BONES: Morgan . . . and Dirk . . . and Black Dog. Aye, they're all here. Stop! Hold your pace. Knives . . . swords! Ah, a fight you want, is it? I'll fight you. I'll fight you for the map. There! There! Devil take you all! *(He slashes with cutlass, growing more delirious. Suddenly he drops his cutlass, grabs his heart, gives an animal-like cry, and falls, bent over and clutching the sea chest.)*

JIM: Captain? Captain!

MRS. HAWKINS: *(Enters UL.)* What is it?

JIM: It's the Captain.

MRS. HAWKINS: Another heart attack! Captain! *(She shakes him, then draws back in fear.)* He doesn't move.

JIM: Is he dead?

MRS. HAWKINS: *(Puts hand near to Bones' nose.)* No breath.

JIM: A blind man came and he gave him the Black Spot.

MRS. HAWKINS: He's dead. We must go for help. But, first, I'll claim the money he owes me. *(Starts to touch the dead body, but pulls back.)* You . . . You, Jim, look in his pocket for a key to the chest.

JIM: Me? *(With fear of the dead, he cautiously searches Bones' coat pockets, giving articles to Mrs. Hawkins.)* A knife . . . tobacco. That's all.

MRS. HAWKINS: The key. I'll warrant he wears the key around his neck. Open his collar.

JIM: *(Rolls Bones forward, off the chest, face up.)* It's here. On a string.

MRS. HAWKINS: Use the knife. *(Jim cuts string.)* Give me the key. Yes, it fits. *(She opens chest, lifting items.)* Some papers tied in oilcloth. Ah! Here it is, a bag of money! Now as my witness, Jim, I'll only take what's rightfully mine, and not a farthing over. *(A loud signal whistle is heard, offstage.)*

JIM: Listen. *(A second whistle is heard.)*

MRS. HAWKINS: Someone's whistling.

JIM: It's a signal. They're coming. Quick!

MRS. HAWKINS: First I'll have the money he owes me.

JIM: *(Third whistle is heard.)* It's the pirates for sure!

MRS. HAWKINS: Pirates!

JIM: They're coming closer. Take the bag of money.

MRS. HAWKINS: Yes!

JIM: *(Hurries her out.)* Quick! Go out the back way!

MRS. HAWKINS: Yes. Come, Jim. Hurry!

JIM: And for the fourpenny you still owe me, I'll take this. *(Holds up oilcloth packet.)* Goodby, Billy Bones. *(He hears Pew, looks toward front, then starts UR, stops when he realizes he is trapped.)*

PEW: *(Offstage.)* Stand guard! Surround the house, mateys. Watch the back door. Shoot if a body moves! *(He enters DR. Black Dog is guiding him. Dirk follows.)* Where be the door? The door?

JIM: *(Desperate, points to closet door.)* I'll hide—in the closet! *(He hides, as Pew and pirates enter "house.")*

DIRK: *(Discovering Bones on the floor.)* What's here? Look!

PEW: What is it?

DIRK: It's Bill. Billy Bones.

PEW: Where? *(Raises his cane to strike.)*

DIRK: He's dead.

PEW: Dead?

DIRK: Laying on the floor.

PEW: *(Feeling the body.)* Are you sure?

BLACK DOG: Aye, dead he is.

PEW: Search him! Find the map. Look in his pockets.

DIRK: Bill's been overhauled.

PEW: Find the key. The key for the chest.

BLACK DOG: The chest is here.

PEW: Where? *(Feels it with his cane.)*

DIRK: Aye, the chest is open.

PEW: The map? The treasure map! Is it there?

BLACK DOG: Nowhere.

PEW: Find it!

BLACK DOG: It ain't here. The map's been lifted.

PEW: It's that boy. He's still in the house. I can smell his kitchen apron. Find him!

DIRK: The closet.

BLACK DOG: Aye, the closet. *(He and Dirk go to closet and start to open the door.)*

PEW: Wait. First, take up old Bill. *(Black Dog and Dirk pick up Bones.)* Put him in his room. Sit him up nice-like in a chair. Show him some respect. He was Flint's first mate. *(They carry Bones off UL.)* Hoist him aloft. Or we'll be cursed forever by Flint's dead eye. Where are you, boy? I'll find you, boy. *(Jim peeks out, sees that only Pew is there, tip-toes out, as Pew, tapping with his cane, searches.)* I hear you. I HEAR you. *(Jim freezes.)* I cannot see you, but I know you're here. *(Pew raises his pistol, advancing toward Jim. Jim holds up knife, tosses it across DR. Pew, alerted by the sound, goes DR, aiming his pistol.)* Ah, there you are! *(Laughs.)* You thought you could trick me. But you won't get away from Blind Pew. *(Calls.)* Ahoy, mates! I've got him cornered.

DIRK: *(Offstage.)* We be coming.

BLACK DOG: *(Offstage.)* Aye, we're with you.

JIM: *(Caught, with no exit, looks up at fireplace.)* No! You haven't got me yet. *(He disappears in the fireplace as Dirk and Black Dog enter UL.)*

PEW: His voice!

DIRK: Where is he?

BLACK DOG: No one here.

PEW: I heard him. He talked! Use your eyes! He didn't go up in a puff of smoke. Smoke! *(Laughs.)* The fireplace. Where be the fireplace?

BLACK DOG: *(Guides him.)* Here.

PEW: We've got you now, boy. *(Three whistles are heard off.)*

DIRK: Three whistles! Morgan's giving us the last warning!

BLACK DOG: Someone's coming.

DIRK: Make for the ship.

BLACK DOG: Aye, we'll have to budge, mates. *(He and Dirk exit DL.)*

PEW: Fools! Wait. You're leaving a fortune behind. We'll be rich as kings when we find the treasure. *(Silence.)* Black Dog . . . ? Dirk . . . ? Where are you? You ain't leaving me behind? Where are you, mateys? *(Desperate to find the way out.)* Help me. Which is the way out? Which way? Which way? *(He falls over the chest, accidently firing the gun. He grabs his chest as he falls, gasping for breath.)*

DOGGER: *(Runs DL.)* I heard a gun shot inside the house, sir. *(Goes in "house" cautiously.)*

SQUIRE: *(He and Doctor enter DL.)* Take care. There's trouble all right. It's good I came with you, Doctor.

DOCTOR: Yes, I'm glad you came, Squire. Is there anyone in the house?

DOGGER: Nay, quiet as a tomb.

DOCTOR: *(He and Squire enter "house.")* Yes, they're gone.

SQUIRE: The rogues. They've escaped before we could have the law on them. *(Sees Pew.)* What's this? Who is he?

DOGGER: One of the ruffians. Been shot in the chest, he has.

DOCTOR: Yes, it looks as if he tripped and shot himself. Come, give him a hand, Dogger. Take him into the back room.

DOGGER: *(Helps Pew, and they exit UL.)* Yes, sir. Up, man.

DOCTOR: I'll see what I can do to save his worthless life. *(Exits after them.)*

SQUIRE: The woman said they were a band of pirates. Gave the Captain the Black Spot.

JIM: *(Offstage.)* Hel-loooo.

SQUIRE: *(Draws pistol.)* Who's that?

JIM: *(Offstage.)* Hel-loooo.

SQUIRE: Who's there?

JIM: *(Offstage.)* Me.

SQUIRE: Who? Where?

JIM: *(Offstage.)* In the fireplace.

SQUIRE: *(Covers fireplace with pistol.)* I have a gun.

JIM: *(Offstage.)* Don't shoot.

SQUIRE: Come down.

JIM: *(His legs appear in fireplace. Offstage.)* I can't. My pants are caught on a peg. O-o-o-o-oh! *(He drops to floor, crawls out.)*

SQUIRE: Up with your hands.

JIM: Yes, sir.

SQUIRE: Why, you're the serving boy.

JIM: Yes, sir.

SQUIRE: Stand up.

JIM: *(Stands, putting hands behind to cover pants.)* My pants are ripped.

SQUIRE: Lucky they didn't rip your belly. Pirates were they?

JIM: *(Nods.)* They were going to shoot me.

DOCTOR: *(Enters UL.)* Who was going to shoot you?

JIM: Blind Pew.

DOCTOR: And instead he shot himself.

DOGGER: *(Enters L.)* Aye, dead he is.

DOCTOR: Pick up the pistol, Dogger, and take the chest away. Now, lad, tell the Squire and me what happened. Are you hurt?

JIM: No, sir.

DOCTOR: Then why are you standing in a twist?

JIM: My trousers are ripped—behind.

DOCTOR: Never mind that. Speak up.

JIM: They were Flint's men.

SQUIRE: Flint's men?

JIM: They came to get the Captain's sea chest.

SQUIRE: Money?

JIM: No, sir. Not money, I think. But—this. *(Holds up oilcloth packet.)* I give it to you, Doctor, for safe keeping.

SQUIRE: What is it?

DOCTOR: *(Puts packet away, and pointedly ignores Squire.)* Now, Dogger, if you will oblige us by putting the chest back in his room, and take the pistol to the Constable. Tell him the rogues are gone, and that Squire Trelawney and I will give him a full report later.

DOGGER: Yes, Doctor. I'll hurry, out the back way. Good day, gentlemen. *(Exits UL.)*

SQUIRE: Good day.

DOCTOR: And now, Squire, what was your question?

SQUIRE: The packet! What is in it?

DOCTOR: *(Toying with packet.)* Suppose it is a clue to where Flint buried his treasure?

SQUIRE: A map?

DOCTOR: And if it is a map?

SQUIRE: I will fit out a ship and we will sail and find the treasure.

DOCTOR: You have made a bargain, Squire. Now, Jim, with your permission, we will open the packet. I need a knife.

JIM: *(Picks up knife from floor.)* Here. It was the Captain's.

DOCTOR: We will open his secret with his own knife.

SQUIRE: Hurry, man! Hurry! Is it? Is it? It is!

DOCTOR: A map!

SQUIRE: Of an island.

DOCTOR: Latitudes and longitudes.

SQUIRE: And three crosses, marked in red. What does the print say in the corner?

DOCTOR: "Bulk of treasure buried here."

SQUIRE: It's Flint's treasure map. Doctor, I will keep my bargain. In two weeks we will have the best ship in England. Jim, you will be the cabin-boy. You will be the ship's doctor. And I will be—Admiral! Ah, I feel like a boy again. Some wine, Jim. We'll drink a toast to our new adventure.

JIM: Yes, sir. *(He crosses, back to audience; remembers his ripped trousers and stops. A piece of bright underwear is seen. He tries to cover it with his hands.)* Yes, sir. *(Exits UL.)*

DOCTOR: Squire. There is one danger. There is one man I am afraid of.

SQUIRE: Who is he? Name the dog, sir.

DOCTOR: You. With your boundless enthusiasm I fear you cannot hold your tongue. This must be a SECRET voyage.

SQUIRE: You are right. My lips are sealed. I will be as silent—as a grave. *(Jim enters UL with tray and three mugs.)* Come, Jim. Join us and lift a cup. *(Holds mug out.)* A toast to our new adventure.

DOCTOR: *(Holds out mug.)* A toast to our secret voyage.

JIM: *(Holds mug out.)* A toast to—Treasure Island!

(Doctor and Squire turn to him and "Sh." The three tip their mugs and drink, as the Toy Theatre curtain drops. Music begins, "The Sailor-oh.")

SCENE 3

The dock. The curtain rises, showing a painted drop. Or the scene may be played in front of the curtain. Also see production notes for a simpler staging. Music dims out as pirates enter. Morgan, a pirate, enters L, carrying a small barrel. Johnny, another pirate, enters R, crosses to L, greeting his mates. Dirk enters L, carrying box. Squire enters R, comically impressive in a plumed Admiral's hat.

SQUIRE: *(In high spirits.)* Hurry along, men. The Captain says we sail with the tide. You, bring the Captain's box.

JOHNNY: Aye, sir. *(Exits L.)*

SQUIRE: *(Inspecting boxes as Morgan and Dirk cross and exit R.)* Gun powder, yes. In the hole by the muskets. Keg of pork? Below, in the storage by the galley. *(Johnny re-enters with small chest, crosses to R and exits.)* Hurry along. *(Sings with comic excitement. No music.)*

The sailor-oh, the sailor-oh,
It's the life for me;
The sailor-oh, the sailor-oh,
It's the life—for me!
Yo-ho! *(Exits R.)*

JIM: *(Runs in L, followed by Doctor.)* Here it is, Doctor! Here is the ship!

DOCTOR: *(Looks off R.)* Yes, the *Hispañiola.*

JIM: It's so big!

DOCTOR: Two hundred tons. We're ready, Jim, to explore—*(Looks about, speaks in low voice.)* our secret island.

JIM: Will there be wild animals?

DOCTOR: Perhaps.

JIM: And wild savages?

DOCTOR: I hope not. Here, have a look at the top of the mast. *(Jim takes small telescope and looks, as Johnny and Black Dog enter R, talking.)*

JOHNNY: Devil take the Captain and his hard work.

BLACK DOG: Aye, matey, the going to the island is sweat enough, but think of the gold coming back.

JOHNNY: The map, they say, 'sgot red crosses where the treasure's buried.

BLACK DOG: *(They see Doctor.)* Sh! *(They give a salute-like gesture to Doctor and hurry off L.)*

SQUIRE: *(Enters R.)* Ahoy, Doctor. Ahoy, Jim. The Admiral bids you welcome.

JIM: Yes, sir. *(Salutes.)*

SQUIRE: Gentlemen, all is ship-shape and ready to sail. Everyone in Bristol has helped, once they got wind of the port we're sailing for.

DOCTOR: They know where we are sailing? *(Pointedly.)* Jim, go ahead. Explore the ship.

JIM: Yes, sir. *(To Squire.)* Yes, sir, Admiral! *(Exits R.)*

DOCTOR: Squire, I am worried. The sailors were talking about the map with the red crosses.

SQUIRE: Put your fears to rest. Good luck brought the very man who could help us.

DOCTOR: Who?

SQUIRE: Long John Silver. Poor fellow, he has only one leg.

DOCTOR: One leg?

SQUIRE: It turned out he not only is a fine cook, but he found the whole crew for the ship.

DOCTOR: The entire crew?

SQUIRE: And every one of them is an Englishman!

LONG JOHN AND JOHNNY: *(Off L, Long John Silver and Johnny are heard singing. No music.)*

The wind blows east, *(Silver beats rhythm with crutch.)*
The wind blows west, *(Silver beats rhythm.)*
Where ever I may roam *(They enter, arm in arm singing lustily. Silver has a peg leg.)*
But east or west,
The wind blows best, *(Silver taps crutch.)*
That blows me back to home. *(Johnny and Silver dance, with Silver beating a rhythmic ending. They laugh. Squire and Doctor applaud.)*

SILVER: *(Bows, extremely humble, pleasant and polite.)* Ah, good day, Admiral. *(To Johnny.)* Get your gear, matey. *(Johnny exits L.)*

SQUIRE: This is the man who has helped us so much. Long John Silver, this is Doctor Livesey.

SILVER: Ah, it's a pleasure to meet you, sir. And thankful I am that we have a good doctor a-sailing with us. One of your kind saved me life, but left me with only one leg.

BLACK DOG: *(Enters L with chest.)* Be this the doctor's box?

DOCTOR: It is my chest of medicine.

SILVER: Have a care, matey! You're holding the good doctor's special chest!

BLACK DOG: Aye, sir. *(Puts chest down carefully.)*

SILVER: And mind you, plant it safe in the ship.

BLACK DOG: Aye.

SILVER: Excuse me, gentlemen. I'll get my darling bird. I never sail without my parrot. By your leave, gentlemen, by your leave. *(Exits L.)*

SQUIRE: You see what a fine fellow he is.

JIM: *(Runs in R, excited.)* The Captain says we're going to sail! And on the deck there's a cannon, and I'm going to sleep in a hammock that swings, and—

SQUIRE: Yes, the time has come! Seaward, ho! I've arranged for a fife and drum and a one-gun salute. Oh, hang the treasure, it's the glory of the sea that has turned my head! Anchors away! *(Exits R.)*

DOCTOR: You, bring the chest along. *(Exits R.)*

BLACK DOG: *(Following with chest.)* Aye, sir. We'll be needing the medicine, sailing south with the heat and the fever.

JIM: His voice. I've heard his voice . . . some where . . . It was one of the pirates! Sir, did you know Billy Bones?

BLACK DOG: Aye? Who?

JIM: Billy Bones.

BLACK DOG: Nay. Never heard of him. *(Exits R.)*

JIM: Was it . . . was it his voice I heard?

SILVER: *(Enters L with bird cage.)* Ahoy, lad. *(Jim turns and sees Silver—with one leg, gives a startled cry.)* Ah, it's my peg leg you're looking at. Pay no mind. It's as frisky as a flea. You must be young Jim Hawkins. Well, pleased I am to meet you. I be the cook, Long John Silver. But me friends call me—and you can call me—Barbecue.

JIM: Yes, sir.

SILVER: Ah, I can tell you and me, we're going to be friendly mates. Now I'll introduce you to me lady-love. I call her Captain Flint, after the famous buccaneer. Look at her. Would you be thinking she's two hundred years old? And I'm warning you, she swears like a blue fire! Here, lift the cover and pipe her a word.

JIM: Good day, Captain Flint.

PARROT: Son of a Dutchman! Son of a Dutchman!

SILVER: See—she likes you. Already you've made two friends today. *(Dirk enters R, followed by Morgan.)* Ahoy, mates. Come and join us, Morgan. I want that you meet our cabin boy, young Jim Hawkins. He's a friend of the Squire and the Doctor. Oh, we'll look after you, lad. Morgan here is handy with the cutlass.

MORGAN: *(Draws cutlass.)* Last blood on it was a thief. Took something off a dead man what wasn't his.

SILVER: And Dirk can carve your coffin with his stiletto.

DIRK: *(Flashes knife.)* Sharp it is. Sharp enough to cut out a tongue what talks too much.

SILVER: You've nothing to fear, my lad, as long as we all be friends together. *(Jim looks at each one surrounding him. Each gives him a big, if ugly, smile. Fife and drum are heard off.)* Listen. That's the Squire's fife and drum. *(Cannon shot is heard.)* And a one-gun salute. We're ready to sail!

DOCTOR: *(Offstage, calls.)* Jim. Jim Hawkins!

SILVER: Run, lad, run! We're off to find—adventure! *(The three pirates give a lazy salute. Jim returns the salute, cautiously, then runs off R. Silver calls to L.)* Come, matey! We're off to sail the seas. *(Johnny enters L.)* Pipe us a tune. And Captain Flint— *(Gives an evil laugh as he motions for Johnny to pick up bird cage.)* Captain Flint will rightly lead the way. *(Johnny leads with bird cage. The pirates sing, without music.)*

PIRATES:

The sailor-oh, the sailor-oh,
Rest is not for me;
What a life, a rollicking life,
It's the life for me.
What a life, a wicked life,
It's the life for me.

Yo-ho!

(There is music of the song as they exit R, and curtain drops.)

SCENE 4

(See production notes on page 251 for a simpler staging. Music changes to "Sailing, Sailing." Curtain rises. The scene is On the Ocean. There is a backdrop with a painted horizon of the ocean. In front are two moving ground rows with peaked waves, the first row is lower than the back row. When one row is pulled to the left, the other row is pulled to the right, making the "waves" move. The "Sailing, Sailing" music continues. A small painted schooner, the Hispañiola, *crosses behind the first ground row, L to R, rocking with the movement of the "waves." As*

it exits R, immediate a smaller size, but identical, schooner crosses from R to L behind the second row. It, too, rocks with the moving "waves," and sails off into the distance. Music dims out as curtain falls.)

SCENE 5

(On the deck of the Hispañiola. *Night. Jim enters L, looking through small telescope. Silver enters R.)*

SILVER: Ahoy, Jim. Be we sailing in the right direction?

JIM: Aye, sir. By the stars, straight south.

SILVER: You've learned to be a good sailor, lad.

JIM: I have a good teacher—you. And a good friend.

SILVER: You'll have to wait 'til the sun be up to see—Treasure Island. Aye, it's no secret, lad. They say it's pirate gold we be digging for.

JIM: I once met a pirate.

SILVER: Aye?

JIM: Billy Bones. I—I could tell you a real secret.

SILVER: Aye, tell me. Friend to friend.

JIM: The map. I got the map from Billy Bones that shows where the treasure is.

SILVER: You have the map?

JIM: No. *(Looks into telescope.)*

SILVER: Where be the map? You can whisper where it is to old Barbecue.

JIM: The Doctor has it. I saw it in his medicine box.

SILVER: In the Doctor's medicine box. Ah, and here comes the fine Doctor himself. *(Doctor enters R.)* Good morning, Doctor. And a good morning, I'm thinking it soon will be. *(Starts L.)*

DOCTOR: Yes, the island is near.

SILVER: I'll be looking after the crew, sir. Excited they are, what with the landing so soon. *(Exits L.)*

DOCTOR: Well, Jim, we're here. How do you feel about our adventure?

JIM: *(Excited.)* I feel—I feel—I feel hungry.

DOCTOR: I'm afraid this morning you'll have a long wait for breakfast. There may still be an apple left in the barrel. *(They go to apple barrel at L. Loud laughing and shouts are heard off R.)* The crew is already celebrating our landing. Too soon, and too much rum, I would say. *(Looks into barrel.)* You are in luck. There are a few apples at the bottom. But you'll need a long arm. *(Exits L.)*

JIM: I'll climb in. *(He starts to climb in. Surprised at the sudden singing, he falls into the barrel.)*

JOHNNY: *(Enters R, with bottle, singing. He is happily drunk.)*
"Yo-ho-ho, and a bottle of rum,
Fifteen men on a—"

MORGAN: *(Enters R.)* Hold your tongue, you fool! The Squire and the Doctor will hear you.

JOHNNY: "Yo-ho-ho, and a bottle of rum—"

MORGAN: Rot your blood and stop your singing! *(Covers Johnny's mouth.)*

DIRK: *(Enters L, sneaking and sinister.)* Are you there, mateys?

MORGAN: Aye.

DIRK: Alone?

MORGAN: Aye. No one else is here. *(Jim peeks out from the top of the barrel.)*

DIRK: Now is the time. This morning we'll take over the ship afore we land. *(Flashes knife.)* I say, kill the Squire. Kill the Doctor.

MORGAN: Kill the boy! *(Jim gasps and disappears in barrel.)*

DIRK: Then come the sun, Flint's treasure will be ours!

JOHNNY: I'll drink to that. "Yo-ho-ho, and a bottle of rum—"

MORGAN: Listen.

DIRK: It's Long John. His peg leg. *(The thump of his peg leg is heard, as Silver enters L.)* We're ready. Give us the word to strike.

MORGAN: Aye, we're ready, John.

SILVER: Is it breakfast you're ready for?

DIRK: We're ready to take over the ship.

MORGAN: Aye, what we should of done long afore.

JOHNNY: I'll drink to that. "Yo-ho-ho—"

SILVER: Silence! Am I your leader? Or do one of you challenge me? *(Draws cutlass. No one moves.)* Then I say, by blazes, you'll spoil it all if you rush it now. This is the plan. *(Jim peeks out from barrel.)* When the sun is up and we see the island, I'll ask leave for the crew to go ashore. We'll leave old Israel behind to watch those on the ship. Then when we return, the Squire and the Doctor, suspecting nothing, will be easy for us to take.

DIRK: Aye, dead they'll be.

SILVER: With them out of the way, we'll take the Captain prisoner—

MORGAN: And the treasure will be ours.

DIRK: *(Walks to barrel.)* And the boy? What about young Jim Hawkins? *(Leans on barrel.)*

SILVER: Ah, the lad has won my heart, he has.

DIRK: Put a bullet in his heart, I say, and I'll do it.

SILVER: Stay your hand and hold your tongue! Yes, alas, the boy must die.

MORGAN: How?

SILVER: We'll take him ashore with us and do it quickly. Now, on deck, you dogs.

MORGAN: First, the map. We be needing the treasure map.

SILVER: And that is why I am your Captain. Here be the map! Treasure Island!

MORGAN: How did you . . . ?

SILVER: Not with a cutlass, Morgan, but with a friendly smile. *(Holds up oilcloth packet.)* Here I hold in me hand Flint's treasure—and it's ours!

JOHNNY: I'll drink to that. "Yo-ho-ho, and a bottle—"

MORGAN: Hold your tongue. They'll hear us.

DIRK: Plug his mouth.

MORGAN: Aye, choke him on an apple. See if there be one in the barrel.

DIRK: Aye, stuff him with a rotten apple. *(Starts to barrel.)*

SILVER: Nay. Scatter, my mates. Whisper the plan to the others. And mind you, for the time, wear a smile on your ugly faces. *(Silver exits R. Morgan exits L. Dirk helps Johnny, who starts to sing, "Yo-ho-ho, and a bottle—")*

DIRK: Hold your drunken tongue! *(They exit R. Jim, frightened, cautiously peeks from the barrel. As he starts to climb out, Johnny is heard singing. Jim quickly hides in barrel again, as Johnny enters, comically drunk. He crosses to bottle which he has left, picks it up, starts to drink, but the bottle is empty. He shakes it, then discards it by tossing it into the barrel, and exits R, singing. Doctor and Squire enter R.)*

SQUIRE: I have given orders to fire the cannon when we sight the island. Egad man, will the sun never rise!

JIM: *(Peeks out of barrel.)* Dr. Livesey!

DOCTOR: Who is that?

JIM: Quick! Help me out! *(They do.)* I have something to tell you.

DOCTOR: You're shaking.

SQUIRE: You are as pale as a ghost.

JIM: Is anyone about?

SQUIRE: We're all alone.

JIM: They are pirates!

SQUIRE: Pirates?

JIM: They are going to take over the ship.

SQUIRE: Who?

JIM: Long John Silver and Dirk and Morgan and—

SQUIRE: John Silver? Poppycock! He is my most trusted man.

JIM: I heard them. They have a map. And they are going to kill you—and you—and me.

SQUIRE: If this is true—

JIM: It is!

SQUIRE: Then this is mutiny!

DOCTOR: Do you swear—swear this is true?

JIM: Yes, I was in the apple barrel and I heard them.

DOCTOR: They will not find the treasure.

SQUIRE: They have the map.

DOCTOR: They have a second map—a fake map which I drew. It is identical to the real map—*(Takes oilcloth packet from pocket.)* which I still have, except on their map there are no signs where the treasure is buried—no red crosses. Now the real map is in danger. They will search me first. You keep it, Squire.

SQUIRE: No, I think, begging to differ, they will search me first.

DOCTOR: Then who? *(They look front, then both turn to Jim and speak, "You.")* Take it, Jim, and keep it hidden.

JIM: Yes, sir. *(Puts packet in pocket.)*

DOCTOR: Now we must make our plans.

SQUIRE: I say, shoot them down like dogs.

DOCTOR: No. We are outnumbered. Our only chance is to outwit them.

SQUIRE: How?

DOCTOR: If they do not know that WE know their plans, we have a chance. They will want to go ashore immediately.

SQUIRE: Never!

DOCTOR: They will probably leave a man on board to watch us. But we will take HIM by surprise. And if the wind will come, we will turn the ship about, leave the pirates on the island, and escape with our lives.

SQUIRE: My plan exactly! *(Offstage there are shouts of "Land, Land, ahoy. Land ahead, etc." The stage has become brighter.)* The island is in sight!

DOCTOR: The sun is up.

SQUIRE: Quick! To the bridge. We must salute as they fire the cannon and sing "God Save the King." *(Exits R.)*

DOCTOR: Come, Jim. We must stay together—keep close together. *(Exits R.)*

JIM: *(Looks through telescope.)* Yes. There it is—Treasure Island. It looks like a great monster rising in the sea. I thought when I saw it I would be glad, but now—it makes me shiver.

SILVER: *(Offstage.)* Aye, mateys! It's Treasure Island.

JIM: Long John Silver . . . I thought you were my friend, and all the time you were waiting to kill me. *(Offstage there is a roll on the drum, fife music, and a boom of the cannon.)* How can you tell who is good and who is bad? *(Voices are heard off R, as pirates enter, crossing to L.)*

JOHNNY: Ashore! We're going ashore! Shore ahoy!

MORGAN: They're letting down the small boats. Into the boats, men.

SILVER: Aye, on mateys! On to Treasure Island. Ah, Jim, my boy, we're here. Come along. We're all going ashore.

JIM: No!

SILVER: *(Sudden silence. All look at Jim.)* Come along with you, lad.

JIM: No!

SILVER: What did you say?

JIM: No!

SILVER: *(With violent authority.)* Bring him along, mates! This is the day we've been waiting for! *(Exits L.)*

DIRK: *(Behind Jim, holds him and puts knife to Jim's face.)* Do as you are told, or I'll put a scratch on your pretty face— *(Dirk pushes Jim forward, following him off L, with knife raised.)*

MORGAN: We'll plant our flag ashore.

JOHNNY: Aye, the Jolly Roger.

BLACK DOG: The pirate flag with skull and cross bones!

MORGAN: Aye, the island is ours!

(They cross and exit L. There is frightening music of "Yo-ho-ho, and a bottle of rum," improvised with sinister bass. The curtain falls. A very large pirate flag—white skull and cross bones on a black background—drops in front of the curtain and is spotted in a single light.)

SCENE 6

(The pirate flag rises. Music stops. The curtain rises. Scene, the island. Painted profile trees stand in front of a sky backdrop. There are sounds of the surf and a bird or two. Jim runs in from R, panting for breath and desperate to escape. He hides, then creeps out, looks through his telescope.)

JIM: They've lost sight of me. I jumped from the little boat . . . waded to shore . . . and ran . . . and ran . . . *(He sinks wearily to the ground. A strange figure, Ben Gunn, enters UL, sees Jim, moves toward him, makes a strange sound, and darts behind a tree.)* What's that? Behind the tree! *(They play peek-a-boo on each side of a tree.)* What are you? A bear? A monkey? A man? *(Gunn comes out, waving his arms.)* A cannibal? *(Jim raises his arm to protect himself. Gunn kneels before Jim.)*

GUNN: *(Speaks in a strange voice.)* Ben Gunn. I'm poor Ben Gunn, I am. And I haven't spoke with a man these three years.

JIM: Three years! Were you shipwrecked?

GUNN: I was marooned.

JIM: Left here? All alone?

GUNN: Aye, three years, and lived on fish and goats. Ah, might you have a piece of cheese? Many's the long night I've dreamed of cheese—but woke again, and here I were.

JIM: No, I don't have any cheese.

GUNN: I want to confess. I've lived a wicked life. But for now on I'm being good. And *(Laughs and looks about.)* I'm rich. Rich, I says. And you'll be rich, too, because you was the first to find me.

JIM: Rich?

GUNN: *(Takes gold from pocket and a dazzling necklace which he puts on.)* Gold . . . gold . . . gold. And jewels. *(Laughs and dances happily about.)*

JIM: How did you . . . ? Where?

GUNN: I'll tell you this and no more. I was a pirate and I were on Flint's ship when he died.

JIM: How did you get here?

GUNN: On another ship I was, and we sighted this island. "Boys," says I, "here's where Flint's treasure is buried." Twelve days we dig for it. Dig, dig, dig. But not a trace. Then all hands go aboard and leave me behind. Marooned.

JIM: Our ships belongs to a good Squire.

GUNN: A good man, you says? Would he be taking me back to my poor mother? Tell him, tell him, I'm rich—rich!

JIM: *(Realizing his desperate situation.)* I'll never get back to the ship. I'll never see the Squire or Doctor again. What am I going to do? *(Sinks, wearily.)*

GUNN: Put your trust in Ben Gunn. He knows many secrets.

JIM: They'll find me. And when they do . . . they are going to shoot me.

GUNN: *(Kneels.)* Here, take comfort on poor Ben Gunn.

JIM: *(Leans against him.)* They're going . . . to kill me. *(Faints in Gunn's arms.)*

GUNN: He's dimmed out, he has. *(Lays Jim on ground.)* Poor lamb. Still believes that all the world is good. Nay, lad, you'll learn there's the bad along with the good. Hot with sweat you are. *(Fans Jim.)* I'm wondering . . . in your pocket, if you have a . . . a bite of . . . cheese? *(Starts to look, stops.)* It ain't that I'm stealing. Nay! But I'm thinking you might be an angel answering my prayers and bringing me a taste of cheese! *(Digs into Jim's pocket.)*

SILVER: *(Offstage.)* On mateys! On to the top of the hill.

(Gunn looks off R, quickly hides behind a tree, then runs off UL. Black Dog, with sack, and Morgan enter R. Silver follows them. Dirk and Johnny, with sacks, are behind.)

MORGAN: *(Sinks to his knees.)* First, catch our breath, and let's have a look at the map.

BLACK DOG: *(Also rests, picks up Jim's telescope.)* What's this?

SILVER: Young Jim's telescope. And here he be! *(They surround Jim.)*

DIRK: *(Over Jim, ready to plunge his knife.)* Let's have done with him, here and now.

SILVER: I found him! He's my booty! Sh. He's coming to. *(Jim moves, opens his eyes, and slowly looks around at the pirates, then suddenly withdraws in fear.)* Well, here's Jim Hawkins, shiver me timber. Sitting and waiting just for me. I take that most friendly.

JIM: No, you're not my friend.

SILVER: What's ailing ye, lad? Where's your smile for old Barbecue?

JIM: *(Confronts him.)* You are going to kill me.

MORGAN: Aye, and we'll do it right now. *(Draws cutlass.)*

SILVER: *(In anger with authority.)* You, batten down your hatches till you're spoken to! *(To Jim.)* I know you're going to listen to what I have to say, Jim. And this is the long and the short of it. You can't go back to your friends and the ship, you may lay on that! So as a friend, I'm giving you a choice.

JIM: A choice?

SILVER: You can join up with us and be a gentleman of fortune—

PIRATES: *(Mockingly elegant.)* Aye, gentlemen of fortune!

SILVER: Or—

DIRK: Or— *(Holds up knife.)*

SILVER: Speak up, lad.

JIM: I was your friend. I thought you were mine. But now I know the truth. I heard—your plans to take over the ship, to kill the Squire and the Doctor.

MORGAN: You heard?

JIM: I was hid in the apple barrel.

DIRK: Cut out his tongue before he blabs.

JIM: Too late. I've told the Doctor and the Squire.

MORGAN: They know! *(He draws his cutlass and Dirk holds knife on the side of Jim.)*

SILVER: *(Draws pistol.)* Move one hand, Morgan, and I'll blow your head off! *(Pirates retreat.)*

JIM: You can kill me, yes, or—you can spare me. Because . . . when you . . . all of you . . . are in court on trial for murder and for piracy . . . I can be the witness who will save you . . . and I will . . . if you save me.

DIRK: He squealed our plans.

BLACK DOG: He stole the map from Billy Bones.

MORGAN: First and last, we spit on Jim Hawkins! *(Pirates start to attack him.)*

SILVER: *(Shouts.)* Avast, there! *(Pirates stop.)* Be you the Captain? By the power, but I'll teach you better. So you want to have it out, do you? Take a cutlass, him that dares, and I'll be quick to show him the color of his own insides! *(No answers.)* No one moves. Then listen and understand King George's English! I be the Captain here by election and because I'm the best man by a sea-mile. If you won't fight, then by thunder, you'll obey. I like this boy. He's smart, figured out how to save his life. He's more of a man than any of you cowardly rats. And he who lays a hand on him—beware! *(Moves and takes out map.)* And now we'll take a look at the map. *(Pirates gather about eagerly.)* Here's the harbor where we anchored. And in the center is Spy Glass Hill.

MORGAN: Where be—the red crosses?

DIRK: Aye, them that mark where the treasure be!

BLACK DOG: There ain't no red crosses!

DIRK: It's a fake! You've been swindled!

SILVER: By thunder, it ain't Flint's map!

MORGAN: You've bungled it again, Silver. The Squire and the Doctor have the ship. And we be marooned with no map.

BLACK DOG: I've stood your bossing long enough.

DIRK: Aye, your time is up, Silver.

BLACK DOG: We're with you, Morgan.

MORGAN: I say—speaking for the crew— *(Pirates nod and say, "Aye.")* we have our right to step aside and hold a council.

SILVER: Aye, I know the rules. Hold your council.

MORGAN: Come, all of ye. *(Pirates exit L.)*

SILVER: *(His back to Jim, speaks softly.)* Jim, don't look at me. They mustn't know we're talking. But listen.

JIM: *(His back to Silver.)* I can hear you.

SILVER: Didn't I stand by ye through thick and thin?

JIM: I thought you were my friend, but you—

SILVER: We'll make a bargain. You be my witness in court, save me from hanging, and I'll save you from walking the plank.

JIM: You want to be my friend?

SILVER: I'm wanting to save my life—and yours.

JIM: Save my life? Here, you take it. *(Gives Silver oilcloth packet.)*

SILVER: What is it?

JIM: The real map. With the crosses—where the treasure is.

SILVER: The real map! They're coming. *(Pirates enter L.)* Well, step up mates. Don't be afraid. Hand it over. I know what you have. *(Morgan with a nod from pirates, gives Silver the Black Spot.)* The Black Spot.

MORGAN: Aye, this crew, according to the rules, has tipped you the Black Spot.

SILVER: *(Reads.)* "Deposed."

MORGAN: Aye, you're no longer our leader. *(Pirates agree, "Aye.")*

SILVER: Not so fast. I still be your Captain tills you out with your grievances.

MORGAN: You made a hash of this trip and that's our grievance.

DIRK: We ain't got the map. We ain't got the treasure.

BLACK DOG: And that boy is a bag of trouble.

SILVER: Now I'll answer you. First, kill the boy? Nay. If there is trouble, he's our hostage. And—the Squire and Doctor, being good men, won't sail without him. So when they come to fetch him—

DIRK: Aye, we'll kill them and take the ship!

JOHNNY: I'll drink to that.

SILVER: And about Flint's map. What would you say if I told you that the boy has the real map? *(Pirates move toward Jim.)* And while the likes of you was squabbling, the lad gave it to me—to his new Captain.

MORGAN: You have the map?

SILVER: Aye, mateys, Jim Hawkins has joined our side. Here be the map.

MORGAN: *(Morgan grabs map, and the three pirates eagerly inspect it.)* It's Flint's, sure enough. J and F writ right there.

DIRK: With a clove hitch to it, the way Flint always did.

JOHNNY: And the red crosses! Where the treasure's buried!

DIRK: Three of them. Plain as print!

SILVER: Now who's your Captain? Pipe up and let's hear the vote. *(Together the three shout, "You. You, Silver. Long John Silver, etc.")* And the Black Spot? Ain't worth a biscuit. *(Tosses it over his shoulder.)* So I say—get your sacks, follow the map, and on to Spy Glass Hill. Are you with me? *(All answer, "Aye," and get sacks.)* And Jim—you stay beside me. Head up, lad. You are now a bad, brave buccaneer.

JOHNNY: *(Behind tree, picks up skull by his sack.)* What's this?

DIRK: *(Takes it.)* It's a skull! *(Tosses it to Black Dog.)*

BLACK DOG: A dead man's skull! *(Tosses it to Johnny.)*

JOHNNY: What's been eaten and rotten away.

SILVER: Where did you find it?

JOHNNY: Beside the sack, it was.

SILVER: *(Looks behind tree.)* Let me see. By thunder, there's a mess of bones—a human skeleton. Look how straight he is, his bony feet pointing one way, and his hands pointing the other way. Morgan, let's have a look at the compass. Take a bearing along the line where them bones point.

MORGAN: East, South, East and by East.

SILVER: This here is a pointer! By thunder, this is one of Flint's jokes. A dead man he laid here, pointing straight to the treasure. *(Stage grows darker.)*

BLACK DOG: It's enough to run a chill through you. *(A bird screeches.)*

JOHNNY: What's that?

BLACK DOG: Birds a-screeching.

DIRK: Vulchers, I'm thinking, waiting to eat the dead.

JOHNNY: It's getting darker.

BLACK DOG: There's a cloud over the sun.

MORGAN: I saw Flint die. Hollering he was for rum and singing, "Fifteen men on a dead man's chest."

SILVER: Flint is dead.

GUNN: *(Offstage, sings in an eerie trembling voice.)*
"Fifteen men on a dead man's chest,
Yo-ho-ho, and a bottle of rum."

DIRK: It's Flint. It's Flint's voice.

GUNN: *(Offstage, wails.)* Darby McGraw . . . Darby McGraw . . . Fetch after the rum, Darby.

MORGAN: Them was Flint's last words.

JOHNNY: It's his ghost. Flint's ghost is come to haunt us.

BLACK DOG: Aye, them was Flint's last words.

SILVER: But not his voice.

MORGAN: Nay, but 'twas a voice like one I remember. *(Stage grows bright again.)*

SILVER: By the powers, it sounded like Ben Gunn.

JIM: Ben Gunn? Ben Gunn! Where? *(Looks about.)*

MORGAN: *(Laughs.)* Then there be no worry. Nobody minds Ben Gunn, dead or alive. *(Turns and shouts at Jim who starts to make a run for it.)* You lad! Where are you going? *(Jim stops.)*

DIRK: Wanting to walk, eh? I say, let him walk the plank. What's your answer, John?

MORGAN: Aye, John, trying to give us the slip, he was.

SILVER: Aye, trying to escape. I judged him wrong.

BLACK DOG: He ain't one of us and never will be.

SILVER: Aye, you're right.

DIRK: *(Holds up knife.)* What do you say, John?

SILVER: I say—when the treasure's ours, we'll be done with him.

JIM: *(Confronts him.)* I thought you were my friend.

SILVER: You've this to learn, my lad. There's many a clean glove that covers a dirty hand. *(Laughs.)* Shoulder your sacks, mates, and on to the top of the hill. *(Pirates get sacks.)* And you, Master Jim Hawkins, will lead the way. March.

DIRK: *(Points the way.)* It's the end of the journey. *(Holds knife to Jim.)* And the end—of you.

MORGAN: Him, a pirate! He's a cowardly little lubber. Listen. You can hear his heart beating . . . thump . . . thump . . . louder . . . *(A low beat of a bass drum begins.)* and louder . . . cause he knows he's walking to his death.

(As Jim leads, they go to L. Trees move to R and off. A large tree enters L and stops at C. Drum beat grows louder, and then stops as Pirates re-enter L.)

SCENE 7

(At the site of the treasure. Pirates rush to big tree.)

DIRK: There's the big tree!

MORGAN: The big tree! Like on the map!

JOHNNY: We've found the treasure!

BLACK DOG: Aye, the treasure! *(They search behind the tree.)*

MORGAN: What's this? A hole's been dug!

JOHNNY: *(Holds up a scrap of wood.)* Piece of packing-case. Says, "Walrus."

MORGAN: That's from Flint's ship.

DIRK: Where be the treasure?

BLACK DOG: It's been lifted!

MORGAN: The treasure is gone! *(Pirates search the ground behind the tree.)*

SILVER: *(At side with Jim.)* Jim, take this and stand by for trouble. *(Gives Jim pistol.)*

JIM: So you've changed sides again?

SILVER: I'm wanting to be on the side that gets out alive.

DIRK: Where be the treasure, John Silver?

JOHNNY: Aye, you be the man that never bungled nothing!

BLACK DOG: Look at him. He knew it all along.

MORGAN: What are we waiting for, mates? There's only the two of them. One's a cripple and the other's a cub that I mean to have the heart of. Are you with me, mates?

PIRATES: Aye!

SILVER: *(As pirates step forward, Silver pushes Jim forward and holds him in front of Silver.)* In front, Jim! If you kill the boy, you kill our chances of going home. He's our living hostage.

MORGAN: Dead he'll be. And so will them that come for him. At 'em, mateys!

JIM: *(Holds out pistol and aims.)* Stop! Stand back. STAND BACK! *(Pirates stand back.)* Or I'll shoot.

MORGAN: Nay, you won't shoot.

JIM: Yes, I will. *(Moves pistol. Pirates move back.)*

MORGAN: *(Sarcastic, as he inches forward.)* You're a good boy. Good boys don't shoot. Good boys—

JIM: I am good! And you—all of you are evil.

MORGAN: *(Laughs.)* Good against evil. Aye! We'll see which be the winner. Avaunt, mates!

SILVER: By fire and brimstone, I'll slash you to pork! *(Raises cutlass.)*

MORGAN: Kill him!

SILVER: Shoot, Jim!

(Pirates start toward Jim and Silver, at L. Squire, Doctor and Gunn appear at R with pistols drawn.)

JIM: Doctor Livesey!

MORGAN: *(Pirates turn to see.)* Whose there?

DOCTOR: Drop your weapons! All of you! Or we'll shoot!

MORGAN: Nay! It's pirates we are, and like pirates we'll fight. And the devil take you all!

(Pirates attack. Doctor, Squire and Gunn fire pistols. Three loud gunshots ring in the air. Dirk, Johnny, and Black Dog are hit. They fall to the ground.)

SQUIRE: *(Rushes to Jim.)* Jim, my boy!

(Morgan, alone, fights Doctor with his cutlass; knocks pistol from Doctor's hand; backs Doctor up, with violent slashing.)

JIM: *(Sees danger Doctor is in.)* Doctor Livesey!

SQUIRE: *(Turns and sees situation.)* Jim, quick! Your pistol! *(Takes Jim's pistol, aims it at Morgan.)* You villain! *(Morgan turns to Squire, raises cutlass. Squire shoots. There is a loud gunshot report. Morgan drops cutlass, cries, grabs his chest, and runs off R, crying in pain.)* Yes, the devil has taken you all.

DOCTOR: Jim, my boy, you're safe.

JIM: Yes.

DOCTOR: We came ashore to find you.

SQUIRE: And Ben Gunn found us, and led us here to save you.

GUNN: Aye, good gentlemen they be, says I. Taking me back, they are, to me dear mother.

SILVER: Ben Gunn? It was you we heard in the woods.

SQUIRE: You, John Silver, I will take back to England as a prisoner and there you will be hung as a pirate.

SILVER: Nay! Speak out, lad. Tell him our bargain. Tit for tat.

JIM: I promised—if he saved my life—

SILVER: And I did! I did!

JIM: I would save his.

SQUIRE: Never! He is a pirate and disgrace to England.

JIM: Doctor, I gave him my word. I promised.

DOCTOR: Then you will keep your promise. Silver, you will return a free man.

SILVER: Thank you, sir.

JIM: You see, John Silver, I was right. It is the good side that wins!

GUNN: Aye, and the good ones win the treasure. Rich, rich we are! All of Flint's treasure, chest and chest of gold. Buried here it was. Dig, says I, and I did. Dig, dig, dig. And safe it all is in my cave.

DOCTOR: And so, young Jim Hawkins, your adventure to Treasure Island comes to an end. *(Doctor, Squire, Silver, and Gunn move and stand together at L.)*

JIM: *(Recalling it all.)* Yes . . . it was an adventure . . . with a buried treasure . . . with pirates and a pirate ship . . .

DOCTOR, SQUIRE, SILVER, GUNN: *(Sing with music.)* You were the hero of our story.

JIM: And a treasure island in the sea . . .

DOCTOR, SQUIRE, SILVER, GUNN: *(Sing.)* Who fought for right and glory.

JIM: Yes! It was an adventure. A glorious adventure! *(Leaves stage.)*

DOCTOR, SQUIRE, SILVER, GUNN: *(Sing.)*

Now the treasure's found, our story told,
Goodby we say to pirates bold;
(Jim waves to them from audience.)
We take our leave, and bow from view,
And say goodby, goodby, goodby, goodby, goodby to you.

(They nod, turn and exit L. Jim is seated again in the audience. The Toy Theatre curtain falls. Music continues for curtain calls.)

CURTAIN

PRODUCTION NOTES

To help the actor who plays Long John Silver hide his real leg, which can be belted up behind him, he can wear baggy knee pants; a knee-length coat of the period, full in the back; and a rapier, which he never uses, but the handle is seen at his side in front, and the pointed end is seen extending from his coat behind, the rapier keeping the coat always extended which completely hides his real leg. He may have a short knife in his belt which he does use when he threatens the pirates.

For a simpler staging the following changes can be made:

SMALLER CAST (10)

The actors playing the parts of Billy Bones, Dogger and Blind Pew can double and also play the parts of Johnny, Morgan and Ben Gunn.

FEWER SETS (3)

Scene 4 may be omitted and scene 2, on the dock, can be combined with scene 3, both being played on the ship, with a light change and music—"Sailing, Sailing"—showing a passage of time. Between the first and second part of scene 2, a passage of time can also be indicated by Black Dog crossing, as the music of "Sailing, Sailing" is being played, and adding a lighted lantern to the deck scene.

The play in three sets is staged:

Scene 1. England, at the Admiral Benbow Inn
Scene 2. Aboard the *Hispañiola*
Scene 3. Ashore on Treasure Island

Although the concept of staging the play as if performed in a life-size Toy Theatre is effective, any other appropriate style can be used.

NOTE: The term "Toy Theatre" as used in this script may for some readers require further explanation. During the nineteenth century in Europe and the United States, one immensely popular toy was a model theatre—about the size of an ordinary doll house—with a brightly painted proscenium arch. Scripts for well-known stories could be purchased, complete with printed pictures of the characters and the scenery. These sketches could be colored if they had been bought "plain." Then they were cut out and attached to cardboard for support. Backdrops were inserted and characters manipulated across the stage by means of sticks or wires projecting through the open top and sides of the theatre. As the script was read aloud by one or more persons, the flat paper-doll "actors" were moved about. The main characteristics of this homemade drama were bright colors and exciting tales; elaborate characterizations were harder to achieve since the two-dimensional "actors" were locked into a single position and expression, with only their human voices as expressive tools.

A logical next step was for a creative child to make up his own stories, to draw pictures as needed, or to playact roles himself. Among children who treasured toy theatres were Lewis Carroll, Hans Christian Andersen, Tad Lincoln, and Robert Louis Stevenson, who received one on his sixth birthday. Its importance to him and to his developing imagination is detailed in his 1883 essay "A Penny Plain and Twopence Coloured," an allusion to the price of the picture sets he had lovingly selected for his diminutive theatre at a nearby stationer's shop. Thus the life-size Toy Theatre staging for Aurand Harris's *Treasure Island*, as developed for its premiere production, seems particularly fitting.

THE WIND IN THE WILLOWS

by

MOSES GOLDBERG

freely adapted from the book by Kenneth Grahame

THE WIND IN THE WILLOWS

CHARACTERS

Mole
Rat
Otter
Toad
Badger
Weasels
Policeman
Alice

SETTINGS

Scene 1. Rat's house.
Scene 2. The high road.
Scene 3. The wild woods.
Scene 4. Badger's house.
Scene 5. Toad Hall.
Scene 6. A street in the village
Scene 7. Rat's house.
Scene 8. Toad Hall.
Scene 9. A jail cell.
Scene 10. Badger's house.
Scene 11. Toad Hall.

SCENE ONE

The action of this play should be continuous, so that whatever changes are performed on the set, they should be nearly instantaneous; whether by means of wagons, revolves, flies, etc. Sets may be changed in view of the audience, but must be smoothly flowing, so that the action is not interrupted. Lighting effects carry a big burden for setting the mood and locale. Throughout it is important that the animal characters and settings be handled realistically, although greatly simplified. The actors playing animals are not to wear masks, but may use headpieces with ears attached, leaving a hole for the face. Makeup is simplified, but authentic. Human machines, by contrast, should be exaggerated and stylized; (the hobby horse, the cars, etc.); and the human characters may be masked. The general atmosphere is one of a blend, with Riverbank, Wild Wood, Toad Hall, and Wide World all contributing their special flavors. There is also a certain rural English elegance about the animals and their homes, especially Badger, Rat, and Toad Hall, (although pre-Civil War Confederate elegance would probably work just as well.) The overture starts and the house lights dim. It is night on the riverbank. We are at Rat's house, just where his front door issues out onto the River itself, with his small front yard separating the porch and its thatched roof from high tide. It is nearly dawn, and as the overture dies the sun begins to rise. The music of the wind plays under the following scene. (Not a symphony, please. A solo flute or oboe is sufficient.) Rat emerges slowly from sleep and from his hole. He yawns magnificently and inspects the beauty of the world he loves. Rat is the stable, understanding, gentlemanly poet of the play. He has a natural and uncultivated upper class manner; is extremely tolerant of the faults of others—and has depth of sensitivity which is all too rare. He makes his mistakes, like the rest of us, but he can always rise above them.

RAT: *(After a pause.)* Listen! Listen to that wind! *(Nodding his head.)* It's going to be a beautiful day. *(Pause.)* Mole! Moley! Where are you? Come out. Smell this breeze!

MOLE: *(Sticks his nose timidly out, afraid to leave the security of the hole. Mole is sympathetic, warm, and sensitive. He is too naive, perhaps, and certainly unpolished, but his faith in others redeems both him and them. Black glasses protect his weak eyes.)* Oh! *(He ducks back.)*

RAT: Come out, Mole. It's dawn! *(Pause, while Mole partly emerges, blinks at the sun, looks pleadingly at Rat, and hesitates.)* Well? *(Mole gathers his courage and his legs, and leaps out, losing his balance and almost falling down. Rat catches him, but lets him go as soon as he is sure Mole will not fall.)* Easy. It's still here. *(Pause.)* Listen to that wind!

MOLE: *(Listens blankly, he cannot hear anything.)* What wind? What does it sound like?

RAT: *(Nods.)* Can't hear it? Well, you will. Too many years living underground—your eyes and ears are out of practice. Just keep trying.

MOLE: *(Pause.) (Shrugs, and shakes his head—he still can't hear it.)* Maybe. But not today. *(A long pause as they sample the dawn.)* I'm glad I came to live with you, Ratty.

RAT: So am I. *(Pause.)* Deep Breath! *(Mole takes a deep breath, and starts to cough.) (Rat chuckles.)* Easy! Easy!

MOLE: Just think—all this has been going on here all the time, every single day, and I was down underground—just like all the other moles in my family, and never knew about the wind, or the trees, or the fresh air. *(He takes another deep breath, and holds on to it a little better. He takes a third and starts to relax with it.)* Ah! *(Suddenly he lifts his head and listens hard. Then sadly he shakes his head again; he almost thought he heard the wind.)*

RAT: Go slow! You'll hear it! Takes time! *(The music fades out.)*

MOLE: *(Pause.)* Rat?

RAT: What, Mole?

MOLE: Can I learn to swim today?

RAT: Go slow!

MOLE: I know. I'm sorry. Everything is so new and exciting though. I never dreamt that when I left my stuffy hole there would be so many new things to do—swimming, and boating, and sunshine, and wind, and . . . I can hardly wait.

RAT: I know. I know. Something new comes along and you want to explore it. Fine. But start out slowly. Animals who go rushing around too fast get into lots of trouble. You don't want to be the kind of an idiot who is always trying out new things and never having fun with the old ones!

MOLE: No. I guess not.

RAT: You don't want to be the kind who never tries anything new, either. If you did, you would never have left your hole.

MOLE: That's right. I guess I want to be someplace in the middle. *(Pause.)* *(Mole takes another deep breath.)* Well, you tell me then, what shall I learn today?

RAT: *(Sniffing the air.)* I'm not sure it's warm enough for the water. Spring hasn't really started yet. How about a picnic?

MOLE: A picnic? Oh, Rat. Can we go somewhere new? I mean . . . if you think I'm ready.

RAT: All right, all right. We'll head toward the High Road—that's someplace you've never been. And I'll try to invite some of the others to come along.

MOLE: Oh, good—thanks, Ratty.

RAT: Wait here; I'll get a lunch packed. *(Exits into the house.)*

MOLE: *(Yawns.)* Oh, maybe I shouldn't have gotten up so early. But on a day like this, how can any animal stay in bed? *(Otter enters.)* Oh, hi! It's Otter!

OTTER: *(Otter is largish and quick in his movements, but he is also on the fringe of the good life, as opposed to Rat, who is at the center. Otter is sensitive and presumptuous, in love with the status quo, and unashamedly hypocritical. He bullys anybody he can, and flatters the rest. Still he means well, is quite good natured, and can be forced to come through when the chips are down. His personal loyalty is to his comfort, but Rat is one of his favorites.)* Howdy! How's little Mole?

MOLE: Oh, fine, er . . . how's big Otter?

OTTER: Not too bad. Not too bad. Well—how do you like the River?

MOLE: *(Somewhat taken aback.)* Oh, I . . . well, I haven't really . . .

OTTER: Good. Good. Well, if mean old Rat gives you any trouble, you can always move in with me! Just you remember that.

MOLE: Thank you. But Rat isn't . . . I mean he doesn't . . . well . . . thank you.

OTTER: You're welcome. You are welcome. What's up?

MOLE: A picnic! Would you like to come?

OTTER: Sure! Why not! What about right here by the River? Perfect spot!

MOLE: I sort of wanted to go to the High Road. I've never been there and I . . .

OTTER: Yech! The High Road is a terrible place! Moley, you're new here, so I hope you'll take a little advice. Leave the High Road alone! Why, that leads out to the Wide World, and there's nothing out there but people and trouble!

RAT: *(Returns with the loaded picnic basket.)* Here it is! Hello, Otter! You coming along? We're going to the High Road!

OTTER: Oh? Yeah! Fine idea. I'd love to come. Haven't been to the High Road for months. Good spot.

RAT: Let's go. I brought extra food in case we run into Badger or Toad.

MOLE: But I thought you said the High Road . . .

OTTER: Oh! Toad! He'll probably be along! Yech! Moley, let me warn you about Toad!

MOLE: What's the matter? Is he bad?

OTTER: Bad? Worse! He's an idiot! Toad is an idiot!

TOAD: *(At this instant Toad is heard galloping along on the back of some noble horse. He rides into view on the back of a broom with a horse's head tied onto the handle. Toad is modern and progressive. He has a quick mind and an agile tongue, coupled with a love of life and a minimum of scruples. This makes him a delightful rogue—if a dangerous one. The problem with Toad is he wants to be a modern, and is completely unsuited for it, having been brought up in a respectable upper class tradition. He tries though—he tries very hard! Just now he is trying so hard to ride that he rides over the picnicbound threesome, knocking them into a heap.)*

TOAD: Wahoo! Gidyap! Wahoo! Wahoo! Ride 'em Cowboy! *(Exits.)*

OTTER: *(As they untangle.)* TOAD! TOAD! Come back here! Come back here this instant!

TOAD: *(Obliges by riding over them again.)* Here comes Toad—the two-gun kid. Wahoo! *(Exits.)*

MOLE: Is that Toad?

RAT: That's Toad!

OTTER: Look out! He's coming back! *(They duck this time, and as Toad returns they grab him and force him to the ground. Otter sits on his legs and Rat holds his shoulders down. Mole stands in wonder.)*

TOAD: Gidyap! Wahoo! Wahoo! Toad rides again!

MOLE: Rat. Ratty. What is it? Shall I get the doctor?

RAT: Hold on. He'll be all right.

TOAD: *(Subsides into a semi-trance.)* Wahoo . . . c'mon horse!

OTTER: Useless Moron! He thinks he's riding a horse!

MOLE: A horse? Does he get like this often?

RAT: Every once in a while. He gets a new idea in his head, and everything else blanks out. We just watch him till he settles down. It shouldn't take long.

OTTER: Settle down? Yech! When does Toad ever settle down?

TOAD: MMMMMMMMMMMM.

RAT: I think it's safe now. Let him up. *(They release him.)*

TOAD: *(Sits up as if nothing had happened.)* Hi! Beautiful day, huh? Oh, who's that?

RAT: This is Mole. I wish you had set him a better example, Toad; he's new to the Riverbank.

TOAD: New to the Riverbank, huh? How do you do? How do you like my horse?

MOLE: Oh, I . . . how do you do?

TOAD: Of course, this isn't a real horse.

OTTER: At least he knows it isn't real!

TOAD: *(Directs himself to Mole.)* But I'm going to buy a real one. And Moley, I might even let you help pick it out.

MOLE: Really! Oh, Rat, he said I could help him. *(A look from Rat sobers him quickly.)* . . . Thank you, Toady.

OTTER: Yech!

TOAD: Don't pay any attention to them. You see, Mole, I'm having a whole set of stables built at Toad Hall. So I can have a whole fleet of horses. White ones and gray ones and red ones and black ones . . . I think I'll even let you ride sometimes!

MOLE: Really?

RAT: Mole! Go Slow!

TOAD: Can you see me riding about, or rather flying about, on the back of some great steed? Poetry in motion. I'll admit I've had some silly ideas before—but this is really it! Horses! Wahoo! Let's go buy a horse right now! *(Starts to drag Mole away.)*

RAT: Moley! I thought you were coming on the picnic.

MOLE: Well, yes . . . but . . . Toad invited me to help him . . . that is, I . . .

OTTER: Little Mole, don't talk to the moron! Come with us!

TOAD: Come on, Moley, let's go. *(Climbs on horse and starts out, stepping on Rat's foot.)*

RAT: That's my foot, Toad!

MOLE: Oh, Rat! Are you all right? Please be careful, Toady.

TOAD: Wahoo! Gidyap! Neeeigh!

RAT: Calm down, Toad, please! We were just starting a picnic. Interested?

MOLE: Yes. Come along on the picnic, Toady. We can go look at horses later.

TOAD: Picnic? What a splendid notion! Where are we going?

MOLE: To the High Road!

TOAD: To the High Road! Maybe I'll see a horse!

OTTER: That does it! I'm through. I take no picnics with morons! If he goes, I don't.

RAT: Otter, you lead the way. This is no time for YOU to get silly.

OTTER: I wasn't being silly! But that moron . . . oh, all right. I'll go ahead. But make HIM stop being silly. He's the one who's an idiot! *(Starts out.)* Horses! Yech!

RAT: Coming, Toad?

TOAD: Sure!

MOLE: Good!

RAT: All right. But no mention of horses.

TOAD: I'll try. I will. But I can't promise; and if we should actually see a horse . . .

RAT: Toad!

TOAD: Oooops. I mean if we should actually see a whatcha-macallit. Well, I can't promise at all. After all, whatcha-macallit is a whatcha-macallit.

RAT: Well, try! *(He catches up with Otter, and they go off.)*

MOLE: Come on, Toady, to the High Road! And on the way you can tell me what kind of horse you are going to buy.

TOAD: Mole, I like you. You are an animal with real understanding. I only want the kind of horse that suits my character—big, white, ferocious, and fast as the wind . . . *(They exit, following Rat and Otter and the scene changes to:*

SCENE TWO

The High Road. A broad highway, with a low bank on the upstage side. The scenery is barer, the trees less green. Perhaps there is a milestone, brightly painted, showing "2 miles to the Red Lion Inn." The sounds of a real horse are heard in the distance. Instantly Toad is there, followed at a more leisurely pace by the others.

TOAD: It was a horse. It was. A real horse. Aah! Ooh! EEEh!

OTTER: Yech!

TOAD: What beauty—what grace.

RAT: Toad—you promised!

TOAD: No I didn't—I said I'd try. And I have tried! But a real live horse; and we just missed him! *(He pretends to be riding a horse up and down all through the following.)*

OTTER: I can't stand it! Leave him alone! Let's get on with the picnic.

MOLE: But look at Toad!

OTTER: I'd rather not. Let's eat. I'm starved.

RAT: He'll come over in a minute. Mole. Don't worry. *(He starts to unpack the picnic basket, pulling out a fancy tablecloth and several wineglasses, followed by the wine, the cheese, the half turkey, the ham, the mustard pot, the cake, the jam, the buns, the cloth napkins—quite a spread.)*

MOLE: Oh! This is the High Road!

OTTER: This is it, little Mole. What do you think? Down that way is the village, where all the people live, and beyond there, the Wide World!

RAT: You could help me unpack! *(They do.)*

TOAD: Gidyap! Neeeeeeigh! *(The music of the wind is heard.)*

MOLE: Oh, Rat—it's different from the River. I can't explain it—it just seems, well, not as nice, somehow.

RAT: It's different . . . listen!

MOLE: *(Cocks his ear and tries to hear, without success. Otter and Toad are oblivious. The music stops and Rat signals Mole it is over. Mole sighs. Pause.)* Why is the Road—well—so dirty?

OTTER: That's because of the people, and their crazy inventions. People are never satisfied, always moving around, inventing new machines. I like it just like it is!

MOLE: Yes, but suppose I'd said that. I'd still be back in my hole.

TOAD: Neeeeigh! *(He gallops around, stepping on some of the picnic.)*

OTTER: Moron! You stepped in the lunch! See what happens when you get crazy ideas all the time. You end up like Toad!

MOLE: I don't think Toad's that bad. I mean . . . well, who is right, Rat, me or Otter?

RAT: Both of you. Hand me the caviar dish, please. *(At this moment, Badger appears through the bushes.)* Badger! Quick, Mole. Look!

MOLE: Oh!

RAT: Badger. It's only us. Come out.

OTTER: Quiet, Mole. He'll go away if he thinks it's too noisy.

TOAD: Go for your gun, bang, bang! Got ya! That'll teach you to mess with two-gun Toad! *(Badger disappears.)*

OTTER: He's gone! Idiot. You scared him off!

MOLE: Oh, Toady! I wanted to meet him. Where does he live?

RAT: *(As they resume eating.)* In the Wild Woods. He's the only friendly animal that dares to live there. He's so big, not even the weasels will bother him!

MOLE: Oh! Why is he so shy?

OTTER: Hates company! Tough as they come on the outside, but a heart of gold on the inside. Badger comes from a fine family. Anybody needs help—anybody—Badger's always ready to help them.

RAT: Never seems to be around when you need him though.

TOAD: Whoa, horse. I reckon I'll go over and get some grub. You set right here. *(Dismounts and joins the picnic.)* What's for lunch?

OTTER: For you—fried horse!

RAT: Otter! *(Pause as Toad settles and they eat.)*

MOLE: Can I have an apple, Ratty, please?

(At this moment a shrill whine is heard—the approach of a motor-car. Brilliant red, stylized to represent the human world, and emitting an incessant "poop-poop," the car streaks across and off, scattering the animals in its wake. Toad is drawn to center, where he sits dazed on the road. The others are flung to one side or another, but are instantly on their feet.)

OTTER: I'll sue! Teenage drivers! Call the Police!

MOLE: Rat, help! A monster!

RAT: Easy, Mole. Everybody all right?

OTTER: Yech! People and their new ideas. Now what do you say, little Mole?

RAT: All right, Mole?

MOLE: Yes, I guess. What was it?

TOAD: *(From a deep trance, where he sits.)* Poop-poop, poop-poop.

MOLE: A what?

TOAD: Poop-poop-poop-poop-poop-poop.

RAT: Toad. Where you hit?

TOAD: OOOOOOH! Did you see it, or was it a dream—

MOLE: Is he all right, Ratty?

TOAD: That vision. That cloud of light. Poetry in motion. Poop-poop. Poop-poop. What a way to travel—the only way to travel. Horses? I was silly. I was childish! A horse is nothing! A motor-car! A motor-car!!

MOLE: A motor-car? How does it work?

OTTER: Oh, no—not again?

RAT: Watch him, Otter.

TOAD: Poop-poop, poop-poop. *(Finally he breaks loose, crashes into Mole, who goes down with his glasses broken; and streaks out after the motor-car, all the while with a silly look on his face and a continuous "poop-poop, poop-poop.")*

RAT: *(Pause.)* Gone!

MOLE: Where to?

RAT: Don't know. Don't like it! He looks pretty bad.

MOLE: But . . . what happened to him? He's broken my glasses! Look!

RAT: The motor-car. He's gone wild for cars. Last time he got like this was the first time he saw a canoe. He spent half his money on canoes in three weeks, and nearly drowned everybody on the River.

MOLE: Oh!

OTTER: Maybe the idiot will actually buy a car and crash it. Then we'd be rid of him!

RAT: Otter! *(At this point a weasel peeks out at them.)* Look out. Weasel! *(Rat throws something at the weasel, who vanishes. There can be as many weasels as desired, and they may be cast with girls, especially if they are dancers. The weasels are have-nots, they are care-*

less and destructive, and they have little respect for elegance. They are not evil, however, just sloppy and unkempt.)

MOLE: I think I'm going back to my hole.

RAT: Relax, Mole—go slow!

MOLE: What was it?

OTTER: Just an ordinary old weasel! Harmless—as long as we have them outnumbered.

RAT: I'm worried. Those weasels have an instinct for trouble. They must have seen Toad run off like that. We'd better get to him before the weasels do. They'd take advantage of any silly thing he did. I don't think they like Toad much.

OTTER: Or any Riverbankers for that matter.

RAT: Are you all right, Mole? Can you see?

MOLE: A little. I guess I'm getting used to the sunlight. Things happen pretty fast up above ground, don't they?

RAT: *(Nodding.)* Let's pick up this mess. *(They get some of it up, when the car is heard returning! This time Toad is at the wheel. The friends again scatter as the car streaks out of sight, but Otter is hit on the foot. Toad waves gaily and continues tooting the horn.)*

RAT: Toad!

OTTER: OUCH! Oh, Rat. OW! My toe!

MOLE: That was Toad driving! What's happened?

RAT: He's bought a car! Otter, are you all right?

OTTER: My toe! I think it's broken!

RAT: Better get you to the doctor's. Come on, quick!

MOLE: What about Toad, though? Suppose he crashes? Suppose the weasels get him?

RAT: No time to look after Toad now. Otter needs help first. You go back home and wait. Just follow the same trail and you won't get lost. I'll be home in an hour.

MOLE: All right. *(Unconvinced.)*

RAT: Can you see well enough to get home?

MOLE: Yes. I see much better now.

OTTER: Hurry up, Rat. It really hurts.

RAT: Let's go.

OTTER: Blast that Toad!

RAT: Lean on me. *(They limp off slowly.)*

MOLE: Poor Toad. Isn't anybody going to help him? He'll hurt himself! Ratty? . . . *(Pause.)* Badger! Otter said Badger could help anybody! I'll go get Badger and he can help Toad to go slow with new ideas; just like Rat's teaching me . . . Only, Rat said to go home! . . . I've just got to get Badger. What if the weasels get to Toad before Rat comes back? The Wild Woods! That's where Badger lives. The Wild Woods. I hope I can find his house. *(Mole goes off haltingly. Instantly a weasel pops up, chuckles maliciously, and follows after Mole. The stage is empty for a moment, then Toad drives across, tooting his horn. He gets out of sight, and we hear a frightful skid, followed by a crash and a thud. Toad staggers back onstage, clears his head, and removes a large branch from around his neck. He recovers himself and searches in his pockets. He finds his money and starts out again at top speed, imagining himself on the track at Sebring, and giving off his traditional poop-poop. He is off to buy another car, as the lights fade and the scene changes to:*

SCENE THREE

The Wild Woods. The stage grows dark and eery, and a light, early Spring snow fall begins. Backlit trees take on weird shapes, and mosses fly in to entangle the wanderer. A weasel sneaks across the stage, chuckling, he sees Mole coming and hides offstage. Mole enters, weary and cold.

MOLE: Badger! Hello? Badger, where are you? Oh, it's snowing! Where am I, Badger? *(He exits. A weasel follows him on, chuckles, and follows him off. There is a moment of silence. Then Mole re-enters from a different direction.)* Badger, where are you? Help! Oh—I'm lost! Badger! Hello! Why is it so cold? *(Shivers.)* Hello Ratty, where are you? Where's Badger's house? Hello!

A VOICE: Hello! *(An echo picks up the voice and it seems to come from many directions. Mole starts to panic and bolts off. Two weasels enter following him, a third pops out and joins them. All three laugh as they go out after Mole. There is a long pause. Suddenly the voice is heard again, it is Rat! He enters with a huge club.)*

RAT: Hello! Mole! Where are you? Mole? Why didn't he wait at home? Mole? Hello? *(He exits after the mob.)*

MOLE: *(Enters from a third direction, running and very scared.)* Help—oh, help. Badger! Rat! Anybody!

VOICE: Anybody? *(Echo: anybody?)*

MOLE: Who's there? Who is it? Rat?

RAT'S VOICE: Mole, where are you?

MOLE: Rat! It's Rat! Here I am! Help! Help! *(He starts off toward Rat's voice, but quickly backs up. There are weasels in the shadows before him. He backs up and they advance, surrounding him.)* Rat . . . *(Weakly.)* you aren't Rat. Who are you? Are you . . . Weasels?

WEASELS: Moooooole! *(Echo: Moooooole!) (They chuckle and advance. Mole is on the verge of tears. Suddenly Rat enters.)*

RAT: Mole? WEASELS! *(He springs into action wielding his club. The weasels offer little resistance and flee.)*

MOLE: Rat, oh, Ratty!

RAT: Are you all right? What are you doing out here?

MOLE: Oh I'm sorry! I wanted to find Badger—I wanted him to help Toad! It got so cold all of a sudden! And I got lost!

RAT: Go slow, Mole. Go slow, please! Weather is tricky this time of year and weasels are always tricky! They would have enjoyed dragging you around in the woods. It's their idea of fun!

MOLE: I'm sorry. I wanted to help Toady, though. None of you seemed to care about him.

RAT: Easy! Otter was hurt; and you have to let Toad run his own life. He knows cars are silly! He doesn't always remember, but he knows. And he's old enough to take care of himself.

MOLE: I know—and I should be too. Thanks for saving me!

RAT: No more of that. Let's get to Badger's. Toad is pretty bad this time, you're right. He did hurt Otter's foot, and that means it's time we took some action. I remember the canoes. Nobody's really safe when Toad starts one of his crazy ideas.

MOLE: How is Otter?

RAT: He's all right. The doctor fixed him up as good as new! This way to Badger's . . . But don't expect too much. Maybe Badger will have an idea on how to bring Toad back to his senses, and maybe he won't—Badger's pretty old, and he doesn't like to get involved.

MOLE: Well, as long as we're here, we might as well try. *(They go off together, as the scene changes to:)*

SCENE FOUR

Badger's House: An underground warren, with provisions left over from the mild Winter hanging in the dining room itself. An old table and bench, old wall paper, and an old Badger. All is somewhat elegant however, or at least it once was. On the wall is Badger's collections of clubs and shilelaghs, and a picture of a younger Badger in splendid military uniform. Badger enters with Rat and Mole. Badger, besides being old, lives in the past. This makes him absent minded, garrulous, and gruff. Yet he is really very considerate, and even fond of weaker animals and children. He does help them when he notices that they need help, but he is too wrapped up in his reminiscences to be very reliable in the average difficulty.

MOLE: And that's the whole story, Mr. Badger . . . You've just got to help Toady!

RAT: Mole's right, Badger. Toad's in bad shape. We could use your help.

BADGER: *(Not paying much attention.)* Humph!

MOLE: Will you help us? I'm sure if you told him to, he'd go slow; about new ideas, I mean.

BADGER: Now Old Toad, Toad's father—he wasn't that sort of animal at all. A more cautious animal you'd never find. Always saving his money; taking good care of things; that's how Toad Hall got to be such a fine estate in the first place! I can remember Old Toad—so clear, it seems like yesterday. He was a gentleman! He was! They don't make them like that anymore, no sir!

MOLE: Then you'll help us talk to Toad?

BADGER: Ah, Old Toad—those were the days. 'Fore these weasels got so mean . . . weren't any people around much in those days, either. None of these . . . motorcars! No wonder that rascal son of Toad's acts so strange. The world ain't what it used to be, no sir! Time somebody put a stop to all this foolishness!

RAT: Then you'll help?

BADGER: Help what? What in blazes are you youngsters chattering about? Come to the point; I ain't got all day to waste on foolishness.

MOLE: It's very simple, Mr. Badger. I think if you came with us we could persuade Toad to take it easy with these motor-cars. He could hurt himself. He's already hurt Otter and broken my glasses. And the weasels are following him all over, just waiting for him to make a mistake—Won't you please help us talk to him? Please?

BADGER: Humph!

RAT: If we stick together we might save ourselves some nasty trouble. Toad's likely to get worse before he gets better.

MOLE: Please, Mr. Badger.

BADGER: Sounds like you really need help with this one. Wish I could help you! But I never go out much anymore. I used to go out a lot. Me and Old Toad used to go everywhere together, before he died—ah, there was an animal who stood for something! Not like today, no sir. World ain't like it used to be!

MOLE: If only you'd talk to him . . .

BADGER: I can remember back—oh, must be forty years. Old Toad used to go rowing every Sunday—had a fine old rowing boat. Oak oars—nothing but the best for Old Toad!

RAT: It's no use, Mole. He can't get used to anything new. That's why he lives out here by himself—so he won't have to see any of the changes going on in the world. *(Suddenly there is a noise offstage—Otter's voice is heard, and then he bursts in, carrying a cane.)*

OTTER: Badger? Are you home? Rat? Ratty? Where is everybody?

RAT: Here, Otter. What is it?

OTTER: That idiot! That moron!

MOLE: Toad?

OTTER: You'll never guess! How many cars has Toad crashed today? One? Nope! Two? Nope! Three? Three cars in one day! I've had enough! I came for help to grab and turn him over to the police. I told you this nonsense of his would mean trouble. I told you!

MOLE: Poor Toad! Was he hurt?

OTTER: No, blast it! He never seems to get hurt. It's always the other guy—first my toe, and now my house. He smashed into my front porch with the last car—wrecked everything! But before I could even grab him to give him a punch in the nose, he was off to buy ANOTHER motor-car! He isn't even sorry about the crashes!

RAT: We'd better get to him fast!

OTTER: There's more! There are about five weasels following him now!

RAT: *(Pause.)* The weasels. Badger, you've got to help us. If we stick together we can stop Toad. Badger!

MOLE: Please!

BADGER: Humph! Crashes! Three crashes! What would Old Toad say? Humph! I'm going to bed. Can't stand all this nonsense. If that Toad was right here, I'd give him a spanking he wouldn't forget in a hurry. Mind you don't slam the door when you go out. *(He goes out muttering.)* Never saw the likes of it! What would Old Toad say? Now, Old Toad—there was an animal . . . *(He is gone.)*

MOLE: Oh, Ratty. He didn't even hear us!

RAT: I know. Let's not waste any more time with Badger. He'd be a big help to us—even Toad won't talk back to Badger; but we'll just have to try and talk to him ourselves.

OTTER: I aim to do more than just talk. That idiot has a punch coming, and I'm going to see that he gets it.

RAT: Won't help, Otter, and you know it. Let's get to him before he wrecks another car. Toad Hall. Come on.

OTTER: I told you it would be like this. I told you so! Toad is an idiot! *(They exit quickly as the scene changes to:)*

SCENE FIVE

Toad Hall. The front gate, and the main Banquet Hall. Toad Hall is a magnificent palatial country estate; a sort of cross between Buckingham Palace and Versailles, with touches of Scarlet O'Hara's "Tara." A huge ornate gate comes in first, in front of which Toad drives on in the motorcar, singing a song:

TOAD:

The world has held great heroes,
  As history books have showed;
But never a name to go down to fame,
  Compared with that of Toad!

(He drives off into the garage, and keeps on going! There is the customary crash, after which Toad staggers on wearing the steering wheel draped around his neck. He slowly recovers and discards the wheel. He reaches happily into his pockets, but discovers they are, alas, empty. Dauntless he sails through the gate, which disappears, and into the Banquet hall. In this room is the splendor of the animal world, the epitome of objets d'art animals. Old Toad was justly proud of this room, as it contains exquisite tapestries, a chandelier, fine furniture and other evidence of taste and wealth. Toad is only interested in one of the objets, however. He grabs his piggy bank from the corner, shakes it to verify the amount, and starts off to buy another car. He is, of course, proceeding rather rapidly when Rat, Mole and Otter enter. There is a huge collision which re-damages Otter's foot, and leaves Toad sitting on top of the surprised Rat.) Poop-poop, poop-poop.

OTTER: OUCH! MY TOE!

RAT: Get off of me!

TOAD: Watch out, you fools, the yellow flag is up! Poop-poop.

OTTER: Toad! You are a nincompoop!

TOAD: Poop-poop. Nincompoop! Poop-poop!

RAT: You might at least manage to stay on the road!

TOAD: Oooops! Sorry. While you're here, though—how about some breakfast? I have some first-rate pancakes?

RAT: No, Toad! No breakfast!

TOAD: Lunch?

MOLE: I'm afraid not, Toady!

OTTER: You've asked for it, Toad—now you're going to get it!

RAT: Otter, let me talk to him.

TOAD: Now, fellows—let's discuss this like civilized animals. I know I shouldn't have run into you like that, but it was only in fun. I'm sorry—I really am.

OTTER: Fun, he says. FUN! Nincompoop.

TOAD: But a little fun never . . .

RAT: This is more than a little, Toad. New ideas are one thing—but three crashes in one day . . .

TOAD: *(Weakly.)* Four.

RAT: Four!

MOLE: Oh, Toady. Another one? *(Toad nods.)*

OTTER: You're wasting money! You are wasting money! Cars are expensive and you've bought four in one day! Idiot.

MOLE: Four crashes, Toady—you could have been killed four times.

OTTER: Everybody's talking about you, Toad! Everybody! *(Toad beams.)* And not very nicely either! You are bringing shame on all your friends.

RAT: The weasels are following you everywhere! They'd love to see you get into trouble or go to jail for reckless driving, so they could drag you around a little or wreck your house!

TOAD: Weasels don't scare me at all! And it's my money I'm spending; so just leave me alone!

OTTER: Toad, you are behaving like a person! No, I mean it! an irresponsible, short-sighted, muddled-headed person!

MOLE: Toady, go slow! At least learn how to drive first! We're all terribly worried. We really are!

OTTER: It's no use. This is a job for the police! I'll go get them!

TOAD: The police? Now wait a minute!

RAT: You're making us do this, Toad. Just say that you'll never drive another car, and we'll go away and leave you in peace. You're too dangerous a driver and that's all there is to it.

TOAD: You'll go away if I promise never to drive again?

RAT: Yes, Toad, we will.

TOAD: OK. I promise never to drive another car!

OTTER: He has his fingers crossed!

MOLE: Toad, do you?

RAT: I'm sorry, Toad. From now on one of us will have to watch you at every moment. We are going to take turns keeping you under strict guard until you come to your senses. It's for your own protection.

TOAD: But . . . but . . .

MOLE: It's no good, Toady. We've made up our minds! Who's going to guard him first?

RAT: I will. Otter, you can come relieve me in a little while.

OTTER: All right. Come on, little Mole. You can help me start fixing my porch. With this hurt toe, I don't think I can work too hard.

MOLE: *(As they exit, leaving Rat and Toad.)* Thank you, Otter. I think it would be fun to build a porch! *(They are off.)*

RAT: I've got some writing to do, Toad. Just make yourself comfortable. And please try not to disturb me . . . I'm working on a poem! *(The wind music starts up, Toad does not hear it, but Rat does.)*

TOAD: *(Sits on the table, watching Rat work. Slowly he gets an idea and slumps down until he is lying flat.)* Agh!

RAT: Sh! I'm working!

TOAD: Agh! Oogh! EEEEEEGH! *(The music stops.)*

RAT: What is it, Toad? Have you been hurt in one of the crashes?

TOAD: The pain—oh!

RAT: Come on, Toad. I'm trying to think.

TOAD: Oh! He's trying to think! I'm lying here dying, and what is he doing? He's thinking! OOH!

RAT: Nobody's dying, Toad, sh!

TOAD: Nobody's dying! *(He goes into convulsions and shock. Rat drops his poem and stares at Toad.)*

RAT: Toad—Toad—what is it?

TOAD: Oh—doctor! Please, doctor. Oh—Ratty.

RAT: A doctor? Toad! Hang on; I'll be right back. *(He rushes out, then remembers his poem. As he comes back to pick it up he catches Toad starting to sit up. Toad instantly goes back into convulsions.)* Toad. Have you been fooling me?

TOAD: No! Oh! The pain! *(More convulsions.)* Ratty, quick—and get my lawyer, too. I must make out my will! AAAAAGH!

RAT: All right. All right. Lawyer? A minute ago he was fine! Oh, dear. I'll be right back—you won't escape? *(Toad shakes his head.)* Oh, dear. *(Rat exits.)*

TOAD: Agh! *(Sits up cautiously.)* OOGH! *(Waits, and then goes to the door.)* EEEEGH!!! hahahahahaha! I've done it! Oh, clever me. Clever Toad! Poor Rat! He means well—but how could he hope to outwit me? After all, I'm not just an ordinary animal. I am Toad! The great Toad! I tricked him so well! But of course it was easy for me. Hahahaha. He thought I was dying. I would make an excellent actor. "Agh," "Oh, dear," he said. Poop-poop. I'm free. Poop-poop, poop-poop. I'm free! Poop-poop-poop-poop. *(He runs off.)*

(No sooner is he gone, however, than the lights start to fade. First one, then two, and finally five or six weasels materialize into the room. Slowly they creep in, hesitantly touching tapestries, etc., delighted to find the palatial Toad Hall unguarded. After making sure the place is deserted,

they discover the piggy bank! As their confidence grows, they make a few attempts to get it open, without success; then they start playing ball with the bank. They all join in and toss it back and forth until finally it falls to the floor and breaks, scattering money everywhere. Joyfully, they swoop down on it, scooping up the money, and chasing each other to increase their share. They end up by chasing each other off the stage. The stage remains deserted for a moment and then the scene changes to:)

SCENE SIX

A Street in the Village. A large policeman drives on in a police-car, which is very much like the other car, except it carries a stripe or pennant that says "POLICE." The policeman gets out and stretches, and goes off swinging his billyclub. The street itself may be a simple wall with many bills posted, including one which says "Red Lion Inn, one block." After a few seconds Toad comes gayly on. He sees the abandoned car, but not the POLICE sign.

TOAD: Well, look at that! Somebody has left an old motor-car just standing about on the street. Tch, tch . . . that's dreadfully careless. Why someone could come along and just steal it! Not that I would do anything like that, of course. Hmmm. I wonder whose it is? Perhaps it's broken? Maybe that's why they left it here. It probably won't even start! Hmm . . . Maybe, with my mechanical genius I could fix it! Wouldn't they be grateful if I did—they might even give me a ride! . . . I wonder if it will start? *(He cranks it and it starts.)* It does! I've fixed it already! Oh—perhaps it won't run? Poop-poop, poop-poop. I really ought to test it before I tell them that I fixed it. *(He climbs in.)* Maybe there's something else wrong with it? Just to make sure it works I really ought to drive it around the block—just once! *(He revs the motor.)* Hmm—it seems to be all right! *(He starts up and gathers speed as he careens out of sight. We hear him coming to the corner at high speed. The car hits a store window and we hear crashes and tinkles for quite a while. Then the Policeman strolls back on, munching an apple. He looks frantically for his car. Finally, he notices with shock that it stands offstage in a heap. He runs off and returns immediately dragging Toad, who has gotten his head wrapped in a sign that used to say "Red Lion Inn." The Policeman is quite upset, but Toad is calm and happy.)*

POLICEMAN: You've smashed me car! Ye villain! Ye arch-scoundrel! I'll be after seein' ye thrown in the callaboose, I will.

TOAD: I fixed it! It was broken, and I fixed it!

POLICEMAN: Well, I'll fix you, I will, I will. Get along with ye there. The judge'll be having a word to say to ye, I'm thinking. It'll be the jail for you, me buckoo!

TOAD: The jail? No wait! I was only fooling. It was only in fun. *(He is dragged off unceremoniously.)* Honest. I was only fooling . . . HELP! *(He makes his farewells as the scene changes to:)*

SCENE SEVEN

The River: In front of Rat's house. Rat and Mole enter from the wings.

RAT: I'm sorry, Mole. I thought he was sick. He really fooled me! I can't explain it—I—I—well, I was pretty silly.

MOLE: That's all right, Ratty—I'm sure he would have fooled me, too.

RAT: If I hadn't been concentrating on my poetry . . . *(The music starts.)* I . . . *(Rat hears the music.)*

MOLE: The wind, Ratty?

RAT: Yes. Can you hear it?

MOLE: No. I can see much better though. I really feel at home. Helping you and Otter save Toady—well, I mean—trying to save Toady. *(Pause.)* Where do you think he's gone to? *(The music stops.)*

RAT: Don't know.

MOLE: Well, I think I'll go over to Toad Hall and wait for him. I've baked him a little cake. I was going to give it to him to cheer him up; but maybe I shouldn't now that he's run away.

RAT: No. Go ahead. I'll stay here and wait for you. He ought to be home soon, and he likes you—maybe you can get him to take it easy.

MOLE: I'll try. Bye. *(He exits.)*

RAT: Really fooled me. Huh! *(Shrugs it off, sits down by the river.)*

OTTER: Rat! Rat! *(He limps in.)* Run for the hill—get out of here!

RAT: What is it?

OTTER: Don't stop to talk—move. I'm getting as far away as I can. The weasels are in Toad Hall! Anything could happen!

RAT: The weasels! Toad Hall! But Mole's headed that way! We've got to catch him before he gets there. Mole! Wait! *(He runs out after Mole. Otter shrugs and goes off the other way.)*

OTTER: Every man for himself—I'm getting out of here! Weasels! Yech! *(He flees cowardly as the set changes to:)*

SCENE EIGHT

The Banquet Hall: The weasels start to enter in groups, carrying Toad's belongings. They display with pleasure, and grunts of delight, the articles they have found. Alternately they rip them to pieces or put them to some foul use. Toad's finest hats get trampled or holes punched in them. Wine bottles are smashed or spilled. Shirts are torn up. One weasel appropriates a cape, and converts it into a hideous hood. Another is throwing darts at the elegant picture of Old Toad. A third tortures the ancient cuckoo clock, etc., etc. Suddenly Mole's voice is heard. The weasels scurry about for a second, and then they all hide.

MOLE: Toady, Toady, are you home? *(Enters and sees the mess.)* I've brought you a . . . cake. Oh! *(Slowly Mole comes down into the room. He sets the cake down and regards the shambles. Then he bends down and starts to straighten up. The wind music starts softly as the weasels sneak out behind Mole, and come toward him with an old sheet spread out as a net. The music suddenly becomes a warning of a fierce storm. Mole straightens up and cocks his ear—he has almost heard the message—but too late! The weasels fling the sheet around Mole and wrap him in its folds. With hilarious whoops and chuckles they push him around, and finally drag him off. Mole fights to keep his self-control, and the music mounts in volume and in agony as they drag him off with kicks and shoves. The music reluctantly dies away as the scene changes to:)*

SCENE NINE

A Jail Cell. A narrow spot of dim light in a black void. A set of bars separates the cell from a passage, lit from a different direction. A Policeman drags Toad on and thrusts him into the cell. Toad sits, sincerely repentant, and extremely dejected. The Policeman exits.

TOAD: Oh. *(Pause.)* What a foolish Toad I've been! Stole a police-car! Stole a police-car? How could it happen? OH! Forty-nine years in jail. And I deserve it; I deserve it. Oh, Rat . . . and Mole . . . oh, how can I look them in the eye again. Well, that's one problem I won't have to worry about for a while. By the time I get out of here they probably won't even remember me! *(He cries.)*

ALICE: *(Enters with a tray of food.)* Hello! [NOTE: *If the ghost of Tenniel will forgive, I see Alice as a caricature of his immortal heroine of Wonderland. She is simple and pretty, in pinafore and Alice-blue gown.*]

TOAD: Go away!

ALICE: Poor thing . . . Come on, let's have a smile! *(Toad grimaces.)* Poor thing. Here, I've brought you your food. I'm Alice, and I'll be bringing you your food every day.

TOAD: No food . . . NO! I don't deserve to eat! Oh, what a foolish Toad!

ALICE: Oh, dear. I can't stand to see an animal in tears. Poor Mr. Toad. I can't stand it! *(She starts to cry, too. Toad is challenged, and so he cries louder; so she gets louder; so he gets louder. Finally, it becomes obvious that she has him outclassed, so he shrugs and gives up sincerity for his usual "show-off"—man-ship.)*

TOAD: Well, what's the matter with you?

ALICE: I can't help it . . . an animal in trouble always makes me cry.

TOAD: Well, no sense in both of us crying. *(He starts to recover, when suddenly an idea strikes him.)* OH! How cruel life is. OH! *(Watches her carefully.)* Misery. Wrongfully imprisoned—oh, oh, oh. *(Peeks at her.)*

ALICE: What is it?

TOAD: I was framed! It wasn't me that did the crime—it was some other Toad. Oh, my poor Mother, this will break her heart. I'm innocent, completely innocent; and yet I'm doomed to suffer in this cruel penitentiary for the crimes of another. Oh, is there no justice in the world?

ALICE: Are you innocent?

TOAD: Innocent. Innocent. Oh, innocent. What is more—I am not guilty. When my Mother finds out that I am in jail, it will break her heart. She will die from grief, when she finds out. Any minute now she'll find out.

ALICE: *(Bawls.)* Oh.

TOAD: Unless . . .

ALICE: Unless what?

TOAD: Yes. I must do it! I hate to break the law but I must save my poor sweet Mother. I must escape!

ALICE: Escape?

TOAD: Yes. And you must help me!

ALICE: Yes—I will help you. Oh, what a brave Toad. Risking everything for his poor old mother. I will help you.

TOAD: Good! But how? How will you help me escape?

ALICE: *(After a few seconds' pause.)* I have it! I have an old dress that used to belong to my aunt, who was a very respectable washerwoman.

TOAD: A washerwoman?

ALICE: Yes. Quick—you wait here and I'll get the dress. You can put it on, and in that disguise no one will recognize you. You can just walk out the door.

TOAD: A washerwoman! I don't know. It doesn't sound very romantic. Still I suppose I'm not in any position to choose. DONE! Where is this famous disguise?

ALICE: Oh, you brave animal. Wait here. I'll see you out of this cruel prison within the hour. *(She exits, and Toad breaks into gales of laughter.)*

TOAD: Hahahahaha! "Poor thing," she said. "Oh, my poor dear Mother," I said! hahahahah. Oh, the poor girl! No match for me at all. No match for the clever intelligent fantabulous stupendous colossal brain of Toad! haha . . .

ALICE: *(Returns with a hideous and overlarge housedress and an equally distasteful scarf.)* Here, Mr. Toad. Put this on. *(She helps him quickly don the outfit, to his disgust. He curtsys grotesquely, and straightens his girdle.)* Good. Follow me. *(She exits, he curtsys once more and follows her off. The set changes to:)*

SCENE TEN

Badger's House: Badger enters with Otter.

OTTER: Well, where in the world is Rat? I don't understand why he sent me that message to meet him at your house if he wasn't going to be here! I've got better things to do than sit around and wait for Rat!

BADGER: Simmer down! Rat'll be here. If he says to meet him here, he'll be here. Humph! Can't say as I approve of all the excitement, though. Bet you anything you like it's got something to do with that young rascal of a Toad.

RAT: *(Enters breathlessly.)* Both here! Good!

OTTER: I want you to know that I was just leaving to spend a week with my cousins down the River, when I got your message! What do you want?

RAT: Good of you to come, Otter . . . Mole's been captured by the weasels!

BADGER: What's that?

RAT: I tried to stop him but I was too late. The weasels have taken over Toad Hall; and Mole just walked right in! There's no telling what they're doing to him—right now!

OTTER: Little Mole captured? I don't believe it! The weasels wouldn't dare. It's impossible!

RAT: Go look for yourself. All the windows are broken, there's furniture all over the yard, and I could see Mole tied up in front of the banquet hall window!

BADGER: I knew it would happen. I could see it coming. Ever since Old Toad died those weasels have been getting more and more uppity! When he and I were still young, they wouldn't have dared touch a Riverbanker. The world's going to pot. Yes, sir, going to pot!

RAT: No it isn't, Badger—it's changed, that's all. The weasels still wouldn't be able to stand up to us! Not if we all fought together. We've got to get Toad Hall and Mole back. We've got to fight!

OTTER: Fight! Ratty, be serious! We wouldn't have a chance!

RAT: Yes we would. The weasels are disorganized, and we could be a team!

OTTER: But fight? That's silly! I'm sure they'll let Mole go in a couple of days. They're only trying to scare us. And as for Toad Hall—it's Toad's fault the whole thing happened; I say he deserves to have his house wrecked for him!

BADGER: Hold your tongue! Toad Hall was Old Toad's pride and joy. No weasel's going to set foot in that place while there's still a breath in my body!

OTTER: Badger? Do you mean, you're actually going to go with Rat? And fight?

BADGER: You bet I am—and so are you! Once the weasels get the idea they can get away with capturing Mole, they'll never be stopped! I'm getting old—but I can still swing a club! Let's go get 'em, Rat. I'm with you!

OTTER: But . . . but . . . *(Shrugs.)* ME TOO! Let's go!

TOAD: *(Entering from offstage.)* Badger! Rat! Are you here? *(He comes in, still in his disguise.)* Oh, hi, fellows!

RAT: Can I help you, madam?

TOAD: It's me! It's Toad! I've just escaped from jail! *(Discards dress.)*

ALL: Jail?

TOAD: I was just on my way to Toad Hall to tell you how clever I've been . . . when . . . oh, Ratty, the weasels are running all over my house . . . and they have Moley a prisoner!

RAT: We know.

OTTER: It's all your fault, nincompoop! Horses! And Motor Cars! Yech!

TOAD: You're right. I know it. I've been so stupid. Help me please! I'll never do anything silly again. I promise! But I've got to get Toad Hall back.

RAT: I hope you mean that, Toad.

BADGER: Humph! Get the clubs, Otter. *(He gets them off the wall and passes them out.)* Now everybody hush, I have a plan! It's almost suppertime, and if I know weasels, and I ought to by now, they'll be having some sort of celebration over the capture of Toad Hall. All we have to do is sneak through the secret tunnel, take them by surprise, and send them into such a fright they won't stop running for a week.

OTTER: Secret tunnel? Is there a secret tunnel into Toad Hall?

TOAD: There most certainly is not! If there were I think I should know about it, and I've never heard of such a thing—never!

BADGER: My dear Toad—your father was a very sensible animal—which is not true of his son. Old Toad was much too clever to let an irresponsible scalawag like you know about such a valuable thing as a secret tunnel. But he told me all about it; with instructions to make use of it only in case of great emergency. I think the time has finally come to make use of that secret. So follow me! *(They start off.)*

TOAD: A secret tunnel? A secret tunnel! *(They are forced to wait for Toad.)* What fun! How splendid! I can see it all now! The weasels will calmly be drinking their beer—or rather my beer—when up from the most secret secret secret in the whole castle, the mighty TOAD, armed to the teeth!, fighting off dozens at a time—slashing here—stabbing there—*(He is fighting the army off singlehandedly, by now.)*—one by one, the weasels will die! On fights Toad! Until, at last, only ONE weasel, the toughest, is left! Gradually the great Toad backs him into the staircase

(Suiting action to words.) . . . parrying . . . thrusting . . . en garde . . . OH! He got me! Everything is going black! . . . but first, take that! *(He stabs the opponent and lightly tosses his sword away.)* Oh! I'm going . . . farewell . . . ugh. *(Dies, downstage center.)* . . . *(Sits up.)* Pretty good, huh?

OTTER: Baby! I don't think I want to save Toad Hall for that idiot!

RAT: Toad, do you want help or don't you? *(Toad nods.)* Then please behave yourself.

TOAD: I'm sorry.

BADGER: Humph! How could Old Toad have such a nitwit for a son?

TOAD: I've reformed! I have. I promise! I'll never do another silly thing! Honest!

RAT: You've got one more chance, Toad. Even I'm getting a little annoyed.

TOAD: I promise! You'll see—I'm a new Toad!

BADGER: Humph! Let go!

RAT: You lead, Badger—but remember, we don't want a massacre; we only want Toad Hall and Mole back! *(They follow Badger off and the scene changes to:)*

SCENE ELEVEN

The Banquet Hall: The weasels are having a party. They whoop, grunt, and laugh as they drink beer and wine, continue to smash Toad's belongings, swing from the chandelier, throw food at each other, and occasionally taunt Mole, who has been pushed in and is kept in a corner. One weasel saws at the furniture. Mole's cake is brought in, they all take turns licking at it, finally placing it on the table, where they return for occasional finger's-full of icing, which they flick at each other or at Mole. They are a little tipsy, but not drunk. After a few moments of loud destruction, the action onstage freezes, the lights die away, and we are left with a party tableau. Slowly a trap door opens way downstage. Badger appears from the secret tunnel; followed by Rat, the Otter, and finally Toad.

TOAD: Hey, fellows!

ALL THREE: SHHHH!

TOAD: Oops! *(Whispers.)* Hey, where are we?

BADGER: Under the banquet hall. If you took the trouble to be quiet, you could hear the weasels right above us!

TOAD: Well, let's go get 'em!

RAT: Go slow, Toad. We must first make sure that Mole's all right.

OTTER: Shall we all attack at once? Who's giving the signal?

BADGER: I am! When I say "go," make as much noise as you can! Our best hope is to scare the living daylights out of them. Then we only have to fight the ones who don't run very fast! Well, are you ready? Report!

OTTER: I'm ready, Badger. Whenever you say.

RAT: Ready!

TOAD: I'll learn 'em to mess with my house!

OTTER: Moron! It's teach 'em, not learn 'em—teach 'em!

TOAD: But I don't want to teach 'em. I want to learn 'em—and learn 'em good!

RAT: All right. Shh!

BADGER: Follow me! *(They start out. Toad tries to get to the front, but Otter makes sure he comes last.)*

TOAD: *(As he disappears.)* I'll learn 'em and learn 'em and learn 'em . . .

(The lights come back up onstage, and the party continues. One weasel pulls down Old Toad's portrait from the wall, and crashes it onto Mole's head. Two of them start trying to pull the picture off. Inadvertently they pull Mole into the center of the room. They get the picture off but continue to pull at Mole. The others join in, until there is a circle around Mole and they are all grunting and gesturing wildly at the helpless victim. They get more and more primitive, and finally they are doing a savage rhythmical dance and chant around Mole's prostrate form. As they stop to breathe—there is suddenly a blood-chilling yell piercing the

room. It is the terrible Badger battle-cry. Rat, Toad, and Otter join the screeching, and confusion reigns among the panicky weasels. The weasels manage to draw their swords, just as the friends sweep into view. For a minute the weasels fight united, and succeed in forcing back the charge. At last, however, Badger breaks into the ranks and the pack splits. Rat helps Mole to get free, and he seizes the saw and joins the fight. In smaller groups the weasels are outclassed and one by one they are overtaken, disarmed, and sent packing. Toad several times comes close to a fight, but each time succeeds in avoiding any conflict. Finally he hides behind the table, to escape notice. One weasel, cleverer than the rest, pretends he is hit, and falls to the floor. By now the weasels are beaten and they all surrender and run for the protection of their Woods, leaving pride and weapons behind them. The Riverbankers are congratulating themselves on their victory, when the shamming weasel slowly rises, and, sword in hand, makes straight for the unsuspecting Mole. Suddenly they all see him threatening—but they are too far away to prevent Mole's certain death! At that instant, Toad comes up from behind the table, grabs the cake, and places it square in the face of the threatening enemy. The last weasel drops his sword in disgust, and is quickly ushered out by Rat and Otter. They all stand, victoriously, regarding the mess and disorder of the once palatial Toad Hall.)

OTTER: Toad Hall is ours!

RAT: Good fighting! Thanks, Badger, Otter!

BADGER: Humph! Can't say them weasels were much of a challenge. I can remember really having to fight, course that was back a few years—Old Toad and I held off a pack of wolves once—just the two of us! This was easy!

RAT: Anyway, they won't be back for a while!

MOLE: Thanks, Toady—you saved my life!

TOAD: Oh, it was nothing, for an animal like me! *(The others stare at him fiercely.)* I mean . . . er . . . it was the least I could do! You all risked your lives to help me, and I certainly didn't deserve it.

OTTER: Well, I hope you realize it.

TOAD: I know I've been foolish, and believe me, Ratty, and Otter, and Badger, you, too—I'm sorry! Getting thrown in jail, risking the lives of my friends, and the name of animals everywhere . . . *(The sound of an airplane is heard.)* . . . I have been . . . what's that noise? . . . I . . . *(Looks up at sky.)* . . . I was foolish and . . . oh. *("That" look comes into his eyes.)* Oh, did you see it? Or was it a dream?

MOLE: See what?

TOAD: That little yellow airplane! Those lovely wings . . . what grace . . . what a way to travel . . . Poetry in motion! *(He becomes aware that the others are advancing on him with mayhem in their eyes.)* Er . . . er . . . I was only kidding, fellows—honest—I'm a reformed animal—a new Toad! I am! Help! *(The four close in on him. Rat hands him a broom and gestures to the mess. Toad starts to clean up the mess, quite sincerely interested in creating a good impression. He picks up the mutilated picture of Old Toad, which Badger promptly snatches from him. Toad keeps right on working and Badger beckons to them all and starts out. Otter follows him and these two go out. Rat and Mole start out together, when the wind music starts up again.)*

MOLE: Oh, Rat—the wind! I think I hear it!

RAT: Of course! Come on—I think today I can teach you how to swim. *(They go off, but Moley turns back to the door to the hard-working Toad.)*

MOLE: Bye, Toady—hurry up and finish this, then you can come swimming— *(He rushes off.)*

(Toad stops and sighs—gradually he begins to think about the plane, and the broom in his hands starts to turn into the wings of a yellow airplane. He starts to fly around the stage gathering speed, the sound of the plane is his accompaniment. As he approaches the exit, however, he checks himself, and sadly returns to sweeping. The sound of the plane continues to swell as Toad imagines he is firing rockets, etc. But he continues to sweep the floor—or does he?)

CURTAIN

JIM THORPE, ALL-AMERICAN

by

SAUL LEVITT

with music by Saul Levitt

JIM THORPE, ALL-AMERICAN

CHARACTERS

Jim Thorpe
Black Hawk
Hiram Thorpe
Nikifer
Welch
Colonel Pratt
Pop Warner

SETTING

The action of the play takes place in Oklahoma; Lawrence, Kansas; Texas; Carlisle, Pennsylvania; the football stadia of the nation; at the 1912 Olympics in Stockholm; in California and in the spirit world of the great Indian Chiefs.

(A tape of Harrison Fisher's music for this play can be ordered from Anchorage Press.)

A semi-circle of poles around the edges of an inclined circle; a "wagon" or low-lying platform on wheels which can be moved about.

At opening: Jim Thorpe is on platform DR which now serves as a classroom. Other chiefs are reclining at their spots on set.

SONG: *(All but Thorpe.)* Hi ya way ya ya, etc.

BLACK HAWK: My brother chiefs of the Indian nations, I, Black Hawk, call you out of the great dark to witness this youth who struggles to be free . . . *(They appear as he calls . . .)* Cochise of the Apache tribe, Tecumseh of the Shawnee, Kicking Bird of the Kiowa, Crazy Horse of the Sioux, Seattle of the Northwest Suquaimish.

CRAZY HORSE: Why are we summoned, Black Hawk?

COCHISE: The light blinds me—

KICKING BIRD: *(Overlapping.)* What is there to see?

TECUMSEH: *(Indicating Thorpe.)* Who is this?

SEATTLE: Why should we watch him—

COCHISE: Is he a chief's son?

BLACK HAWK: He is Jim Thorpe. His Indian name is Wa Tho Huk which means Bright Path.

SEATTLE: Of what tribe is he?

BLACK HAWK: He is of my tribe, the Sac and Fox and of my clan, the Thunder Clan. Born—by the white man's reckoning—1888. Look at him.

COCHISE: He moves as if caged.

BLACK HAWK: He is held within the white man's walls.

CRAZY HORSE: Then he will never be free.

KICKING BIRD: It is painful to watch and remember . . .

CRAZY HORSE: Let us go back into the dark . . .

SEATTLE: Back to the long sleep . . .

BLACK HAWK: Wait . . .

CRAZY HORSE: For what? We were mighty warriors. Great chiefs.

TECUMSEH: Fearless against the white man . . .

KICKING BIRD: And we lost . . .

COCHISE: And if we could not be free, then how . . .

BLACK HAWK: Wait!

CRAZY HORSE: For what? He has no weapons. No braves follow him. Our Indian life is gone forever . . .

COCHISE: It is useless.

BLACK HAWK: My brothers, didn't I say that myself when I was beaten by the white man? Wasn't mine the darkest heart among you? Yet in this youth I feel the roots of Indian life still live. My brother chiefs! *(He waits for them to place their hands on his.)* I ask you to watch Jim Thorpe's struggle to win against the white man.

(Teacher Scene. All Chiefs have put on gray coats.)

CRAZY HORSE: You've got to stay in school!

COCHISE: You have to learn to read!

TECUMSEH: Learn to write!

KICKING BIRD: Learn to spell!

SEATTLE: Spell freedom!

(Break out.)

SONG: Hi ya way ya, etc.

(Black Hawk steps toward pole [it will be Thorpe's pole], and unwinds rope from it, carrying it toward others.)

BLACK HAWK: Listen to me, my brother chiefs. I have a vision of the life to come of Wa Tho Huk or Jim Thorpe. Here is his lifeline . . . *(Hands rope off.)* I see him winning many victories . . . but I do not see everything clearly . . .

CHORUSING VOICES: Try. Try, Black Hawk . . .

BLACK HAWK: I see him running across a field knocking down enemies . . . I see great crowds watching him . . . Medals of gold will be hung around his neck . . . He will be given gifts by mighty kings . . . It is not easy to see him further.

VOICES: Try, Black Hawk . . .

BLACK HAWK: I see a fire stick carried onto a field, where many watch. I see the flags of many nations. I see him run . . . I see him hurl a spear . . . I see him leap . . . I hear the crowd roar . . . He wins great glory . . .

KICKING BIRD: And what then?

BLACK HAWK: Beyond that it grows darker . . . *(He cries out as the rope is joined behind him.)* But from the beginning he howled in pain when the walls were around him. He could not endure being held in . . . Will he win or lose? We shall see . . .

(The Chiefs step away, leaving only Black Hawk.)

(Thorpe leaps into arena. Spreads arms in joy. His movements are as if he is in a wooded area . . . Finds his hidden "shotgun" and puts it over his shoulder . . . sights game . . . points gun . . . fires . . . moves to game . . . which he carries back to "fire." Lies down near fire, relaxed and happy . . . Hiram Thorpe, Jim's father, observes scene. Hiram sneaks up and kicks Thorpe on the butt.)

THORPE: Pa!

HIRAM: Knew where to find you alright. Along the river always near this old cottonwood. Every time you bust out of school. An' there ain't but one thing to do when you bust out an' that's to whup you.

THORPE: Pa, put me back there, and I'll bust out again—that's for sure.

HIRAM: Dammit, you got to learn . . . *(Strikes him. Chiefs wince.)*

THORPE: Don't like that learning. White man learning.

HIRAM: Great grandfather of yours was a white man. You ain't all Indian.

THORPE: Indian enough . . .

HIRAM: We ain't blanket Indians anyway . . .

THORPE: Indians all the same.

HIRAM: Want you to have it better, and don't know how. Put you to the Mission School five miles away and you walk home. Put you to the Agency School, that's twenty miles away, figurin' you won't walk back twenty miles—an' you walk back twenty miles . . . What do you tell them teachers when you bust out?

THORPE: Tell 'em . . . I got to be outside . . .

HIRAM: What's that mean, "outside"?

(Thorpe waves hands inarticulately . . . the gesture seems to express something about space—the sky.)

HIRAM: *(Looks up and around.)* What you gonna do with all that "outside"? *(Spots shotgun and "goose.")* See you got yourself a goose . . . *(Hefts it.)* Nice size bird . . . Ain't much game left anymore. All of us outside once . . . hunters. *(Black Hawk nods in agreement.)* No more buffalo, no more livin' like the Sac and Fox used to . . . *(Shouting.)* and you're goin' to school . . .

THORPE: Ain't neither . . .

HIRAM: Yes, you're goin' alright and you'll never walk back from this one.

THORPE: Which one?

HIRAM: Haskell Indian School. That's off in Lawrence, Kansas . . .

THORPE: Lawrence, *where?*

HIRAM: *Kansas.* An' that's three hundred miles. An' you ain't walking back three hundred miles.

(Thorpe is hustled out of clearing by his father. They disappear. Thorpe is pushed by his father aboard platform which is now a train . . . We might hear the chugging sound of the steam engine . . . The train whistle sounds . . .)

CONDUCTOR VOICE: Arriving in Lawrence, Ka-a-a-nsas. Home of the Haskell Indian School.

(Thorpe reappears on wagon platform which is now a classroom . . . The others become "teachers" donning their gray coats. They block his way.)

SEATTLE: Where are you going . . . Jim?

COCHISE: You've got to stay.

CRAZY HORSE AND KICKING BIRD: Stay and learn.

(Thorpe breaks out.)

SONG: Hi ya way ya, etc.

CRAZY HORSE: Where are you going, Jim Thorpe?

THORPE: I'm catching the first train out of here, no matter where it goes. *(We hear train sounds. Thorpe leaps aboard platform, now a train, rolling over . . . Railroad man, in white mask, enters "car" . . .)*

RAILROAD MAN: *(Calling offstage.)* Hey, Joe! You're right on time. Crossin' into Texas . . . *(He spots Thorpe.)* Well, now . . . *(Peers.)* Damned Injun . . .

ALL SING: Hi ya way ya, etc.

(Railroad Man swings "billy" which Thorpe evades . . . leaps off . . . He reappears in arena which is now a corral.)

RANCHER: *(Enters with horse.)* Hey, Thorpe. Nobody on this ranch has been able to break this bronco, an' I'll bet you can't either.

THORPE: We'll have to see about that. *(Business of rancher holding down horse's head . . . horse plunging . . . Thorpe mounts.)* Let him buck! *(Chiefs whoop it up. Spectacle of breaking horse . . . horse growing tired . . . leaps shorter.)* OK, you pony . . . gettin' used to me now . . . sure . . . easy now . . . easy . . . easy . . . Well, I guess I'll be goin' . . . I've saved some money and I'd like to buy this pony.

RANCHER: Can't get you to stay? You can't work every ranch in West Texas, y' know. It's too big. Stick around. I'll give you a raise . . .

THORPE: See that pony, Mr. Smith? . . . You see him nice an' quiet? Ready to be rode? Well now, that's what I don't want happening to me . . . I don't want to be broke and bridled and rode . . . Just want to feel free.

RANCHER: *(Laughing.)* Well, if you ain't something! *(Rancher laughs, nods, disappears. Thorpe reappears in arena as if riding horse . . . dismounts to face father . . . Black Hawk puts horse's head on Thorpe's pole.)*

HIRAM: There you are. They wrote me you left school. Where you been?

THORPE: Texas.

HIRAM: What you got to say about Texas?

THORPE: *(Scratches head, thinking.)* There's lots of it.

HIRAM: Damn near fourteen months you been down there. Learn a thing or two? *(Chief hands Thorpe lasso.)*

THORPE: Sure did. *(Twirls lasso expertly.)*

HIRAM: Now that you learned a thing or two in Texas . . . you're gonna learn another thing or two in Pennsylvania . . .

THORPE: *Where?*

HIRAM: Carlisle Indian School in Pennsylvania . . .

THORPE: Ain't goin' to no school nowhere . . .

(Hiram swings at Thorpe who evades his father. Hiram swings again and this time Thorpe grabs his arm . . . Hiram forcing, Thorpe holding . . . a silent duel of strength . . . Hiram gives up . . . They step apart looking at one another.)

THORPE: You ain't hittin' me again . . .

(They circle and fight until Thorpe gets Hiram in airplane spin as Chiefs whoop. Thorpe sets Hiram down.)

HIRAM: Growin' up strong, ain't you?

THORPE: Pretty strong.

HIRAM: And dumb . . . That's how you're gonna be . . . just like your old man—puttin' in time in the Black Dog saloon.

THORPE: No, I ain't, because I ain't stayin' here.

HIRAM: Where you goin'?

THORPE: Somewheres . . . Somewhere where there's lots and lots of outside. *(Making a widearmed gesture.) (Black Hawk plays flute softly, refrain heard earlier . . . Thorpe seems to cock head toward sound.)*

HIRAM'S VOICE: *(Calculatingly indifferent.)* Suit yourself. Thought you might want to be somebody someday.

THORPE: *(Uncertainly.)* Well . . . sure.

HIRAM: Have money in your pocket . . .

THORPE: Well, *sure* . . .

HIRAM: Then you got to go to school . . .

THORPE: *(Nods reluctantly . . . the nods become slower and slower . . . stopping . . . and then . . .)* No more hunting deer, turkey, quail?

HIRAM: No more—

THORPE: No more fishing, no more breaking wild horses?

HIRAM: No more—

THORPE: I ain't goin'—

HIRAM: *(Starts offstage.)* Suit yourself. That's your business . . . You're gettin' big enough an' strong enough to do whatever you want . . .

THORPE: Why should I listen to you?

HIRAM: So you don't have to become . . . what I am . . . *(Pause.)*

THORPE: Where did you say this school was?

HIRAM: Carlisle, Pennsylvania. An' if you go there, you got to forget about walkin' back, because you *can't* walk back from there.

THORPE: Why not?

HIRAM: Because it's a thousand miles and even if you was the walkin'est Indian in the world, you ain't walkin' back a thousand miles.

THORPE: *A thousand miles!* What's that place?

HIRAM: I told you. Carlisle, Pennsylvania. *(Scene of new Indian arrivals at Carlisle. They include Thorpe and Others whom we will get to know. All of them wear their hair long, some with knots in the back, all in Indian style dress. They look about uneasily. "Colonel Pratt," superintendent of Carlisle, appears on the platform—talking as he is pulled across stage.)*

PRATT: My name is Colonel Pratt, Superintendent of Carlisle Indian School—welcome to the greatest training school for Indians in the country. Look around, boys. Look at those fine buildings all around this green. I'll bet you never saw a place that looked as civilized as this. Not a tepee or a hogan or a lean-to in sight. Civilized. And that's what we're going to make you.

(Thorpe cocks his head—flute sound heard in distance—Pratt continuing:)

PRATT: The Indian comes into Carlisle as a savage and goes out civilized. We civilize you. *Civilize.* You don't talk Sioux or Apache or Chippewa talk here; you talk and read and write English. Every time you talk Indian you will lose privileges. You're going to forget your Indian ways because they're no use in the United States of America. We're here to help you fit in . . . for your own good . . . Now you've got to live among us, and that's a fact, isn't it? So you might as well forget your ways, and learn ours . . . for your own good . . . *(Walking among them.)* You'll sleep on mattresses—under roofs. You'll learn to brush your teeth—take baths—learn a trade. We are going to civilize you. *Civilize. Civilize. Civilize . . . (Pratt's voice penetrating.) You . . . (Pratt is looking at Thorpe.)* What's your name?

THORPE: James Thorpe . . .

PRATT: You want to learn to pay attention, Thorpe.

THORPE: Yes, sir . . . *(Students bring out mat. Thorpe whispers to boy next to him, Welch.)* I'm ready to leave now.

WELCH: Take it easy!

THORPE: What's your name?

WELCH: Gus Welch—Chippewa.

THORPE: Sac and Fox.

(They handwrestle.)

WELCH: Say, Thorpe, let's bunk next to each other.

THORPE: OK.

BUNK SCENE

NIKIFER: They expect us to sleep on these things? I don't like this place one bit.

ED: It's scary.

THORPE: How much do we have to take from this white man, Colonel Pratt?

ED: Let's run away.

EMIL: That's not a bad idea.

NIKIFER: We can't. We have to get civilized.

WELCH: They'll tell us all over again how Columbus discovered America.

THORPE: Ain't that a laugh!

NIKIFER: Even though we Indians were here all the time.

EMIL: Nobody's cuttin' my hair.

ED: Mine either.

WELCH: What are you goin' to do to stop it?

NIKIFER: I think I'm goin' to be sick.

WELCH: I'm thinking about how a loon cries waiting for a wind to help it off a lake . . . in Wisconsin.

THORPE: I'm thinking of a bird too . . . a high-flying bird over the North Canadian in Oklahoma. He's looking down . . . he sees all the way down to where a mouse moves under the leaves.

WELCH: A hawk . . .

THORPE: A black hawk . . . I wish I was where that hawk is . . . in those woods.

EMIL: This is no place for the fighting Cheyenne.

THORPE: Cheyenne! Sac and Fox, Jim Thorpe—Oklahoma Territory.

EMIL: Emil Wauseka, Nebraska.

ED: Ed Two Hearts—Sioux.

THORPE: *(To Nikifer.)* Hello, little fella.

NIKIFER: Hello, big fella. *(They shake hands and Nikifer flips Thorpe on his back. Thorpe laughs.)*

THORPE: Say, what's your name?

NIKIFER: Nikifer Shouchuck. *Inuit*—Eskimo to you.

VOICES: Eskimo . . . Is that Indian? . . . Where you from?

NIKIFER: Alaska. Of course we're Indian. Just different, that's all.

WELCH: Eskimos hunt seals, don't they?

NIKIFER: *(Leaping on Welch . . . they roll down mat.)* Harpoon 'em . . . and eat 'em and wear the furs. And live in snow houses. We call them igloos.

THORPE: Say, I noticed something about you.

NIKIFER: *(Grins; makes a face.)* I think I know what you're going to say.

THORPE: What?

NIKIFER: *(Turning here—there—)* I have the sharpest teeth you've ever seen . . . *(Inviting inspection; they crowd around him.)*

VOICES: Yeah . . . Holy Smoke . . . Gee whiz . . .

NIKIFER: Know why we sharpen 'em?

VOICES: Why?

NIKIFER: So we can strike a flint on 'em and make sparks—to start a fire!

VOICES: No kidding! . . . Wow! . . . Never heard . . .

NIKIFER: And if you believe that, I'll tell you another— *(He laughs.) (Advances mock-menacing on Thorpe as he speaks:)* I can make a face so ferocious that I can scare a polar bear. *(Thorpe "rears up" playing polar bear . . . then falls down "dead.")*

THORPE: *(Standing up.)* Make a noise like a seal. *(Nikifer gets down on his knees and moves about like a seal using flippers . . . barks . . . a loud seal bark.)*

MONITOR: Hey, no dogs allowed in the dormitory. *(Monitor bursts into dorm, peers.)* OK, you guys, where's the dog?

VOICE: What dog?

NIKIFER: *(Overlapping.)* *(Winking—signalling.)* Yeah, sure . . . *(Indicating.)* Went under *there,* didn't it? *(As Monitor turns and bends to search . . . Nikifer barks. Monitor whips around . . . Everybody "looking" for dog.)*

VOICES: This way . . . under my bunk . . . yeah, this way . . .

MONITOR: What's it look like?

THORPE: *(Behind Monitor's back: holds hand level with top of Nikifer's head.)* Big . . . real *big* . . . and it's got the sharpest teeth you ever saw— *(On this, Nikifer rushes swiftly behind Monitor and bites him on leg. Monitor cries out.)*

MONITOR: Wise guys. You better behave if you know what's good for you. Now it's time for lights out. *(He goes out.)*

THORPE: *(Shouts in Sac dialect.)* Mah no chee na way nee way tah. *(Monitor bursts in again.)*

MONITOR: Alright. Who talked Indian talk in here?

ALL: *(Snores.)* *(Stares hard at Thorpe.)* Somebody around here's starting off on the wrong foot. *(Snores.)* Lucky I don't understand Sac talk . . . *(Snores.)*

VOICES: Hey, Thorpe, what did you call him?

THORPE: I called him big chief pain-in-the-neck.

(Bell.)

MONITOR: Rise and shine. Jim Thorpe, front and center. It's your turn, Thorpe. *(Haircut—on counts—Monitor pulls out Thorpe's braids. Then bell.)* Fall in! Two minutes to drillfield, or you lose your weekend privileges. One-two-three-four. One-two-three-four.

(All run out. Bell rings. Re-appear in marching formation. Step forward in one-two-three-four as Monitor plays Drill Sergeant. As Monitor goes on they will shift to the right and then to the left—and then face around to march forward.)

MONITOR: Shop class in two minutes, or you lose your recreation period. One-two-three-four. One-two-three-four. *(Bell rings.)* One minute to bakery class *(Activity.)* One-two-three-four . . . *(Bell rings.)* Thirty seconds to Print shop— *(Activity.) (Bell rings. They shift to left.)* Hup-tup-thrup-four— Nothing flat to the Tailor Shop! *(Bell rings.) (All appear in "Tailor Shop." Thorpe arrives late. He works with needle and thread in growing frustration. Other students are busy operating "sewing machines." One student "presses" a pair of pants. Thorpe puts down cloth and throws away needle and thread with violent motion, cries out, "No!"—stalks out—Welch after him.)*

WELCH: Jim . . .

PRATT'S VOICE: Where are you going, Thorpe? *(They move as if through hall—"walking" rapidly, Welch tagging after Thorpe.)*

WELCH: What are you going to do?

THORPE: Walk back to Oklahoma.

WELCH: I'm willing to give Carlisle more of a try . . .

THORPE: But I'm not . . . *(Scene continues "outside.")* . . . I'm just going to keep on going!

WELCH: Where?

THORPE: Where it's wide open—Texas—

WELCH: And do what?

THORPE: Break wild horses . . . *(Welch turns back—discouraged—disappears as Pratt appears.)*

PRATT: You've got it the wrong way around, Thorpe. You Indians have got to be broken like wild horses.

WARNER: What's a track-and-field team without a decent high-jumper? Okay guys, let's try again! *(He picks up "cross-bar.")* Next! *(Man jumps.)* Next! *(Man jumps.)* Next!

THORPE: Nobody's breaking me! Nobody! *(Pratt turns and disappears. Thorpe runs and then takes off in high jump.) (As Warner measures off Thorpe's leap . . . Music.)*

BLACK HAWK: Listen to me, my brother chiefs . . . *(As they appear at their poles.)* You see how he leaps . . . It is his feeling to be free that gives him his power . . . *(Begins to tap softly on drum . . .)* It begins now . . .

CHIEFS: What?

BLACK HAWK: Jim Thorpe's discovery of a path.

WARNER: Hey, you! Know what you've done? Damn near broke the American record for the high jump . . . Ever high jump before?

THORPE: Nope.

BLACK HAWK: For an Indian, it is right, is it not?

CHIEFS: *(Chanting.)* It is right for us to jump . . . very right.

WARNER: My name's Pop Warner—

THORPE: Everybody knows who you are. I'm Thorpe. Jim Thorpe.

(Warner disappears but goes on speaking.)

WARNER'S VOICE: Think you can run too?

THORPE: I can run some.

CHIEFS: Being Indians—of course.

WARNER'S VOICE: Jump hurdles?

THORPE: Maybe. *(Track suit flies out—Thorpe grabs it.)*

WARNER OFF-STAGE: Played any baseball? *(Throws him bat.)*

CHIEFS: Did we not all our lives have to leap over rocks and streams? *(Black Hawk drumming continues.)* Were we not athletes in order to survive?

THORPE: Little bit. *(Thorpe takes bat and swings it as if facing pitcher.)*

WARNER OFF-STAGE: Football? *(Gives him helmet.)*

THORPE: Once or twice *(Thorpe takes football stance . . . A football flies out, Thorpe catches it, hefts it . . . Football equipment flies out at him . . . pants, helmet, Carlisle red jersey . . . He puts on gear.)*

BLACK HAWK: Didn't we need the hawk's eye to hunt with? The wolf's instinct to track? The spring of the antelope in our legs to run down the enemy? The power of the bear's paw to knock him down? And for our very lives to win our hunting grounds?

(In counterpoint to song Thorpe has run "down field" and has "scored" . . . touches ball to ground . . . raises it in air in a victory salute . . . then tucks football under arm in a familiar Thorpe pose, holds helmet in other hand—.) (Warner appears.)

WARNER: He's ready.

CHIEFS: He has found a path— *(Black Hawk drums louder—the steady beat carrying over into next scene and then lowering . . . but it stays . . . Warner blows whistle . . . The Chiefs become the Indian players . . . Warner stands along edge of "field.")*

WARNER: Shouchuck! . . . *(As Warner calls out names of players, they will jog out on field, in the high-stepping jogging style of players running onto a football field.)* Welch! . . . Thorpe! . . . *(Now there are Thorpe, Welch and Shouchuck on field . . . They run in a slow trotting motion around the field as Warner exhorts . . .)*

WARNER: *(Claps hands in a staccato beat.)* Men, you're off to a season of showing this country Indians can play the best football it's ever seen. You're going to be outweighed and outmanned, but what's that to Indians? Haven't they always been outmanned—outgunned? You've got to make up for it with speed, kicking, and great plays they've never seen . . . and tomorrow you play . . . Army! One of the powerhouse teams of the east— *(The three Carlisle players move faster now . . . We are still listening to the drum beat of Black Hawk . . .)* Army, men, Army. I want you to remember the massacres at Sand Creek and Wounded Knee . . .

BLACK HAWK: Remember, remember . . .

WARNER: The Trail of Tears to Oklahoma . . .

BLACK HAWK: Too many tears! . . .

WARNER: The massacre at Fort Lincoln—

BLACK HAWK: Too much death! . . .

NIKIFER: What does he want us to do—scalp them?

WARNER: That's right, Shouchuck! On the scoreboard.

(Whistle begins and ends each game.)

Opposing Indians: "Army" Scene

(Game is played: music and drumbeat of Black Hawk . . . Enact snap from center by Shouchuck to Welch and handoff to Thorpe who runs and straightarms and goes through two "Army" players to cross the goal.

Warner shows score on blackboard. "Carlisle 27 Army 6." Chiefs whoop. All run off field . . . The three Carlisle men appear and pattern of pre-game is repeated as Thorpe trots with slight limp . . .)

Opposing Indians: "Pennsylvania" Scene

WARNER: *(As game progresses.)* You better take Penn . . . You've gotta take Penn . . . You're gonner take Penn . . . You've taken Penn! 16 to nothing. *(As he says this we are in Penn game. A fake handoff to Thorpe but it goes to Welch with Thorpe taking out a Penn defense man . . . and Welch scores . . . "Warner" carries sign across "field," "Carlisle 16, Penn 0)*

WELCH: And now—Harvard!

CONDUCTOR: *(Calling.)* All aboard for Boston . . . Boston, Massachusetts next stop . . . *(Beat.)* Tickets . . . tickets, please. *(Conductor goes.)*

NIKIFER: Say, Conductor, how long till we get into Boston?

CONDUCTOR: You fellas keep asking me that, you in some sort of a hurry?

ALL: We can't wait to beat Harvard!

CONDUCTOR: You can't beat Harvard. *(Conductor exits.) (Waiter appears as they study menu.)*

WAITER: Orders, please.

THORPE: I'll have two double sirloin steaks . . . rare.

WAITER: For breakfast?

THORPE: Oh yeah. Breakfast. The steaks and scrambled eggs . . . half a dozen eggs.

WELCH: Fried oysters . . .

WAITER: How many? *(Welch shows him.)* That many?

NIKIFER: Wait'll you hear this. I'll have a seal steak. Medium rare.

WAITER: We don't have seal steak.

NIKIFER: Roast leg of polar bear— *(As Waiter dumbly shakes head.)* Boiled seagull? Seal-blood soup? All right. Then make it toast and marmalade.

THORPE: And for dessert . . . Harvard upside-down cake. *(Team whoops, Reporter appears.)*

REPORTER: No, sir. Harvard's having the dessert—Carlisle Indian pudding!

NIKIFER: Says who?

REPORTER: Says this reporter, who happens to know his football. And no bunch of savages is going to beat Harvard. *(Nikifer gives Reporter a look which makes him jump back several feet.)*

THORPE: Gus, tell him what we're going to do to Harvard—

WELCH: We're going to do what Sitting Bull did to Custer at the Little Big Horn—

THORPE: Nikifer!

NIKIFER: *(Raising arm in gesture of throwing spear.)* What my father, the great hunter, did to the giant polar bear . . . *("Throws" harpoon.) (Waiter, Conductor appear and join Reporter.)*

WAITER, CONDUCTOR, REPORTER: *(In unison.)* You-can't-beat-Harvard.

Football Sequence
Opposing Team: "Harvard"

COMMENTATOR: Ladies and Gentlemen, this man is terrific. The more you ask that Thorpe to do, the more he does . . . He's scored one touchdown and three fieldgoals. Carlisle's ahead—15 to 9. *(Effect of "Harvard" putting in new men.)* What's going on? Harvard's bringing in new men. Warner's looking at his bench. *(2 guys yell, "Harvard!")* He hasn't got another man to put in . . . He's got no fresh men. His team is bushed. *(Football play: blocked kick.)* Harvard has blocked Thorpe's kick. A Harvard man has got the ball—he's breaking tackles—he scores—it's tied, 15 to 15. Can Carlisle hold them the rest of the way? Harvard's coming on. Carlisle's tiring.

WELCH: How's that sprained ankle?

THORPE: It hurts some.

WELCH: Too bad, you're going to have to do it anyway.

COMMENTATOR: What's this? Welch calling for a field goal on fourth down? Who ever heard of a 53-yard field goal against the wind. How much can this big Indian be asked to do? Only 1 minute to play. If he doesn't make it Harvard can still score.

THORPE: Who ever heard of a place kick from this far away.

WELCH: You can do it, set, hike. *(Freeze—Dance—Kick.)*

COMMENTATOR: It's good. Carlisle's won. The score posted: "Carlisle 18—Harvard 15" *(The Chiefs take up positions at poles.)*

TECUMSEH: How well our young brave maneuvered.

KICKING BIRD: Thorpe should have scalped Harvard after the victory, as he was justly entitled to do.

CRAZY HORSE: Our young men have won today!

BLACK HAWK: *(Softly.)* Is it a sign?

Scene: *(Welch and Thorpe.)*

WELCH: Jim! Listen to what the newspapers are saying. A young Indian at Carlisle promises to become the greatest athlete in the world. *(Warner enters.)*

WARNER: To really prove that you've got to compete and win against the best athletes in the world . . . And that means . . . the Olympics! *(Thorpe says nothing.)* Think of what that would mean for Carlisle, Jim . . . of what Carlisle's done for you . . . *(Thorpe stares at Warner . . . touches hand to back of his head where Pratt cut his hair . . . remembering . . .)*

THORPE: I'll think about it . . .

WARNER: Good.

BLACK HAWK: It's not as simple as it appears . . .

CRAZY HORSE: What do you see?

BLACK HAWK: Jim Thorpe will make a choice which will lead to victories . . . and yet . . .

THORPE: Guess I won't go back to the Carolina League this summer.

WELCH: I'd say the Olympics are more important.

THORPE: The Olympics are glory—but you get paid cash for playing baseball in the Carolina League, and the Thorpe family could sure use cash.

WELCH: You know what winning in the Olympics would mean? How great an Indian can be, today in sports, tomorrow in something else. An Olympic gold medal means a first place in the whole world for an Indian.

THORPE: I never said I wasn't going.

BLACK HAWK: The vision becomes clearer. The test will be in skill, in strength, in sharpness of eye, and in the will to win for men of many nations.

(Olympic scene created . . . Black Hawk and one other Chief speak of the ceremony as it is enacted. Four "white men" carry flags into "arena" marching in formation . . . Olympic March.)

CRAZY HORSE: I see the flags of many countries but none which speak for the Indian nations. Where are the Indian streamers? For whom will Jim Thorpe race and leap?

BLACK HAWK: For the United States—

CRAZY HORSE: How can he be an Indian and of their country?

BLACK HAWK: In his heart he is an Indian. *(Thorpe prepares to throw the discus.)*

REPORTER: Here we are at the 1912 Olympics in Stockholm, Sweden. The Olympic audience is seeing American Indians at the games for the first time. Jim Thorpe of Carlisle has already won one gold medal in the pentathlon, a series of five events, and seems on his way to a second, in the decathlon, a series of ten events . . . He's preparing to throw the discus . . . *(Thorpe throws discus . . . whoop.)*

REPORTER: He wins first place in the discus! His feats have fired the imagination of the world . . . Now he prepares for the broad jump . . . *(Thorpe broad jumps . . . whoop.)* Another first for Thorpe . . . He is close to another gold medal . . . and now the last event! He's preparing to throw the javelin . . . *(Whoop.)* Thorpe has won his second gold medal at the Olympic games! *(Thorpe steps toward "the King of Sweden.")* He is stepping up to receive them from the King of Sweden . . . *(The King of Sweden takes his place on "reviewing stand" . . . Thorpe moves to face King, who puts gold medal around his neck . . . Applause.)*

KING: I, Gustavus Adolphus of Sweden present you, Jim Thorpe, with these medals. Sir, you are the greatest athlete in the world. *(Thorpe acknowledges with a slight bow of the head. Applause . . . Thorpe steps forward to acknowledge it . . . He stands alone in middle of arena . . . Chiefs have re-assembled . . .)*

THORPE: *(As if speaking to himself: possible song.)* From breaking horses in Texas . . . from growing up Indian in the Oklahoma territory, here I am and it's like the whole world's watching me. *(Looks up.)* And there's the black hawk crying out . . . what's it saying? . . . Jim Thorpe feels good right now . . . feels leaping . . . feels singing . . . feels laughing . . . feels cheering . . . feels flying . . . feels . . . free . . .

CRAZY HORSE: They honor him with their medals . . .

KICKING BIRD: Medals are powerful . . .

CRAZY HORSE: In our time we were given many medals by white chiefs—

BLACK HAWK: Then the white man betrayed them—

TECUMSEH: *(Voices going higher: intense: foreboding.)* What do you see now, Black Hawk?

BLACK HAWK: I see the sun and rain clouds in the sky at the same time!

CRAZY HORSE: Will it be sunlight, or rain?

BLACK HAWK: The sky grows darker! *(Chiefs silent . . .) (Two Reporters appear . . . Thorpe is pulled in on platform acknowledging applause . . .)*

FIRST REPORTER: Welcome to New York, Jim Thorpe! *(Turns to other Reporter.)* Say, I've been watching Thorpe and I've been thinking I've seen him somewhere . . . and I think I know where . . . and if that's so . . .

SECOND REPORTER: Well! Come on! If that's so, *what*?

FIRST REPORTER: He might not have those medals long.

SECOND REPORTER: That's a news story that would break all over the world!

1ST MAN: *(French accent.)* Ze American Indian, Zhim Sorpe, may lose his Olympeec honors for playing professional baseball.

(At various places on stage we see men purchasing and reading newspapers . . .)

2ND MAN: *(Reading out.)* Jim Thorpe, once called the greatest athlete in the world, may lose his honors.

3RD MAN: *(In accent.) (Says same thing but the words "Indian," "Jim Thorpe," "baseball" will convey idea.)*

4TH MAN: *(Cockney-accented English.)* Jim Thorpe, the great Indian athlete, charged with playing professional sports and may lose his Olympic prizes . . . It's a blooming shame, that's what it is.

(Reporters surround Thorpe on platform.)

KICKING BIRD: What have you got to say about those medals, Jim?

CRAZY HORSE: Will you ever get them back, Jim?

SEATTLE: Why did you play professional ball, Jim?

TECUMSEH: What are your plans for the future, Jim? *(Thorpe spins away.) (Thorpe stands facing away from Welch . . . as if looking out of a window . . . Welch enters.)*

WELCH: Jim . . . They've done it . . .

THORPE: I don't understand.

WELCH: *(Very tight: holding himself under control.)* Your Olympic victories and your name have to be wiped out of the record books because you were paid money for playing baseball in North Carolina. They went by the rules. You must be strictly an amateur to compete in the Olympics—

THORPE: *You* know more about stuff like that than I do, Gus. Why didn't you tell me?

WELCH: Because nobody paid any attention to the rules.

THORPE: Only thirty dollars a week—

WELCH: No matter how little money you got, under the rules you're still disqualified—

THORPE: But other college athletes who played professional baseball aren't—

WELCH: They didn't win in the Olympics, their pictures weren't all over the papers. They didn't play under their own names and you did . . .

THORPE: So I'm being nailed to the wall because I played under my own name.

WELCH: You're being nailed because you violated the most important rule the white man has . . .

THORPE: What's that?

WELCH: Don't get caught . . . you dumb Indian, you dumb honest Indian.

BLACK HAWK: *(To assembled Chiefs.)* So the Indian loses . . .

VOICE: Again . . .

BLACK HAWK: Again . . . cheated of our victories . . . Again . . . Again the honors given, then taken away . . .

VOICES: Again . . .

BLACK HAWK: Again . . . Again trapped by them . . . And still not free . . . Still not free . . .

WELCH: What are you gonna do now?

THORPE: *(With passion.)* What I'd like to do's get me a horse. Find a lot of open country to move through—plains country. Hunt and fish. Pitch camp at night.

WELCH: That's an Indian life. Deep down it's what all of us Indians want, but it's gone.

THORPE: What are you going to do now?

WELCH: I'm going to law school.

THORPE: I'll play ball . . . football, baseball, for whoever wants to pay me money and just . . . keep going along . . . *(On the side, Black Hawk and the other Chiefs murmur approvingly.)*

WELCH: Jim . . . Your medals have to be returned. *(Thorpe points to pole. Welch goes to pole and takes them off . . .)*

THORPE: Know what losing them feels like? When I first came to Carlisle . . . Like when they cut my hair . . . Will I ever get them back?

WELCH: I don't know if anything of what was taken from us is ever coming back. *(Music.)*

THORPE: I won't ever think about those medals again. *(Thorpe disappears.)*

CRAZY HORSE: *(Chiefs assembled.)* Nothing of ours remains . . .

BLACK HAWK: Except our spirit . . .

KICKING BIRD: Jim Thorpe's circle is broken and cannot be made a circle again . . .

COCHISE: The Indian circle is broken and cannot be a circle again.

SEATTLE: The buffalo . . .

CRAZY HORSE: The clear waters . . .

TECUMSEH: The mighty forests . . .

KICKING BIRD: The Indian earth . . .

SEATTLE: Nothing of ours remains . . .

BLACK HAWK: Except our spirit.

TECUMSEH: Our power is broken.

BLACK HAWK: But not our spirit! . . . Listen to me, my brother chiefs. We must breathe out our spirit so that our children, wandering and lost in the white man's world, will feel it . . . so that they will hold onto the Indian way in their hearts . . .

CRAZY HORSE: And will the Indian way come back?

TECUMSEH: The songs?

SEATTLE: The language?

KICKING BIRD: The clear waters?

COCHISE: The medals of Wa Tho Huk? Will they come back?

BLACK HAWK: We must hold on. Our children must hold on . . . until . . . I cannot see so far . . . We must hold on! *(Thorpe goes down field evading invisible tacklers . . . Again he gets ball and runs . . . By now the game is "real," and several players try to tackle*

Thorpe . . . At last he's brought down. Warner rushes over to him, Thorpe gets up slowly.)

WARNER: Jim, you ok? Want to rest till the 2nd half?

THORPE: Just need a little rest, that's all.

WARNER: *(Aside.)* Can ole Jim last another season? Pro ball for ten years now. *(Crosses to him.)* Jim, you're still the greatest. Wait till they see you next week in Canton! *(Thorpe runs again.)* We'll rest you till the 2nd half, Jim.

THORPE: Maybe I won't play the second half.

WARNER: Alright. Then you'll be fresh for next week's game in Toledo.

THORPE: Maybe I won't play next week, either . . . *(Thorpe goes by Warner . . . He disappears.)*

WARNER: *(Calling after him.)* Maybe two weeks from now in New York . . .

THORPE'S VOICE: *(As if from a distance . . .)* Maybe. *(Thorpe appears as if leaving park. Moves slowly. Reporter appears.)*

REPORTER: This your last game, Jim? *(Thorpe shrugs.)* Been playing pro ball ever since you left Carlisle . . . Must be fifteen years . . . Say, Jim, what have you got to say about those Olympic medals they took away from you?

THORPE: Never think about it. *(Scene conveys action of Thorpe wielding a shovel and digging a ditch. He's older and heavier. A second Reporter and Photographer rush up.)*

PHOTOGRAPHER: *(To 2nd Reporter.)* What do you want with this guy . . . a ditchdigger?

2ND REPORTER: He happens to be Jim Thorpe . . .

PHOTOGRAPHER: Never heard of him.

REPORTER: Just take the picture. The caption under the picture will be 'Jim Thorpe, the Indian called the greatest athlete in the world, digs ditch at construction site for the Los Angeles County Hospital.' Jim, hold up that shovel the way you did the javelin in the Olympics? *(Thorpe starts to strike pose . . .)*

REPORTER: Jim, that's good! *(Thorpe angrily throws "shovel" away.)* Hey, Jim! C'mon!

THORPE: Nothing doing.

REPORTER: Got something to say about those medals they took away?

THORPE: I never think about it.

COCHISE: Will the medals come back?

BLACK HAWK: I cannot say. We must hold on.

(Thorpe sits on what will represent a pier, fishing. He is now 64 years of age, heavyset and tired.)

1ST REPORTER: *(Approaches.)* Hi, Jim. Tracked you to California. How's the fishing—catch any big ones lately?

THORPE: *(Squinting—tries to recognize Reporter.)* Haven't I seen you someplace before?

REPORTER: *(Evasively.)* Maybe. Been a long time since Carlisle, hasn't it?

THORPE: *(Jiggling "line.")* Might have a fish . . . no . . . yeah, been a long time.

REPORTER: Forty years . . . lots of ups and downs . . . *(Thorpe shrugs.)* Say, Jim, the paper's got a terrific idea for a Thorpe story: Jim Thorpe tells how he feels forty years later about losing his Olympic medals!

THORPE: I never think about it.

REPORTER: Ever think about those great days at Carlisle?

THORPE: You reporters said we couldn't beat Harvard!

REPORTER: That was a mistake . . .

THORPE: And you guys said savages can't learn the rules . . .

REPORTER: Well . . . that wasn't exactly a mistake . . .

THORPE: You swim?

REPORTER: Not this time of the year . . .

THORPE: *(Picks up Reporter by scruff of neck and holds him over edge of "pier.")* You tracking me down here—*that* was a mistake . . .

REPORTER: Hey! What are you doing? You're not going to throw me in the water, are you? *(Thorpe "drops" him in "water.")*

THORPE: See any big ones down there?

SON: How's the fishing, Dad?

THORPE: Not so good.

SON: Dad, I feel we should try and get your medals back.

THORPE: I don't like to talk about those medals.

SON: It wasn't fair to take them away.

THORPE: Lots of things are unfair. Forget it.

SON: I can't.

THORPE: Well, I'm getting old. Get them back if you can . . .

SON: Dad . . . if you were young now, an Indian in the white man's world, how would you live?

THORPE: It's always been hard to figure . . . *(Beat.) (Yawns.)* I'm tired . . . Guess I'll go home and lie down . . . *(Thorpe lies down to rest, hands folded on chest. After a little while, one hand falls lifelessly down.)*

BLACK HAWK: *(Softly.)* Wa Tho Huk— *(Blows softly on reed flute.) (Thorpe rises and joins Black Hawk.)* Come, stand by my side, Wa Tho Huk Jim Thorpe. Here you may be free in spirit, come, take your place among us. Here you may roam the great plains where the Sac and Fox roamed . . . You are the great hunter. This is surely a great thing to do.

THORPE: A great thing . . .

BLACK HAWK: Here you may live in the old way. But if you were young now, an Indian in the white man's world, how would you live?

THORPE: *(He becomes charged . . .)* How would I live? I'd be all Indian . . .

BLACK HAWK: *(Chant.)* Hiya, hiya, ya, ya, etc.

THORPE: I'd get back the language . . .

ALL: *(Chant.)* Hiya, hiya, ya, ya, etc.

THORPE: I'd celebrate the earth . . . *(all chant.)* I'd call for the Indian pride to grow stronger.

BLACK HAWK: *(In Sac: same words.) (All chant.)*

THORPE: The Indian way brought back to life! That's the game to win! *(Calls.)* Welch . . . Nikifer . . . We've got a big game to win now . . .

WELCH: Bigger than beating Harvard?

THORPE: *(Claps hands.)* The biggest one we ever played. Let's line up . . . *(They do.)*

WELCH: It looks like you're going to have to kick a long one now. The longest you've ever tried . . .

THORPE: That goal looks far away . . .

WELCH: You can do it . . .

THORPE: Against the wind?

WELCH: Hasn't it always been against the wind? Set. Hike. *(Thorpe nods . . . steps back . . . kicks . . . All watch flight of ball.)*

NIKIFER: Straight as an arrow . . .

WELCH: It's going . . . *good.*

ALL: Chant. *(All follow the flight of the ball.)*

CURTAIN

RIDE A BLUE HORSE: ADVENTURES OF THE YOUNG JAMES WHITCOMB RILEY

by

AURAND HARRIS

RIDE A BLUE HORSE
ADVENTURES OF THE YOUNG JAMES WHITCOMB RILEY

CHARACTERS:

James Whitcomb Riley: The young poet
Mrs. Riley: His mother
Mr. Riley: His father
John Riley: His older brother
Noey Bixler: A neighbor boy
Gypsy Woman
Schoolteacher
Three School Children
Mary Alice Smith: An orphan
Sarah: A neighbor woman
First Slave Hunter
Second Slave Hunter
Slave
Dr. S.B. McCrillus: A Medicine Show Man
Daisy: His niece
James (Mac) McClarnahan: A drummer
Medicine Show Helper
Crowd and Halloween Ghosts

SETTING

Indiana.

TIME

1849–1916

NOTE: *(The cast of 19 can be performed by doubling with 9 actors, as suggested below:*
Riley
Mother
Father
John
Noey/Second Hunter/Medicine Show Helper
Gypsy/Ellsworth/Sarah/Daisy
Teacher/Slave/Doctor
Rolling/First Hunter/Mac
Bassett/Mary Alice.)

(Lively band music. On the stage R is a hat rack with various hats. At L are four stools. Riley enters, wearing a stylish top hat. He smiles and tips his hat to audience. He is in high spirits. Music out.)

RILEY: How do you do. I am very honored—I am very pleased that you—and children everywhere in America—on this day October 7, 1915—are celebrating—MY birthday. I thank you for the hundreds of letters you have sent telling me that you like the poems which I write. *(With childish enthusiasm.)* Today is, indeed, a special birthday—bands playing, flags unfurled, parades—almost as good as a circus. *(Takes off hat.)* I bought this hat for this occasion. I will keep this hat and it will be my memory of you and of today's celebration. *(Remembering.)* I have many memories. *(Looks at hat and chuckles.)* And I have worn many hats. *(Goes to hat rack, R.)* I don't remember my FIRST hat, but they tell me it was a small, home-made, baby's bonnet. *(Puts top hat on rack. Takes bonnet off rack and puts it on his hand. His hand becomes a puppet, his fingers and thumb "talking" as the mouth.)* And they said, even as a baby, the first sounds I made were little gurgling RHYMES. *(Holds hand up for baby and "talks" with great fun, stressing the rhymes.)* "Yoo-hoo, Coo-coo, Ba-ba, da-da. Moth-er, broth-er. See-me, Need-me, *(Cries.)* FEED-me!" *(Cries comically like a baby, then cradles bonnet in his arm. He smiles happily.)* Yes, I have many memories of my childhood. Some of my memories I write in my poems. I remember my loving mother. *(Mother enters.)* My good father *(Father enters.)* And John, my older brother, who was my best and truest friend, always. *(John enters.)*

MOTHER: *(Holding an imaginary baby, crosses, and she, Father and John stand in a family group.)* We will call the baby James Whitcomb, after our friend, the Governor of Indiana.

FATHER: *(To baby.)* It is an important name, young man. A name you must live up to!

MOTHER: *(Visualizing.)* James . . . Whitcomb . . . Riley. It has a nice sound.

FATHER: John.

JOHN: Yes, sir.

FATHER: Say "Hello" to your little brother.

JOHN: *(Eagerly.)* Can I hold him?

MOTHER: *(Gives imaginary baby to John.)* Be careful. He is so little, so helpless.

JOHN: Look. He's smiling right at me. He likes me! *(Tickles baby and talks baby talk.)* Citchy-chitchy coo-oo. Coo-oo-oo-OO-oo.

FATHER: Now, John, you have a buddy.

JOHN: That's what we'll call him. Hello—BUD! *(Family freezes.)*

RILEY: The first hat I do remember was a little brown cap with a round button on top. *(Takes hat from rack.)* And I do remember the first time I wore it. It was a memorable day—a day I will never forget. We hitched the horses to the buggy and Mother and Father and John and I drove down the pike—and went to the county fair. *(He puts cap on. Music: "The Animal Fair." All the cast enters—a balloon seller, school children, acrobat, juggler, etc.)* All sing:

We went to the county fair,
Oh, the sights that we saw there;
(All freeze in moving position, while one actor speaks.)
A woman that be, as tall as a tree,
And a man with rubber hair.
(All move and sing.)
We went to the county fair,
We saw a juggler there,
(All freeze. One speaks.)
Who hung by his toes, and on his nose

Balanced a kitchen chair!
(All sing and move.)
We went to the county fair,
Oh, the music we heard there;
(All freeze. One speaks.)
A fiddle played "Hi Diddle Diddle,"
To dancers in a square.
(All move and sing.)
We went to the county fair,
Rides and glides were there;
(All freeze. One speaks.)
A big balloon, as big as the moon,
Went sailing up in the air!

(Music continues as all exit humming. Riley stands alone.)

RILEY: There were balloons and banners, and the smell of pop-corn and sausages. But most of all I remember—the merry-go-round. *(Carousel music.)* The tinkling music—it went round and round, and the horses—went up and down. It was a wonder to behold! But there was one horse—one horse that was different from the rest. He was—a little BLUE horse. And it seemed to me he lifted HIS feet—to different music. I rode the BLUE horse, and we went around and around. Oh, the joyous feeling that bubbled inside me! I wanted to sing out, to tell the world the joy I felt! But I didn't know what words to say. *(Carousel music up softly.)*

Ride a blue horse,
There's one waiting for you;
Ride a blue horse,
Make a dream come true.

(Riley goes to hat rack, puts cap on peg and exits.)

NOEY: *(Noey Bixler, a young boy, barefoot, runs in L, calling excitedly.)* Come on, John. Let's go swimming. Out to the old swimming hole! John? Whatcha doing?

JOHN: *(Enters, barefoot.)* I'm making a bird house—with a sloping roof and a real lightning rod!

NOEY: We've fixed a jumping log at the swimming hole. We can dive in the water! *(Has great fun, holding nose, jumping up as if jumping off a log.)* Yippee! Ee-ee-ee-EE! Splash! Come on.

JOHN: I have to look after Bud. Mama's gone to Church Circle.

NOEY: Bring him along.

JOHN: He can't swim. Bud's too little.

NOEY: Put him on the bank. Come on!

JOHN: Bud. Bud! Get your straw hat. We're going to the swimming hole. *(Boys cross L, singing lustily, "Old Dan Tucker," playing tag or leap-frog. They circle to C.)*

JOHN: Don't it feel good to have your shoes off and go barefoot! *(Boys pantomime taking off ALL their clothes, as they talk.)*

NOEY: And shed your winter flannels, and feel the sun hetting up your chest. Yippee! *(Pounds "bare" chest happily and gives an Indian cry.)*

JOHN: Papa says over near Terre Haute there's a swimming hole so deep they ain't no bottom.

NOEY: They say river pirates buried their treasures in some of the deep holes.

JOHN: Treasures? Maybe there's gold buried in OUR swimming hole!

NOEY: Let's find out! *(Stretches.)* Ain't it grand to have your clothes off—and go *(Laughs, delighted with the daring of it.)* — NAKED! Come on!

JOHN: *(Riley enters, wearing knee pants and a little straw hat.)* You sit there, Bud, and be a good boy. The water's too deep for you.

RILEY: *(Sits cross-legged.)* I'll make mud pies!

NOEY: Naw. That's woman's work.

JOHN: You can make up words. Sky.

RILEY: *(Enjoying the game.)* Fly.

JOHN: Trees.

RILEY: Bees.

JOHN: Blue bird.

RILEY: *(Worried.)* Don't know a word.

NOEY: Why is he making rhymes? That's girl stuff! He ought to climb a tree, rob a bird's nest.

JOHN: You guard our clothes, Bud. Don't let no bears get them.

RILEY: I won't. I'll watch them.

NOEY: And don't let no gypsies get them. There's a camp up the road. Come on. Last one in the water is a pickled pear! *(Noey and John exit with loud cries of joy, R.)*

RILEY: *(Happy making imaginary mud pies, he sing-songs to himself.)* Patty-cake—patty-cake; Make it—bake it; Buy! A schalocate pie!

GYPSY: *(Enters L, with bag. She does not see Riley. He is too busy to see her. She stops, looks off.)* Who is in the water? Splashing up the mud! Two skinny little monkeys! Ha, you take from me—my pool. I take from you— *(Sees their imaginary clothes.)* Yes! I take your shirts, your britches, and—your underwear! *(Laughs. Pantomimes putting clothes into bag.)* May a big turtle squeeze your nose and bite your toes!

RILEY: *(Sees her.)* Hello.

GYPSY: *(Surprised.)* You?

RILEY: Do you want to buy a pie?

GYPSY: I want to go into the water.

RILEY: No GIRL goes in the swimming hole!

GYPSY: I go! In the daylight! In the night!

RILEY: You swim at NIGHT!

GYPSY: I float—and I sing to the moon. Sometimes I long to be a mermaid. *(Explains to him.)* A fish.

RILEY: A fish? I druther be a bird—and fly.

GYPSY: Ah! If I were a fish, and you were a bird, together—we would make merry and sip dew—from the dewberry. And eat bread with butter—from the buttercup.

RILEY: *(Joining in her game, happily.)* And butter from the butterfly.

GYPSY: *(Exploding with joy.)* Oh, little one! We sing songs together!

Let me see your hand. I will tell your fortune. *(Takes his hand.)* I see—

RILEY: What?

GYPSY: Look! LOOK! *(Amazed.)* There is a STAR in your hand!

RILEY: A Star?

GYPSY: You are a special person.

RILEY: I am?

GYPSY: *(Impressed.)* You will become great. You will become known, acclaimed, applauded!

RILEY: Me?

GYPSY: Oh, little one. I must come bearing gifts to you. *(Mysteriously.)* I will give you a magic, gypsy rhyme.

RILEY: Magic?

GYPSY: But remember, you can only use it once, so say it ONLY when you are in great need. *(With musical lightness.)*

"Oh, gypsy fiddle,
Fiddle-dee-de;
Grant a wish to me."

RILEY: *(Delighted, chants the rhyme and imitates her gesture.)*

"Oh, gypsy fiddle,
Fiddle-dee-de;
Grant a wish to me."

JOHN: *(Offstage.)* Look, Bud! We got something for you.

NOEY: *(Offstage.)* He's a little fellow, just like you! *(Boys enter R.)* See. We grabbed a little fish. Catch! *(Throws imaginary fish to Riley.)*

JOHN: Look! There's a WOMAN!

NOEY: A GYPSY WOMAN!

JOHN: We ain't covered!

NOEY: We ain't got no clothes on! *(They try to cover themselves with their hands.)*

JOHN: What'll we do?

NOEY: Hide!

JOHN: Where?

NOEY: Behind a bush! *(Hides behind an imaginary shrub.)*

JOHN: A tree! *(Hides behind an imaginary tree. Riley puts "fish" in his straw hat which is on the ground.)*

GYPSY: Yes, hide! Hide, little naked jay birds!

NOEY: *(Peeks over top of "bush.")* Where's our clothes?

JOHN: They ain't here!

NOEY: Bud, you was to watch them! I'll get you, Bud Riley!

GYPSY: Touch him NOT! He is a special one.

NOEY: We ain't got no clothes.

JOHN: *(Points at Gypsy.)* You stole them.

NOEY: You took them!

RILEY: Did you? *(Pause.)* Did you take them?

GYPSY: Yes! You take my pool. I take your britches and your underwear. *(Laughs. Boys look down at their "naked" bodies, give a cry of alarm and "hide.")*

RILEY: I promised—I promised to guard them. Give them back.

GYPSY: To them, I give the back of my hand! *(Turns to go.)*

RILEY: Wait.

GYPSY: What?

RILEY: *(Loudly.)*

"Oh, gypsy fiddle,
Fiddle-dee-de;
Grant a wish to me."

GYPSY: *(Smiles.)* Ah, little one, you are smart. *(Laughs.)* You are brave. What is your wish?

RILEY: Give them back their shirts.

GYPSY: Close your eyes. And when your name is twice-told, open your eyes, and behold. *(He closes eyes. She mimes throwing clothes from her bag to ground near him.)*

JOHN: She's giving us back our clothes. Why?

NOEY: She's gone batty. She's gone cuckoo!

GYPSY: It is done. Open your eyes, little one. Goodby, special one. *(Exits L.)*

RILEY: *(Opens eyes.)* They're here! Thank you, Miss—Gypsy. *(Looks around.)* Miss—Fish?

NOEY: Bud got our clothes back!

JOHN: How did you do it?

RILEY: Words. Words can make magic. *(Gets up, holding imaginary wriggling fish.)*

JOHN: Where are you going?

RILEY: To throw the fish back in the water.

NOEY: What for?

RILEY: And it will float, like her—and tonight—they will both sing to the moon! *(Exits R.)*

NOEY: Now HE'S batty! He's gone cuckoo.

JOHN: Get your clothes on.

NOEY: Afore she comes back! *(They quickly grab imaginary clothes.)*

JOHN: Here's your pants!

NOEY: Where's my underwear?

JOHN: Hurry! Come on!

NOEY: Wait for me! *(They ad lib excitedly, and run off R.) (A hand school bell is heard ringing. Then Teacher enters L, still ringing the bell. He is impressed with his importance and is comical in his affectation.)*

TEACHER: Lesson time. Lesson time. Take your places, young ladies and gentlemen. Take your seats, properly and with decorum. *(Two school girls and a boy enter L, representing the whole class. They put stools in place and sit.)* Good morning, dear scholars. Good morning to you. *(He motions for them to rise, and he sounds a musical note, "Ah.")*

THREE CHILDREN: *(Stand and sing loudly, bored and off-key.)*

Good morning to you,
Good morning to you,
We're all in our places

With bright shining faces;
Good morning to you,
Good morning, dear teacher, to you.

(He motions. They sit.)

TEACHER: *(Delighted, having an audience, he comically exhibits his learning.)* First, the morning roll-call. Mistress Rollins.

ROLLINS: *(Stands.)* "Work ILL done must be TWICE done." *(Sits.)*

TEACHER: Be certain YOU masticate and assimulate those instructive words. Master Ellsworth.

ELLSWORTH: *(Rises, mind blank, then grins and shouts.)* "Do unto others as you would have them do unto you." *(Sits.)*

TEACHER: You have—with repeated repition—recounted that same axiom each morning. Mistress Bassett.

BASSETT: *(Rises. Teacher's pet.)* "Respect those who know more than you. And speak only what is true. *(Sits.)*

TEACHER: Well enummerated and well ennunciated. Master Riley. *(No answer.)* Master James Whitcomb Riley. *(He looks at empty stool. Children giggle.)*

RILEY: *(Runs in, out of breath.)* Yes, sir. *(Sits on stool.)*

TEACHER: You are late AGAIN.

RILEY: Yes, sir. I—

TEACHER: Do not inform me that you were detained conversing with a butterfly!

RILEY: No, sir. That was yesterday. *(Children giggle.)*

TEACHER: Silence. Remember you are young ladies and gentlemen. *(To Riley.)* I am waiting, Master Riley, for an answer to my interrogation.

RILEY: I stopped—

TEACHER: Yes?

RILEY: And helped—

TEACHER: Yes?

RILEY: A doodlebug. *(Children giggle.)*

TEACHER: James Whitcomb Riley, this time you have digressed, dallied—DOODLED!—once too often. You will sit in the corner— *(To class, changing his voice.)* which is the right angle of a square— *(Again commanding.)* —and place upon your head a conical shape on which are fashioned these letters: D-U-N-C-E. *(Pulls Riley up by his ear.)*

RILEY: Yes, sir. *(Children giggle, as Teacher places stool. Riley sits, facing audience and puts on dunce cap which Teacher gives him.)*

TEACHER: Silence! And now young scholars, the clock has crept to that happy hour—multiplication time! Master Riley, being at the bottom of the class, you will recite and reiterate the Three Times Table.

RILEY: *(Stands.)* One times three is three. Two times three is—is—is six. Three times three is—is—is ten.

TEACHER: Certainly NOT. Class, three times three is . . . ?

ROLLINS: Eight.

ELLSWORTH: Eleven.

BASSETT: Nine.

TEACHER: Drill! We will DRILL until three times three is DRILLED into each and every cranium. Begin.

CHILDREN: One times three is three— *(Riley continues to mouth the table, as the three children turn and tease him.)*

Bud Riley, he-he-he,
Is as dumb as he can be!
(Innocently.)
Four times three is twelve.
(Repeat teasing.)
He's so dumb—that
He can't spell dog or cat.
(Innocently.)
Seven times three is twenty-one
(Repeat teasing.)
He's got freckles. He's a laugh!
(Innocently.)
Nine times three is twenty-seven.
(Repeat teasing.)

He's got spots like a giraffe!
(Innocently.)
Eleven times three is thirty-three.
(Repeat teasing.)
Nobody likes Bud Riley.

TEACHER: Now pencil and tablet and each will write, precisely and punctiliously, the previously declaimed TIMES TABLE. Begin. *(Children mime writing. Riley studiously mimes drawing and printing.)* One times three is . . . ? Two times three is . . . ? Work ILL done must be TWICE done! Three times three is . . . *(He becomes suspicious of Riley's industriousness. Slips up behind him.)* Four times three is. . . ? Five times three is . . . ? *(Grabs imaginary tablet.)* Master Riley! Is this what you call a TIMES TABLE?

RILEY: Yes, sir.

TEACHER: You have drawn a picture of a clock—on a table. And what is this scribbling?

RILEY: *(Reads.)*

This is a clock,
Tick-tock;
It is on a table.
It is able
To tell the times. So this is—
A TIMES TABLE.

(Children giggle.)

TEACHER: Master Riley! You are an idler, inattentive, impertinent, impetuous, incorrigible, incomprehensible, irretrievable, irreDEEMABLE! *(An imaginary paper falls from Riley's pad.)* And what is this?

RILEY: My penmanship.

TEACHER: Penmanship! It is another drawing—of a peculiar looking man—and a poem. *(Reads.)*
"My teacher."

My teacher is tall and neat,
He stand on two big feet,
With hair like gingerbread,
On his CABBAGE HEAD . . .

(Children giggle, saying and pointing, "Cabbage head . . . Ginger bread . . . etc." Teacher re-reads.) "Cabbage head! Gingerbread!" *(He gasps for words and breath.)* The switch!

RILEY: The switch?

TEACHER: THE SWITCH!! And bend yourself—horizontally—over the bench!

RILEY: No! No, sir! *(Frightened, he throws dunce cap down, and runs away, circling the stage and stops at other side, R.)*

TEACHER: *(At the same time.)* Stop, you bad boy! Come back! *(As Riley runs, we hear what he is thinking, the chanting of the children. The Children, as they chant, exit with Teacher, who picks up dunce cap. All back off at L.)*

Bud Riley, he-he-he,
Is as dumb as he can be.
He's got freckles. He's a laugh.
He's got spots like a giraffe.
Nobody likes Bud Rile-y-y.
He-he-he-he-HE!

(Teacher, last to exit, rings bell. Riley sits at R, with book. John enters.)

JOHN: Bud? Bud? Whatcha doing—hiding behind the rainbarrel?

RILEY: I'm sitting.

JOHN: Whatcha holding?

RILEY: It's my secret. My book.

JOHN: Where'd you get it?

RILEY: At the store. I charged it.

JOHN: Charged it?

RILEY: Then you don't have to pay for it.

JOHN: *(Takes book.)* It's a book of poems.

RILEY: When I'm in trouble—I hold it.

JOHN: Are you in trouble?

RILEY: I ran away from school.

JOHN: Why?

RILEY: Because I have to wear a dunce cap. Because I can't do numbers.

JOHN: You can read.

RILEY: *(Almost crying.)* They laugh at me. I have to sit in the corner. And—I look funny. I got freckles—SPOTS! They call me polka-dot, and they won't let me play. They make faces. 'Cause I'm dumb—

JOHN: No you ain't.

RILEY: And teacher took the switch and was going to whip me.

JOHN: What did you do?

RILEY: I want to be good, like Mama says. I try. Nobody likes me.

JOHN: I do.

RILEY: I hate school. I hate—me. I don't want to be different. I don't want to be a speckled egg.

JOHN: At the store, there's a sign says they've got stuff that will take spots off your hands.

RILEY: Take off freckles?

JOHN: I reckon. Where are you going?

RILEY: *(Leaving.)* To the store.

JOHN: Wait, Bud.

RILEY: It's got to! And then I won't be different. And I can have a friend!

JOHN: You ain't got the money.

RILEY: Don't need money. All you have to say is, "Charge it." *(Riley exits at L. Mother enters C, with towel.)*

MOTHER: John. John? Come and sit with me—on the porch. *(Wipes forehead and sits, happy with the beauty of the day.)* Oh, it's too pretty a day to be inside. It makes you feel like— *(Enjoying the luxury.)* —like doing nothing.

JOHN: *(Teasing.)* Mama, you got spring fever.

MOTHER: Yes, it's that time of year— *(Embracing all of Indiana.)* —knee-deep in June.

FATHER: *(Offstage.)* Elizabeth. Elizabeth!

MOTHER: It's your father. He's home and he sounds a bit vexed.

JOHN: I'll go feed my rabbit. *(Anxious to leave, exits.)*

FATHER: *(Offstage.)* Elizabeth!

MOTHER: I'm out here, dear.

FATHER: *(Enters L. He is indignant and his anger builds during the scene.)* Where is he?

MOTHER: Who?

FATHER: Our son, James Whitcomb Riley.

MOTHER: Is something wrong?

FATHER: Wrong! Mrs. Sheldon came by the court house. She says each morning Bud stops and splashes her white fence with mud.

MOTHER: But he likes her very much.

FATHER: Likes her? Then why does he take the red clay from the ditch and dab it on her fence!

MOTHER: RED clay? *(Laughs.)* That explains it.

FATHER: *(Angrily.)* Explains WHAT?

MOTHER: Bud says she wants flowers along her walk, and that he is helping her—to grow RED ROSES on her fence.

FATHER: Well, he will stop throwing mud! AND—I was presented with a dun from the store. James Whitcomb Riley bought a book—a book of poems!

MOTHER: Poems?

FATHER: And—he CHARGED it! Where is he? *(They freeze.)*

RILEY: *(Enters R, stands at side, holds small jar.)* It doesn't smell much. Tastes kind of funny. But it's thick and sticky. I'll rub it all over my face. Then I'll listen, so I can hear the freckles when they drop off—ping! ping! ping! *(Turns back to audience and smears yellow ointment on his face.)*

FATHER: *(They unfreeze, at C.)* Where is he?

MOTHER: Bud ran away from school today.

FATHER: RAN AWAY!

MOTHER: Bud drew a picture of the teacher with a cabbage head and hair like ginger bread.

FATHER: He did WHAT? Oh, wait! Wait until I get my hands on HIS hair.

RILEY: *(Calls.)* Mama. Papa! *(He runs to center scene, his face a bright yellow mask. He poses, happily, facing front.)* Look at me!

FATHER: He's turned yellow!

RILEY: How do I look?

FATHER: Like a colored Easter egg!

MOTHER: What have you put on your face?

RILEY: Stuff—to take the freckles off! And I won't look funny, and they won't laugh.

FATHER: Where did you get it?

RILEY: At the store.

FATHER: *(With mounting anger.)* How did you pay for it?

RILEY: I charged it.

FATHER: *(Exploding.)* CHARGED IT! Listen to me, young man. There will be no more charging. No more drawing pictures of cabbage heads! And no more running away from school! Oh—why can't you be like John? Be like ME! I am ashamed of you. Go! Wash your face! And off to bed—without any supper! *(Exits.)*

RILEY: *(Crushed.)* Yes, sir.

MOTHER: *(Wiping off ointment with towel.)* It's all right. It wipes off easily.

RILEY: And the freckles? Are they gone?

MOTHER: No. They are still there.

RILEY: Every one of them?

MOTHER: Everyone.

RILEY: *(Turns away.)* I wish—I wish I was with old Towser.

MOTHER: Our dog is dead.

RILEY: I wish—I wish I was dead.

MOTHER: Oh, no, dear. No! You must never say that, never think that.

RILEY: *(Sits on floor. She, on stool, continues wiping his face.)* I look funny. I'm a dunce. I'm bad.

MOTHER: Now stop this nonsense! You don't look funny. You are not stupid. And certainly you are not bad. You are—different. Yes, you are special.

RILEY: Nobody loves me.

MOTHER: I love you. Father loves you.

RILEY: He's ashamed of me.

MOTHER: No, dear. Father loves YOU. But—but he does not always like what you DO. *(Wipes his fingers.)* It isn't easy—when you're different.

RILEY: They make faces at me.

MOTHER: *(Rises.)* Yes. Instead of marbles, your pockets are full of words and rhymes. Like your Grandfather. He wrote poems. Yes, you ARE like him. I think—you are a budding poet.

RILEY: A poet?

MOTHER: Now wash your face. Remember, dear, freckles are on the OUTSIDE, and they will fade. The important thing is what is INSIDE. And what is in you, will bloom and grow. You must remember, always be brave. *(Kisses him. Starts to exit. Stops.)* Surely of all the words we know, "Brave" is the most beautiful. *(Exits.)*

RILEY: A poet? *(Soft carousel music is heard. He smiles with new hope.)*

Ride a blue horse,
There's one waiting for you;
Ride a blue horse,
Make a dream come true.

(Music ends. He goes to hat rack and picks up a stocking cap.)

Later, when I grew older, I remember I had a stocking cap—one my mother knitted. A warm stocking cap—like John's. *(Puts it on.)* And I wore it, down over my ears—like John.

JOHN: *(Enters, wearing stocking cap.)* Come on, Bud. We're going to get our pumpkins for Halloween.

RILEY: I want a big pumpkin and I'll cut out a big scary face.

JOHN: *(Mimes finding a pumpkin.)* Here's a fat one.

RILEY: And we'll dress up like ghosts and sing around the bonfire.

JOHN: You want to come along afterwards. You know, Halloween pranks?

RILEY: Just you and me.

JOHN: No. There'll be the other fellows.

RILEY: No. They don't want me. *(Mimes seeing a pumpkin.)* Look! Here's a whopper!

JOHN: By jings, it is! We'll take that one. *(Mimes cutting with knife on an imaginary pumpkin.)*

RILEY: Oh, John, it's going to be the best Halloween we ever had!

JOHN: *(Rises, rubs fingers, blows on them.)* Frost is getting kinda nippy!

RILEY: Yes, frost is on the pumpkins and the fodder is in the shock. Oh, John, don't it make you feel the best?

JOHN: *(Looks off.)* Bud! There's a wagon stopping. A GIRL is getting out.

RILEY: Who is she?

JOHN: Don't know. Let's go—and find out. *(They exit R.)*

MOTHER: *(At the same time, enters L.)* Come in, dear. Come inside and warm yourself.

MARY: *(Mary Alice Smith enters. She is a young girl, full of imagination and energy. She is poor, dressed shabbily with a funny little hat and a thin ragged shawl. She is from the backwoods, but holds herself with graceful dignity.)* Thank you. I am cold. I'm a-shivering, I am. And see—I got goosebumps all over. *(Proudly.)* But my nose—it ain't a-drippin'.

MOTHER: Boys! Boys! Come and meet—our new friend. *(John and Riley enter C.)* This is John and this is Bud.

JOHN AND RILEY: *(Speak together.)* How-do-do. *(John takes off his cap.)*

MARY: Pleased to meetcha. *(Curtsies.)* I'm an orphant, I am. I ain't got no place to stay this winter. So—here I am. And who might I be? Mary Alice Smith.

MOTHER: I'll put your things away.

MARY: I ain't got nothing—but my hat and Mama's shawl. They was going to bury Mama in her shawl, but I snuck it out, I did. *(Feels shawl lovingly.)* And now—it's all I got—of Mama.

MOTHER: I have a little jacket that's just for you. Now I'll take—*(Mary hugs her shawl protectingly.)* your hat, and we'll have some hot cider and Bud's favorite cookies.

RILEY: Walnut and molasses!

MOTHER: *(Takes Mary's hat.)* You boys show Mary Alice the house. It's going to be her home for a while.

MARY: Oh, I'll earn my board and keep. You a-wantin' me to be making the beds. Or gathering in the eggs? I got a friendly way with chickens. I cluck-cluck-cluck-cluck-cluck to them, I do. And they cluck-cluck-cluck-cluck-cluck to me, they do. And then they lay a heap of eggs! 'Cause they like Mary Alice Smith.

MOTHER: There will be plenty for you to do. *(Exits C.)*

JOHN: *(Indicating.)* This is the front hall, and over here's the parlor.

MARY: Oh—OH! Look at the stairs! Up—up—up.

RILEY: Papa hand-carved the railing.

MARY: So many steps. And I'll name each one of them.

JOHN: Name the steps?

MARY: *(Thinking and enjoying the game.)* The first step I name—"Adam." The second step I name—"Eve." The next step is—is "Hazeletta." She's my favorite friend. I talk to her, and when I play the pianna she sings—oh, so sweetly. *(Speaks in Hazeletta's funny voice.)* "I want to sing now." She says she wants to sing now. *(In Hazeletta's voice.)* "I have cleared my throat with honey." You have? Well, I've dipped my fingers in spring water. So let's begin. *(Suddenly she starts playing, fingering up and down on an imaginary key board. She "Da-da's" a few bars of "Buffalo Gal." Then sings the words in Hazeletta's voice, still playing the "piano.")*

"Buffalo Gal, won't you come out tonight?
Come out tonight? Come out tonight?
Buffalo Gal, won't you come out tonight—"

(Stops suddenly. Speaks in own voice.)

She won't come out. And do you know why? *(Boys look at each other.)* It's a riddle.

JOHN: A riddle?

MARY: You give up? *(Boys look at each other, then nod to her. She laughs.)* The answer is: She ain't coming out because—it's DAYLIGHT! *(She laughs. Boys laugh.)* Oh, I'm glad I've come to live in this-here house. You know why?

RILEY: Why?

MARY: 'Cause when I step up these-here stairs, I can play like I'm climbing up—up—up to the Good World where my Mama is. That's why. *(Looks at Riley.)* You keep your cap on 'cause you ain't got no hair?

RILEY: I've got hair. See. *(Takes off cap.)*

MARY: *(Mysteriously.)* Once there was a boy and he didn't have no hair, 'cause once he pulled the tail of an old black cat. And that night, the old black cat turned into an old witch! And this-here witch came ridin' on her broom—and she pulled his hair plum out. Hair—by hair—while he mo-oaned and gro-oaned in his sleep, he did. And—NO HAIR EVER GROWED BACK AGAIN. *(Cheerfully.)* I know heaps of stories, and when it's dark and candletime, I'll tell them to you. 'Cause that's the time goblins wake up, and come to getcha, if you don't watch OUT!

MOTHER: *(Enters C.)* Children, cookies are ready. Come to the kitchen.

MARY: I'm right empty, I am. And after we eat, I'll red-up the dishes. I'll wash and wipe 'em clean as a whistle. *(Chants.)*

"Oh, the knife is David-Mason-Jeffrie, and the fork is Mary-Alice-Smith, for he's the one for her." *(Speaks.)* The riddle is: What became of the spoon? If you don't know that riddle, you don't know your hi-diddle-diddle. You give up? *(Boys nod.)* The answer is: The PLATE ran away with the spoon. And—that's all. *(Exits C.)*

JOHN: She sure is something! *(Shakes his head, and exits C.)*

MOTHER: *(Smiles.)* Yes, she is a fanciful child. I think there is a little elf that whispers in her ear.

RILEY: No. It's Hazeletta. I saw her. And I heard her sing—oh, so sweetly.

MOTHER: I'm sure you and Mary Alice are going to fill the house with sprites and elves. Come along, dear. *(Exits.)*

RILEY: *(Looks about and calls.)* Hazeletta? Hazeletta? Come out tonight, Hazeletta. 'Cause there'll be witches and cats! Goblins and bats! *(Excited with a new idea.)* I'll make a rhyme! I'll make up a song! And we'll sing it tonight—with the ghosts—at the bonfire. *(Throws his cap in the air and gives a happy, spooky cry.)* Whoo-oo-oo-oo-oo-oo-OO. *(Exits C.) (Lights start to dim to night. John and Noey enter L, excited and out of breath. John carries an imaginary basket of leaves. Noey carries some imaginary tree branches. They build an imaginary bonfire C.)*

NOEY: I reckon this will be the biggest bonfire in Greenfield.

JOHN: That's a high heap of leaves we've stacked up. And here goes some more. *(Throws "leaves" on "pile.")*

NOEY: These old branches will keep the fire burning a long time. *(Puts "branches" on "pile.")* I snuck that old scarecrow out of Mitchell's garden, and I put it up against Miss Sophie's window. And when she sees a MAN peeking in—Lawsay! She'll die of palpitation!

JOHN: I snitched some of Mama's washing soap. We can smear up all the windows at the schoolhouse.

NOEY: Is Bud coming along?

JOHN: No.

NOEY: He sure is different.

JOHN: He's made up a good song for us to sing tonight, about Halloween. Look. Here comes Willie Pierson—and Frances, with their jack-o-lanterns.

NOEY: And here comes Jess and Cyrus, dressed up like ghosts.

JOHN: There's Bud—and Mary Alice.

NOEY: They're all a-coming! Spark the fire and let her blaze!

JOHN: Here—she—goes! *(John mimes lighting the bonfire. Bonfire light begins to glow. Music begins. From all directions come white-covered figures, with eye-holes so they can see, carrying lighted jack-o-lanterns. They make spooky sounds of cats, goblins and ghosts. Riley's head is the only one which is not covered. His lighted, open-top jack-o-lantern shows his happy face. John and Noey, quickly off stage, put on white sheets and carry jack-o-lanterns, and join the group. All sing and sway, and "dance" to the tune of "My Bonnie Lies Over the Ocean.")*

SONG:

(Chorus.)
It's Halloween, Halloween.
OOO-ooo, Ooo-ooo,
Tonight is Halloween.
(1st verse.)
Tonight all the witches are flying,
On broomsticks they fly in the sky;
Tonight jack-o-lanterns are glowing,
And winking a wicked eye.
(Repeat chorus.)
(2nd verse.)
Tonight ghosts and goblins are out,
Floating and flying about;
Tonight to the moon the cats cry
A scary lullaby.
(Repeat chorus.)
(3rd verse.)
Tonight is the night to act brave,
When skeletons dance on a grave;
Tonight is the night to say, "Boo!"
Before the goblins get YOU.

(Repeat chorus.)

(Ghosts all exit with "Oo-oo-oo's," and spooky sounds. Music stops.)

RILEY: *(Stands alone.)* All the ghosts sang MY song! *(He exits joyously, with musical "oo-oo-oo's," stops and shouts to audience.)* BOO! *(Lights come up bright. Mother enters L.)*

MOTHER: Bud. Bud? Sarah says she can come over to see your play. Bud! *(He is not there. She sees imaginary clutter on floor.)* Oh, what a clutter you have left! I had the dining room all cleaned up for your play. *(Kneels and mimes picking up.)* Paints and paste. *(Smiles.)* You're making valentines! With pictures—and verses. *(Reads imaginary valentines.)*

"As sure as vines grow round the stump, You are my sweet, sugar lump." *(Laughs.)* "I like you—and better, too—Than angel cake or rabbit stew."

Oh, Bud, you are a poet. *(Touched.)* "Of all the rest, I love my mother best." I do believe you are happy ONLY when you are making rhymes.

(Father enters, cautiously, from kitchen, followed by a man whose face is hidden. Father sees Mother, stops, and motions for person to go back. Person exits R.) Well, I'll put these all back in the box for you. *(Is aware of Father.)* Bud? Oh, it's you, dear. Why are you using the kitchen door? Oh, I was afraid you would be late and miss the children's entertainment. *(Listens.)* There is Sarah now, coming up the walk.

FATHER: I wish we had not invited her.

MOTHER: *(Sympathetic.)* You are tired. You are making too many speeches.

FATHER: There is a cloud of WAR hanging over us.

MOTHER: Abraham Lincoln WILL be elected President.

FATHER: But slavery will still be a problem.

JOHN: *(Enters L, excited. He carries a brown hood with openings for eyes.)* Sarah's here! She's coming up the walk. How do you like my costume? *(Puts on hood, which completely covers his face.)*

FATHER: What is it?

JOHN: I'm a bear! Gr-r-r-r-owl! *(Exits L.)*

MOTHER: I'll let Sarah in. Hurry, Reuben. *(Mother exits L. Father quickly and cautiously goes to kitchen "door," R, and motions. Person enters.)*

FATHER: This way. Come in. Sh! Quiet. Don't talk. You can hide in the cellar. You'll be safe there. *(Figure exits at cellar door, CL.)*

RILEY: *(Enters DL, followed by John and Mary Alice who wears a brown coat and carries a coonskin cap.)* Come on. We'll get our places and be ready—for the play! John, you put a chair there for me to stand on. *(John places a stool at R.)* Mary Alice, you come in from the kitchen. And remember—growl loud!

MARY: Don't you fret. I'll growl louder than a toothache! Gr-r-rowl! *(Exits R.)*

RILEY: John, you come in from the cellar.

FATHER: The cellar!

RILEY: We're all ready. *(Calls.)* Come on in, Mama. The show is going to start. *(Exits R.)*

FATHER: Son.

JOHN: Yes, Papa.

FATHER: In the cellar—be careful in the cellar.

JOHN: Careful?

FATHER: Very careful!

JOHN: Yes, sir. *(John exits CL at cellar "door," as Mother and Sarah, a neighbor lady, enter DL.)*

MOTHER: Come in, Sarah.

SARAH: I brought some taffy for the children.

MOTHER: You ARE a good neighbor. Reuben, pull up the chairs.

SARAH: Is it going to be a real play?

MOTHER: Bud has written a story—in verse—which he is going to recite, while the others act it out. Do sit down. *(Sarah sits on stool at L.)*

RILEY: *(Appears R.)* Mama! There's some men looking in our barn and in the woodshed!

FATHER: Men? Are you sure? *(Two Slave Hunters enter DL. Riley exits R.)*

FIRST HUNTER: *(Speaks loudly.)* I'm a-wantin' your attention, folks.

MOTHER: Who are you?

FIRST HUNTER: I'm prepared to search this house. We're hunting for a runaway slave.

SARAH: Oh, my goodness!

FATHER: You cannot burst into my house like this!

FIRST HUNTER: I got the legal paper, writ and signed, right here. I got a witness that says you're harboring a fugitive slave.

MOTHER: Reuben!

FIRST HUNTER: Men are searching the outbuildings. I'm searching inside.

MOTHER: Indiana is a free state. We do not have slaves. And I will not have you in my house!

FATHER: It's all right, Elizabeth. It's legal.

MOTHER: *(Exasperated.)* And—AND you have interrupted our entertainment.

SARAH: You certainly have!

FIRST HUNTER: There'll be real entertainment when we catch the runaway! All right, Jim. We'll start upstairs and work to the cellar. *(They exit DL.)*

MOTHER: Well, I never in all my life!

FATHER: *(Calming her.)* Elizabeth. Go ahead with the play. I will see if the actors are ready. *(Exits at cellar "door.")*

MOTHER: We certainly will go ahead.

SARAH: He's that slave hunter from Kentucky. All HE wants to capture is a big reward.

RILEY: *(Peeks out, R.)* Mama. Mama! We're all ready!

MOTHER: Yes, and so are we. *(Father and John, without costume, enter. Father sits L. John sits on floor.)* Now, without further ado we will begin our—entertainment. It is entitled "The Bear Story."

(She sits. All applaud. Riley enters R, carrying his little-boy straw hat. He smiles and bows.)

RILEY: "The Bear Story" by James Whitcomb Riley. This is a story told by a LITTLE boy. *(Puts hat on. He sees John in audience.)* John? You should be ready—in the cellar.

FATHER: Go ahead, son.

RILEY: But John is supposed to be in the cellar.

FATHER: *(Slowly, and emphatic command.)* GO AHEAD, SON, WITH THE PLAY!

RILEY: Yes, sir. Yes, sir.

MOTHER: We're all waiting and ready.

RILEY: *(Looks doubtful. Father nods. Mother nods. He takes a deep breath and begins, reciting with great enjoyment and dramatizing each scene.)*

Once there was a Little Boy went out
In the woods to shoot a bear.
(Walks.)
And he was going along—and going along, you know,
And pretty soon he heerd something go—

MARY: *(Offstage. Loud and prolonged.)* Grrr-r-rrow!

RILEY: Just thataway—"Grrr-r-row!" And he was *skeered.*
(Shakes.)
He was. And so he runned.
(Runs.)
and clumbed a tree.
(Stands on stool.)
And then he heered it again; and he looked down,
(Mary enters, comical with the tail of the coonskin cap hanging down over her face.)
And it was a BEAR!—a great-big-sure-nuff Bear!
(From cellar, a "bear" enters, covered with brown blanket and with a hood covering face. Riley is surprised.)
No. It was *two* Bears—two great-big-sure-nuff Bears—
And they both went—
(Bears go, "Grrr-r-row!")
and then the Little Boy He was skeered worse'n ever!
(Shakes.)

And here come the great Big Bear a-climbing the tree.
(Mary mimes.)
Oh, no!
It was *Little* Bear.
(Mary stops, motions, and the other bear mimes climbing.)
So here he come
Climbing the tree—and climbing the tree! Then
The Little Boy he just pulled up his gun
And *shot* the Bear, he did,
(Mimes shooting imaginary gun.)
and killed him dead!
Spling-splung! he falled plum down, he did,
(Bear falls down.)
And then the Big Bear's awful mad, and so here
(Mary growls and mimes.)
He come to climb the big old tree and get
The Little Boy and eat him up! And then
The Little Boy climbed 'til he can't climb no higher
(He mimes.)
And old Bear he climbs 'way out
(Mary mimes.)
On a limb, and the Little Boy
He takes his ax and chops off the limb.
(He mimes.)
Old Bear falls *k-splung:* clean to the ground.
(Mary mimes.)
And bust and kill himself plum dead, he did!
And then the Little Boy—

FIRST HUNTER: *(Two Hunters enter DL.)* He ain't upstairs.

SECOND HUNTER: We searched it good.

MOTHER: Of course there is no slave upstairs!

FIRST HUNTER: And we've looked down here. All except the kitchen and the cellar.

SECOND HUNTER: I'll look in the kitchen part. *(Exits R.)*

FIRST HUNTER: Where's the cellar?

FATHER: The cellar door is there.

MOTHER: You won't find anyone there. And don't break any glass jars of my canned fruit! *(Hunter exits at cellar "door.")*

FATHER: Quiet, Elizabeth, quiet. Go on with the play, son.

RILEY: It won't be any good now.

MOTHER: It will be fine.

FATHER: Go ahead.

SARAH: Do go on. I want to know what happens to the Little Boy.

FATHER: I said, GO AHEAD, SON!

RILEY: Well—
(Takes a deep breath, determined to make it good.)
And then the Little Boy commenced a-climbing down.
(He mimes.)
And sir! When he was purt'-nigh down,—why, then
Old Bear he jumped up again! And he
Ain't dead at all—just pretending thataway.
(Mary mimes.)
So he can get the Little Boy and eat
Him up! But Little Boy, he was too smart
To climb clean *down* the tree—and the old Bear
He can't climb *up* the tree no more—'cause when
He fell, he broke one—he broke *all*
(Mary mimes, growls a surprise at one broken leg, then a bigger surprise when all legs are broken.)
His legs! So he growls 'round the tree, he does—

MARY: Grrr-r-rowl! Grr-r-rowl! Grrr-r-owl!

RILEY: He stay up in the tree—all night—
And without no supper neether! Only they
Was apples on the tree! And Little Boy
Ate apples all—night—long.

SECOND HUNTER: *(He enters R, and First Hunter enters CL.)* No one in the kitchen part.

FIRST HUNTER: No sign of him in the cellar.

MOTHER: I told you so.

FIRST HUNTER: Nothing left to search but this room. *(Looks around.)* Any closets? Clothes press?

FATHER: No.

RILEY: *(Irritated.)* You stopped the play twice—and right at the best part.

FIRST HUNTER: Play-acting, huh? You ought to be out shooting a gun, 'stead of this tomfoolery.

MARY: Gr-r-r-rowl!

FIRST HUNTER: What are you?

MARY: I'm a BEAR! Grrr-r-rowl! *(Growls fiercely and claws at him.)*

FIRST HUNTER: *(Backs away, then turns and pushes with his foot the other bear, who is curled up on the floor.)* And what's that? A sack of potatoes? *(Kicks bear with a loud stomp on the floor.)*

RILEY: Don't you kick him! He's a dead bear!

FATHER: If you have finished your search . . . ?

FIRST HUNTER: He ain't here. No slave escapes from me.

FATHER: Then you will kindly leave my house.

FIRST HUNTER: I'm leaving, but mind you this: We're stopping this underground railroad through Indiana. Them slaves is property! We got hounds. We got guns. We got the right to catch them!

FATHER: Good day, sir!

FIRST HUNTER: Good'ay. Come on. *(He and Second Hunter exit DL.)*

FATHER: Now, son, tell us how the story ends.

MOTHER: Yes, go ahead, Bud.

RILEY: Well—
(Takes a deep breath to finally finish the story.)
Then when it was morning and Old Bear went—

MARY: *(Mimes.)* Grr-r-rowl!

RILEY: Then he finds the Little Boy's gun, he did,
(Mary mimes.)
And so Old Bear thinks he'll shoot the Little Boy—
But *Bears* they don't know much 'bout shooting guns:
The Old Bear got the *other* end of the gun
(Mary mimes.)
Ag'in his shoulder, 'stead of *th' other* end—

So when he try to shoot the Little Boy,
(Mary mimes shooting with sound effects.)
It shot *the* Bear, it did—and killed him dead!
(Mary falls dramatically.)
And then the Little Boy clumb down the tree
(Mimes.)
And took bof' bears home, he did,
And he cooked 'em, and he ATE them! And that's all.
(He bows. Bear exits CL into cellar. All applaud and ad lib *their praise.)*

FATHER: That was a fine Bear Story, son.

MOTHER: *(Rushes to him and hugs him.)* Oh, you were splendid, Bud! I'm so proud of you.

SARAH: I thought for sure the bear was going to eat the Little Boy!

MOTHER: *(Overly excited, trying to forget the Slave Hunters.)* Now we'll all go in by the fire and have refreshments. *(As they exit L, she chatters.)* Sarah, you must sing for us and I'll play the melodian, and we'll forget all about the slave hunters. *(All exit L, except Bud and John.)*

JOHN: You did a fine thing, Bud.

RILEY: You mean you like the poem?

JOHN: I mean, you saved— *(Smiles.)* Yes, I like the poem. Come on before they eat the cookies.

RILEY: John? Who was the other bear?

JOHN: Don't you know?

RILEY: No.

JOHN: Then I'll tell you. *(Puts Riley's hat on Riley's head, and speaks secretly.)* Keep this under your hat. It was a real bear! *(Riley looks surprised. John exits L.)*

RILEY: *(Laughs.)* Oh, you're joshing me! *(Seriously.)* Ain't you? *(Speaks to audience.)*
I never knew who it was. But that night I said an extra prayer, just in case, it was—a run-away slave—hiding in the cellar. *(Singing begins, off, with a good vigorous beat. Riley puts hat on rack, as singing continues.)* SONG:

Tramp, tramp, tramp! The boys are marching,
Cheer up, comrades, they will come—they will come—
And beneath the starry flag we shall breathe the air
again
Of the free land in our own beloved home.

(Singing continues under dialogue, but only words are: Tramp, tramp, tramp, etc.)

RILEY: WAR! Civil War was declared. North against South, fighting a war to free the slaves. My father was the first to volunteer. I remember we all watched and waved goodbye, as they marched—with their guns—off to war. *(Noey and John run in, stand and wave. Song changes to a loud stirring singing of):*

Glory, glory Hallelujah!
Glory, glory Hallelujah!
Glory, glory Hallelujah!
His truth is marching on.

(Boys' dialogue is over the singing and at the same time.)

NOEY: Ain't it grand!

JOHN: Bands and flags and parades!

NOEY: If this fighting goes on long enough, I'll be old and I can join up and *(Shouts joyfully.)* —GO TO WAR! HURRAH! *(They join in the singing of the last Line: "His truth is marching on." They sing loudly as they march off.)*

RILEY: The war went on and on. War brings death so near. It makes you know how PRECIOUS life is. My life—what am I going to do with my life? I'm old enough to decide. I know what I WANT to do. I want to write poems that are singing inside of me—words that tell the joy of living. I want to be—a poet! *(Carousel music is heard.)*

Little Blue Horse,
Where are you? Where?
I am ready to ride.
Are you there? Are you there?

(Carousel music dims out. Loud music of a bass drum and tambourine, or other instruments, is heard. Riley goes to hat rack, as Mac, a spirited performer, beating a bass drum, and Daisy, a pert young girl, beating a tambourine, enter L, stepping high, dressed in "show" costumes. There

can be a man carrying a big banner saying: McCrillus Medicine Show, following them. Last in the procession is Dr. S.B. McCrillus himself, flamboyant in dress, manner, and speech. As they enter, they sing to the tune of "Come to the Church in the Wild Wood.") SONG:

Oh, come, come, come, come to see our sho-o-ow
tonight,
Oh, come and join in the fun.
There'll be music and songs in our show tonight,
So come, everyone.
Come, come, come, come, our show is-s-s well known,
Oh, give a beat to the drum!
Our show will tickle your funny bone,
So everybody come.

DOC: Come, come, come, come— *(Shouts.)* to McCrillus famous Medicine Show! *(Raises hands in greeting. Music stops.)*

My friends, my friends. How my heart rejoices to be in Greenfield, the jewel of Indiana. *(Drum roll.)*

I bring to you joy and health in each and every bottle of my medicine. McCrillus Popular Standard Remedies will take away your aches and pains of today and give you vim and vigor for tomorrow. Tell your neighbors, come one, come all, to my free show tonight. We will have lively music. *(Mac plays the drum, with Doctor leading the applause.)*

We will have harmonious singing. *(Daisy sings, with great showmanship, second verse of "Polly-Woddle-Doodle," with Doctor leading the applause.)*

Now I say, bless you, until tonight when I will see you again at McCrillus famous Medicine Show! *(All sing as they march off.)* SONG:

Oh, come, come, come, come to see our sho-o-ow tonight,
Oh, come and join in the fun.
There'll be music and songs in our show tonight,
So come, everyone.

(Riley, who has put on a sign painter's cap, approaches Daisy, who returns for her tambourine.)

RILEY: *(Shyly.)* Hello.

DAISY: *(Always animated.)* Hello!

RILEY: It must be grand to travel—all around.

DAISY: It is! And I get to *(Comically demonstrates.)* PERFORM every night. I'm going to be an actress—a famous one.

RILEY: An actress?

DAISY: On a show boat! But first I have to gain *(Strikes a dramatic pose.)* EXPERIENCE. So Mama let me come this summer with Uncle Silas, and every night I *(Dramatically.)* PERFORM in his Medicine Show. And when I get enough *(Poses.)* EXPERIENCE, I'll be a real actress on a real show boat. It's my heart's desire! My name is Daisy.

RILEY: I'm—Jim.

DAISY: *(Curtsies.)* How do you do.

RILEY: *(Takes off cap.)* How do you do.

DAISY: What's your heart's desire?

RILEY: Huh?

DAISY: What do you want to do?

RILEY: You won't laugh? I want to be a poet.

DAISY: *(Impressed.)* A poet!

RILEY: *(Imitating her.)* A famous one!

DAISY: You'll need— *(Dramatically.)* EXPERIENCE!

RILEY: Yes, I'd like to travel, like you. Instead—here I am—a sign painter.

DAISY: *(Beaming with an idea.)* You paint signs?

RILEY: Yes, 'mam. On barns and fences. Sometimes I put a verse in my signs.

DAISY: A poem?

RILEY: "For horses young and able—come to Hutt's Livery Stable."

DAISY: *(Bubbling.)* It rhymes! And you want to leave?

RILEY: Yes, 'mam. Folks here don't take friendly to a poet.

DAISY: You stay right here. *(Calls.)* Uncle Silas!

RILEY: What are you doing?

DAISY: *(Calls.)* Uncle Silas.

DOC: *(Enters.)* And why is my darling Daisy calling, "Uncle Silas—Uncle Silas"?

DAISY: Uncle Silas, this is—is Jim.

RILEY: *(Takes off cap.)* Jim Riley.

DOC: *(Shakes hands.)* How do you do, son. Yes, you do look a bit pale, a bit peaked. But one bottle of my liver tonic will fix you up.

DAISY: No, no. He is not sick.

DOC: No?

DAISY: He looks that way because he's a— *(Dramatically.)* A poet.

DOC: Oh!

DAISY: And a sign painter!

RILEY: *(Puts cap back on.)* Yes, sir.

DAISY: And right now he is asking you for a job.

DOC: *(Re-acts, surprised.)* He is?

RILEY: *(Re-acts, more surprised.)* I am?

DAISY: You are! He can paint signs—with rhymes—announcing the Medicine Show.

RILEY: Yes, I could! Did you see my sign on the covered bridge? "New Cider Press. A wonder. Jenkins Hardware, by Thunder."

DOC: Could you make a rhyme about my medicine?

DAISY: Of course he can! Think— *(Dramatically.)* —aches and pains.

RILEY: "Banish— *(Imitating Daisy.)* aches and pains— *(Thinks.)* —and grief, Use Standard Remedies— *(Smiles.)* —for RELIEF!"

DOC: That is very good. Yes! YES!

DAISY: Yes? Uncle Silas has said, "Yes" he'll take you with us.

DOC: *(Surprised.)* I did?

RILEY: *(Elated.)* He did?

DAISY: You did.

DOC: So you're a poet who wants to run away—to FIND yourself. What kind of verse do you write?

RILEY: Poems like Tennyson and Longfellow.

DOC: No, no, son. You live in Indiana. Write about swimming holes, apple orchards, and people you know. Write what you HEAR, what you FEEL. Yes, you can come along with me.

DAISY: *(Elated.)* You can get— *(Dramatically.)* EXPERIENCE!

DOC: If you can write some poems about us HOME FOLKS before we get to Kokomo, I'll take you on for the summer.

RILEY: I'm much obliged. *(Takes off cap. Shakes hands.)*

DOC: I like to help folks. *(Joyfully.)*
Folks with liver trouble, stomach trouble and rheumatism—and I like to help young folks—find themselves.

DAISY: Oh, Uncle Silas! *(Kisses him.)*

DOC: A wise man once said, "The gates of great events often swing on small hinges." Now be up and ready tomorrow morning. We leave for Kokomo at sun rise. *(Exits.)*

DAISY: *(Dramatically.)* "Goodby, goodby, parting is such sweet sorrow;
Goodby until it be 'morrow." Shakespeare! *(Exits.)*

RILEY: And the next morning the rooster crowed, calling forth a new day; and I was up—and on my way! *(Riley describes the wagon, as others take their places. Mac and Banner Carrier enter, kneel about eight feet apart, facing R, spacing a "wagon." Each has a red ribbon streamer on a stick. Doc enters, places a stool and sits facing R, ready to drive at the front of the "wagon." Daisy enters, places a stool, sits at back of "wagon," holding the banner. Riley stands upstage of "wagon.")* The wagon was big and painted bright red, with golden letters on the side, spelling "McCrillus Medicine Show." The doctor sat in the driver's seat, holding the reins of the horses. But to me—he was a magic wizard, holding the reins of two swift dragons! And the wagon—it was a flying carpet—and I was going along! *(Steps forward.)* I climbed up on the wagon. I was ready to start—on a wonderous, magic journey. *(He stands in C. of "wagon," facing audience, with imaginary pencil and pad.)*

DOC: *(Mimes driving "horses" with reins.)* Gette up! Gette up! We're a-going! *(Cracks imaginary whip.)* We're off to Kokomo! *(Mac and*

Banner Carrier whirl red ribbon streamers in circles, like wheels turning, and make vocal sound effects for horses' hoofs: Clippity-clop, clop-clop, etc. Daisy and Doctor tap their heels to help make sound effect. It is a joyous ride. Doctor, at the front, pantomiming driving. Riley in the center of the "wagon" looking at the countryside as they pass.)

RILEY: We went past the houses . . . hollyhocks and fences . . . down the road to the open sky. A scarecrow waves . . . as I pass by. Past a school house with pump and hitching post . . . *(Writes.)* "Smell of apples, ripening in the air, Smells of honeysuckle, peach and pear." *(Pleased.)* Yes! YES! It's poetry! Poetry that's part of me! Poems that I can write! *(Shouts, overflowing with rhymes.)* "Ho! Greenfields and running brooks, Knotted string and fishing hooks!"

DOC: Whoo-o-oa! *("Wheels" and sound effect stop. Mac and Daisy and Banner Carrier exit.)*

RILEY: We arrived—in Kokomo! And I—I was knee-deep in poems! *(Goes to side, writing.)*

DOC: How is the poetry going?

RILEY: I've got a pocket full of rhymes!

DOC: Good. We'll hear them tonight.

RILEY: Tonight?

DOC: You will recite them as part of the entertainment.

RILEY: In front of people?

DOC: It is the PEOPLE who will tell you if your poems are good. Now spruce yourself up. Tell Daisy to find you a hat. Tonight, you're going to perform! *(Exits.)*

RILEY: Perform! What if my poems aren't good? And people don't like them? *(Smiles.)* But what if they ARE good, and people applaud! Why am I shaking? *(Swallows.)* What if I lose my voice? What if I can't speak! Yes, give me a hat. A hat full of prayers. A hat full of courage! *(Riley exits. Daisy, with tambourine, and Mac, with bass drum, enter, stepping high to their music. Doctor enters, stands at C. Music stops.)*

DOC: My friends, my friends, How my heart rejoices to be in Kokomo, the jewel of Indiana. *(Drum roll.)* Welcome to the Mc-

Crillus Medicine Show. Tonight we present an entertainment of music and novelty. *(Drum roll.)* Yea, verily! I, also, bring you joy and health in each bottle of my Standard Remedies. Are you weak, sluggish, dispirited? Have you bad dreams, spots before your eyes? If so, do not go away. I have cures for ALL! But first some entertainment. It is with great pleasure I introduce to you my niece, my darling Daisy, who will enliven your spirits with a lively country dance. Miss Twinkle Toes! *(Doctor claps his hands and taps his foot. Mac beats the rhythm on drum. They both sing "Turkey in the Straw," as Daisy does a short, spirited dance, with bows and applause.)* Tonight is a special occasion! I have the honor of presenting a new Hoosier poet, who will recite his own poem. Let us welcome him to the platform and welcome him into our hearts. Mister—James Whitcomb Riley.

RILEY: *(Enters, nervously. He looks at Doctor, who nods and encourages him. He looks at Daisy, on the other side, who nods. He bows. He opens his mouth, but is speechless. Daisy and Doctor try to encourage him. He swallows, tries again, and speaks in a low voice.)* I will recite a poem I have written. A poem—

DOC: Louder, son. Speak up. Speak out!

RILEY: *(Looks at Doctor, nods. Looks at Daisy, who motions him to go ahead. He speaks very loud.)* A POEM WHICH IS ABOUT YOU—ABOUT ME—ABOUT INDIANA. *(Looks up, sees hat, quickly takes it off, nods a bow, and then recites with joy, feeling and the skill of an actor.)*

"When ever'thing's a-goin' like she's got a-goin' now—
The maple-sap a'drippin', and the buds on ever'bough,
The ice is out the crick again, the freeze is out the ground,
And you'll see faces thawin' too, if you'll just look around!
The sun ain't just pretendin' NOW!—the ba'm is in the breeze,
The trees'll soon be green as grass, and grass as green as trees.
When things is goin' THISAWAY, why, that's the sign you know,
That ever'thing is goin' like we like to see her go!"

(Doctor and Daisy lead the applause, Daisy encouraging the audience to applaud, Riley bows, puts hat on, takes it off, bows again, puts hat on.

He is flushed with excitement. He holds up his hands to stop the applause.)

I have another poem! It's about a little boy—a YOUNG boy and his drum. It is entitled "Billy and His Big Bass Drum." *(He uses Mac's drum, as he marches and beats it for sound effects. He recites with childish enthusiasm.)*

"Ho! it's come, kids, come!
With a bim! bam! bum!
Here's little Billy banging on his big bass drum!
He's marching round the room,
With his feather-duster plume
A-nodding and a-bobbing with his bim! bam! boom!
I'm a-coming; yes, I am—
Jim and Sis, and Jane and Sam!
We'll all march off with Billy and his bom! bim! bam!
Come HURRAWING as you come,
Or they'll think you're deef-and-dumb
If you don't hear little Billy and his big bass drum!"

(He beats a final boom-boom on the drum and keeps bowing. Doctor and Daisy applaud and encourage audience to join them. Mac takes drum and beats it for applause.)

DAISY: They like your poems! You're going to be a real poet!

DOC: Son, I think you have just shook hands with success. *(He shakes hands with Riley. Then Doctor, Daisy and Mac exit with drum beating.)*

RILEY: *(Steps forward.)* I kept writing more poems and reciting them. They were printed in newspapers and books—and the world applauded. To the question we all ask—the question: Why?, I found MY answer. Ride a blue horse and light up the sky! *(Carousel music.)*

Ride a blue horse,
There's one waiting for you;
Ride a blue horse,
Make a dream come true.

(Carousel music continues.)

My poems are made of memories—childhood memories of places, of people, of dreams. *(He motions and Father enters, stands DR. Riley exits.)*

FATHER:

"When Me and my Ma and Pa went to the Fair,
We drove the sorrel team and the buggy to go there.
And inside we found—a merry-go-round;
And Pa says, says he, 'Ain't nothing there
Too good for my boy,' when we went to the Fair."

(Carousel music fades out.)

NOEY: *(Enters and stands CL.)*

"Oh! the old swimmin' hole! Where the crick so still and deep
Looked like a baby-river that was laying half asleep.
Tracks of our *bare-feet* in the lane, heel and sole,
Told there 'as lots of fun at the old swimmin' hole."

MOTHER: *(Enters, stands DL.)*

"Tell you what I like best—
'Long about knee-deep in June,
Like to just get out and rest
On a hot lazy afternoon.
Just a-resting through and through,
With nothing else at all to do.
It's my kind of afternoon—
'Long about *knee-deep in June.*"

JOHN: *(Enters, stands CR.)*

"When the frost is on the pumkin and the fodder's in the shock,
And you hear the kyouch and gobble of the struttin' turkey cock,
O, them's the times of all the rest,
A feller is a-feelin' at his best,
When the frost is on the pumkin and the fodder's in the shock."

MARY: *(Enters, stands C.)*

"Little Orphant Annie's come to our house to stay,
An' wash the cups an' saucers up, and brush the crumbs away,
An' shoo the chickens off the porch, an' dust the hearth, an' sweep,

An' make the fire, an' bake the bread, an' earn her board-an'-keep;
An' all us other children, when the supper-things is done,
We set around the kitchen fire an' has the mostest fun
A-list'nin' to the witch-tales that Annie tells about,
And the Gobble-uns 'at gits you IF YOU DON'T WATCH OUT!"

RILEY: *(Enters, dressed as he was in the beginning, dark coat and tie.)* I have written many poems, and I have many memories. *(Smiles, goes to hat rack, takes top hat.)* And—I have worn many hats. This hat may be my best memory of all, and what a glorious occasion it is! The President of the United States has declared that all schools in America shall set aside this day, and observe it as "James Whitcomb Riley Day." America is celebrating MY birthday, Bands are playing, children are marching—it is! It is BETTER than a circus!

(Loud circus music begins. All the cast march in a circle, like a circus ring, around Riley, who stands on a stool, waving his hat. Each character after circling, pauses down center and bows, taking a curtain call, and then exits. Riley, last, bows, steps off stool, puts on his hat, and marches off with a happy step. Circus music continues.)

CURTAIN

DANDELION

by

JUDITH MARTIN, DIRECTOR OF THE PAPER BAG PLAYERS

MUSIC BY DONALD ASHWANDER

DEVELOPED WITH IRVING BURTON AND BETTY OSGOOD

A Fantasy Based on Darwin's Theory of Evolution

DANDELION

CHARACTERS

This play is written for four actors and two musicians. If desired, different actors could play each scene so that the entire play could provide parts for as many as thirty performers.

Drawings and notes that describe how to make the costumes and props are contained in the acting edition of the play published by Baker's Plays. Also, the complete score for voices and piano (four hands) may be purchased from the publisher.

SCENES

INTRODUCTION AND BEFORE
EARTHSHAKE
TOO MANY FISHES
DINOSAUR
DANDELION
NATURE'S WAYS
  PART I: MOTHER DUCK
  PART II: THE CATERPILLAR AND THE BIRD
  PART III: FOX AND PHEASANTS
LETTUCE
DARK SKIN, LIGHT SKIN
ON THE ROAD TO CULTURE
BOW WOW

INTRODUCTION

The stage is bare except for a piano extreme downstage right and a cluster of cardboard boxes and paper props center stage. The entire play is performed without interruption. The curtain is never drawn.

The use of the actors' real names give a sense of informality and intimacy. Personal names are dropped when the action becomes formal or abstract points are illustrated.

The musicians take their place at the piano. They play the Introduction. On Music Cue the actors run up the aisles of the theatre onto the stage. Each actor carries a piece of cardboard scenery. One very large piece is carried by two actors. The actors have the air of going someplace important. After circling the stage, they come to a halt with a flourish facing the audience.

Music ends.

(The cardboard the actors are carrying will be used as illustrations in the short scenes to follow.)

JUDY: We're The Paper Bag Players. I'm Judy.

BETTY: I'm Betty.

CHARLIE: I'm Charlie.

IRVING: I'm Irving.

DONALD: *(From the piano.)* And I'm Donald.

JUDY: Today we're going to do a play for you that takes place a long time ago.

IRVING: Long before The Paper Bag Players.

BETTY: It was long before that.

CHARLIE: And we're going to show you just how long ago it was. *(Music.) (There is a great deal of scurrying about. Everyone sets their cardboards down slightly upstage. Judy and Irving then come downstage and open a folded cardboard. It is a painting of the city.)*

JUDY: It was before New York City.

CHARLIE AND BETTY: Honk, Honk. Toot, Toot.

(Charlie and Betty pretend they are in cars. They ride back and forth in front of city. They use their voices as horns, almost collide and abruptly freeze.)

CHARLIE: It was long before New York City!

(Judy and Irving fold up city. Irving and Charlie take the "city" offstage and return immediately. Meanwhile Judy and Betty unfold another piece of cardboard downstage to face the audience. It is a painting of an Indian in a canoe.) (Music ends.)

CHARLIE: It was before the American Indian.

(The actors all stand behind the painting posing like stock pictures of Indians.)

IRVING: Before the Indian even came to America.

JUDY: Before anyone came to America.

BETTY: Before there were any people on this earth . . .

CHARLIE: At all! *(Music.) (Now the "Indian" cardboard picture is folded and taken off the stage by Betty and Judy. Meanwhile Charlie holds up cardboard "tree." The cast rushes to the "tree.")*

JUDY: Before there were trees!

BETTY: Before trees?

(Charlie folds "tree" and runs offstage with it. Runs back on stage without prop to rejoin the action. Irving picks up small squares of cardboards. On each square is painted a picture. Holds up a picture of a flower.)

IRVING: Before flowers. *(Tosses "flower" into wings. Then holds up picture of "cat.")* Before cats. *(Tosses "cat" into wings. Then holds up picture of "bird.")* Before birds. *(Tosses "bird" into wings. Then holds up picture of "mosquito.")* And even before the mosquito.

(Cast goes up to "mosquito" picture; slaps hands as if killing a mosquito. Irving exits with "mosquito" while making a buzzing sound. Then Betty, Judy and Charlie talk directly to the audience.) (Music ends.)

BETTY: In fact, you may find this hard to believe but it was long before there was any living thing on earth.

JUDY: Way back when the earth itself was a bubbling, boiling pot of soup.

CHARLIE: Way back at the beginning of the world.

(Music.) (The Actors' attention is caught by a huge paper "blob" moving slowly across the stage. It is Irving, completely enveloped in a paper bag, coming from stage left. He is crawling on the floor and is about to impersonate the formation of the earth. Judy and Betty back off toward stage right. Charlie stands at extreme stage right to narrate.) (Music ends.)

EARTHSHAKE: DANCE AND NARRATION

NARRATOR: The beginning of the world. *(Music.) (Music pauses for narration and speeches. Dance starts as Figure in paper slowly rises and falls.)* Four million years ago the earth was a mass of hot gases. *(Figure jumps from a low position on floor to as high as possible.)* The earth was covered with molten lava. *(Figure rolls on floor.)* Rocks and mountains were just forming. *(Figure runs about the stage while striking jagged poses.)* And as the earth spun it cooled. *(Figure spins and dancing slows to a stop.)* Its crust began to harden. *(Shape of Figure contracts.) The following speech is spoken over music.* And the waters rushed down to form oceans, lakes, and rivers. *(Figure makes a trembling pulsating motion and exits.) (Music ends.)*

(As Figure exits Judy runs on stage watching the disappearing Figure. When it is gone, she picks up a box painted blue (to suggest water) from the cluster of boxes on the stage and places it downstage. She addresses audience.)

JUDY: In those days the earth was mostly water. And in this water were many living things.

TOO MANY FISHES

(Music.) Judy picks up a red cardboard "fish" which is set inside the box, pops her head through hole in the cardboard fish and dances in the "water box." Betty, in a blue fish costume, enters from stage right and goes directly to the box. (Music ends.)

BLUE FISH: Excuse me please, but would you mind moving over? I'd like to get into the water. *(Climbs into box.)*

RED FISH: You know, there isn't that much room in here.

BLUE FISH: Oh, I'll manage. *(Music. The two Fish dance. Enter Charlie in green fish costume. Music stops abruptly.)*

CHARLIE THE FISH: Hummph. Is there room for one more?

RED FISH: I'm sorry but I really don't think so.

BLUE FISH: Definitely not.

RED FISH: Really!

CHARLIE THE FISH: What are you talking about? Looks like plenty of room to me. *(Climbs into box too. Music. Fish sing and dance in box. Dance is a simulation of swimming motion.)*

TRIO:

Too many fishes, too little water,
Somethin's gonna happen soon!

Too many fishes, too little water,
Somethin's gonna happen soon!

(Fish collide. Dance abruptly stops. Music ends.)

CHARLIE THE FISH: Somebody pushed me.

RED FISH: I think it's terrible the way things are getting so crowded around here.

BLUE FISH: Watch your tail, will you?

RED FISH: Who's breathing down my fin?

CHARLIE THE FISH: Somebody pushed me right in the mud.

BLUE FISH: Well don't look at me. I'm all muddy, myself.

RED FISH: Say, if you two are looking for clear water, you won't find it here.

CHARLIE THE FISH: Well, where will we find it?

RED FISH: Don't ask me. *(Fish start to sing again.)*

TRIO:

Too many fishes, too little water,
Somethin's gonna happen soon!

Too many fishes, too little water,
Somethin's gonna happen soon!

(Fish dance and repeat song.)

Too many fishes, too little water,
Somethin's gonna happen soon!

(Song becomes faster and more excited.)

Too many fishes, too little water,
Somethin's gonna happen soon!

(Movements of Fish become frenetic and chaotic. Charlie jumps out of "water" and lands on his side stage right. Music ends.)

BLUE FISH: Charlie! Charlie, you crazy fool!

RED FISH: You crazy fool fish. Come back in the water.

CHARLIE THE FISH: Gasp . . . Gasp . . . Gasp. *(Music. Irving runs on, stands stage left and narrates in excited voice over music.)*

IRVING: Will Charlie the Fish live or die? *(Charlie the Fish using cardboard fish continues to indicate a fish out of water gasping for breath.)* Is it the beginning or is it the end? *(More gasps from Charlie.)* His gills must turn into lungs. *(Charlie starts to rise.)* His fins must turn into legs. *(Charlie is on his knees.)* He's crawling. *(Charlie moves forward on his knees. Now Charlie is moving on the words.)* He's breathing. *(Charlie pants audibly.)* He's standing. *(Charlie struggles to his feet.)* And in a mere million years, Charlie the Fish has changed into a frog. *(The cardboard fish is now in a vertical position. Charlie the Fish is standing with legs apart. He looks like a Frog.)*

CHARLIE THE FROG: RIBBIT! RIBBIT! RIBBIT! *(Charlie the frog exits leaping. Music ends. Betty and Judy put down their fish costumes and cheer.)*

BETTY: Hooray for Charlie.

JUDY: Good for Charlie.

BETTY: Charlie the Fish has made it! *(Betty and Judy applaud briskly. Music begins for next scene during applause.)*

DINOSAUR

Enter Dinosaur on music.

A 15' paper bag with a Dinosaur skeleton painted on it enters from stage left, crosses in front of Betty and Judy while they are still applauding. They can no longer be seen by audience. Inside one end of Dinosaur stands Irving—at other end stands Charlie. They support the Dinosaur as Betty slips into the Dinosaur from the upstage side. A paper window in Dinosaur's body opens and Betty's head pops out. Dinosaur stops moving for Betty's recitation which should be brisk.

BETTY: Here we have the bones of a dinosaur that lived one hundred million years ago. Dinosaurs were the largest reptiles that ever walked the earth. They liked warm weather, but the weather changed and it got cold. They got cold. They laid eggs and their eggs got cold. They were cold blooded and couldn't warm up so they all became extinct. *(Music ends.)* That means dead. They all died. You won't find any dinosaurs around here any more. *(Closes window. Music. Dinosaur slowly exits. Music ends.)*

(Judy has been kneeling behind Dinosaur. She can now be seen. She is holding a large yellow flower. The end of the stick is on the floor as if it were still in the earth.)

(Judy plucks flower.)

(Music.)

JUDY: What a pretty yellow flower. I wonder what it's called. *(Enter Charlie singing carrying a book.)*

CHARLIE:

Dandelion, Dandelion, don't you know a Dandelion?
Dandelion, Dandelion, can't you tell a Dandelion?

(Charlie and Judy talk to the audience and to each other.)

JUDY: I wonder how it got here. *(Charlie points to his book.)*

CHARLIE: Look, first a flower, then a fluff, then a seed, then a plant.

JUDY: First a flower, then a fluff, then a seed, then a plant? Is that the end?

CHARLIE: No, there is no end. It happens again and again.

JUDY: *(To audience.)* Did you know that?

CHARLIE: *(To audience.)* You know, Judy understands things better if you sing to her. *(Sings to Judy.)*

Dandelion, Dandelion, same old story every time.
Dandelion, Dandelion, same old story every time.

JUDY: That's a nice song, Charlie, but I don't get it.

CHARLIE: *(To audience.)* Maybe if we all sing to Judy, then she'll understand.

JUDY: *(Gestures to audience.)* You're not going to ask all these people to sing, are you? They don't even know the words.

CHARLIE: Well I'll just teach them the words. *(To audience.)* The words are:

Dandelion, Dandelion, same old story every time.
Dandelion, Dandelion, same old story every time.

Now let's sing it to her.

CHARLIE AND AUDIENCE:

Dandelion, Dandelion, same old story every time.
Dandelion, Dandelion, same old story every time.

JUDY: I like the way everybody sings, but I still don't get it.

CHARLIE: *(Calls offstage.)* Irving. . . . Betty. . . .

(Enter Betty and Irving each carrying book.)

BETTY AND IRVING: Yes Charlie?

CHARLIE: Can you help me make Judy understand about the Dandelion?

BETTY: Oh sure Charlie. *(Betty crosses over to Judy and opens her book.)*

BETTY: You know, Judy, it's like the cat and the kitten.
First, the cat has a kitten, the kitten becomes a cat.
The cat has a kitten, the kitten becomes a cat.

The cat, the kitten, the kitten, the cat.
The cat, the kitten, the kitten, the cat.

(Irving and Charlie join Betty.)

TRIO:
The flower, the fluff, the seed, the plant.
The flower, the fluff, the seed, the plant.

JUDY: Is that the end?

BETTY: No, there is no end.

JUDY: I didn't know that.

BETTY: *(To audience.)* Tell her.

TRIO AND AUDIENCE:
Dandelion, Dandelion, same old story every time.
Dandelion, Dandelion, same old story every time.

JUDY: I don't get it.

IRVING: Judy, I'll explain it to you. Look, it's just like the chicken and the egg.

JUDY: The chicken and the egg?

IRVING:
The chicken lays an egg, the egg becomes a chicken.
The chicken lays an egg, the egg becomes a chicken.

The chicken, the egg, the chicken, the egg.

BETTY:
The cat, the kitten, the kitten, the cat.
The cat, the kitten, the kitten, the cat.

TRIO:

The flower, the fluff, the seed, the plant.
The flower, the fluff, the seed, the plant.

JUDY: Is that the end?

IRVING: No, there is no end.

JUDY: Well I didn't know that.

IRVING: *(To audience.)* Tell her.

TRIO AND AUDIENCE:

Dandelion, Dandelion, same old story every time.
Dandelion, Dandelion, same old story every time.

JUDY: I don't get it.

CHARLIE: Judy, it is so simple. It's just like the caterpillar and the butterfly.

The caterpillar spins a cocoon, out comes a butterfly.
The caterpillar spins a cocoon, out comes a butterfly.

IRVING: The chicken, the egg, the chicken, the egg.

BETTY:

The cat, the kitten, the kitten, the cat.
The cat, the kitten, the kitten, the cat.

TRIO:

The flower, the fluff, the seed, the plant.
The flower, the fluff, the seed, the plant.

JUDY: Is that the end?

CHARLIE: No, there is no end.

JUDY: I didn't know that.

CHARLIE: *(To audience.)* Tell her.

TRIO AND AUDIENCE:

Dandelion, Dandelion, same old story every time.
Dandelion, Dandelion, same old story every time.

JUDY: I still don't get it.

(Betty, Irving, and Charlie confer).

BETTY: Tadpole!!!

The tadpole comes from out of the egg, which comes from out of the frog.
The tadpole comes from out of the egg, which comes from out of the frog.
The frog, the egg, the tadpole.
The frog, the egg, the tadpole.

CHARLIE:
Caterpillar spins a cocoon, out comes a butterfly.
Caterpillar spins a cocoon, out comes a butterfly.

IRVING: The chicken, the egg, the chicken, the egg.

BETTY:
The cat, the kitten, the kitten, the cat.
The cat, the kitten, the kitten, the cat.

TRIO:
The flower, the fluff, the seed, the plant.
The flower, the fluff, the seed, the plant.

JUDY: Is that the end?

TRIO: No, there is no end.

JUDY: I didn't know that.

TRIO: *(To audience.)* Tell her.

TRIO AND AUDIENCE:
Dandelion, Dandelion, same old story every time.
Dandelion, Dandelion, same old story every time.

JUDY: But I don't get it.

IRVING: Judy, I'll explain it to you one more time and please listen carefully.

JUDY: I've been listening.

IRVING: All right, it's just like the mother and the child.
The mother has a child, the child grows up, becomes a mother.
The mother has a child, the child grows up, becomes a mother.

The mother, the child, the mother, the child.

BETTY:
The frog, the egg, the tadpole.
The frog, the egg, the tadpole.

CHARLIE:

Caterpillar spins a cocoon, out comes a butterfly.
Caterpillar spins a cocoon, out comes a butterfly.

IRVING: The chicken, the egg, the chicken, the egg.

TRIO:

The cat, the kitten, the kitten, the cat.
The cat, the kitten, the kitten, the cat.

The flower, the fluff, the seed, the plant.
The flower, the fluff, the seed, the plant.

JUDY: Is that the end?

TRIO: No, there is no end!

JUDY: Wait a minute. I think I have it.

(Trio gasps.)

JUDY: Does this happen to a popsicle?

TRIO: NO!

JUDY: Well then, I don't get it.

TRIO: Forget it! *(Trio despairing of ever making Judy understand hands her the books, turns away from her and exits singing.)*

TRIO:

Dandelion, Dandelion, same old story every time.
Dandelion, Dandelion, same old story every time.

(Trio exits. Judy starts to follow them—then stops. Turns to audience and says:)

JUDY: *I don't get it! (Judy exits.)*

NATURE'S WAYS

Scene change.
Enter Betty and Charlie with a large folded screen, about one half the length of the stage. They place it in front of the cluster of boxes. They unfold it and hold it taut to display a sign painted "Nature's Ways."
They stand at either end of screen.
Music ends.

BETTY: Nature works in curious ways.

CHARLIE: As we will show in three short plays.

(Music.) (They lift paper painted "Nature's Ways" and flip it over back of cardboard screen, revealing another painting. This is a landscape of a pond. They adjust cardboard so it is self-standing. Music ends.)

PART I: MOTHER DUCK

CHARLIE: A mother's love in any form,

BETTY: Will keep her children safe and warm.

(Betty and Charlie exit behind screen. Enter Judy as Mother Duck from stage left. She has a beak, goggles and is wearing a white cardboard carton. She waddles in front of the pond. All the sequences of Mother Duck take place in front of this "pond.")

DUCK: Quack . . . Quack . . . Quack . . . Quack . . .

(Enter Irving as a Turtle in a cardboard box. Irving is on his hands and knees in the box with his head protruding.)

TURTLE: Oh me oh my oh me oh my oh me oh my oh me . . .

DUCK: Poor Mrs. Turtle. What's the matter?

TURTLE: I am simply exhausted.

DUCK: What from?

TURTLE: I just laid my eggs.

DUCK: Just laid your eggs? Quack . . . Quack . . . Quack . . . Who's sitting on your eggs?

TURTLE: Why nobody's sitting on my eggs. I left them over there in the sand.

DUCK: You left your eggs in the sand? What kind of a mother are you?

TURTLE: I always leave my eggs in the sand. They'll be all right.

DUCK: I never heard of such a thing.

TURTLE: What do you do with your eggs?

DUCK: I sit on my eggs until they're hatched and even then my baby ducks are always within calling distance. Quack . . . Quack . . . CHILDREN!!!

(Enter Betty and Charlie as Baby Ducks. They have costumes like their mother. They quack in unison. They obediently follow their mother as she waddles about the stage. Then they exit.)

DUCK: Now that's what I call taking care of children.

TURTLE: Well thank goodness my children can take care of themselves. Oh me oh my oh me oh my.

(Turtle exits. From around the other side of the screen Betty enters as a Fish. The fish costume is similar to the fish earlier in the play—a cardboard-shaped fish with a hole for the face where the eye of a fish would be.)

FISH: Gulp, gulp, gulp, gulp, gulp.

DUCK: What are you so excited about?

FISH: I just laid my eggs.

DUCK: How many eggs did you lay?

FISH: Oh, about a thousand.

DUCK: A thousand? What do you do with all those children?

FISH: I eat them.

DUCK: Q U A C K!

FISH: Oh don't get so excited. I don't eat all of them.

DUCK: What are you anyway?

FISH: I am a Fish. Gulp . . . Gulp . . . Gulp . . .

(Fish exits around the same corner of the screen as did the Turtle.)

DUCK: Oh a fish. What can you expect from a fish?

[NOTE: While the characters are behind the screen they have ample opportunity to change costumes. All the costumes are part of the preshow setup and have been part of the scenery since the show began.]

(From the other side of the screen enters Charlie as an Ostrich. Ostrich costume is a pair of goggles with a beak worn on his face. The body is a cardboard box with layers of newspaper suggesting long white feathers.)

DUCK: Quack . . . Quack . . . Quack . . . Quack . . . What are you?

OSTRICH: I am an Ostrich.

DUCK: What's an Ostrich?

OSTRICH: A bird.

DUCK: I'm a bird too. Quack . . . Quack . . . I'm a Duck. Say, how do you know you're a bird?

OSTRICH: I have no teeth.

DUCK: I have no teeth either. Quack . . . Quack . . . What else makes you think you're a bird?

OSTRICH: I lay eggs.

DUCK: Oh you must lay a beautiful egg.

OSTRICH: And I have feathers.

DUCK: Say, you must fly very high.

OSTRICH: Fly? Fly? I wouldn't dream of flying!

(Ostrich exits with great hauteur. Duck is speechless, then gathers herself together for a defiant response.)

DUCK: I never heard of a bird that didn't fly!

(Duck utters a sound reminiscent of a razzberry in the direction of the no longer present Ostrich. Irving, Betty and Charlie enter from behind the screen. They are now Mice. The Mice costumes are goggles and black turtleneck shirts with no sleeves. The actors' arms are folded underneath the shirts. The Mice are very excited, run about and finally cluster together.)

MOUSE 1: Eeeek, eeeek, eeeek, eeeek . . .

MOUSE 2: Eeeek, eeeek, eeeek, eeeek . . .

MOUSE 3: Eeeek, eeeek, eeeek, eeeek . . .

DUCK: Oh, you're so peculiar. What are you?

MICE: We could tell you . . . eeeek . . . eeeek. . . .

DUCK: No, no, no, no. Let me guess.

MICE: Okay.

DUCK: Are you snails?

MICE: No.

DUCK: Are you snakes?

MICE: No.

DUCK: Now don't tell me, don't tell me. Let me guess. Have you got bones?

MICE: Sure, we got bones.

DUCK: Do you lay eggs?

MICE: No.

DUCK: Are you warm blooded?

MICE: Yes.

DUCK: Do you carry your babies here? *(Places her hand on her stomach.)*

MICE: Yes.

DUCK: You're mammals!

MICE: Eeeek . . . eeeek . . . she's got it . . . she's got it . . . eeeek. . . .

DUCK: What kind of mammals are you?

MICE: Mice.

DUCK: Oh I like mice.

MICE: She likes mice . . . eeeek . . . eeeek . . . eeeek. . . .

(Duck suddenly looks serious. She is no longer interested in the Mice. Something urgent and internal has seized her attention.)

DUCK: Q U A C K . . . Excuse me, Mice, *I think I have to go lay an egg.* Quack . . . Quack . . . Quack. . . . *(Exits, moving very gingerly.)*

MICE: Must be a bird . . . has to lay an egg . . . eeeek . . . eeeek. . . .

(Two Mice exit behind left side of screen. Third Mouse peeks around corner of screen where Duck has disappeared, "eeeks" and then follows the other Mice.)

(Music. Judy and Charlie now appear at either end of screen. They flip the painting of the pond over the top of the screen and reveal a landscape of three trees on a hill very simply painted.) (Music ends.)

PART II: THE CATERPILLAR AND THE BIRD

JUDY: Should caterpillar choose a leaf which is green,
He is safe, will not be seen.

CHARLIE: But should he play another hunch,
The bird will have him for his lunch.

(Judy and Charlie are about to illustrate with a pantomime of two cardboard puppets the encounter of a Caterpillar and a Bird and how protective coloring works. In the pantomime, a green Caterpillar crawls along the brown earth. A red Bird sees him and gives chase. The green Caterpillar hides in a green bush and cannot be seen by the Bird. When the Bird is not looking, the green Caterpillar leaves his green bush. He is spotted again by the Bird who gives chase. This time the green Caterpillar hides in an orange bush and is easily spotted by the Bird who seizes the Caterpillar in its beak and goes off.)

(Charlie exits behind screen. Judy remains in front of screen. She is handed a cardboard caterpillar, from behind the screen. She kneels to place cardboard caterpillar on the edge of the landscape.)

(Illustrations and directions of the cardboard fantasy follow on the next page.)

(Music.)

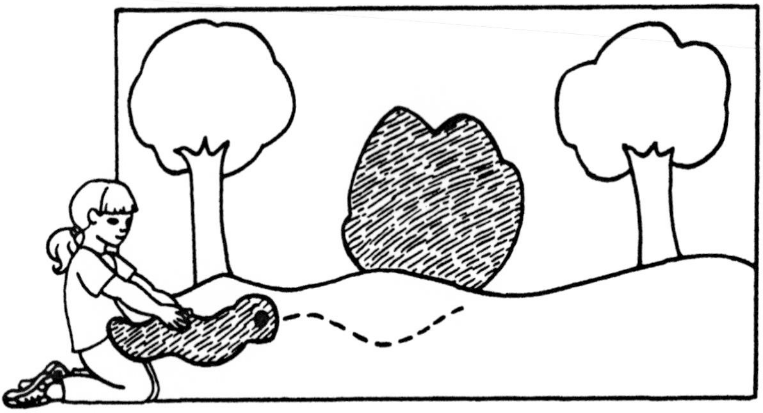

(Picture covers entire screen. Sky is blue. Ground is brown. Trees are orange. Bush and Caterpillar are green. Bird has a hopping motion. Caterpillar has a rocking motion. In these sketches only the first and last appearance of the actors are shown. But they are always seen operating their characters. Actor is on knees.

(Actor holding Bird is behind screen. Bird pops up. Actor's hands holding Bird are visible. Bird is a flat profile painting of a bird. A paper clip is glued to his beak.)

(Bird is brought down alongside of screen. Actor holding Bird is now in full view. He is standing.)

(Bird and Caterpillar come together. Both pause.)

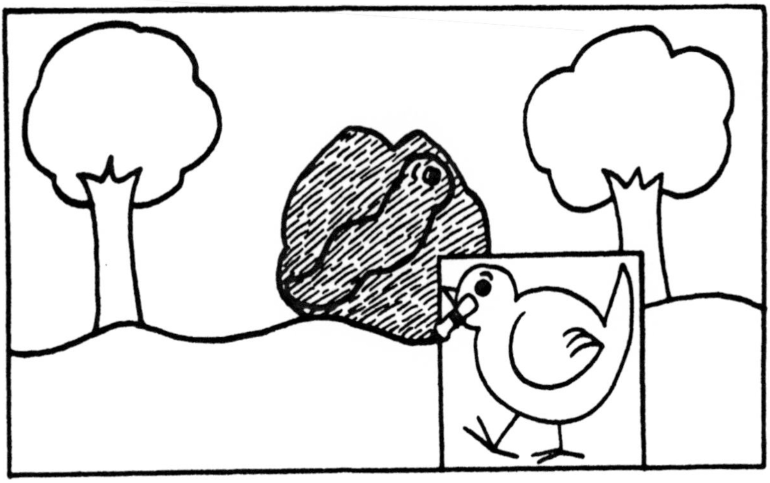

(Caterpillar in quick upward movement reaches bush. Is now camouflaged. Bird pauses.)

(Bird turns to leave.)

(Caterpillar comes down from bush.)

(Caterpillar and Bird go in opposite directions.)

(Bird unexpectedly turns and sees Caterpillar. Turn is accomplished by flip of bird prop. Bird is painted on both sides of cardboard.)

(A chase. Bird, hopping, pursues Caterpillar. Gets closer.)

(Chase continues. Bird catches up to Caterpillar.)

(Caterpillar, in quick upward movement, reaches tree. He is now on orange and can be clearly seen.)

(Bird seizes Caterpillar in its "clip" beak.)

(Bird turns and hops along top of screen. Actor holding Bird remains in front of screen. Actor who has been holding Caterpillar, stands, makes gesture of disappointment, and exits behind screen.)

(Actor holding Bird walks triumphantly in front of screen.)

(One last view of Bird before it disappears behind screen.)

PART III: FOX AND PHEASANTS

(Irving and Betty enter from behind screen and stand at either side. They flip green and orange painting to reveal another landscape. This painting is all in browns, tans, and rust.)

(Music ends.)

BETTY: Never be jealous of anyone's looks.

IRVING: The color you are may save you from crooks.

(Betty and Irving exit behind screen.)

(Music. The head and nose of the Fox appear over the edge of the screen. Then the Fox stalks in front of the landscape. Fox has a costume of goggles with a large paper nose. He also has mittens and tail.)

FOX:

Fox, Fox, looking for a pheasant.
Nice fat juicy bird.

Fox, Fox, looking for a pheasant.
Nice fat juicy bird.

(Music ends.)

Aaooooaaoooo!!! Am I one big hungry fox. Oh, would I love to find a nice fat juicy pheasant. But they're so hard to find. A brown bird in a brown tree in the brown grass on a brown road. Aaooooaaoooo!!! But I have a feeling today is going to be my lucky day.

(Music. Fox exits. Music changes and enter Irving as pheasant. He wears goggles and beak on his face. On his body he wears colored paper to indicate feathers. He enters briskly with nervous birdlike movements. He looks to the left and right and then calls to his mate.)

MR. BIRD: You can come out dear.

(Enter Betty as hen pheasant dressed like her mate except that the papers she wears are brown and drab. She too is nervous and also looks left and right. Music ends.)

MRS. BIRD: Is it safe here, dear?

MR. BIRD: Yes, dear, it's safe. You know, dear, you blend right into this background. Why, your tail looks exactly like these hills.

MRS. BIRD: I am sick and tired of looking like these hills. Why, look at you, you have such gorgeous feathers. And look at me, I'm so drab.

MR. BIRD: I have to be attractive dear. Why else did you marry me?

MRS. BIRD: I always did say you were a beautiful bird.

MR. BIRD: Cheeep. . . . Cheeep. . . .

MRS. BIRD: But nevertheless, it just isn't fair.

MR. BIRD: I have to be brightly colored. This is a safety measure.

MRS. BIRD: Safety measure? Why, anybody could see you for miles around.

MR. BIRD: Cheeep . . . Cheeep. . . . It's not that I'm a show-off. Don't you forget that, in case of danger, I attract the enemy and not you.

MRS. BIRD: Oh, I've heard that a thousand times.

(Music. Birds sense danger and use their protective coloring to hide by standing against the landscape. Mrs. Bird's dull colors blend in with the landscape while Mr. Bird's bright colors stand out. Fox enters, stops, senses pheasants—slowly turns his head and sees male pheasant.)
(Music ends.)

MR. BIRD: Fox!

FOX: Pheasant!!!

(Music. As Mrs. Bird runs behind screen Mr. Bird jumps at Fox and screams. Mr. Bird runs behind screen with Fox following. Mrs. Bird reappears and hides by covering herself with her long tail. Fox runs in and stops abruptly. He does not see her, but senses her presence. Unaware of Fox, Mrs. Bird starts to tiptoe away. Unwittingly she moves closer to the Fox. As he is about to pounce on her, Mr. Bird rushes in and distracts Fox with a shriek.)

MR. BIRD: "Eeeeek!"

FOX: "Pheasant!"

(Both Birds run behind screen. Fox remains, crouches down, covers his face with his tail and blends into the landscape as Mr. Bird enters. Thinking he is safe, Mr. Bird relaxes. He sits on Fox. Fox grabs at Bird.)

MR. BIRD: "Eeeeek!"

(Another chase. Mr. Bird pulls screen around himself and spins. Fox continues to chase. The landscape slowly stops spinning, but the pheasant is still hidden in the landscape which is wrapped around him.)

(Music ends.)

FOX: Ooooooo, doggone that show-off bird. He fooled me again. How does he do it? *(Exits.)*

(Music. Mr. Bird peeks out from enveloping landscape, then opens screen fully.)

MR. BIRD: You can come out dear.

(Mrs. Bird enters. Music ends.)

MRS. BIRD: Is he gone?

MR. BIRD: Yes, he's gone and we are safe.

MRS. BIRD: Cheeep. . . . Cheeep. . . .

MR. BIRD: Now what do you think of my brightly colored feathers?

MRS. BIRD: Oh, you were right dear. Your brightly colored feathers saved our lives.

MR. BIRD: It wasn't only my feathers. It was my quick thinking.

MRS. BIRD: Well, dear, I always did say you were a very smart bird.

MR. BIRD: Cheeep. . . . Cheeep. . . .

MRS. BIRD: And he was a pretty dumb Fox.

(Music. Birds exit as Judy and Charlie enter and fold screen. Music ends.)

JUDY: Charlie, these plays we saw, are they all true?

CHARLIE: Why sure, they are; I thought you knew.

JUDY: But I feel sad about some of these plays.

CHARLIE: Don't feel sad, Judy; those are nature's ways.

(Music. Judy and Charlie exit stage left carrying off screen. Meanwhile behind the screen, Irving and Betty have taken off their bird costumes and piled up all the remaining costumes and props into the large "water" box. They exit stage right pushing off the props. Stage is cleared.)

(Music ends.)

LETTUCE

Throughout this skit the music follows the action closely. Consult score for cues.

Enter Betty. She is bent over so that her hands touch the floor—monkey fashion. She beats her chest with her fist and roars Tarzan style.

BETTY: Aaaaaaaaaaaaa. I wonder where all those other monkeys are.

(Enter Irving with the same monkey walk. He roars.)

IRVING: Aaaaaaaaaaaaa.

(Music. Irving and Betty run to greet each other.)

BETTY: Irving!

IRVING: Betty! Say, what are we having for breakfast?

BETTY: Bananas.

IRVING: What are we having for lunch?

BETTY: Bananas.

IRVING: And what are we having for dinner?

BETTY: Bananas.

IRVING: It's a good thing I like bananas.

(Betty and Irving jump about with their hands on the floor grunting and making ape-like movements.)

IRVING: Say Betty, couldn't we have something else besides bananas?

BETTY: Sure, what would you like? Some lettuce?

IRVING: Yeh, lettuce.

BETTY: I knew you were going to say lettuce. Haven't I told you a thousand times that lettuce is the worst thing for a monkey.

IRVING: But I like lettuce.

BETTY: You're always talking about lettuce. Lettuce. . . . Lettuce. . . . Lettuce. . . . Lettuce!

(Music ends. As Betty shouts angrily "lettuce-lettuce-lettuce," she begins to stand. On the last "lettuce" she is at her full height with her hands in the air.)

IRVING: What are you doing standing up there? You get down here where you belong.

(Music. Betty is surprised herself at her upright position. Gets back down, hands on the floor without a protest. Music changes and Betty continues argument.)

BETTY: And another thing, I don't know one other monkey besides you who even likes lettuce.

IRVING: Don't you tell me what to like. I like lettuce.

BETTY: LETTUCE . . . LETTUCE . . . LETTUCE . . . LETTUCE.

(Music ends. Again as Betty shouts "lettuce," she stands to her full height. She is startled and pleased.)

IRVING: I will not continue to talk to you unless you get down here where you belong.

BETTY: I'm not getting back down there 'til bananas turn purple. *(Takes a few awkward but deliberate steps.)*

IRVING: Where do you think you're going?

BETTY: I'm going for a walk!

(Music. Betty exits triumphant, upright and walking very fast. Irving jumps up and down and yells in outrage. Enter Judy and Charlie. They, too, are on their hands and feet, ape fashion.)

CHARLIE: Irving, what's the matter?

IRVING: Betty stood up on two feet and walked away.

JUDY: On two feet and walked away? Irving, what did you say to Betty to make her do a thing like that?

IRVING: I don't know. We were just talking and all of a sudden she started screaming . . . lettuce . . . lettuce . . . lettuce . . . lettuce! *(Music ends.)* And she stood up just like this.

(Irving demonstrates Betty's action and stands. Judy who is watching him intently is astonished.)

JUDY: Irving, you're standing up too.

IRVING: Wait a minute. I can think much better standing up on my feet. I think, I think, I think I'll go get her.

(Music. Irving runs out after Betty with fast and clumsy steps.)

JUDY: Say, did you ever see anything like that in your life?

CHARLIE: Uh . . . uh.

(Betty comes running back across the stage with Irving in pursuit. They are shouting and obviously enjoying the new experience of standing and running. They both exit. Music ends.)

JUDY: Say, that looks like fun. I'm going to try standing up too.

(Music. Judy with tremendous effort stands up. Music ends.)

JUDY: Look, Charlie, look at me, I'm standing. Come on Charlie, you can stand up, too.

CHARLIE: Oh, no. I'm staying right down here where I belong.

JUDY: Well, you can stay down there where you belong, but I'm going for a walk.

(Music. Judy starts to walk, then jumps and runs and calls to Irving.)

JUDY: Irving . . .

(Enter Irving running.)

IRVING: Here I am.

JUDY: Look at me. I'm standing.

IRVING: Good for you.

JUDY: Catch me.

IRVING: Oh, boy.

(Irving chases Judy in a wild romp around the stage. Charlie is on the stage watching them unbelievingly. They ignore him. Finally Irving catches Judy by the leg. Music ends.)

(They are both making loud flirtatious noises. Their backs are to Charlie. Charlie stands up in anger and in a cartoon-like gesture hits Irving soundly on the head. Irving falls down on his back. Judy and Charlie watch Irving fall, but Judy is mainly impressed with Charlie's new stance.)

JUDY: Charlie, you're standing!

CHARLIE: Yes, I am!

JUDY: Catch me. *(Music.)*

(Charlie chases Judy around the stage. They ignore Irving and jump over him. Judy exits squealing, with Charlie chasing her. As they exit, Betty enters passing them. Seeing Irving on the floor, she stops abruptly. Music ends.)

BETTY: Irving, you're lying down. I thought you were standing up. What happened?

(Betty helps Irving stand.)

IRVING: I don't know. First, you stood up, then I stood up, then she stood up, then he stood up, then he hit me on the head. You know, things are happening too fast around here.

BETTY: Never mind, Irving, we're both standing up now.

IRVING: Yes, we are.

BETTY: What do you say we go for a nice walk?

IRVING: Okay.

(Music.)
(Betty and Irving start to walk.)

BETTY: Say, Irving, when we get home, I'm going to make you a nice big salad.

IRVING: With lettuce?

BETTY: Lots of lettuce . . . and a few slices of bananas.

(Music.)
(They exit arm in arm.)

DARK SKIN, LIGHT SKIN

Narrator enters and walks to center stage. He is wearing a raincoat and rainhat, an outfit suitable for fierce storms. He is wearing a false beard of black wool.

NARRATOR: It was a million years ago. The age of the glaciers.

(Music.)
(The Glaciers [large cardboard boxes painted white and stacked high on each other] slowly move on stage pushed by three players who are concealed behind the boxes. Narrator talks as Glacier moves.)

NARRATOR: Masses of snow and sheets of ice moved down from the north. Glaciers of rock and ice covered half the earth and in this ice and snow and freezing wind, man lived.

(Glaciers stop moving. Three actors wearing brown paper cut-out shapes of human figures emerge from behind the Glaciers and stand in front of them. Music ends.)

FIRST FIGURE: It's been snowing for days.

SECOND FIGURE: And the winds are still howling.

(Music.)

FIRST FIGURE: It's colder now than it was before.

THIRD FIGURE: More ice and more snow.

SECOND FIGURE: Whatever happened to the sun?

THIRD FIGURE: I think we had better move again.

(The Figures move left to exit. The Narrator pushes Glaciers in their direction. The two Figures seem to be slowly retreating from the Glaciers. As they finally exit, the Glacier, too, is pushed offstage by the Narrator.)

(The Narrator stays on stage and so does the First Figure. Narrator addresses the audience.)

(Music ends.)

NARRATOR: And so the Ice Age gradually disappeared.

(First Figure speaks to Narrator.)

FIRST FIGURE: Say, can you tell me where I am?

NARRATOR: Why, sure, you're in the temperate zone where it's hot in the summer and cold in the winter.

FIRST FIGURE: Well, it must be winter 'cause it sure is cold and there's hardly any sun.

NARRATOR: You know I think you'd be better off with a lighter skin.

FIRST FIGURE: A lighter skin?

NARRATOR: With a lighter skin your body will be able to absorb more sunshine in the cold weather.

FIRST FIGURE: Ohhhhhh.

NARRATOR: *(To audience.)* And you know in a few thousand years, this man could change the color of his skin.

(Music.)
(First Figure slowly and deliberately turns brown paper cutout shape around. On the side now facing the audience, it is painted white. From now on this character is referred to as White Figure.)
(Music ends.)

WHITE FIGURE: Say, my skin is much lighter and I feel great.

NARRATOR: *(To audience.)* This man was doing very well until . . .

WHITE FIGURE: *(Sneezes.)* Aaaaaaachoooooo! Aaaaaaachoooooo!

NARRATOR: Do you know why you're sneezing?

WHITE FIGURE: No. Why?

NARRATOR: You're breathing in too much cold air. What you need is a longer nose.

WHITE FIGURE: A longer nose?

NARRATOR: Why yes. With a longer nose you'll be able to warm the air up on the way in.

WHITE FIGURE: But I don't want a longer nose. It won't look good on me.

NARRATOR: It's not what you want, it's what you need.

(Narrator takes small cardboard nose out of his pocket and attaches it to the face of the White Figure.)

NARRATOR: There!

WHITE FIGURE: You're right. I can breathe much easier now.

NARRATOR: And all over the world people were living in different climates.

(Music.)
(White Figure moves upstage. Reenter other Two Figures. Second Figure moves to stage right; Third figure moves stage left.)
(Music ends.)

(Narrator gestures toward Second Figure.)

NARRATOR: The tropic zone. . . .

SECOND FIGURE: It's so hot, I'm burning up.

(Narrator gestures toward Third Figure.)

NARRATOR: The polar regions . . .

THIRD FIGURE: It's cold, I'm freezing.

WHITE FIGURE: Say, what's going to happen to them?

(Narrator pointing to Second Figure.)

NARRATOR: This lady lives in the tropics. *(To her.)* What you need is a darker skin.

SECOND FIGURE: Why?

NARRATOR: Because with a darker skin you can protect yourself from the hot rays of the sun.

SECOND FIGURE: Well, let's get started.

NARRATOR: All right, but it's going to take a little time.

(Music.)

(Second Figure slowly and deliberately turns brown paper cutout shape around. On the side now facing the audience, it is painted black. From now on this character is referred to as Black Figure.)

(Music ends.)

BLACK FIGURE: That took a little time all right.

NARRATOR: It took fifteen thousand years.

BLACK FIGURE: But my head is still hot.

NARRATOR: What you need is some special hair.

BLACK FIGURE: Special hair?

NARRATOR: Yes. Special hair, like this. *(Points to his beard.)*

BLACK FIGURE: Let me try it on.

(Narrator takes off his beard, turns it upside down and places it on Black Figure's head. It now looks like black curly hair.)

BLACK FIGURE: My head feels much better.

WHITE FIGURE: You look great and I like your special hair.

THIRD FIGURE: Say, I want a color skin just like that.

NARRATOR: You don't need a skin just like that. You see she lives in the tropics where she needs a darker skin; whereas you live in the Polar region. You need a color skin that is suitable to an altogether different climate.

THIRD FIGURE: Whatever it is, let's get going.

NARRATOR: All right, but it's going to take a little time.

(Music.)

(White Figure, Black Figure and Narrator form a group upstage. They are motionless as Third Figure slowly and deliberately turns brown paper cut out shape around. On the side now facing the audience, it is painted

red. From now on this character is referred to as Red Figure.)
(Music ends.)

(The Narrator moves toward the Red Figure.)

NARRATOR: Well, how's that?

RED FIGURE: My skin feels better but I'm still cold.

NARRATOR: Now, you're going to have to change the shape of your body. You're going to have to look like all the other animals up here; like the seal, the penguin, and the walrus.

RED FIGURE: I don't want to look like any walrus.

NARRATOR: Oh, come on. They all have short arms, short legs, and they have lots of layers of fat on them to keep them warm.

(As Narrator speaks, he adjusts Red Paper Figure so that the arms are shorter and the body is wider.)

RED FIGURE: How do I look?

BLACK FIGURE: That's a beautiful color skin.

WHITE FIGURE: You look just like a walrus. Haaa . . . haaa.

RED FIGURE: I told you I didn't want to look like a walrus. I want to be tall and thin just like him.

WHITE FIGURE: And I want some of that special hair.

BLACK FIGURE: And I want a longer nose.

NARRATOR: And I want and I want and I want. Everybody wants something that they don't have. What are you people making such a fuss about? Don't you realize that there are sixty-seven different races living in this world?

RED FIGURE: Sixty-seven?

NARRATOR: Sure, and they all have long noses, short noses, straight hair, curly hair, big feet, little feet, dark skin, light skin.

(Speech of Three Figures becomes excited and rhythmic.)

BLACK FIGURE: Long noses, short noses.

WHITE FIGURE: Straight hair, curly hair.

RED FIGURE: Big feet, little feet.

THREE FIGURES: Dark skin, light skin.

(Music.)
(Narrator exits. Black, White and Red Figures dance and then exit.)
(Music ends.)

ON THE ROAD TO CULTURE

In this scene, music cues and sound effects are essential to the action. Refer to score.

Enter Narrator. He is sitting on a wooden dolly with his feet in the air. The dolly has been pushed on to the stage from the wings so his entrance has considerable speed. He is holding a cardboard tube and a piece of flat cardboard.

NOTE: *In this skit, the tube will be used as a stick and the flat cardboard as lumber.*

When the dolly reaches stage right, the Narrator makes his announcement.

NARRATOR: On the road to culture!

(He springs up and adjusts the dolly so it stands with its wheels facing the audience.)

NARRATOR: Here we have the wheel, lumber, cardboard. These things didn't happen overnight, you know. Now culture began a long time ago when mankind was very young. A Cave Lady . . .

(Enter Cave Lady. She is wearing a paper wig which looks like long unruly hair.)

NARRATOR: She's about to take a walk.

(Music.)
(Cave Lady walks in place.)
(Music ends.)

NARRATOR: It starts to rain.

(Music.)
(Cave Lady holds out her hand to feel raindrops.)

CAVE LADY: Oh dear, I'm going to get soaking wet. What'll I do?

NARRATOR: She walked until she came to a tree.

(Tree [an actor holding green leafy branches] enters and stands center stage with arms extended. Cave Lady runs to Tree and clutches the trunk. She huddles under the leafy branches. The leafy branches of the Tree lower to give the Cave Lady protection.)

(Music ends, indicating rain has stopped. Cave Lady puts out her hand.)

CAVE LADY: It stopped raining. Now I can go on with my walk. *(She starts to walk, then stops.)* Wait a minute! What if I run into another rainstorm and I'm not near a tree with big branches. I'd better take one of those branches with me. . . . *(Pulls branch from the Tree. The Tree winces. Cave Lady holds the branch over her head.)* Just in case.

NARRATOR: Little did she realize, she had just invented—the—umbrella.

(Music.)
(Tree exits as Cave Lady, holding the umbrella high, continues her walk until she meets a Tiger [an actor with a cardboard Tiger mask] who springs out from the wings. The Tiger chases the Cave Lady around the stage. She stops frightened and cornered.)
(Music ends.)

TIGER: Grrrrrrrrr.

CAVE LADY: It's a wild tiger!

TIGER: I'm hungry. Grrrrrrr. . . . *(Tiger grabs the Cave Lady's arm.)*

CAVE LADY: I think it wants to eat me. What'll I do?

NARRATOR: She just happened to be near a Heap of Bones.

(Heap of Bones enters very quickly [an actor holding large white cardboard bones.] Heap of Bones falls on the floor at the feet of the Cave Lady.)

(Music changes.)
(She withdraws her arm from the Tiger's grasp and carefully selects a bone and offers it to the Tiger.)

CAVE LADY: Here Tiger, here's a nice juicy bone. It's much better than eating me. *(Tiger lets go of Cave Lady, takes bone, growls and exits. Music Ends.)* Whew, what a close call. *(Resumes her walk and then stops abruptly.)* Wait a minute! What if I run into another one of those wild tigers and I'm not near a heap of bones? I'd better take one of these bones with me. *(She runs back to Heap of Bones and delicately separates one bone and holds it up.)* Just in case.

NARRATOR: Little did she realize that she had just invented Cat Food.

(Music.)
(Heap of Bones rolls offstage as Cave Lady continues her walk.)
(Music ends.)

(Enter Raging River [an actor waving blue plastic shower curtain].)

NARRATOR: She came to a Raging River!!!

(Music.)
(Raging River runs about stage constantly blocking the Cave Lady's path. Then the Raging River flings itself on the ground in front of the Cave Lady who stops short.)
(Music ends.)

CAVE LADY: How am I going to get across that Raging River?

NARRATOR: She just happened to see a big log.

(Music.)
(Narrator gives piece of cardboard [representing log] to Cave Lady who

places it over the Raging River. She steps on cardboard log and crosses the Raging River.)

(Music ends.)

CAVE LADY: Now I can go on with my walk. *(She resumes walk, then stops abruptly.)* Wait a minute! What if I come to another one of those Raging Rivers and I'm not near a big log? I'd better take this log with me. . . . *(She goes back to River and picks up cardboard log.)* Just in case.

NARRATOR: Little did she realize she had just invented the first portable bridge!

(Music.)

(Raging River exits waving shower curtain. Cave Lady continues walk as Snake [two actors wrapped in striped paper) enters].)

(Music ends.)

NARRATOR: She heard a hissing sound.

(Music.)

(Snake hisses, then unwinds to a length of about 20 feet. Head of the Snake directly confronts Cave Lady and hisses again.)

CAVE LADY: It's a snake!

(Snake moves in a large circle around the Cave Lady, confronts her again and hisses.)

CAVE LADY: It's a crawling snake!

(Snake chases Cave Lady around stage and finally wraps itself tightly around her body.)

(Music ends.)

CAVE LADY: It's a poison snake! What'll I do?

NARRATOR: She just happened to see a big stick! *(Runs to Cave Lady and gives her a stick [the cardboard tube].)*

NARRATOR: Here you are.

CAVE LADY: Thanks.

NARRATOR: You're welcome.

(Cave Lady whacks the Snake four times with stick. Snake collapses. Cave Lady climbs out of snake coils.)

CAVE LADY: Another close call. *(She returns the stick to the Narrator.)* Wait a minute! *(She takes the stick back.)* What if I run into another one of those poison snakes and I'm not near a big stick? I'd better take this stick with me . . . just in case.

NARRATOR: Little did she realize she had just invented the first Snake Knocker.

(Music.)
(Snake exits as Cave Lady continues her walk. She stops to rest. Another Cave Lady, her friend, enters. She also wears a paper wig.)
(Music ends.)

CAVE LADY: Hi!

FRIEND: Hi!

CAVE LADY: Say, where are you going?

FRIEND: Oh, I'm on my way to Cavesville.

CAVE LADY: Cavesville? I just came from Cavesville and I had nothing but trouble, trouble, trouble, and trouble. You'd better take some of this stuff with you. Here's a Snake Knocker. *(Gives Friend stick.)* Here's a Water Crosser. *(Gives Friend log.)* Here's a Rain Stopper. *(Gives Friend branch.)* And here's some Cat Food. *(Gives Friend bone.)*

FRIEND: Gee, you've got some neat things.

CAVE LADY: Well, they're your things now.

(Cave Ladies freeze in a happy pose.)

NARRATOR: Little did she realize she had just passed on culture!

(Music.)
(Narrator sets dolly down on wheels. Both Cave Ladies sit on it very pleased with themselves. Narrator pulls them out.)

BOW WOW

Music continues from previous scene and accommodates setup for Bow Wow. Charlie pushes in a pile of large boxes. They are the glacier boxes turned around. On each box (on the side facing the audience) is painted a large black rock. He arranges the painted boxes so they form a cave. He signals to his family.

Ma, Pa and Judy enter dressed in burlap bags. They look like cave dwellers. They do a funny walk around the cave in time to the music. Ma, Pa and Charlie go into the cave, snuggle around each other and go to sleep.

Judy remains outside, wide awake. Music ends.

JUDY: There's my whole family asleep inside the cave. What a bunch of deadheads!

(Family snores. Judy paces up and down humming and singing to herself.)

Nothing to do. Nobody to talk to. I think I'll go down to the river and get myself a dog. Then I'll have somebody to talk to. They won't even know I'm gone but . . . *(To audience.)* If Ma wakes up and asks "WHERE IS JUDY?," you say "BOW WOW" . . . then she'll know I went down to the river to get myself a dog. Now if Ma asks "WHERE IS JUDY?," what are you going to say?

AUDIENCE: BOW WOW.

JUDY: Louder!

AUDIENCE: BOW WOW!!!!

JUDY: Thanks. *(Exits. Ma crawls out of the cave.)*

MA: Well, it's time to clean up the cave. How can I sweep with everyone fast asleep? There's my son, Charlie. . . . *(Charlie mumbles in his sleep.)*

MA: And there's Pa. . . . *(Pa mumbles in his sleep.)* But where is Judy?

AUDIENCE: BOW WOW!

MA: BOW WOW? Judy's being chased by a mad dog! I'd better go help her. Listen, if Pa wakes up and asks, "WHERE IS MA?," you just tell him I went down to the river to help Judy. No, that's too long. If Pa asks "WHERE IS MA?," you just say BB-BLLLLLLLL. . . . BBBLLLLLLLL. . . .

(Ma makes a rippling motion with her hand to accompany the sound BBBLLLLLLLL. [Audience usually imitates Ma's hand movements].)

AUDIENCE: BBBLLLLLLLL. . . . BBBBLLLLLLLLL. . . .

(Ma exits.)

PA: Such a racket going on here. I can hardly get any sleep. *(Crawls out of cave and looks at sleeping Charlie.)* There's my son, Charlie. He sleeps all the time. He's either asleep or he's in trouble. Nobody else is home. *(To audience.)* Where is Judy?

AUDIENCE: BOW WOW.

PA: BOW WOW? Judy's been eaten by a mad dog! Where is Ma?

AUDIENCE: BBBLLLLLLLL. . . . BBBLLLLLLLL. . . .

PA: BBBLLLLLLLL? Ma fell into the river! I'd better go help her. *(Runs to go offstage, but comes back to cave. He bends down to wake Charlie.)*

PA: Charlie, get up, your sister's been eaten by a mad dog, and Ma fell in the river. *(Charlie mumbles and remains asleep.)* Oh, never mind. *(To audience.)* Listen, if Charlie should wake up and ask, "WHERE IS PA?" you just tell him to stay right here and use his head. Noooo. That's too long. Just tell him to use his head. Noooo. Listen, you just say BONG BONG. *(Makes a knocking motion on his head with his fist.)* Then he'll know he should stay right here and use his head. Now if Charlie asks "WHERE IS PA?" what are you going to say?

AUDIENCE: BONG BONG!

PA: Goooood. Maaaaa, I'm coming. *(Exits. Charlie wakes up and crawls out of cave.)*

CHARLIE: Say, nobody's home. *(To audience.)* Where is Judy?

AUDIENCE: BOW WOW!

CHARLIE: BOW WOW? Judy ate a mad dog! Where is Ma?

AUDIENCE: BBBLLLLLLLL. . . . BBBLLLLLLLL. . . .

CHARLIE: BBBLLLLLLLL? Ma fell into the river! Where is Pa?

AUDIENCE: BONG BONG!

CHARLIE: BONG BONG? Pa's having a fight! I'd better help him. No, I'd better go get help. *(To audience.)* If anyone asks "WHERE IS CHARLIE?," you just say "HELP." *(Jumps and waves his hands in air.)* Now if anyone asks "WHERE IS CHARLIE?," what are you going to say?

AUDIENCE: HELP!!!

(Charlie runs off. Enter Judy holding cardboard dog.)

JUDY: Ma, look at my new dog. *(She looks in cave, and then asks audience.)* Say, where is Ma?

AUDIENCE: BBBLLLLLLLL.

JUDY: Where is Pa?

AUDIENCE: BONG BONG!

JUDY: Where is Charlie?

AUDIENCE: HELP!!!

JUDY: H E L P. . . . H E L P. . . . *(Waves her hands in the air. Pa rushes in and grabs Judy.)*

PA: Judy, I thought you were eaten by a mad dog.

JUDY: Oh, no, Pa, but Ma fell in the river.

(Both cry but they are interrupted by Ma rushing in.)

MA: PA!

PA: MA!

MA: JUDY!

JUDY: MA!

PA: Ma, I thought you fell in the river!

MA: No! Judy, I thought you were eaten by a mad dog!

JUDY: No! No! No! But Charlie needs help!

MA, PA, JUDY: *(To the audience.)* Where is Charlie?

AUDIENCE: HELP!!!!!!

(Charlie rushes in. He and Judy collide in an attempted embrace.)

CHARLIE: I thought you were eaten by a mad dog.

JUDY: No, Charlie. You always get messages all mixed up.

PA: Judy, stop picking on your brother.

MA: Children, there must be some way we can straighten this out.

JUDY: Listen, Ma, I know what we can do. The next time I want to go down to the river to get myself a dog, I'll draw a picture on a rock. Here Pa, hold my dog. *(She grabs a piece of chalk that has been taped to the box and draws a picture of her dog on the black rock.)* Now if anybody sees that picture, they'll know I went down to the river to get myself a dog.

MA: Judy, that's good. Now when I want to leave a message that I'm going down to the river, I'll draw this. *(She takes a piece of chalk taped to a second box, and draws two curved parallel lines indicating a river.)*

PA: Ma, that's great. Charlie, my boy, when I say use your head, I'll draw this. *(He takes a piece of chalk from a third box, and draws a circle.)*

PA: Now anybody will know that means use your head.

MA: Now, Charlie, read these pictures.

CHARLIE: The cow looked at the sky and saw the moon.

MA, PA, JUDY: NOOOOOOO!!!!!

JUDY: Listen, the next time I want to leave a message, I'll draw this. *(With her chalk she goes to the fourth box and carefully prints D O G.)* Dog, not cow.

MA: What if there's more than one dog?

CHARLIE: Then we draw this. *(Charlie adds "S" to the end of D O G.)*

MA: What if there are exactly eight dogs?

PA: Then we'll draw this. *(Pa draws the letter "8" in front of D O G.)* 8 Dogs. Children, we've invented writing.

MA: I think I'll write a letter.

JUDY: I think I'll write a poem.

CHARLIE: I'm going to write the story of my life.

PA: And I'm going to write the history of the world.

(Music.)

(Family disassembles the cave. Each character takes a rock and with great excitement begins to write on it.)

(Music ends.)

MUSICIANS: Is this the end?

CAST: No. There is no end.

MUSICIANS: I don't get it.

CAST: *(To audience.)* Tell them.

(Everyone sings Dandelion Song.)

Dandelion, Dandelion, same old story every time.
Dandelion, Dandelion, same old story every time.

MUSICIANS: Is *this* the end?

CAST: No, there is no end.

MUSICIANS: We still don't get it.

CAST: *(To audience.)* Tell them.

(Audience invariably joins the cast in singing the Dandelion Song.)

Dandelion, Dandelion, same old story every time.
Dandelion, Dandelion, same old story every time.

(The song is repeated. The Musicians join in the singing and the Cast exits pushing the boxes offstage.)

CURTAIN

THE FORGOTTEN DOOR

by

GREGORY A. FALLS

from the book by Alexander Key

THE FORGOTTEN DOOR

CHARACTERS

Jon
The Deer, Mary Bean
Gilby Pitts, Jon's father's voice
Emma Pitts, Miss Josie, Jon's mother's voice
The Snake, Rascal, First Farmer, Newscaster, Colonel Quinn
Thomas Bean
Sheriff Anderson Bush, Second Farmer

(The cast of twenty can be played by seven actors if they play multiple roles as grouped above.)

The play is written to be played continuously; therefore, all transitions of place are covered by narration or some action that will permit the necessary chairs, stools, cloths, etc. to be set by actors in the scene. The large black cloth for the void and the large brown cloth for the cave and rocks should be stretchable and at least 20 feet long and as high as the actors can reach up. Then they can be manipulated by actors not in the scene. While the touring production used only a minimum of scenery, adding set pieces and props can enhance the production.

Music is vital and lighting effects are important.

Jon's "thoughts," as well as those of others, can be recorded and played back on cue, or can be live with the use of cordless microphones. Thoughts may also be spoken by the actor if everyone else "freezes" while the thoughts are spoken.

At the opening, a very large black cloth is discovered draped over benches and stools to look like a small hill or rock. It is night and lovely. Music comes up and people with simple but attractive clothes come on, looking at the sky which is alive with shooting stars. The star effect is created with whips made of long strips of silver Mylar that can be whipped into curving patterns about the stage.

Jon is dressed in a fabric cap, shirt, pants and boots, which are similar to ours, but different enough to make him look "different." He addresses the audience as his people watch the wonder of the stars.

JON: We were on top of the hill looking up at the stars and planets. They were like jewels flung across the sky. Everyone, even the children, had come up from the valley to see them. I wanted to see better, so I stepped up on a little rise—and it *happened*!

(The black cloth suddenly stretches up and out, making a black void behind Jon. He tumbles slowly into it, as the music swells and changes. He is falling in space, first this way and then that, sometimes upside-down, until finally his feet touch the floor and the black cloth flings him forward, then seems to pull him backwards as it disappears off stage, and he crashes into a very large brown cloth that looks like the wall and part of the top of a cave. As he falls against it, he hits his head, losing both his cap and his consciousness.

The music changes and he recovers consciousness. His lips don't move but we hear his thoughts.)

OHHHH. MY HEAD. WHAT HAPPENED? STEPPED UP AND FELL THROUGH A HOLE. WASN'T THERE BEFORE. BETTER GET OUT OF HERE! GO BACK!

(He rushes out of the cave into the mountains. The brown cave cloth becomes a rock with a small stream [Mylar strips] on it that activates when Jon sees it. Some actors in brown burlap ponchos enter supporting tree branches. They become stones and parts of the mountains.)

MY KNEE HURTS . . . A LITTLE STREAM!

(Jon limps to the stream and washes his face in the cool water, climbing over the Rocks, running in panic. The Trees rush past him as he runs in place, so he seems to be going very fast.)

BETTER. SEE BETTER NOW. KEEP GOING. WHERE? . . . WHERE AM I GOING? . . . I DON'T KNOW. HELP ME! RUN! RUN!

(Jon is now running through the mountains. Finally he stops, comes down stage and looks out at the audience. The Rocks disappear.)

STOP IDIOT . . . YOU'LL KILL YOURSELF. STOP. THINK, REMEMBER. CAN'T REMEMBER. CAN'T REMEMBER ANYMORE . . . NOT EVEN MY *NAME*.

(He looks around as his loss of memory sobers him.)

THIS PLACE LOOKS FAMILIAR . . . BUT NOT QUITE. THERE'S SOMETHING DIFFERENT ABOUT IT . . . AND ABOUT THOSE FERNS AND ROCKS. I'M IN A STRANGE PLACE AND . . . *I DON'T KNOW WHERE I AM!*

(He kneels down in alarm, but hears the Deer, who enters on the other side. The Deer is feeding, unafraid, but is alert to both sound and smell. Jon thinks out toward the Deer.)

DEER, LOOK OVER HERE.

(The Deer is suddenly alert.)

DEER: SOMETHING'S THERE . . . CAREFUL . . . LISTEN.

JON: HELP ME.

DEER: DANGER THERE . . . HURT THERE.

JON: DON'T BE AFRAID.

DEER: NOT SURE . . .

JON: WON'T HURT YOU.

DEER: NOT SURE . . .

JON: YOU KNOW WE DON'T HURT ANIMALS ANYMORE.

DEER: GO CLOSER. HE'S DIFFERENT. NOT LIKE THE OTHERS.

(The Deer, curious, comes to Jon; he pets her head to reassure her.)

JON: WHERE AM I?

DEER: DON'T UNDERSTAND. CAN'T ANSWER . . . HUNGRY . . . VALLEY DOWN BELOW . . . EAT . . . EAT . . .

JON: YOU'RE SO WILD. I'VE TROUBLE THINKING OUT TO YOU. WAIT. I'LL GO WITH YOU . . . NOT SO FAST . . . KNEE HURTS.

(The Deer starts to travel as Jon follows, limping on his sore knee.)

DEER: FIELD . . . FOOD . . . EAT . . . EAT . . .

JON: A FARMER'S FIELD. MUST BE PEOPLE HERE WHO CAN HELP ME. WHAT IS IT?

(As they arrive at a field, the Deer suddenly starts and listens.)

DEER: LISTEN . . . LISTEN . . . DANGER?

JON: DANGER? WHERE? OH, THERE!

(Gilby Pitts, an old, nosey farmer, dressed in overalls and bill cap, enters carrying his hunting rifle, which he raises when he sees the Deer, aiming at her.)

JON: AAAIIIIEEEEE!

(Jon runs, leaping high in the air, causing Gilby to raise his rifle. The Deer escapes, but Gilby grabs Jon by the back of the shirt.)

GILBY: Hey! . . . Whatcha doin? You ruin't my aim! Blast it, boy, I had that there deer. Hold on there! Emma! Come here.

JON: WHAT IS THIS STRANGE LANGUAGE? HIS MIND IS ALL FULL OF HATE.

(Emma Pitts, Gilby's wife, also dressed in overalls and carrying a hoe, comes in.)

EMMA: How's that, Gilby?

GILBY: Would you look at what I found sneakin' onto our land.

EMMA: Lordie, never seen him afore.

JON: CAN'T QUITE UNDERSTAND THEIR LANGUAGE.

EMMA: Whose young'un is he, reckon?

GILBY: Dunno. Figure he's an Indian, mebbe, from the reservation.

EMMA: Naw, tain't no Indian. Look at that hair and them clothes. Funny lookin' get-up.

JON: BEGINNING TO UNDERSTAND WHAT THEY SAY.

EMMA: You a gypsy boy? Huh? A runaway, mebbe? Answer me!

JON: SHE'S GOING TO *HIT* ME!?

EMMA: Answer me, I say!

(Emma tries to slap Jon, but misses when he pulls away from Gilby and moves away from them.)

GILBY: Hey, hey. Would you look at what we got?

EMMA: We got ourselves a wild boy.

(They intend to capture this "wild boy." They make a team and slowly close in on him, as they ad lib:)

"Come on, wild boy. Let's get ourselves a wild 'un." Etc. etc.

(But Jon is capable of running much faster and leaping much higher than people of our world. As the Pitts come toward him, he makes a quick feint to the left, then the right and with a leap, sails between them. They both move left, then right, then toward each other, knocking the other sprawling on the ground. They watch in amazement as Jon exits with a great leap.)

GILBY: Would you look at him skat out of here!

EMMA: Gil, he jumped over that little tree.

GILBY: And over that high fence—kinda like he *flew* over it.

EMMA: C'mon, Gil. See if we can head him off on t'other side of the ridge.

GILBY: He's a strange 'un . . .

(They exit, chasing after Jon, who now enters from another part of the stage. He has easily escaped them, but doesn't know where he is. Meanwhile, another actor wearing a brown burlap poncho enters and becomes a Rock, on which is coiled a Rattlesnake. This actor can manipulate the Snake's upper body, head and mouth.)

JON: There they go. I'm safe . . . That rattling sound?

(As Jon comes past the rock, the Snake raises its head and rattles a warning.)

SNAKE: STAND OFF! . . . BITE YOU.

(Jon sees the snake. He is curious about it, because there are no snakes in his world and because there people and animals are friendly.)

JON: WHY? I WON'T HURT YOU. YOU MUST KNOW THAT. WHAT KIND OF ANIMAL ARE YOU? NO LEGS, COVERED WITH SCALES, SLIDING ALONG THE GROUND?

(Jon comes closer and the Snake opens its mouth warning "KEEP BACK." When Jon gets too close, the Snake strikes at him, saying "KILL." Jon leaps back surprised.)

ALL RIGHT. I'LL GO AROUND YOU.

(Jon goes around the Snake and travels on; the Snake and Rock exit. Another Rock comes on, as the light fades into twilight. Jon, having been lost all day, is exhausted and depressed.)

WHAT AN ANGRY PLACE THIS IS. WHERE AM I? WHAT AM I GOING TO DO? IT'S GETTING DARK . . . I'M SCARED . . . IN THIS . . . STRANGE PLACE.

(He collapses by the Rock, on the edge of the Beans' front yard. The Beans, Mary and Thomas, moved to the mountains when Thomas came

home from Viet Nam. They are in their late 20's and are warm attractive people. Mary enters from her "front door" on the "porch" of their house. She is expecting Thomas for supper.)

MARY: Thomas? Is that you?

(Thomas comes on.)

THOMAS: Coming, Mary.

MARY: What's that over there?

THOMAS: Where?

MARY: Over there, on the edge of the yard.

(They go toward Jon, who is trying to get up.)

THOMAS: It's a boy. What seems to be the matter?

MARY: He may be hurt. His face is all covered with scratches.

THOMAS: Hey, young fellow. Are you all right? Are you lost?

MARY: Here, let me wipe his face. Are you hurt some place?

THOMAS: I think he's just frightened.

MARY: Can you tell us who you are? We want to help you.

THOMAS: Shock, maybe. Look at his eyes. Haven't seen that look since Viet Nam.

MARY: Can you stand up? Let me help you. That's better. Maybe you're hungry. Like something to eat? Some food? Eat? *(She mimes "eating" and Jon slowly nods "yes" as he begins to understand.)* Good. That's it. Come into the kitchen. We'll get something warm in your stomach. *(Mary leads Jon to the kitchen.)*

THOMAS: You'll be just fine in no time. I'll look around and see if there is anyone else out there. Halllllooooooo? Halllllooooooooo? Anyone there?

(Thomas now addresses the audience, as we hear night noises: crickets, hoot owl.)

THOMAS: There wasn't anyone else. These mountain ridges 'round here are pretty rugged. We figured he had gotten lost from his family. Maybe wandered about all day. Course, we were right about all that . . . but we didn't know then what a strange tale it really was. You'll see.

MARY: *(Enters, carrying Jon's boots.)* He's plain tuckered out. Ate some but wouldn't touch any of the meat. He's asleep now. Out like a light.

THOMAS: Did he tell you anything?

MARY: Nope. But he did smile at me just before he dropped off. Funny thing . . .

THOMAS: What?

MARY: Nothing.

THOMAS: Come on, what is it?

MARY: I have this strange feeling about him. Oh, I don't mean that . . . I'm not afraid of him, he seems like a nice enough boy. It's just that . . . well, look at these boots.

THOMAS: Pretty fancy boots for our mountains. He must be a city boy, wearing cloth boots up here.

MARY: But I've never seen cloth like this before. It's very strong.

THOMAS: Probably some new synthetic.

MARY: Who's that coming up the road?

THOMAS: Maybe it's his parents. Nope. Looks more like Gilby Pitts to me. He's riled about something.

MARY: Wonder what old nosey Gilby wants this time of night?

(Gilby enters, carrying a lantern and rifle. Owl hoots or other night sounds, as he comes to the porch.)

THOMAS: Sh-h-h. We'll find out . . . Evening, Gilby.

GILBY: Howdy, Thomas . . . Mary. You folks seen anything unusual 'round here tonight?

THOMAS: Not 'specially.

GILBY: Uh huh. You still got that there old bloodhound of yourn?

THOMAS: Naw. Traded him to Ben Whipple about six months ago. Picked up a mongrel named Rascal. But I can't do anything with him. Keep him tied up out back.

GILBY: Wish you still had that there bloodhound.

THOMAS: What for?

GILBY: There's a wild boy loose in these parts!

MARY: A wild boy?

GILBY: Dang tootin'! Like an animal. Had my hands on him fer a minute, but he fought like a wild cat. Ran off faster'n lightning!

THOMAS: You telling us a tall one?

GILBY: Nary a whit. He jumped clean over my high fence. At least ten foot in the air.

THOMAS: Awww.

GILBY: I'll swear on a stack of Bibles. Emma seen it, too.

MARY: Hope you aren't going around alarming folks about this?

GILBY: Have to! This warnt no natural thing. He was only a young 'un. But what if there is more of 'em up in the mountains? Grown ones? Why they'd . . . Mary, them's funny looking boots you got there.

MARY: Yes, this boy that . . . uh . . .

GILBY: What boy?

MARY: Uh . . . one that's visiting us.

GILBY: You got a stranger boy visiting you all?

MARY: Well, he's not exactly a stranger.

GILBY: Uh huh.

THOMAS: Son of a friend of mine . . . one I knew in the Army.

GILBY: Reckon he seen that wild boy?

THOMAS: I doubt it. He just came this afternoon.

GILBY: This afternoon, huh. You figure he's the one been pokin 'round my land? Let me see him.

MARY AND THOMAS: *(Together.)* He's asleep. No, not now.

GILBY: Uh huh. Don't want to let me talk to him, huh? I know when I ain't welcome. Maybe I'd better mosey on along. Thought I'd warn you. Them's sure peculiar lookin' boots, Mary, ain't they?

THOMAS: Good evening, Gilby.

GILBY: Yup. Thomas. Mary. *(Gilby exits, but he is suspicious.)*

MARY: Nosey old skinflint.

THOMAS: You think maybe he's the boy Gilby saw?

MARY: The boy asleep in there is no wild boy who jumps ten feet in the air. I'm going in and see if he's warm enough.

THOMAS: His parents'll show up looking for him tomorrow . . . I'm pretty sure they will.

(Thomas now addresses the audience.)

THOMAS: But they didn't. I just knew we'd hear about a lost boy on the radio the next morning. But there wasn't anything on the news. It surprised me some, but not as much as that boy surprised Mary the next morning.

(Thomas exits as Mary and Jon enter talking and carrying a small breakfast table. Jon sits and begins to eat as Mary, who is wearing an apron, watches.)

MARY: I just can't get over how your scratches healed up over night. You're walking just fine now. Sure wish your memory would come back and you'd talk to me. Course, I've been talking a blue streak ever since you got up. I'll bet your family's worried sick trying to find you. Try to remember. Try to speak. Tell me your name.

JON: *(Speaking for the first time—a little uncertain.)* J-J-Jon.

MARY: Jon . . . that's good. Cat's no longer got your tongue! Is it "Jon" as in Jonathan?

JON: Y-yes. Jon . . . as . . . in . . . Jonathan.

MARY: Do you know where you are?

JON: No . . . I . . . do . . . not.

MARY: You are lost, then.

JON: Yes, I am.

MARY: Anyway, I'm glad you're talking. Now you can help us find your family. Want some bacon on that toast?

JON: We don't eat . . . animals.

MARY: Vegetarians, eh?

JON: Yes. Veg-e-tarians.

MARY: Is it hard for you to talk?

JON: It is hard . . . now . . . but it is . . . coming.

MARY: All right. You and I'll talk up a storm. I'll tell you some things about us, then you can tell me some things about you. Let's see . . . You know that I'm Mary Bean, and that my husband is Thomas. We bought this farm right after he came back from Viet Nam, but we soon found out that you can't make a living on a small farm, anymore. So, Thomas started that Rock Shop you can see up there on the road. With the tourist trade, it keeps the money coming in.

JON: Money? What is money?

MARY: You must know what money is. Everybody has to have it.

JON: We don't have it.

MARY: You couldn't live without it . . . how would you eat?

JON: It's a food? You eat money?

MARY: *(Laughing.)* Oh, come now. You don't remember what money is? Not even this penny?

JON: No. It's metal. Hard and round.

MARY: You're just not remembering yet! Let's go around the house and I'll point at things. You tell me which things you remember . . . that are familiar to you.

JON: All right.

(Mary moves about, miming the things she points to, and Jon follows. It is a fun game for both of them.)

MARY: A window?

JON: Yes, familiar.

MARY: A door . . . *(The cave theme music comes up and plays under the scene until Jon says he can't remember.)*

JON: Door! I remember. I fell through a door.

MARY: *(Laughing.)* Well, you didn't quite make it to our door. You fell in the yard. What about this radio?

JON: It carries music and messages?

MARY: Yes, it "carries" music and messages. What about this?

JON: You call it . . . a book?

MARY: Yes. What do you call it?

JON: I don't know.

MARY: Hm-m-mmm. Read me some of it.

JON: I can't read this language . . . yet.

MARY: That's strange. A boy your age, who speaks English as well as you do, ought to be able to read it.

JON: I think there's another language I seem to know.

MARY: Maybe you're a foreigner. Speak in your own language.

JON: *(Upset at his inability to remember.)* I can't remember it.

MARY: Try.

JON: I know it's there, but all I can remember is a little song.

(During this sequence, Jon gets through the song three or four times. First he starts to hum the tune, which leads him to begin moving his arms and hands in a children's clapping game. This leads him to remember the words. Mary is drawn into the clapping game with him until they are doing the clapping faster and faster, ending in a burst of laughter.)

Ahoeeeee, ahoeeeee,
Umanam loee, loee
Umanam la tee, la tee!

MARY: That's great! What do the words mean?

JON: I don't know. I don't even know where I learned it.

MARY: Well, where did you learn English?

JON: I haven't learned English yet. I only began yesterday.

MARY: Say that again.

JON: I'm learning it now from you.

MARY: No, no. You don't understand me.

JON: You were thinking I could not learn English so quickly.

MARY: Of course.

JON: But I am. *(A dog howls off-stage.)* Your dog is thirsty for water.

MARY: Rascal? No, no. Thomas fills his water pan every morning.

JON: He has a dry throat. There is no water in his pan.— You do not believe me! Why?

MARY: Jon, surely you remember the difference between truth and falsehood?

JON: Truth is right. Falsehood is—not right. But you are thinking another word for falsehood.

MARY: A lie.

JON: But I don't lie. I must always speak the truth.

MARY: Now we're getting somewhere.

(During this scene they clear the table off-stage. Rascal enters with a rope around his neck, which is held by an actor as though he were a tree. Rascal has his empty water dish in his mouth. He drops it on the floor and barks. Jon and Mary are still inside the house, but when they come out the whole stage becomes the yard.)

JON: Rascal wants water. I hear him. How can Rascal think a lie?

MARY: Jon! Do you believe you can read his mind?

JON: No. I hear his thoughts.

MARY: Oh, dear. . . .

JON: I will go and see if Thomas is . . .

MARY: What?

JON: You are wondering if Thomas is back?

MARY: Yes, I was. How did you know that?

JON: I heard your thought.

MARY: Jon, don't be silly! Don't tell lies. Come out to the dog pen and I'll show you. But I warn you. Rascal is vicious . . . we have to keep him chained up and in the pen. Thomas is the only . . . why, you're right! It is empty . . . dry as a bone. How did you . . ?

JON: I will fill his water pan. *(He starts toward the pen.)*

MARY: Look out! Don't go in there! He's vicious. . . .

(As Jon approaches the pen, Rascal snarls and barks, pulling at the rope, trying to attack him. Then we hear their thoughts.)

RASCAL: KEEP OFF!

JON: I WON'T HURT YOU.

RASCAL: KEEP OFF!

JON: I'LL GET YOU SOME WATER. *(Jon picks up the empty water pan and mimes filling it at a faucet. Rascal watches him, not quite understanding how a human can talk with him. When Jon returns and holds out the pan toward him, Rascal wants to drink but is afraid.)*

RASCAL: KEEP OFF!

JON: HERE'S WATER.

RASCAL: KEEP OFF!

JON: DON'T BE SCARED.

RASCAL: THIRSTY . . . THIRSTY . . . KEEP BACK!

JON: HERE, DRINK.

(Rascal gradually, guardedly, comes closer, then suddenly throws caution to the wind and greedily laps the water. Jon kneels beside to pet him, and now they are friends.)

RASCAL: WANT TO RUN.

JON: BE PATIENT. SHE DOESN'T UNDERSTAND YET.

(Mary now addresses the audience.)

MARY: It was too much to believe . . . at first. I told Thomas, who didn't believe it either. *(Thomas enters, as though continuing a conversation with her.)*

THOMAS: You're out of your mind. Read your thoughts? Talk to dogs?

MARY: *(To the audience.)* But enough other things happened that day to make him wonder.

(Thomas and Mary watch as the once vicious Rascal plays with Jon. Jon takes the rope off him. Rascal picks up a stick in his mouth, which he lets Jon take. Jon throws it across the stage and Rascal races after it. He picks the stick up in his mouth, but drops it as he comes back toward Jon.)

JON: No, fetch it, Rascal. Bring it back.

(Rascal picks it up again, starts back, drops it again.)

Fetch it. That's it.

(Rascal does the same thing.)

Come on . . . bring it back to me. . . .

(This time, with a rush, Rascal picks up the stick and brings it back to Jon, who takes it and pretends to throw it again. Rascal races after the stick but can't find it, looks at Jon, confused. Jon then shows him the stick, and throws it. Rascal leaps on it, rushes it back to Jon and in shaking his head throws the stick in the air. Jon catches it. They both rush off-stage with Jon leaping high in the air.)

THOMAS: Certainly has a way with Rascal. I wouldn't recognize him as the same dog! Look at him run. Look at him leap. Never saw anybody jump like that!

MARY: He told me he just "lightens his feet." Makes you think.

THOMAS: Yep.

MARY: That he may not be from here.

THOMAS: Oh, I don't doubt now that he's a foreigner.

MARY: I mean *from this world.*

THOMAS: Oh, come on! You've always had a *vivid* imagination. You read too many fairy tales when you were growing up.

MARY: Maybe I did, but I am sure he understands some thoughts. . . .

(We hear the sound of a car driving up and stopping.)

THOMAS: Looks like the Sheriff's car.

(Sheriff Anderson Bush, in a tan uniform, enters, followed by Gilby and Emma Pitts.)

BUSH: Good morning, folks. I'm Sheriff Bush.

THOMAS: Glad to meet you, sir. Seen you around but I don't think we've met. Morning, Emma, Gilby. Nice day.

EMMA: Mebbe 'tis, and mebbe it ain't. We'll find out.

BUSH: A routine investigation. There've been a series of small robberies down at Doc Holliday's summer place. A more serious one yesterday.

GILBY: He lost two fishing rods and a rifle.

EMMA: And a tackle box full of plugs and gear.

THOMAS: Well, Sheriff, I don't see what this has to do with us.

BUSH: Last night there were several sightings of a strange boy running loose in the mountains.

(Jon's music theme comes in.)

EMMA: A *wild* boy. . . .

MARY: Oh, come now. . . .

EMMA: Fierce, Mary Bean, I seen him jump over a small tree and he was runnin' with them deer.

GILBY: Plumb made me miss my shot.

THOMAS: You hunting deer out of season, Gilby?

GILBY: Well . . . now . . . I was. . . .

EMMA: Them crows, weren't they, Gil?

GILBY: That's what it was. Dang crows eating my corn crop.

THOMAS: Sheriff, Gilby told me all this nonsense last night.

BUSH: Is it true you have a boy visiting you . . . a stranger boy to these parts?

THOMAS: Yes . . . Jon.

BUSH: Jon who?

THOMAS: Uh . . . He's the son of a friend of mine.

BUSH: What's his last name?

THOMAS: O'Connell.

BUSH: His parents?

THOMAS: Captain Patrick O'Connell, U.S. Army, and his wife. We were together in Nam. Jon only came last night and couldn't have been involved in those robberies.

BUSH: I would like to see the boy, please.

MARY: He may be asleep.

BUSH: It's important. Please wake him.

MARY: All right. *(She exits into the house.)*

THOMAS: Sheriff, I'd better tell you something. This boy just lost his parents. I don't want him upset.

BUSH: Only a couple of questions.

(Mary and Jon enter.)

MARY: This is Jon.

EMMA: 'At's him! Gilby!

GILBY: Sure is. I'd knowed him any place. Had a good holt on him, but he fought like a wild Comanche. Take him in, Sheriff.

THOMAS: Not on your life, Gilby Pitts!

BUSH: Hold your horses. Both of you. Is your name Jon?

JON: Yes, sir.

BUSH: Were you in this man's cornfield yesterday afternoon?

GILBY: Durn tootin' he was.

BUSH: Mr. Pitts. Well, boy?

JON: THOMAS WANTS ME TO TELL A LIE SO THERE WON'T BE ANY TROUBLE. BUT I CAN'T SAY WHAT'S NOT TRUE. Yes, sir. I was lost and followed a deer into his cornfield. He tried to kill her, but I spoiled his aim.

GILBY: I never did shoot no deer out of season.

BUSH: When you were lost, did you go past Doctor Holliday's place?

JON: I don't know.

BUSH: Think, boy.

JON: I was so confused and lost. I . . . I. . . .

EMMA: Oh, he's the one. Look at them boots. He ain't right!

THOMAS: That's enough, Emma. I'll not permit you all to bother him anymore today.

BUSH: I have a few more questions for him.

THOMAS: Not without a warrant, Sheriff.

BUSH: Are you serious?

THOMAS: Yes, I am.

BUSH: You really want to go that far?

THOMAS: Yes, I do.

BUSH: All right, then, I can get a warrant in short order.

THOMAS: Do it, then.

BUSH: If that's the way you want it. . . .

(Bush exits, followed by Gilby and Emma.)

EMMA: *(As she exits.)* Tain't right, Thomas Bean, letting that boy run loose like a wild Banshee. Lots of folks 'round here gonna get nervous.

(Mary comes forward and addresses the audience.)

MARY: We knew then trouble was coming. We had to find some way to help Jon. And quickly. *(Turning back to Jon.)* Can't you remember anything?

THOMAS: Try.

MARY: Once you told me you "fell through a door." *(Cave music under.)*

JON: All I can remember is that I stepped up on a rise to see better and fell into the darkness and hit my head. When I came to, I was in the cave, but I couldn't remember. . . .

MARY: A cave?

JON: Yes.

THOMAS: But how could you fall *into* a cave?

JON: I don't know.

MARY: Unless, Thomas, it was a fall from *another dimension.*

THOMAS: You've been reading too much science fiction! Jon's too real to be a boy from outer space. But, I do think the cave may be a link to his past. Could you find that cave again, Jon?

JON: I think so.

THOMAS: Then, let's go!

(Mary addresses the audience as Jon and Thomas prepare to go into the mountains.)

MARY: None of us slept very much that night. Our one clue, that cave, would be almost impossible to find in these mountains. But Thomas and Jon set out at dawn.

(Music under as Jon and Thomas travel through the mountains. Actors wearing brown burlap ponchos and carrying branches or small tree trunks become rocks, forests, ledges, all the things needed for creating the travel to the cave. The last obstacle is a narrow ledge that leads to a steep but narrow ravine. On the other side a small tree has grown so that it leans across the chasm. Jon quickly leaps across and swings himself up on the other side. Thomas looks down at the chasm, but with a mighty leap also catches the tree, which bends up and down under his weight. He hand walks himself to the other side, where Jon gives him a hand onto safe land. Jon starts off again, but Thomas stops him.)

THOMAS: Whoa . . . We must've walked fifteen or twenty miles. Does any of this look familiar to you?

JON: I think so. I was so scared and confused. Listen. The deer is near.

THOMAS: I don't see her.

JON: Over on that ridge. *(Jon points in a direction off the stage. While we hear the deer's thought, she does not actually appear on the stage.)* DEER, COME NEARER.

DEER: DANGER.

JON: IT'S JON.

DEER: AFRAID.

JON: DON'T BE. *(Jon turns to Thomas and speaks.)* She's afraid of you.

THOMAS: I see her now . . . way over there.

JON: CAN YOU TAKE US TO THE CAVE?

DEER: CAVE? YES.

JON: She'll lead us toward the cave.

(They travel again. As they move, the cast, which we saw earlier, becomes the brown cloth rock with the little stream.)

THOMAS: By golly, I believe she *is* trying to lead us. Never saw a deer behave like that one. Is it possible that . . . Jon, did you try to communicate with her?

JON: Yes, I thought out to her.

THOMAS: Huh! Maybe Mary's right about you.

JON: This is looking more familiar.

THOMAS: Watch out for the stream there!

JON: We're close now. I remember that spring.

THOMAS: Here's a hand-print in the mud. Put your hand in it.

(Jon puts his hand on the cloth by the stream.)

They're the same! You were here all right.

(Now they travel more quickly forward. The rock transforms back into the cave.)

JON: I crawled along a ledge . . . up a bit . . . then around . . . it should be . . . *Here! (Cave theme begins.)*

THOMAS: Not exactly a cave. More like a split in the layers of rock. Like some gigantic force cracked the rock formation. Let's go in. *(They enter the cave.)*

JON: I can *feel* something in this cave.

THOMAS: Funny. So can I. It's like being inside a bottle . . . Like a compartment. Look at my compass . . . spinning around madly . . . never saw it go so fast.

JON: I feel tingly all over as if . . . I can't say what!

THOMAS: Where were you when you woke up?

JON: Lying here, like this . . . eh? What's this?

THOMAS: A cap. It matches your clothes.

JON: It fits. Must be mine. I had it on when I stepped back and fell through the forgotten door that leads to the other place.

THOMAS: Did you say "The forgotten door that leads to the other place"?

JON: And I woke up here.

THOMAS: Then this must be "the other place."

JON: Yes, it must.

THOMAS: Then you must be from another place . . . maybe not of this world.

JON: Yes. I know that now. It is true. I am from another place. *(Jon addresses the audience.)* I longed to remember that other place. To remember if I have a father and a mother beyond that forgotten door. Will I ever see them again? Will they ever find me?

THOMAS: It's getting late. We'd better start back.

(They start out of the cave, which dissolves. Jon exits, while Thomas addresses the audience.)

It was easy going back. Jon had an uncanny sense of direction. And, of course, I no longer had any doubts that he was truly from another world, where people like us live. While we had been gone, Mary had been having a busy time.

(A phone bell rings. Thomas exits as three local farmers enter, one holding a phone and the others crowded around him. One is Gilby Pitts. They are calling the Beans. Mary enters, center, with a phone.)

MARY: Hello.

FIRST FARMER: Is it true, Mary, you got a wild boy locked up in your barn?

MARY: No!

SECOND FARMER: I heared tell he jumps fifty feet straight up in the air!

GILBY: Spits fire outen his mouth.

FIRST FARMER: Like a dragon?

GILBY: Like a dragon!

FIRST FARMER: He's a dragon boy. Mary, you got a dragon boy up there. The Lord help us!

SECOND FARMER: I sure ain't going up into them mountains. Bet there's a whole gang of 'em up there!

FIRST FARMER: Mary, we're gonna phone the Governor to call out the National Guard to protect us. He ought to . . .

MARY: Stop it! You're all stark raving mad! *(She hangs up. They exit as Thomas and Jon enter.)*

THOMAS: Easy, Mary, easy. We're back.

MARY: Did you . . ?

THOMAS: We found the cave. And now I believe Jon must be from another world and that cave is the key to it.

(As Thomas and Mary hug, Sheriff Bush enters with a summons.)

BUSH: Thomas Bean, I serve you with this summons. You must bring the boy to Juvenile Court tomorrow at 9:00 a.m. Good evening. *(He exits.)*

MARY: Let me see it. Signed by Miss Josie. That's a good sign.

JON: Who is she?

MARY: Miss Josie? Really Mrs. Cunningham: *Judge* Cunningham, but everyone calls her Miss Josie. She's tough, but she's fair. And she understands people.

(Mary addresses the audience as the scene does a transition to the Juvenile Court.)

We took Jon to the Juvenile Court next morning. A mob of folks had gathered there trying to get a look at him, touching his strange clothes and taking his picture.

(Sheriff Bush brings in Miss Josie's table and chair. Gilby and the First Farmer come in gawking at Jon, touching his clothes. The Farmer takes his picture with a small camera and flash attachment. Hubbub as Thomas and Mary try to protect Jon.)

THOMAS: Excuse us, please. Let us through. Thank you.

BUSH: Leave him alone . . . let 'em through, folks. Here comes Miss Josie!

(Miss Josie enters, a middle-aged lady, dressed in a business-like way. She is clearly in command of the court, listens carefully and puts up with no nonsense. She puts a small vase with a flower on her table, then raps her gavel.)

MISS JOSIE: Sheriff, call this court in session.

BUSH: Yes, Ma'am. Juvenile Court in session. Judge Cunningham presiding.

MISS JOSIE: Now then, Sheriff, what's all this commotion about?

(Ad lib explanations from everyone. She raps her gavel.)

BUSH: Quiet, please. Quiet in the court!

MISS JOSIE: Proceed, Sheriff.

BUSH: There've been a series of small robberies at the Holliday place this fall.

MISS JOSIE: What makes you think they involve children?

BUSH: The house was locked, but a small window was broken in. No one but a child could have crawled through it.

MISS JOSIE: Go ahead.

BUSH: Two days ago, several valuable items were stolen.

GILBY: Yah! a rifle, two good fishin' rods and a . . .

MISS JOSIE: *(Rapping gavel.)* What are you doing here, Gilby Pitts?

GILBY: I'm the chief witness, Miss Josie. You all know I'm in charge of Doc's place during the winter. Me and Emma seen that there wild boy running onto . . .

MISS JOSIE: *(Raps gavel.)* Gilby! That's enough of that kind of talk.

GILBY: Yes'm.

MISS JOSIE: What did you see?

GILBY: Me and Emma seen that there wild boy . . .

MISS JOSIE: *(Rapping gavel.)* Gilby!!

GILBY: *(Quickly.)* Youngun! Youngun sneakin' across my upper forty, headed toward Doc's. I nabbed him right away, but he clean got loose. Shook me up some, I tell ya.

MISS JOSIE: Did you see any of the stolen things on him?

GILBY: No, but I thought he was goin' back for *more*. So it was my duty to warn other folks about this wild boy running loose . . . Youngun . . . but that's what he is, Miss Josie, even if you don't like it. Well, when I got to the Beans', they acted kinda peculiar, too, so naturally I reported all this to Sheriff Bush.

MISS JOSIE: Naturally.

BUSH: The Beans were not cooperative when I questioned them, but what's worse, I'm sorry to say, they lied to me about the boy.

MISS JOSIE: About what?

BUSH: They said he was the orphan son of a Captain Patrick O'Connell, but when I checked with the Army, I learned that Captain O'Connell *had no children*.

MISS JOSIE: Thomas, is that true?

THOMAS: Yes, Miss Josie, I'm afraid it is. I misled him only to protect an innocent boy. If you please, there is something special you should know about this boy. I've written it down in this letter for you to read. *(He hands her a sealed envelope.)*

MISS JOSIE: Thank you, Thomas. Young man, come here.

JON: Yes, Ma'am.

THOMAS: Miss Josie . . .

MISS JOSIE: *(Kindly.)* Now then, what's your name?

JON: Jon.

MISS JOSIE: Jon what?

JON: I don't know.

MISS JOSIE: Don't you know your family name?

JON: I can't remember who I am or where I'm from.

THOMAS: Please read my note, Miss Josie.

MISS JOSIE: In good time. Well, Jon, would you like to tell me *all* you know about the Holliday robberies?

JON: I know that Mr. Pitts has already found the stolen things.

GILBY: How'd you know that? You been sneakin' round my place again?

JON: No, sir. But I know you've hidden them in a different place.

GILBY: You bet your boots I have! Not where you're likely to find 'em again.

JON: In your attic. In an old trunk.

GILBY: How'n tarnation do you know that?! I'll be jiggered!

JON: You still believe it was the two Macklin boys who stole them in the first place.

GILBY: I never said nothin' to nobody 'bout that. . . .

JOSIE: Gilby, sit down!! How do you know that, Jon?

THOMAS: Please read my note!

JOSIE: You're out of order, Thomas. You sit down, too! Answer my question, please, Jon.

JON: I heard him think it.

JOSIE: Say that again.

JON: I heard him thinking it.

(Thomas, Mary, and Gilby all leap up and we hear their thoughts overlapping.)

MARY: JON, DON'T. DON'T TELL THEM. DON'T!

GILBY: DONE WHAT? READ MY MIND? THAT'S CRAZY.

THOMAS: WHY COULDN'T YOU KEEP QUIET 'TIL SHE READ MY NOTE?

JON: STOP! PLEASE STOP! YOU'RE HURTING MY HEAD.

(The thoughts stop.)

Your thoughts are so loud.

JOSIE: Young man, do you believe that you can hear his thoughts?

JON: Yes, Ma'am. I know I can. I realize you find that hard to believe, but I think I can prove it to you.

JOSIE: All right, Jon. Prove it to me.

JON: Yes, Ma'am. Would you please think of a number?

JOSIE: All right.

JON: It ought to be a larger number than that.

JOSIE: Uh . . . All right.

JON: *(Quickly and easily.)* Your number is three million, seven hundred and forty thousand, nine hundred and seventy-six.

JOSIE: That's correct!

BUSH: It is?

JON: You, Sheriff, think that it was really the Macklin boys who stole those things.

BUSH: That's right! But I never told anyone about that!

GILBY: He's unnatural!

JON: You've hidden the stolen things in your attic.

GILBY: Where you ain't likely to find them again.

JON: In an old yellow trunk that belonged to your Pa!

(Gilby realizes what Jon can do and we hear his thoughts as he rushes out in a panic. Miss Josie is banging her gavel trying to keep order.)

GILBY: HE'S READING MY MIND! HE'S READING MY MIND! LET ME OUTTA HERE!!

JON: *(Overlapping at the end.)* STOP THINKING SO LOUD. YOU'RE HURTING MY HEAD . . . PLEASE . . . PLEASE . . .

(Mary and Thomas lead him off. Bush, in the hub-bub, takes Miss Josie's desk off stage as she comes down to address the audience.)

MISS JOSIE: The Beans then told me the whole incredible story. How this boy from some other world had fallen through an old, forgotten door onto our earth. A boy who could learn our language in a day, read our thoughts, be unable . . . or unwilling . . . to tell a lie. A boy from a civilization perhaps more advanced, certainly much more civilized than ours. But, also, a boy who could not find his way back to his home. I could only send him home with the Beans . . . but I knew that there would be trouble ahead, bad trouble. This kind of news spreads like wild fire.

(A television newscaster with a lavaliere mike enters and addresses the audience as though it is the camera.)

NEWSCASTER: This is Channel One Evening News. A genius boy has been discovered in a remote area of the state. The boy was found running wild in a heavily wooded, primitive area. First reports indicated he can perform feats of incredible ability, including . . . and you may not believe this . . . the ability to read minds. Our news team is now on its way to the farm where the boy is being held. We will bring you further details on our eleven o'clock News.

(As he exits we see Gilby Pitts sneaking on. He sticks a note on the "front door" and skulks off as the Beans and Jon enter.)

MARY: I was proud of you in court.

JON: I'm sorry to cause so much trouble.

MARY: What's this pinned on the door? "This is a warning. Get rid of that wild boy. Do it quick."

(The phone rings.)

THOMAS: Now, who would do something like that. *(Answering the phone.)* Hello?

(Newscaster enters, speaking on the phone.)

NEWSCASTER: Mr. Bean, this is Channel One News. We want to confirm a report of a "genius boy" you found.

THOMAS: What? No, no, no . . .

NEWSCASTER: We are sending our mobile unit out to interview him, but I would . . .

THOMAS: No, no. You can't!

NEWSCASTER: Then, it is true, you do have him there?

THOMAS: I have nothing to say. Goodbye. *(He hangs up.)*

MARY: Who was that?

THOMAS: Channel One News. They've already found out about Jon. "Genius Boy" . . .

(Phone rings again; Thomas answers it. Miss Josie enters on the phone.)

THOMAS: We're not talking to anyone. Goodbye!

JOSIE: Thomas, wait! It's me, Miss Josie.

THOMAS: Oh, Miss Josie. Sorry. The trouble's already begun.

JOSIE: I know. There's more coming . . . I've had a call from the United States Army Intelligence Corps. A Colonel Eben Quinn.

THOMAS: Colonel Quinn? I know him. He was my Unit Commander in Viet Nam.

JOSIE: He's on his way to see Jon. He said that Army Intelligence is keenly interested in him . . . in his special abilities.

THOMAS: I'll bet they are!

JOSIE: He didn't explain why. But he certainly means business. A very forceful man.

THOMAS: That's Quinn all right, and I know what he wants.

JOSIE: You do?

THOMAS: I wasn't in Intelligence for nothing . . . doing spy work.

JOSIE: Spy work?

THOMAS: Yes.

JOSIE: Maybe we'd better not talk about it over the telephone. Just thought you ought to know.

THOMAS: Thank you kindly, Miss Josie. Bye.

JOSIE: Bye.

(They hang up. She exits.)

THOMAS: Mary! Jon! We've got to clear out of here. Get our camping gear. I'll get the car. Mary! Hop to it!

MARY: Not 'til you tell me what's going on.

JON: He thinks the Army is coming to take me away, to work for them.

MARY: The Army wants Jon to be a spy?

THOMAS: No. For counter-intelligence. To spy on spies. If Jon can read minds . . . *in any language* . . . he would be the most powerful weapon in the world! No foreign spy would be safe around him. No foreign leader could keep a secret from him.

MARY: I see what you mean!

THOMAS: Then, let's clear out of here. Quinn is a tough cookie. C'mon.

JON: I can't. I can't leave here.

THOMAS: Why not? Come on.

JON: Something tells me that I must not go away . . . at least not too far from the cave. . . . I can feel that they are trying to find me. I know they will come to the cave and call out to me. I must be able to hear them. If I go too far away I will never get home!

(Sound of a helicopter approaching and landing.)

MARY: What's that?

THOMAS: An Army helicopter. That'll be Quinn. What do we do?

MARY: We've got to get Jon out of here, quickly.

(Gilby enters, throws a stone with a note at the Beans' porch and runs away.)

GILBY: Bean!

THOMAS: What the devil is this? They're throwing stones at our house. Mary, get me my rifle! Please do as I say! "Bring that wild boy out to us, or we're coming in and get him!" Don't you come near my house! I warn you! I'll defend it!

MARY: *(Giving him the rifle.)* Here. Look over there.

THOMAS: Colonel Quinn.

(Colonel Quinn enters from another direction. He is in uniform, a full colonel, and wears a side arm. Thomas comes off the porch to him.)

QUINN: Captain Bean.

THOMAS: I'm a civilian now, Colonel.

QUINN: You look more like a soldier with that rifle.

THOMAS: Just defending my home, sir . . . in the tradition of mountain men.

QUINN: Admirable, admirable. I'm here to examine that boy you've found. If what I hear is true, he could be of great service to his country.

THOMAS: It's not his country, Colonel. He's here only by accident.

QUINN: Bean, you know what would happen if our enemies got him.

THOMAS: Yes, that's too terrible to imagine.

QUINN: Good. Then bring him out and let's get this show on the road.

THOMAS: No. He doesn't belong to us either. He's from another world.

QUINN: If that's true, he's even more important to us. Well . . . Captain Bean? . . . No? Then I am obliged to take him by force.

THOMAS: I wouldn't try it, sir.

QUINN: Oh, there are *legal* means—with force.

THOMAS: I'll fight you with every legal means at my disposal. You're not going to misuse this boy.

QUINN: But you know you will lose. I'll have him in custody in five minutes. Don't let him out of your sight for a second. Is that clear? *(Quinn exits quickly.)*

MARY: What'll we do?

THOMAS: I don't know.

(Rascal barks off stage.)

JON: Rascal hears the Pitts and some other people coming across the field.

THOMAS: It's getting dark outside. Maybe we can slip through them and hide out in the woods. Mary?

MARY: Look at Jon. What is it, Jon?

(Jon is staring into space. Gilby and Emma enter from the side opposite Quinn, but are "outside." They have a lantern, a pick-ax, and a hoe.)

GILBY: *(Calling out.)* Bean! We're coming in to get that boy! You hear?

JON: I heard something.

MARY: Gilby Pitts.

JON: No. A different voice.

(Sound of a siren and car approaching from the other side.)

THOMAS: Quinn and the Sheriff. We'll be surrounded in a minute.

(Jon now hears his father's voice.)

JON'S FATHER: LITTLE JON . . . LITTLE JON. . . .

JON: Ahhh-h-h.

GILBY: We ain't gonna hurt him none. Jes put him where he'll be safe.

JON'S FATHER: WHERE . . . ARE . . . YOU . . . ?

MARY: What is it, Jon?

JON: My father is calling me. The door must be open again.

MARY: You can hear him?

JON'S FATHER: WE HAVE COME TO TAKE YOU HOME. COME TO US.

JON: Yes, they are with the cave.

(Colonel Quinn and Sheriff Bush enter from the other side. They have flashlights and a bullhorn. The Bean house is now surrounded.)

QUINN: *(On bullhorn.)* Captain Bean! I have a warrant here for the boy. Bring him out.

JON: My parents are there. They are waiting for me.

JON'S FATHER: MAKE YOUR FEET LIGHT. RUN TO US.

JON: I CAN'T. THOMAS AND MARY ARE IN DANGER BECAUSE OF ME.

MARY: What are they saying?

JON: I must try to get to them—with the cave.

THOMAS: There's no moon. We might make it out the back way. *(They start, but he stops.)* But, of course! Jon, you can hear their thoughts . . . *even in the dark.* You could lead us around them and to the cave!

MARY: Come, Jon, help us take you home. *(So begins the long escape to the cave.)*

GILBY: This way, Em.

EMMA: See anything, Gil?

GILBY: Too dark.

(The Pitts come downstage with hoe and pick-ax ready, trying hard to peer into the darkness. Jon leads the Beans down between the Pitts. Gilby keeps thinking he hears something but can never quite make out what is happening. At one point Jon slowly raises the head of Gilby's pick-ax so they can crawl under it.)

EMMA: Hear anything, Gil?

GILBY: How can I hear anything with you yammerin', Emma?

(Mary is just crawling past Gilby when he starts to sneeze. She freezes.)

EMMA: Shhh-h-h.

(Gilby sneezes and then Jon leads them on. Quinn and Bush hear the sneeze and begin searching. There is a near-miss as they pass the Beans, and then sensing the Pitts, they suddenly snap their flashlights at the Pitts. Pandemonium! The Pitts bolt, only to run into each other and go sprawling. Quinn and Bush try to follow them, but in the wrong direc-

tion. Quinn and Bush keep hearing the Beans and Jon, but after several near misses move away and take up an alert position. As the Pitts recover and start to rise, the Beans are stepping over them and around them in the dark . . . near misses again. Then Emma hears them.)

EMMA: I hear 'em, therrr-r-re!

GILBY: I got 'em! Help! Look out!

(The Pitts rush about trying to find the Beans in the dark, and succeed only in frightening themselves and running off stage. Their cries fade in the distance. Quinn and Bush, hearing their commotion, pursue them offstage. Jon and the Beans are at last safe and begin to travel. Cave music comes in.)

JON: We're close now. There!

(The cave cloth enters and Jon leads the Beans inside the cave.)

MARY: I can feel something in the air. It's lovely. A gentle, loving welcome. Thomas?

THOMAS: Me, too. A presence . . . a joyful presence of others. It must be coming from Jon's world.

(Jon is almost in a trance of listening, being in this world but communicating with his own world.)

JON: The door is opening! I can go home again.

(The big brown cave cloth begins to pull away revealing the big black cloth. It stretches into a solid-looking wall of blackness.)

MARY: Goodbye, Jon. I am so happy for you.

JON: Wait! You must come with me.

MARY: Come with you? Into another world?

THOMAS: We can't do that.

JON: Yes, you can. I have talked to my parents. They say you can come and live in peace with us.

JON'S MOTHER: COME TO US, JON. BRING MARY AND THOMAS WITH YOU.

THOMAS: Some day. Tell them, Jon. We may be able to come some day.

JON'S MOTHER: HURRY, JON. DANGER IS APPROACHING. COME, MARY! COME, THOMAS! YOU ARE WELCOME TO LIVE WITH US IN OUR WORLD.

JON: Please come . . . there is so much hatred here.

MARY: Jon, this is *our* world. We must stay here and try to change it.

(The black cloth, pressed against Jon's body, is beginning to turn and take Jon with it.)

THOMAS: Some day we hope to live in peace as you do. Tell . . . them . . .

(The cloth moves upstage, then downstage, then the shape of Jon's body against the cloth is gone. He is home! Thomas takes Mary's hand and they exit. Immediately, from another direction, Gilby Pitts rushes in.)

GILBY: I caught up with—what? He plumb disappeared, right off the face of the earth. Twasn't natural. But I'm glad he is gone. Good riddance! But, you know something? I kindly like to know where he went to . . . wouldn't you? *(Gilby turns and exits.)*

CURTAIN

PART TWO

PLAYS FOR CHILDREN TO PERFORM

THE BREMEN TOWN MUSICIANS

and

THE GOLDEN GOOSE

by

PAUL SILLS

FROM HIS PLAY *STORY THEATRE*

THE BREMEN TOWN MUSICIANS

CHARACTERS

Ass
Hound
Cat
Cock
Chief
Messenger

(Ass enters UR, crosses to DC.)

ASS: The Bremen Town Musicians. A certain man had an ass, which for many years carried sacks of flour to the mill without tiring. At last, however, its strength gave out and it was no longer of any use for work. So its owner began to ponder as to how best to cut down on the ass's rations and indeed how to do away with the beast entirely. But the ass, sensing mischief in the air, broke from its quarters and ran away on the road to Bremen. *(Starts off counterclockwise.)* There, he thought, I shall become a town musician.

(Brays.)

[When he had been traveling a short time, he fell in with a Hound, who was in the road panting as though he had run himself off his legs.]

(Hound enters UR, crosses DL—on knees. Much barking, whining, and panting by Hound. Ass crosses DL to U of Hound.)

Why are you panting so, Growler?

HOUND: Just because I am so old, and every day I get weaker all the time, my master wanted to kill me.

ASS: *(Commiserates with the Hound.)* I'll tell you what, Growler. I myself am on my way to Bremen; there I shall become a town musician. It occurs to me that you can come along with me. I shall play the lute and you can beat the kettledrum.

HOUND: Boom . . . boom . . . boom?

ASS: Yes.

HOUND: Yes.

ASS: Very well then, let's be on our way. *(Hound and Ass circle counterclockwise. Hound urinates DL proscenium. Cat enters DR pit, Hound crosses R to C.)*

[The two began on their journey. A short time later they came upon a Cat sitting in the road with a face as long as a wet week.]

(The Hound goes for the Cat, barking; the Cat arches its back and spits and claws at the Hound. The Hound runs away whining. The Ass gets between the two and tries to make peace.)

ASS: *(To Hound.)* Sit, sit, sit. *(Hound sits DC. Cat hisses at Hound and Hound sits quickly.)* Why are you so unhappy, Whiskers?

CAT: Who can be happy when he's out at elbows? I am getting along in years, my teeth are blunted out, I prefer to sit by a nice warm fire and purr instead of hunting round after mice. Did you ever taste a mouse? Just because of this my mistress wanted to drown me. *(Ass and Hound sympathize with his fate.)*

ASS: Well, sir, I have a suggestion, we two are on our way to Bremen, there to become town musicians. It occurs to me that you are a great hand at serenading.

CAT: Thank you.

ASS: Yes, why don't you come along with us and take your part in the music?

CAT: All right.

ASS: Let's be off. *(Circles counterclockwise to UC.)*

[So the three began their journey once more. After a short while the Hound and Cat began to fight. Just then a Rooster approached them.]

(Cock enters UR, crosses C. Hound and Cat fall back L.)

COCK: Cock-a-doodle-doo! Cock-a-doodle-doo!

(The Hound and Cat quickly take cover and cover their ears.)

ASS: You crow so loud you pierce one through and through.

COCK: Yes, I do, don't I?

ASS: What is the matter?

COCK: What's the matter? Why didn't I prophesy fine weather for Our Lady's Day? FINE WEATHER? Yes, I did. Yet notwithstanding this, because Sunday visitors are coming tomorrow, my mistress has ordered the cook to make me into soup . . . SOUP . . . *(Hound and Ass and Cat lament.)* CHICKEN SOUP.

ASS: There, there, now, Red-comb. I may have a suggestion for you. We three are on our way to Bremen, there to become musicians. Now you have a fine voice . . . *(Hound and Cat start laughing, Ass quiets them.)* And when the four of us make music, there will be quality in it. So why don't you come along?

COCK: All right.

ASS: Let's go then, but stay in line. *(They circle counterclockwise with Cat last. When Cat is UC he taps Cock—replaces him—Cock is now last.)*

[So the four went off together. They could not, however, reach the town in one day, and by night they arrived at a wood, where they meant to spend the night.]

(Night Noises.)

ASS: *(All huddle C.)* It's obvious we can't reach Bremen in one day.

COCK: Why don't we stay here?

ASS: *(Ass and Hound cross DR. Cat is C.)* So the ass and the hound lay under a tree

CAT: . . . and they all lay down

COCK: *(Jumps UC.)* . . . while the cock flew up to the top branches. A light, a light. *(Cock crosses DC to Hound.)* Dog, I see a light. It must be a house.

HOUND: If there's a house, there's a bone

CAT: . . . and maybe some tuna.

ASS: Very well, then. Let's set out but be very quiet. *(Ass crosses DL to pit, motions. Cat crosses DL to pit, motions. Hound crosses DL to pit, motions. Cock crosses DL to pit. Robber No. 1 and Robber No. 2 enter UR, cross to UC.)*

[So they set out in the direction of the light till they reached a brightly lighted robbers' den.]

ASS: Perhaps, I should look in the window before we just barge in there.

HOUND: Watch out.

(Ass crosses R to DC, looks in window, then returns DL.)

CAT: Be careful.

[The Ass crept forward and observed Two Robbers heartily enjoying their meal.]

COCK: What did you see?

ASS: What did I see? Why, I saw a table laden with delicious food and drink, and robbers enjoying it.

COCK: Oh, if only that were us.

ASS: It could be us. I have a plan . . .

(The Animals huddle together to discuss the Ass's plan.)

[The Ass, the Hound, and the Cat were to form a triangle underneath the window and the Cock was to jump onto their backs and through the window: All Four were to perform their music. The Ass brayed, the Hound barked, the Cat mewed and the Cock crowed. Then the other three followed the Cock through the window. The Robbers jumped up at the terrible noise, and fled from the cottage and into the woods.]

(Animals form pyramid DC. Robber No. 1 and Robber No. 2 exit DL. Hound barks after them. Ass taps Hound on shoulder. Hound gives one last bark, joins others at table UL.)

[The Animals then went to the table and began to eat the food.]

(Ass crosses DR.)

ASS: After supper, the ass lay down on a pile of straw.

HOUND: *(Crosses DCR.)* . . . the dog under the table.

CAT: *(CL.)* . . . the cat stretched out by the fire

COCK: *(Jumps UC, blows out candle.)* . . . and the cock flew up to the top rafters, and extinguished the light.

MESSENGER: *(Robber No. 1 and Robber No. 2 enter DL, cross C.)* Soon the robbers returned.

CHIEF: We were saps to run out like that, I hadn't finished eating yet. One of us has to return.

MESSENGER: That's right. Be careful; I'll wait here for you.

CHIEF: What do you mean? Get in there immediately, and report back to me here.

MESSENGER: *(Robber No. 1 crosses U.)* Seeing all was dark, the robber crept inside the broken window to strike a light. Taking the cat's glowing eyes for coals, he held a match up to light them.

[But the Cat would stand no nonsense—it flew at his face, spat, and scratched. He was terribly frightened and ran away. He tried to get out the back door but the Hound, who was lying there, jumped and bit his leg. As he ran across the pile of straw in front of the house, the Ass gave him a good sound kick with his hind legs; while the Cock, who had awakened at the uproar quite fresh and gay, cried out from his perch.]

COCK: Cock-a-doodle-doo.

[Thereupon the Robber ran back as fast as he could to his chief.]

CHIEF: What happened?

MESSENGER: There is a gruesome witch in the house who breathed on me and scratched me with her long fingers. Under the table there stands a man with a knife who stabbed me and a great hairy devil who hit me with a club. And on the roof a judge sits, crying, "Bring the rogue here." So I ran away as fast as I could.

CHIEF: Let's get out of here. *(Robber No. 1 and Robber No. 2 exit DL. Animals group C.)* We'll never go back there again.

COCK: And so the four Bremen Town Musicians

CAT: . . . were very pleased with their new house

HOUND: . . . and they never had to leave it again.

(The Animals sing a barbershop-type chord for finale.)

ASS: Heehaw.

CAT: Meeoooow.

COCK: Cock-a-doodle-doo.

HOUND: Woof, woof.

THE GOLDEN GOOSE

CHARACTERS

Mother
Eldest Son
Second Son
Simpleton
Little Gray Man
First Daughter
Second Daughter
Parson
Sexton
Peasant
King
Princess

MUSIC: "HERE COMES THE SUN"

(At C, clockwise, Simpleton, Mother, Second Son, Eldest Son, playing Odd Man Out, Eldest Son and Second Son, kneeling.)

MOTHER: Once there was a widow who had three sons,

SIMPLETON: . . . the youngest of whom was called Simpleton.

ELDEST SON: *(Slaps away Simpleton's hand. Second Son pushes Simpleton off UR, follows him.)* He was scorned and despised by the others.

SECOND SON: . . . and always kept in the background. Go on, get in the background.

ELDEST SON: *(Crosses D for ax, crosses DL.)* One day the eldest son went into the forest to cut wood,

MOTHER: . . . but before he left, his mother gave him a nice sweet cake and a bottle of wine to take with him so that he might not suffer from hunger or thirst on his way. *(Kisses her son.)*

ELDEST SON: Ahh, ma! *(Mother exits L. Eldest Son circles counterclockwise.)*

MUSIC:

HERE COMES THE SUN,
HERE COMES THE SUN,
I SAY, IT'S ALRIGHT.

(Little Gray Man enters DR as Eldest Son is about to chop tree.)

ELDEST SON: Suddenly there was a little gray man.

LITTLE GRAY MAN: Good afternoon, kind young sir, I wonder if you might not have a piece of cake and a drop of wine to share with a hungry and thirsty old man.

ELDEST SON: If I give you any of my cake and my wine, I shan't have enough for myself. So, be off with you. *(Little Gray Man exits DR pit. Eldest Son chops tree twice before ax head flies off and hits his arm. Eldest Son exits L.)*

[The Little Gray Man left quickly, waving his hand at the Son as he left. The Son had not been long at work, cutting down a tree, before he made a false stroke. He dug the ax into his own arm and he was obliged to run home and have it bound.]

My arm! My arm!

LITTLE GRAY MAN: *(Enters DR pit.)* This was no accident! This was caused by the little gray man! *(Exits DL.)*

(Second Son enters UR, crosses DR, gets ax, then crosses DL. Mother enters L.)

SECOND SON: So the second son had to go out into the forest to cut wood,

MOTHER: . . . but before he left his mother gave him a sweet cake and a bottle of wine, so that he might not suffer from hunger or thirst on his way. *(Kisses son.)*

(Second Son circles counterclockwise. Mother exits L. Little Gray Man enters UL.)

MUSIC:

HERE COMES THE SUN,
HERE COMES THE SUN,
I SAY, IT'S ALRIGHT.

SECOND SON: But there was the little gray man.

LITTLE GRAY MAN: Good afternoon, kind young sir, I wonder if you might not have a piece of cake and a drop of wine to share with a hungry and thirsty old man.

SECOND SON: I have some cake and I have some wine, but I'm not going to share them with a hungry and thirsty old man. So be off! *(Little Gray Man exits DL pit. Second Son chops twice before hitting foot. He falls down C.)*

[The Little Gray Man left quickly, but the Second Son's punishment was not long delayed. After a few blows at the tree, he hit his own leg.]

LITTLE GRAY MAN: *(Enters DL pit, exits DR pit. Eldest Son enters L, crosses to Second Son. Simpleton enters UR, crosses C.)* Guess who!

SECOND SON: Brother! *(The Two Injured Brothers meet C.)*

SIMPLETON: Then it was Simpleton's chance to go into the forest to chop down trees.

ELDEST SON: Simpleton, you know nothing about it. You'll only hurt yourself.

SIMPLETON: But you never let me go outside, even.

[(But Simpleton begged so hard to be allowed to go out that the Brothers finally consented.]

ELDEST SON: *(To Second Son.)* Shall we let him go outside?

SECOND SON: Go ahead then, and when you get hurt, you'll be all the wiser for it.

SIMPLETON: Thank you, brothers, thank you. *(Starts to leave.)*

(Simpleton crosses DR, then L. Eldest Son and Second Son start off L.)

ELDEST SON: Don't forget your ax.

(The Simpleton crosses DR, gets ax, crosses L. Eldest Son and Second Son exit L. Mother enters L.)

[Simpleton went back and got his axe and once again started to leave.]

MOTHER: But before he left his mother gave him a cake which was mixed with water and baked in the ashes, and a bottle of sour beer. Simpleton, please be careful.

(Mother exits L. Simpleton circles counterclockwise into forest.)

MUSIC:

HERE COMES THE SUN,
HERE COMES THE SUN,
I SAY IT'S ALRIGHT. *(Twice.)*

[When he reached the forest, like the others, he met the Little Gray Man.]

LITTLE GRAY MAN: *(Enters UR, crosses to C.)* Good afternoon, kind young sir.

SIMPLETON: Hullo.

LITTLE GRAY MAN: I wonder if you might have a piece of cake and a drop of wine to share with a hungry and thirsty old man?

SIMPLETON: I'm afraid all I have is a cake mixed with water and baked in the ashes and a bottle of sour beer, but if you like such fare, I'll be glad to share it with you.

[The Two sat and ate. But when The Simpleton pulled out his cake it was a nice sweet cake and his sour beer was turned into good wine, and so they ate and drank.]

LITTLE GRAY MAN: You have shared your simple meal with me. You have a pure heart. So I will bring you luck. Over yonder in the forest there stands an old tree. Cut it down. You will find something at its roots. So saying, the little gray man disappeared. *(Exits UR. Simpleton crosses D through thick forest. Backs U through forest. Gets ax, returns DC. Simpleton talks with birds, telling them to fly elsewhere before he chops tree. Simpleton chops tree, pushes it down.)*

[The Simpleton went into the forest, but had to return to where he had eaten because he forgot his ax. He went back into the forest and there he found the old tree. Telling the birds what he was planning to do, he convinced them to leave the tree. Then he cut down the tree.]

HONK! HONK!

SIMPLETON: A goose! With golden feathers. *(Simpleton and the Goose play together. Simpleton opens door DC, turns U, puts Goose down. Then he lies down U of it.)* So Simpleton and the goose went to an inn where they planned to spend the night. All right, little goose, lie down. Time to go to sleep.

[Finally Simpleton pulled the legs from under the goose and he himself went to sleep.]

(First Daughter and Second Daughter enter L to U of Simpleton.)

SECOND DAUGHTER: The innkeeper had

FIRST DAUGHTER: . . . two daughters,

SECOND DAUGHTER: . . . and when they saw the golden goose

FIRST DAUGHTER: . . . they were very curious as to what kind of bird it could be,

SECOND DAUGHTER: . . . and wanted to get one of its golden feathers. *(First Daughter opens window. Both climb through.)*

FIRST DAUGHTER: This is my opportunity to get a feather, I'm the eldest. *(First Daughter crosses DR and sits after plucking bird.)* But as the eldest sister reached to pluck a feather, she found her hand was stuck fast.

SECOND DAUGHTER: Hurry up, sister. I want to get one too.

FIRST DAUGHTER: No, sister, stay away, it's some kind of strange bird.

SECOND DAUGHTER: Don't be so selfish. Why shouldn't I have one if you have one? But as soon as she touched her sister she found that her hand was stuck fast, too.
(Second Daughter attaches to First Daughter and sits.)

FIRST DAUGHTER: And in this manner they had to spend the night.

(Cock Crows. Simpleton crosses R, picks up goose D of First Daughter, while First Daughter grabs back of his belt.)

SIMPLETON: In the morning, Simpleton picked up the goose without even noticing the two girls stuck on behind and set out into the forest. *(Weaves counterclockwise with First Daughter and Second Daughter behind.)*

MUSIC:

LITTLE DARLING, IT'S BEEN A LONG AND
LONELY WINTER,
LITTLE DARLING, IT'S BEEN SO LONG SINCE
IT'S BEEN HERE.

PARSON: *(Enters DR, attaches to Second Daughter's waist.)* In the middle of the fields they met the Parson. Shame, shame on you two young girls, chasing after that young man like that, come away! Come away immediately. If you don't come away, I'll have to pull you away.

[The Parson grabbed the Younger Sister to pull her away but no sooner had he touched her than he felt himself stuck fast and he too had to run behind.]

(Sexton enters L, attaches to Parson's coattail.)

SEXTON: As they passed the church, the Sexton said, "Hallo, Your Reverence, where are you going so fast? Don't forget we have a christening."

[So saying, he plucked the Parson by the sleeve and soon found that he could not get away.]

(Peasant enters UR, grabs Sexton's hand. All exit UR. King and Princess enter DL, cross DC.)

PEASANT: A simple peasant came along the road. Ha, ha, ha!

SEXTON: Give us a hand, simple peasant.

[The Peasant went to help them and grabbed onto the Sexton's hand to free him, but immediately he too was stuck fast. So now there were five people running behind Simpleton and his goose.]

KING: By and by they came to a town where ruled a king whose only daughter was so solemn

PRINCESS: . . . that nothing and nobody could make her laugh.

KING: So the king proclaimed that whoever could make his daughter laugh should marry her.

(Simpleton whistles. King motions him on. Procession weaves counterclockwise to U of Princess.)

[When Simpleton heard this he took his goose with all his following before her and when she saw these five people running one behind the other, she burst into fits of laughter and it seemed as if she could never stop.]

MUSIC:

HERE COMES THE SUN, KING,
EVERYBODY'S LAUGHIN', EVERYBODY'S

LAUGHIN',
HERE COMES THE SUN, KING.

KING: You have made my daughter laugh, I now pronounce you man and wife. *(Takes goose from Simpleton as First Daughter goes from Simpleton's belt to King's coat.)* Give me the goose, you won't need it on your honeymoon. *(Leads all off UR. Simpleton and Princess fall in embrace C.)*

[The King took the goose and the Five People and left Simpleton and the Princess to their honeymoon.]

MUSIC:

LITTLE DARLING, THE SMILE'S RETURNING
TO THEIR FACES.
LITTLE DARLING, IT'S BEEN SO LONG SINCE
IT'S BEEN HERE.
HERE COMES THE SUN, HERE COMES THE
SUN,
I SAY, IT'S ALL RIGHT, IT'S ALL RIGHT, IT'S
ALL RIGHT!

CURTAIN

HOW THE CAMEL GOT HIS HUMP

and

HOW THE FIRST LETTER WAS WRITTEN

by

AURAND HARRIS

FROM HIS PLAY *JUST SO STORIES*

FROM THE BOOK BY RUDYARD KIPLING

HOW THE CAMEL GOT HIS HUMP

CHARACTERS:

Djinn, a magician
Man
Dog
Horse
Camel

TIME

When the World was so new-and-all

SETTING

In and near a cave

Magic music. Djinn, a spirit of magic, enters at center, between the main curtains. From his sleeve he pulls a red piece of cloth, whirls it in his right hand. Lights become red. From his other sleeve he pulls a green piece and whirls it with his left hand. Lights become green, then he whirls both colors. Lights change quickly to and from many colors. He stops, holds both hands high and lights become bright. He puts red piece back into his sleeve. He drops green piece which bounces back to his hand. A rubber ball is sewn inside. He casually puts piece in his other sleeve. Or he may do any other quick dramatic bit of magic. He holds one hand out, palm upward. From the center of the curtains an invisible gloved hand places a large book into his waiting hand. He opens book, on the cover of which in large letters, can easily be read, JUST SO STORIES. He holds the open book up in front of his face. The curtains open, showing a bare stage. Music stops. He lowers the book, smiles and announces with excitement and anticipation.

DJINN: Hear and attend and listen. I shall show you a story which befell and behappened and became and was. The story is—HOW THE CAMEL GOT HIS HUMP. When the world was so very new in the very beginning, all the Animals were called and came and worked for Man.

MAN: *(An energetic cave man runs in, sings.)*

Oh, it's another day to find a way
To do the things *that* have never been done before.
(Talks over music patter.)
Yesterday I found a way:
To hoe a seed and make it grow,
To carve a flute that toots when you blow,
To dig a pit and make a trap,
To tap a tree—drip—maple sap,
To squeeze some berries and paint a tiger on the wall,
To make the wheel, the best invention of them all!
(Sings.)
Oh, it's another sun. I'll work some more
And do the things *that* have never been done before.

(Man puts finger in his mouth and whistles loudly. Dog runs in. Man whistles again. Horse runs in from the other side. The three sing.)

ALL:

To—geth—er—We'll work and work from morning 'til night,
A community will grow.

We'll work and work 'til everything is right.
Set! Ready! Go!

(They dance.)
We'll give a—

MAN: Push.

HORSE: And a pull—

DOG: And a helping hand.

ALL: We'll start the world to spin. We'll make a—

MAN: City.

HORSE: And a farm.

DOG: And a promised land.

ALL: So let's begin.
(They mime working and exit, as Djinn speaks.)

DJINN: They did their part. They hauled and they carried in a cart. Together they gave their milk, their wool, a feather, their ivory, their tallow, their leather. They brayed and they neighed and they laid a fresh egg. They scurried and ran, all in a hurry to finish before history began. And in the middle of this busy, busy Far-Off Time, there was—in the middle of the desert—a lazy, lazy—Camel. He didn't like work. He didn't want to work. And so—he did not work. Oh, he was a howler in the howling desert as he ate a stick and a thorn and a core and munched a tamarack clump, and when anybody spoke to him he said, "Humph!" Just "Humph!" and no more.

(Camel music, lumbering, lazy, with sudden spurts of joy. Camel enters from back of the auditorium and comes down right aisle. Djinn exits on stage at right, unnoticed. Camel should not in any way be frightening to the children with whom he will have close contact. Rather he should be lovable, fun, and touchable in looks and actions. At the end of the aisle, by the stage, he stops and gives a loud "Humph!" to audience and crosses in front of the stage, still in the audience, to center. The music picks up and he dances comically, then walks to piano or to the raised stage and lays his head on it to rest. Music stops. Camel raises his head and gives a loud "Humph!" and rests his head again. Dog runs in on stage at left, barking. He comes to front and talks with Camel over footlights.)

DOG: Camel, O Camel, you do not come when Man calls. You do no work at all.

(Camel lifts head and looks at Dog.)

Come. Come and fetch and carry like the rest of us. Oh, there is so much to do with the World so-new-and-all.

CAMEL: Humph!

DOG: What did you say?

CAMEL: Humph!

DOG: *(To audience.)* What did he say?

(Camel leads audience in saying, "Humph!")

Did he say Humph? That's what I thought he said. O Camel, is that all you have to say?

(Camel nods his head.)

Very well! I will go and tell the Man. We must each work and do our part or—how in the world is the world ever going to start?

(Barks as he exits right.)

CAMEL: Humph!

(Camel music. Camel moves in rhythm, dances when music is lively, scratches his back on piano, etc. He sees a conspicuous flower standing upright on a lady's hat who is seated in the front row on the aisle, goes to her, smells the flower. Raises head.)

Humph!

(Suddenly he takes flower in his mouth and waves the flower. Lady protests, "Go away, etc." Camel dances back to piano.)

Humph!

(Music stops. He rests his head on piano.)

HORSE: *(Gallops in on stage at left.)* O Camel, O brother, why do you run wild while there is so much to do with the world so-new-and-all? Come. We will carry and haul and pull together.

CAMEL: Humph!

HORSE: What did you say?

CAMEL: Humph!

HORSE: *(To audience.)* What did he say?

(Camel leads audience in saying "Humph!")

Humph? That's what I thought you said. What kind of four legged word is that? Is that all you have to say?

(Camel nods.)

Then I will go and tell the Man.

(Proudly raises his head.)

And the world will know: Camel is a lout; Horse is proud to help out!

(Horse trots off left.)

CAMEL: Humph!

(Camel music. Camel dances, plays with audience and goes to Lady on the aisle, smells her hat and says, "Humph!" Then pulls her hat off by his mouth. She protests, "Stop! Give me back my hat, etc." Camel waves hat and starts to run with it across the front of the stage. She chases him and hits him from behind with her purse. Camel turns and charges after her. She screams, runs back across in front of the stage, calling for help and exits up the aisle. Camel in close pursuit after her.)

(Music changes to "Work Together" song. Man strides in at right, quickly chops down an imaginary tree, shouting, "Timber!" Dog runs in at right, barking, followed by Horse. Music stops.)

DOG: We have run to tell you—

(Turns to Horse. They nod to each other.)

that there is one—a lazy one—

(They nod to each other.)

who will not help the world to begin.

(They shake their heads to each other.)

MAN: Who?

DOG: Who?

(They speak together.)

The Camel!

MAN: I knew he would be the one. What does he say?

DOG: All he says is—

(They nod and speak together.)

Humph!

MAN: Humph?

DOG: *(Together.)* Humph!

MAN: Something must be done.

(They nod.)

At once.

(They nod.)

DOG: What will we do?

MAN: Since the Camel shirks his work—

(They nod.)

you and you—the two of you—

(They nod.)

will have to do his work, too, by working double time.

(They start to nod, but shake their heads.)

It is—togetherness. It is—the new way. Be about! Time is running out. It is already Thursday. So much to do, with the world so new-and-all.

(Man exits right.)

DOG: *(Angrily.)* Did you—ever feel indignation?

(Horse nods in agreement, angrily to audience.)

Irritation?

(Horse nods.)

Extreme vexation?

(Horse neighs.)

I would like to give a snap, a bite, a chew!

HORSE: I would like to give a kick or two!

DOG: Let's do!

(Dog growls, snaps and shakes his fists at right. Horse snorts, paws, and kicks at left.)

DJINN: *(Enters right.)* What is this?

(He points at Dog, who suddenly freezes in growling position. He points at Horse who suddenly freezes with foot up in a kick.)

DOG: I cannot bark!

HORSE: I cannot kick!

DOG: *(Djinn waves his right hand.)* I see a whirl of sand.

HORSE: *(Djinn waves his left hand.)* It is the Djinn of the land!

DJINN: *(Releasing them from the freeze.)* What is this about?

DOG: Oh, Djinn, I ask you, is it right for anyone to be idle when the world is so new-and-all?

DJINN: Certainly not.

DOG: Well! There is one in the middle of the howling desert, one with a long neck—

(Dog and Horse nod together.)

and long legs—

(They nod together again.)

who hasn't worked a day since Monday.

(They shake their heads.)

DJINN: Who is this one?

DOG: Who?

(They speak together.)

The Camel.

DJINN: By all the gold in Arabia, I knew he would be the one. What does he say?

DOG: Humph.

HORSE: Humph.

DJINN: Humph?

DOG: *(With the Horse.)* Humph!

DJINN: Something must be done.

DOG: It isn't fair.

DJINN: I agree.

HORSE: He should do his share.

DJINN: Certainly!

(Thinking.)

Humph, he says . . .

DOG: Humph.

HORSE: Humph.

DJINN: If you will wait, you will see that he will get a humph from me! First I will make a pool of water in the sand.

(He tosses a shower of sparkling powder into the air, or pulls a piece of blue cloth from his sleeve and puts it on the ground, either with magic music.)

He will come and he will stand and look at his reflection. And while he admires his gangly grace and the whiskers on his face, I will think of—and I will do—a magic—that will put him in his place. Hide.

(Points to right and to left.)

There and there. And you will see what will happen to him if he gives a humph to me! Quick—for here he comes.

(Camel music. Horse and Dog look up aisle, then quickly tip-toe off, Dog to right, Horse to left, and hide in wings. Camel enters and comes down aisle, nodding and giving some "Humphs." He stops at the edge of the stage. Djinn motions over pool of water. Camel looks up and smells, and walks up onto the stage. Djinn motions over water again. Camel comes to pool and gives a "Humph." Djinn circles back and watches. Camel looks at his reflection, lifts his head and gives a "Humph," looks again and gives several pleased "Humphs," then settles down on his knees and gazes fondly at himself, unaware of the others. Dog and Horse peek from each side, but duck back when Djinn comes near to Camel.)

(To audience.)

He smiles . . . he nods . . . he winks at himself. Did you ever wonder what a Camel thinks while he looks at himself? I'll tell you.

(Imitating.)

Oh how beautiful the world would be if everyone was a beautiful Camel like me.

(Dog and Horse peek from each side and shake their heads.)

My eyes . . . my nose . . . my chin . . . my teeth so wide and my ears so thin. But best of all—my back! So straight, so smooth, so fine. No one has a back as beautiful as mine.

(Has an idea.)

His back . . . ? Ah, he has given me a magic clue. Oh, Camel, you will wish you could take back the words you said about your back when I am through with you.

(Motions to Dog and Horse.)

Come.

(Horse and Dog appear at each side.)

Look at the Camel's back. See it now, for nevermore shall it be the same.

(To Camel.)

Camel! Why do you sit while the others work?

(Camel raises head.)

Answer me!

CAMEL: Humph.

DJINN: What did you say?

CAMEL: Humph!

DJINN: That's what I thought you said.

CAMEL: Humph! Humph! Humph!

DJINN: Ha! You have humphed three times too much.

(To audience.)

I will give a "umph," but which "umph" shall I do? I could give him a thump . . . a lump . . . a plump . . . a bump . . . a jump . . . a hump! Shall I give him a hump?

(Listens.)

I will! And—where?

(Listens.)

On his back? Yes! I will! Thank you. That is exactly what I shall do!

(To Camel.)

Oh Camel, I will be fair. I will give you one last chance to work with the others. Will you do your share?

(Camel looks at him.)

Answer me!

(Camel lifts head.)

And take care what word you use.

CAMEL: Humph!

DJINN: Ha! And a humph you will have today—and wear for always. For on your back when I clap my hand, a bump will grow and the bump will grow into a lump, and the lump will grow into a—hump! All who see it will know forever that Camel his part did not do, when the World was so very new.

(Djinn points at Camel who rises and stands in profile.)

Rise—and learn a lesson. Grow, O Hump, when I clap my hand. Grow, O Hump, on his back like a pile of sand.

(To audience.)

Come, you do the magic, too. Say the word when I do and clap your hands. First slow—and watch the hump—grow.

(Speaks softly and points at Camel's back.)

Humph.

(He claps his hands softly and continues rhythmic pattern of one clap, then saying "hump," clap, "hump," etc., encouraging the children to do the same. On the back of the Camel a hump starts rising and continues growing bigger and bigger as the clapping and chanting grow louder and louder. At the climax, Djinn holds up both hands and shouts to audience.)

Stop!

(Points at hump.)

That is your own hump you have brought upon yourself by not working.

(Camel turns and sees it in the water, gives a loud comical cry.)

Today is Thursday and you have done no work since Monday. To catch up you will work now for three days without eating or drinking. You will live on—your—hump. Now go to work—and behave!

(Djinn points for Camel to join Dog and Horse who line up at center. Camel sings reluctantly.)

DOG, HORSE, CAMEL: *(Sing.)*

To—geth—er
We'll give a

HORSE: Push—

CAMEL: And a pull—

DOG: And a helping hand,

ALL: And start the world to spin.
We'll make a—

HORSE: City

CAMEL: And a farm

DOG: And a promised land.

ALL: So let's begin! *(They dance off.)*

DJINN: And from that day until this the Camel always wears a hump, but he has never caught up with the three days he missed at the beginning of the world, and he has never yet learned how to behave. *(He closes book as curtains close. Magic music begins.)*
Now I close my book and say. This remember, all you have seen and heard, it was so—just so—a long time ago. *(He bows and disappears between the curtains. Music stops.)*

CURTAIN

HOW THE FIRST LETTER WAS WRITTEN

CHARACTERS

Djinn: A magician
Man
Woman
Taffy: Their little girl
Stranger
Cavelady: A neighbor
Chief
Cavemen and Cavewomen

TIME

When the World was so new-and-all

SETTING

In and near a cave

Magic music. Djinn, a spirit of magic, enters at center, between the main curtains. He does a visual, dramatic bit of magic. Then he holds one hand out, palm upward. From the center of the curtains an invisible gloved hand places a large book into his waiting hand. He opens book, on cover of which in large letters can easily be read, JUST SO STORIES. Music stops.

DJINN: Hear and attend and listen. I shall show you a story which befell and behappened and became and was. The story is—HOW THE FIRST LETTER WAS WRITTEN. Once upon a very early time when Man and his family lived in a cave, he couldn't read and he couldn't write and he didn't want to. He and his wife and his little daughter named Taffimai Metallumai, which means "Small-person-without-any-manners-who-ought-to-be-spanked," but we will call her Taffy—all three lived as happy as could be in their cave in the High and Far-Off-Times.

TAFFY: *(A little cavegirl, enters and pins an irregular-shaped drawing-skin on the front curtain. She gets small pottery jar from right, and taking no notice of the audience, she hums and begins a large finger-paint sketch of a funny looking stick-girl, first the head. She turns to audience and smiles.)*

I like to draw.

(Continues humming and paints eyes, nose, hair standing on end; turns to audience.)

I draw every day in the cave.

(Hums and paints neck, shoulders, arms and fingers. To audience.)

I draw with berry juice. I squeeze the berries—and make different colors.

(Paints again, the body draped with animal skin. To audience.)

Berry juice is pretty—and it tastes pretty, too.

(Licks fingers and then paints again, legs and feet.)

There. Can you tell who it is?

(Stands proudly by picture.)

It's a picture of me!

(Comes to footlights.)

Everyday is something new. Last week Mummy invented a feather pillow and Daddy ate the first oyster. We have neighbors in other caves and they borrow fire and a cup of honey. And today I am going fishing with Daddy. He says I can if I don't talk. So today I'll draw pictures in the sand. Of course, sand doesn't taste as good as juice paint.

(Licks fingers and calls.)

Daddy. I'll call him and tell him it's time to go. I'll be his clock, because clocks haven't been invented yet. Daddy!

(The main curtains open. The stage is bare except for an open cave with an entrance at the side. Taffy walks into the scene.)

Daddy! It's half past time to go. Dad—dy!

MAN: *(A caveman enters with spear.)* Come. *(Motions her to follow.)*

TAFFY: *(To audience.)* Goodby. We're going down through the beaver swamp to the Wagai River where there are lots of fish.

(Taffy and Man go in circle down left. Djinn appears down right.)

And I can't talk because I'll scare the fish away, then Daddy will get angry—very angry. So I'll draw pictures in the—

(Djinn raises hand. Magic music. He points at the two. They freeze in walking position and hold the pose as if in a picture. Music stops.)

One day—this day—Taffy makes a new discovery.

(He motions. Magic music. Man and Taffy continue walking. Music stops.)

TAFFY: —and draw pictures in the sand and let the water squash and mush between my big toes and middle toes and my little—

DJINN: *(He motions. Magic music. Man and Taffy freeze.*

In the river the Man saw a school of carp fish swimming by.

(He releases them with wave of hand and magical sound.)

TAFFY: —And my little toes.

MAN: Quiet! *(He jabs with spear in imaginary water.)*

TAFFY: Did you . . . ? *(He jabs again.)* Did you . . . ? *(He jabs and lunges forward.)* You caught a fish!

MAN: No. I broke the spear! *(Holds up broken spear.)*

TAFFY: Oh dear. I know! I will go to the cave and get your other spear.

MAN: No.

TAFFY: Why?

MAN: You are too small. You will fall into the beaver-swamp and drown and die. *(Sits on rock, or floor, down left, with back to her.)* I will fix and mend the ends together.

TAFFY: How?

MAN: With some strips of leather. *(Takes strips from pouch.)*

TAFFY: Oh, but that will take forever—half a day! And look—there goes our dinner—swimming away! If—If I could write. Yes! If I could write, I could send a message for the spear. Oh, Daddy, wouldn't it be wonderful if we knew how to write a letter!

MAN: Yes. And how to catch a fish in a net. But we don't know how. Not yet.

TAFFY: *(Walks away.)* Well, I'll think—I'll think of something that will help. Something *I* can do—

(Whistles.)

Something that's new—

(Whistles.)

I can think better when I whistle. Can't you?

(Whistles, then stops.)

STRANGER: *(He is a caveman from the Tewars Tribe. He enters right.)*

Walk . . . walk. I've walked from there to here. I've walked where I've never been before. My feet say stop. But my head says—explore!

(Taffy whistles.)

I hear a bird!

(He imitates her whistle.)

TAFFY: I hear a bird!

(She whistles. He whistles an answer. They continue the whistling conversation and slowly turn and see each other.)

STRANGER: It is not a bird. It is a little girl.

TAFFY: It is not a bird. It is a stranger-man.

STRANGER: She is of another tribe. I do not understand her words.

TAFFY: He is of another tribe. I don't know what he says. Hello.

STRANGER: *(Tries to imitate her word.)* Hel—lo.

TAFFY: *(Has an idea.)* I know what I can do! I can't go to get the spear, but since you are here, I—can send you.

(Imitates her mother.)

Now listen and attend. Do you know where I live? Where my cave is? Do you?

STRANGER: She stamps her foot and makes strange faces. She must be the daughter of a Chief. And there he sits! He must be a great Chief because he takes no notice of me.

TAFFY: Please listen. I want you to go—go to *my* cave because you are tall and you won't fall into the beaver-swamp, and bring back Daddy's other spear. Now is that clear?

STRANGER: She waves her arms and talks, but I don't understand what she says. I will give her a present—a piece of birchbark.

(Gives her a large piece of bark which is tucked in his belt.)

TAFFY: For me? Oh, I see—you want me to write where I live—my cave address. But I don't know how to write! Writing has not been invented yet. But—but I can draw! I'll *draw* you a picture to show you where my cave is, then you'll know where and you can go there. But I need something to scratch with . . .

(Points at his necklace.)

Your big tooth! May I use it! Thank you, I will.

(Pulls it off.)

STRANGER: *(Aside.)* That is a magic tooth and anyone who touches it will immediately swell or burst.

(Looks expectantly.)

But she does not swell up or burst. I will be more polite.

(Bows.)

TAFFY: Now I will draw you a picture.

(Holds bark with one hand and draws with the other. Stranger looks over her shoulder.)

First I will draw Daddy with his spear that's broken.

STRANGER: *(Aside.)* A man holding a spear.

TAFFY: And then I'll draw the other spear which he wants. Oooophs! I slipped. It looks like the spear is in Daddy's back.

STRANGER: *(Aside.)* Someone is being struck with a spear!

TAFFY: This is me, explaining it to you.

STRANGER: *(Aside.)* Someone is scared—so scared his hair is standing on ends!

TAFFY: This is you and I'm putting Daddy's spear in your hand so you won't forget.

STRANGER: *(Aside)*. Another man with a spear in his hand! It is a war! She is showing me there is going to be a battle!

TAFFY: And this is the beaver-swamp. Mind you don't fall in. I'll draw lots of beaver heads.

STRANGER: *(Aside)* Heads! Enemy heads peeking out!

TAFFY: There! It is the best picture I've ever drawn!

STRANGER: *(Looks around.)* Enemies must be hiding in the bushes. That is why the Chief turns his back on me, while this wonderful child draws a picture to show me his danger. How clever! I will go. I will go at once and get help before he is killed!

(Grabs bark.)

TAFFY: Hurry.

(Stranger gives a loud war cry.)

Quiet! You'll scare the fish and Daddy will be very angry.

STRANGER: *(Loudly.)* I will go! I will bring back *all* his tribe!

(Gives a jump and war cry.)

TAFFY: Sh!

(Whispers.)

Goodby. Go.

(Waves.)

STRANGER: Hello.

(Waves and exits up aisle with a leap and a yell.)

MAN: *(Turns toward Taffy.)* What have you been doing, Taffy?

TAFFY: I—I am making you—a surprise! Oh, you don't know how surprised you're going to be.

MAN: Quiet! I see another shoal of fish!

(He jabs with spear.)

TAFFY: Promise me, Daddy, promise me you'll be surprised.

MAN: Quiet!

(Jabs again.)

TAFFY: Promise!

(He jabs and lunges.)

Did you catch a fish?

MAN: *(Shaking with anger.)* No! I broke the spear again!

TAFFY: Where?

MAN: There!

TAFFY: What are you going to do?

MAN: What every man will do! I am going to swear!

(In rage he raises spear and fist and opens his mouth. Djinn raises his hand and freezes Man and Taffy.)

DJINN: And all the words which you cannot hear him say are the words which, when Man is angry, he still says today.

(Djinn motions to them. Magic music starts. Man exits at left, twisting his face, mouthing words, and shaking his fist. Taffy's eyes open wide in surprise and her mouth forms an "O" in a gasp. She covers both ears and follows off left. Music stops. Djinn reads.)

The Stranger ran and he ran.

(Stranger enters at back of auditorium and runs down aisle.)

He ran through pits and bogs, over logs and frogs and polliwogs.

(Stranger leaps and gives a war cry.)

He ran FAST past a lion's den—

(Stranger speeds up running.)

Then with a splash and a dash and a tromp, he crossed the beaver-swamp.

STRANGER: *(Runs across front of auditorium.)* What a lot of little beavers.

(Waves at children and runs up aisle.)

DJINN: He ran through duckweed, briar, and fern, made a turn to the right and was out of sight.

(Stranger exits at back. Djinn, as he talks, goes to rock flats, opens front one which makes the cave.)

Meanwhile in the cave, which was just ahead, down the path, all was as usual inside the room, as if it were an everyday—not a day that a new discovery would soon be made.

(Woman enters from right, carries cup and walks into cave set.)

Taffy's mother—you remember her from Story One—was entertaining a neighbor, a cavelady.

(Cavelady enters from right and carries cup.)

She had come to see how Taffy's mother made a double braid, marmalade—and to chat a little. So she—and she—were chatting socially and—having tea.

(The two women in cave Sing.)

WOMAN: *(They both sing a vamp of "Chatter, chatter, chatter, chatter, chatter, etc." Woman announces.)* Weather!

CAVELADY: Such a lovely, lovely day.

WOMAN: The wind has blown the clouds away.

CAVELADY: I think that spring is here to stay.

WOMAN: Winter was cold, ice, and sleet.

CAVELADY: Summer thunder, floods and heat!

WOMAN: Cold or hot—

CAVELADY: Weather!

BOTH: We'll have weather whether or not.

(They vamp an introduction again of "Chatter, chatter, chatter, chatter, chatter, chatter, etc.")

WOMAN: *(Announces.)* Have you heard!

CAVELADY: He laced some leather and called them sandals.

WOMAN: She burned some wax and named them candles.

CAVELADY: Strange cups, the first with handles.

WOMAN: Button holes, needles, thread.

CAVELADY: *Legs* on a table, a chair, a bed!

WOMAN: I'm amazed!

CAVELADY: Perplexed!

BOTH: What will they do that's new and think of next!

(Stranger enters and runs down aisle giving a variety of war whoops.)

CAVELADY: What is that?

WOMAN: Coming near.

CAVELADY: Down the path!

WOMAN: Coming here!

CAVELADY: What can it be?

WOMAN: I'll look and see.

(Quickly peeks through arch and around cave.)

CAVELADY: Is it a lion? A tiger? A coyote?

(Gasps.)

A chimpanzee!

WOMAN: *(Re-enters cave.)* It is a stranger!

(Stranger gives a wild yell. Women jump.)

A wild stranger from another tribe. Get a club!

(Gets large one.)

CAVELADY: And a rope to bind him!

(Gets it.)

WOMAN: We will attack from the front!

CAVELADY: And behind him!

STRANGER: *(Runs on the stage with a yell, stops when he sees cave.)* A cave. I've found it at last.

(Pants.)

No one is about. I must call them all to come out.

(Gives a yell. Women shake.)

It is quiet. Perhaps they are asleep. I'll take a peep inside.

(He tip-toes to arch.)

WOMAN: *(Women stand ready on each side of arch, club and rope held high.)* Steady.

CAVELADY: Ready.

WOMAN: Spread.

(They take a step backwards.)

CAVELADY: Aim at his head!

STRANGER: *(Enters cave and calls hopefully.)* Yoo-hoo.

WOMAN: A yoo and a hoo to you!

(Hits him over the head.)

Yoo-hoo! Cuckoo!

(Keep hitting him.)

STRANGER: *(Raises hands.)* Help! Help! Help!

WOMAN: He holds his hands up.

CAVELADY: He gives up.

WOMAN: We have won. Who are you?

CAVELADY: Why do you come?

WOMAN: What do you want?

STRANGER: I wonder what they are saying?

(He suddenly lifts hands and shouts.)

Battle!

(Women raise their clubs.)

Enemies attack Chief by the river.

WOMAN: I wonder what he is saying? Do you want food? Are you hungry?

(Rubs her stomach and makes faces.)

STRANGER: She is sick.

CAVELADY: Are you weary? Are you tired?

(Droops and limps.)

STRANGER: She is crippled.

WOMAN: Are you lost? Can't you see your path?

(Shades her eyes, looks to right and left.)

STRANGER: She is blind. Poor woman.

BOTH WOMEN: Well?

STRANGER: What can I tell them? I will *act* it out!

(Comically and with great exaggeration he pantomimes.)

Small girl—small—small—small—

(Measures smallness.)

girl—girl—girl.

(Fixes hair, walks and twists daintily and makes cooing sounds.)

WOMAN: Poor man. He has lost his wits.

STRANGER: By the river—river—river.

(Makes waves with hands.)

Water—water—water.

(Splashes water on his face, raises chin and drinks with gurgling sounds.)

Fish—fish—fish.

(Swims, making splashing sounds.)

CAVELADY: He is having fits!

STRANGER: Father—big Chief—Chief—Chief!

(Prances like leader.)

Enemies!

(Scowls.)

Enemies all around hiding with spears.

(Crouches, holding spear.)

Attack! Fight! Hit! Battle! Kill!

(Jumps, hits in a wild fight. Stabs his own chest, yells, struggles, and falls dead on the ground. Women, in silence, lean over and look in awe at him. Suddenly Stranger jumps up and shouts, terrifying the Women.)

Save girl! Save Chief! Help! Help! Help!

(Throws arms in air and yells.)

WOMAN: He is as silly as a goose that's loose!

STRANGER: *(Remembers.)* Picture!

(Hands bark to Cavelady.)

CAVELADY: It is a drawing. Of Taffy? Of your husband?

(Hands bark to Woman.)

WOMAN: *(Looks at it and screams.)* Oh! Oh! Ooooooooooh.

STRANGER: They understand. Now they will thank me.

WOMAN: You have struck my husband—full of spears!

STRANGER: I am glad you are pleased.

WOMAN: Poor Taffy! Look, so scared her hair is standing on ends!

(Stranger nods smiling.)

And more, more heads—enemies ready to attack!

(Stranger nods.)

And you bring me this horrible picture to show me how it was done!

STRANGER: You are welcome.

WOMAN: Oh! You brute! You beast! You mad dog!

STRANGER: Thank you.

WOMAN: At him! Tie him up! Bind him up!

(Cavelady quickly circles around Stranger with rope.)

STRANGER: What is this they do? What a strange way to say thank you.

WOMAN: You savage, butcher, barbarian! My husband—my little girl. You heartless, mindless ape!

(Hits him on head with club.)

You worm, you toad, you baboon!

STRANGER: Help! Help!

(Cavelady puts an apple in his mouth.)

WOMAN: Beat the drum! Call the Warriors! Call the Chief!

(Cavelady runs out behind cave and beats drum. Woman points for Stranger to go out of cave. She follows him out, hitting him on the head with each beat of the drum. Off left, another drum is heard. Chief, in all his primitive finery, enters left. He may enter alone, or may be followed by as many Cavemen Warriors as desired. Chief raises his hands. Drums and everyone stops. Cavelady enters from behind cave.)

CHIEF: Why do you beat upon the Reverberating Tribal Drums? Why do you call the Chief of the Tribe of Tegumai? Explain! Explain! Explain!

CAVELADY: *(Comically nervous, confronted by Chief.)* O brave Chief, I am so glad you've come. A stranger—a loose goose—came down the path.

(She imitates his yelling and running.)

He came into the cave—yoo hoo! We bopped him on the head—Pop! Bound him around with a rope. He brought a picture—showing how—where—Taffy's hair! A battle! A fight! What a sight! He is there! A wild baboon!

CHIEF: *(To Stranger.)* Explain! Explain! Explain!

STRANGER: *(Mouth plugged with an apple, makes loud strange sounds. Chief takes it from his mouth.)*

Quick! Down by the river. They are in danger! Enemies all around—with spears. Save him! Save him!

(Chief puts apple back in his mouth.)

CHIEF: I do not understand his words.

WOMAN: It is here—told in a picture. See! My husband with a spear in his back! Taffy with her hair on ends! Enemy heads! Another tribe!

CHIEF: *(Looks, then gives a roaring battle cry.)* Beat the drums! To the River. We will attack first! This is war!

(All give war cry. Drums beat. Chief leads a short war dance around Stranger. Then all in a war procession march off the stage into the audience. They cross, on the war path, in front of the audience. At the same time, Djinn quickly closes the first flat of the cave, making it again a large rock. The war procession stomps back up on the stage with yells and dancing.)

TAFFY: *(Runs in left.)* Quiet! You will scare the fish away and Daddy will be very angry!

WOMAN: Taffy!

TAFFY: Mummy?

WOMAN: You are safe.

(Embraces her.)

CHIEF: Flay the bushes! Slay the enemy! Attack!

MAN: *(Enters left.)* Quiet! I say! Quiet! You've scared the fish away!

(Cavemen give a yell and come at him with spears, or Cavelady and Chief hit him with club.)

Stop! I am of your tribe.

CHIEF: Explain! Explain! Explain!

MAN: *(Angrily.)* I am fishing quietly, catching carps, and trouts, and you come—yells, cries, shouts! And scare the fish thirty days away! Explain. Explain. Explain.

CHIEF: Enemies all about! War!

MAN: Enemies?

CHIEF: Another tribe!

(Points at Stranger.)

STRANGER: *(Cavelady takes apple from his mouth.)* Now they are going to reward me.

CHIEF: Chop off his head!

STRANGER: Thank you.

(Men raise spears.)

TAFFY: No! Let him go!

(All look at her.)

He is a nice Stranger-man.

MAN: What do you know about this?

CHIEF: Explain. Explain. Explain.

TAFFY: I sent him. I drew the picture.

(Takes picture from Chief. First Cavelady, then Woman, then Man, etc., ask, "You?," "You?," "You?".)

CHIEF: Small-person-without-manners-who-ought-to-be-spanked, you?

TAFFY: He is my—surprise! I did surprise you, didn't I, Daddy?

CHIEF: Explain! Explain! Explain!

TAFFY: It is very simple. Daddy broke his spear. I wanted the Stranger-man to go and get Daddy's other spear, so I drew a picture . . . Daddy with the broken spear . . . Then a beaver-swamp with lots of beaver heads, to show him the way—And me explaining it. It is my best picture! Now untie him and let him eat his apple.

(Chief looks at picture and grunts, looks at Taffy and grunts—it is a moment of suspense—and looks at the Stranger and grunts, and then the grunts build into a laugh.)

MAN: He laughs.

(Man laughs, then one by one, each joins the laughing, Stranger last. They laugh uproariously, hitting on backs, doubling over, holding stomachs. Suddenly Chief raises his hand. All is still.)

CHIEF: A new discovery has been made!

(Points at Taffy.)

O Small-person-without-any-manners-who-ought-to-be-spanked, you have hit upon a great invention.

TAFFY: I didn't intend to.

CHIEF: Never mind, it is a great invention. Today you have made a picture-letter. A time will come when it is called writing. We will have an alphabet—letters—all twenty-six of them. Then we will be able to read and to write.

(Points at Taffy.)

And you can send a letter with no pictures and no danger of it being mis-read!

(Looks at picture.)

Beaver-heads . . . enemies!

(Chief laughs. Points at Stranger.)

Wild baboon!

(Chief laughs. Stranger laughs and points at Chief.)

Unbind him. I adopt him into the Tribe of Tebuami. His name will be—Man-with-big-feet-who-runs-fast. He will be my—letter carrier!

(Points to Taffy.)

You—will be my—letter writer! I give you a new name—Little-person-who-made-great-invention. Now we will celebrate!

(As men spin Stranger around untying him, Djinn speaks.)

DJINN: And so that is how the first letter was written in the Far and High-Off Time.

(Drums beat. Chief takes Taffy and they lead, with the others following, in a short tribal dance of a joyful celebration. At the climax, Djinn motions and all on stage suddenly freeze in an effective picture.)

There are other stories of how and why, when the world was so new-and-all. These you will need to read yourself and enjoy. For now—I close my book and disappear.

(Closes book. Lights on stage change and fade in beautiful colors.)

But this remember—all you have seen and heard while you were here, it was so—just so—a long time ago.

(Magic music. There is a sudden puff of smoke in front of Djinn and he disappears, as the curtains close on a still and colorful scene of the Far and High-Off Time.)

CURTAIN

WHO LAUGHS LAST?

by

NELLIE McCASLIN

from a Polish legend

WHO LAUGHS LAST?

CHARACTERS

The Announcer
King Jan
The Queen
Matenko: The Jester
Elzuňia: his wife
Lords
Ladies
A Beggar

SETTINGS

Scene 1. The palace.
Scene 2. The cottage, several months later.
Scene 3. The cottage, an hour later.

SCENE ONE

THE PALACE

For the first scene, two large, ornate chairs (placed, preferably, on a small platform) should be located at RC, facing DL. A bench DR (optional) and another UL will complete the furniture requirements. Whatever can be added to give the room a regal appearance will be in order, although such embellishments are optional.

ANNOUNCER: Many, many years ago when Poland was ruled by King Jan, there was a jester in the palace named Matenko. He had served a lifetime in the court, and for years had been the favorite clown. But in his old age, his joints became so stiff and his wits so dull that even the lords and ladies who loved him best yawned behind their handkerchiefs when he performed. They begged King Jan to dismiss him and get a new clown. The first scene is in the palace. The characters are the King, the Queen, Matenko, his good wife Elzunia, and the lords and ladies of the court.

(He bows and goes off. As the Curtains open, all are laughing and talking together. The King and Queen sit on their thrones.)

FIRST LORD: *(Interrupting the conversations.)* Matenko! Matenko! Perform for us! Of what use is a jester who sleeps in his corner?

(The other Lords and Ladies take up the cry, ad libbing as follows: "Yes, Matenko, come out! . . . Where are you? . . ." etc. Matenko hobbles out stiffly, tries to bow, but fails. He addresses the King.)

MATENKO: What is your will, Master?

KING: Some trick, if you please! We have had nothing but gossip in the court all morning.

MATENKO: *(Scratching his head.)* Yes . . . there was a joke. . . . I had it a moment ago. . . . If you will be patient . . . *(He goes into a study as he tries to recall it.)*

FIRST LORD: It must be good if you make us wait for it!

SECOND LORD: No doubt it will be like the last one—heard a dozen times before! Where have your wits flown to, Matenko?

THIRD LORD: Time was when one joke followed another so quickly no one could keep up with you!

FIRST LORD: Never mind, old clown. By the time you have thought of it, no one will be listening.

SECOND LORD: Your Majesty, why do you not get us a new jester—one whose movements are active and whose jokes will amuse us?

THIRD LORD: Matenko has had his day. Why not let him spend his old age in some peaceful place where tricks are not asked of him?

QUEEN: There is something in what they say, my lord. They do not mean to be unkind; but look, how tired the old man is! He is no longer happy in the palace.

KING: Perhaps you are right. Matenko has been in this palace for fifty years. Longer than I, myself. He was my father's jester. My first plaything was his old cap with the bells.

MATENKO: *(Trying to spring up.)* I have it! Listen! "Why is a morning in the palace like a day at the market?" *(Looks about him.)*

LADIES: Oh, we have heard it before!

FIRST LORD: An old one, Matenko. *(To the King.)* You see, Your Majesty?

MATENKO: *(Bewildered.)* Have I told it before?

KING: Yes, my good Matenko, many times.

MATENKO: Then I must think of another. Wait . . . *(Goes into another study.)*

KING: No, my faithful old clown. I have a better plan. For a long time we have known that some day you would be leaving us, and I have a cottage near the palace grounds prepared for you. I had not thought it would be so soon. But the place is ready; so put away your bright jester's clothes and become a citizen of Poland.

MATENKO: *(Astonished.)* A cottage for my own?

QUEEN: And for your good wife, Elzunia. Bring her in to us.

(A Lady in Waiting goes for her, and returns with a plump, jolly old woman.)

ELZUNIA: *(As she enters.)* You have sent for me, Your Highness?

QUEEN: Yes, Elzunia. The King has something to tell you.

ELZUNIA: I am in the midst of baking a big cake for Your Majesty's dinner, but I can stay for a minute.

KING: No, Elzunia. This time you are not to return to the kitchen. Let someone else finish the cake for you.

ELZUNIA: *(Alarmed.)* Someone else? Has Elzunia's hand with the pastry grown heavy in her old age? *(Looks anxiously at the King.)*

KING: No, Elzunia. No. But the time has come for you and Matenko to retire and enjoy your old age in the peace of your own home. I have bought a small cottage for you on the edge of the palace grounds, and today you shall move into it.

ELZUNIA: Oh, Your Majesty, it is too much! I had expected to die in your service.

QUEEN: Well, you shall not. You and Matenko have served faithfully for many years and deserve a good rest.

KING: There will be money for you to live on. But you must come to see us sometimes, even though we have a new jester.

MATENKO: *(Bewildered.)* Yes, Your Majesty. And thank you for your kindness.

KING: Will someone take them to their cottage at once? *(A Lord steps forward.)* Everything is ready for you. Good-by, Matenko!

MATENKO: *(Stumbling out the door after the Lord.)* Good-by, Your Majesty.

ELZUNIA: You have been good to us!

QUEEN: No better than you deserve. Good-by, Elzunia!

(There is a confusion of voices, as the Lords and Ladies call, "Good-by! Good luck, Matenko!" etc. And the Curtains close.)

SCENE TWO

THE COTTAGE, SEVERAL MONTHS LATER

For this scene, the benches and throne chairs have been removed. A small table, with plain chairs R and L of it, is placed slightly below C. A small cupboard against the wall L completes the necessary requirements for the humble cottage of Matenko and Elzunia.

ANNOUNCER: Several months have passed. King Jan has found a new jester who pleases the lords and ladies mightily. Poor Matenko and his wife are all but forgotten. The King and Queen have not even remembered to send the money they promised, to keep up the cottage and buy food. The next scene is in the old couple's kitchen, where we find the jester and his wife wondering how they can get themselves some kind of living.

(As the Curtains open, the jester and his wife are sitting despondently at the empty table.)

MATENKO: Poor Elzunia! To end your days in hunger and want.

ELZUNIA: Poor Matenko! Once the favorite clown in His Majesty's service—and now no richer than a beggar!

MATENKO: If only I could find work. But no one will hire an old man who knows nothing except playing the fool!

ELZUNIA: If only I could have the food that is wasted in one day at the palace! It would be enough for us to live on for a month.

MATENKO: Why do you suppose the King has never sent so much as one gold piece to us since we left?

ELZUNIA: Perhaps he has forgotten us. They say there is a new jester at the palace, and there have been many court balls to take up his mind.

MATENKO: If only I dared go to him and ask for the money! But I cannot! *(Drops his head on the table.)* Is there nothing in the house for supper?

ELZUNIA: Nothing, my husband. We ate the last slice of bread for breakfast. Even the hens have stopped laying. There is not so much as one egg. Just this old dried onion is left. *(She tosses the onion to him. He takes it and fingers it as she talks.)* Let us go to bed and forget our hunger. *(She rises, but he jumps up and goes after her.)*

MATENKO: Wait! I have an idea! Things will get no better. You must go to the Queen and tell her I have died. First rub your eyes with this onion. If we cannot eat it, let it bring us some food.

ELZUNIA: But suppose she should discover you are living?

MATENKO: She has never come this way. And perhaps she will give you the money for a decent burial that she has not given us for these last years on earth.

ELZUNIA: Very well, then. I will do it.

(They rub her eyes with the onion, and she takes a handkerchief from her pocket.)

MATENKO: A little more, wife. Let us make them red and swollen, as if you had been crying all the night.

ELZUNIA: *(Pretending great grief.)* There! Am I wretched enough to go to the palace?

MATENKO: *(Rubbing his hands in delight.)* Yes, yes! This is my very best trick—if it works! Now go at once!

ELZUNIA: I shall be back as soon as possible, my husband. Wish me luck in my sorrow!

(She runs out the door, laughing, old Matenko watching her. The Curtains close.)

SCENE THREE

THE COTTAGE, AN HOUR LATER

ANNOUNCER: An hour passes, and Elzunia is running down the road to the cottage. Matenko is waiting for her at the open door.

(The announcer leaves and the Curtains open, to reveal Elzunia, running up to the cottage door.)

MATENKO: What luck, wife? What luck?

ELZUNIA: It was easy! It's too bad you can't die every day. Look! Fifty gold pieces to give their old jester a decent burial!

MATENKO: Did you see the King?

ELZUNIA: No. I found the Queen alone in the garden. I sobbed out my story, and she felt so badly she gave me all the money she had in her little blue purse. She said this would be enough to bury you, and still leave me money to live on!

MATENKO: *(Grabbing her around the waist and twirling her.)* Wife, it's a wonderful trick! And now it's your turn to die! I shall go to the King and tell him you have left me alone and desolate.

ELZUNIA: But suppose he should find out the truth?

MATENKO: That difficulty we shall have to solve if the time comes. Meanwhile, I must try my luck with King Jan. Where is the onion? *(She gets it, and they rub it on his face.)* Ouch! . . . There! *(As she puts the onion down on the table.)* Now I am ready to go and tell him that my dear wife is dead, and I am alone in the world and penniless. *(He is the picture of misery as he leaves the house. He sobs, and his shoulders shake.)* Where is the basket? If the King gives me gold, I shall stop at the market for food.

ELZUNIA: *(Calls after him.)* Good-by, old man. Good luck! *(Sighs.)* Well, it will not hurry him to wait by the open door. Now that we have gold pieces, we shall have dinner. I may as well put the plates and cups on the table.

(She bustles about the room, getting dishes from the cupboard and setting the table. There is a rap at the door; she goes and finds a beggar standing outside it.)

Yes, old fellow?

BEGGAR: *(Slyly.)* Could you give an old man a crust of bread?

ELZUNIA: Alas, sir, we haven't a bite of bread in the house.

BEGGAR: But you are setting the table with plates and bowls.

ELZUNIA: I am waiting for my husband to come home from the palace. He has gone to get food.

BEGGAR: *(With a sneer.)* He will get no food at the palace, my good woman. Many a time I have waited by their kitchen door. But perhaps you have gold pieces in some crock or pot? *(Sidles into the room.)* Some you can spare?

ELZUNIA: What would a poor woman without so much as a loaf of bread be doing with gold pieces?

BEGGAR: *(Peering here and there.)* You wouldn't mind if I looked about?

ELZUNIA: *(Angrily.)* Yes, I would mind. If you will come again when my husband gets back, there will be plenty to eat!

BEGGAR: *(Snatches up the dried onion from the table.)* What is this?

ELZUNIA: That? Why, that's just an old dried onion—one that's brought us good luck.

BEGGAR: Good luck, eh? Then I'll take it along for myself. Does it put gold in your pockets?

ELZUNIA: *(Beginning to twinkle.)* It has.

BEGGAR: Then I'll take the onion and go. Never mind the supper, old woman. I'll see what good luck this will bring. At least I can put it between two slices of bread. Some good wife will see to that! *(He puts it in his pocket, and skips out.)*

ELZUNIA: *(Laughing heartily as he goes.)* Too bad, old dried-up onion! But you have served us well. One bag of gold already—and if you have kept a thief from the cupboard, I guess we can let you go. Who knows? Perhaps it is best to get rid of you now! You were our very best trick! What will Matenko say when I tell him I gave you away? *(Looks out the door again.)* But here he comes now! Down the road as fast as his legs will carry him. What luck, Matenko? What luck?

MATENKO: *(Entering with a heavy bag and a basket of food.)* My dear wife, the King's sympathy is worth even more than the Queen's! Two hundred gold pieces! Enough to bury you. Enough to stop my grief. And enough to keep us the rest of our lives. *(Puts the bag on the table.)*

ELZUNIA: Let us count it out now. Here, Matenko, you take that pile; I'll take this.

MATENKO: Very well.

(They begin to count.)

ELZUNIA: Ten, twenty, thirty, forty, fifty . . . and a hundred gold pieces! What a wonderful trick! *(Laughs heartily.)* But suppose the King should tell the Queen?

MATENKO: Sixty, seventy, eighty, ninety—one—two—three—four gold pieces! And here, wife, in the basket, is food. More food than has been in our kitchen for a long time. Bread, meat, butter, milk, flour. So you can bake a cake for the funeral feast! I bought it on my way home from the palace.

ELZUNIA: Well, let us have some bread at once. *(She cuts off two slices, and they sit down to eat.)* Tonight we shall have a banquet. I shall make soup, roast the meat, bake the cake, and— Why, what is it, husband?

MATENKO: *(He has been looking out the window, and is suddenly the picture of distress.)* Wife! *(His mouthful of bread chokes him, and he can hardly get the words out.)* Wife, look! The King and Queen are coming! Far up the road I can see them!

ELZUNIA: *(Runs to look where he is pointing.)* Are you sure?

MATENKO: Of course; their gold crowns are bright in the sunshine. Come, we had better lie down on the floor and pretend we are really dead, in case they come here!

ELZUNIA: Let us put a coating of flour on our faces and place a candle at our heads and one at our feet!

(Both smear flour on each other with much giggling. Elzunia lights the candles.)

MATENKO: Hurry, wife! They are almost to the cottage!

ELZUNIA: Well, lie down then. I am ready.

(He lies down, and she does likewise.)

MATENKO: Stop laughing, Elzunia! They will never believe we are dead!

ELZUNIA: You stop! Whenever you giggle, I have to!

(They both lie very still, as the King and Queen come to the open door.)

KING: Now we shall see which of them is dead.

QUEEN: *(Arguing.)* I *know* it was Matenko, my dear.

KING: But didn't I say that Matenko himself came to me not half an hour ago? I say it was Elzunia!

QUEEN: Look! Here they are—both of them—dead!

KING: Together on the floor. Then each of us is right. Poor old souls. I'm afraid I have neglected them these last few months.

QUEEN: I wonder what it was that took them?

KING: He was the best jester that ever played a joke in our court. It's too bad his poor wits failed him.

(Wipes his eyes.)

QUEEN: We have never had a cook with the skill of Elzunia. Poor woman! *(Wipes her eyes.)* Well, my lord, there is nothing we can do now but bury them. Let us go and take care of it.

KING: Very well. I do wonder, though, which of the two old folks died first.

MATENKO: *(Rising up suddenly.)* Your Majesty, though my wife died first, I assure you, I was dead before!

KING: *(Greatly startled. Then he laughs.)* You rascal! Get up immediately and tell us what this trickery means!

MATENKO: *(He and Elzunia both rise shamefacedly.)* We were penniless, Your Majesty; for the money that you promised never came.

ELZUNIA: And no one would give work to two such old people. There was nothing in the house to eat. Just one old dried-up onion.

MATENKO: So I thought of this trick, and it worked so well when Elzunia tried it, that I played it, too!

KING: *(Thoughtfully.)* I see, my old friend. It is really I who am to blame. And for that I shall give you two hundred more gold pieces—enough to keep you both as long as you live. But I leave it on one condition—that you promise never to use your wits dishonestly again!

ELZUNIA: I promise, my lord. In fact, I have given the onion away.

MATENKO: *(Solemnly.)* And I promise, my lord. I do indeed. The next time I die, you will know that I am really dead!

(All laugh.)

CURTAIN

THE CHINESE CINDERELLA

by

LOWELL SWORTZELL

from a Chinese fairy tale

THE CHINESE CINDERELLA

CHARACTERS

Wing-Woo: the stage manager
Pear Blossom (or Little Pigling)
Stepmother
Stepsister
The white doves
The cow
Members of the procession:
  Acrobats, tight-rope walkers,
  lantern and dragon bearers
Lin Yun
Four property men

SETTING

In Old China.

The scene is a bare stage. Wing-Woo, dressed in an elaborate gown, enters. He strikes a gong which he carries.

WING-WOO: Honorable ladies and gentlemen *(Bows to right, left, center.)* Kind permission to present a play about Pear Blossom, a little girl of Old China. I assure you, ladies and gentlemen, that it is a simple play and will not tax your minds. The property men will first set the stage. They are supposed to be invisible to your eyes, honorable ladies and gentlemen. *(He strikes a gong and four property men dressed all in black enter. They arrange several stools. When Wing-Woo strikes the gong again, two property men go to the left side of the stage and two to the right. They kneel facing the audience.)*

In the story we enact for you today, Pear Blossom, the young girl you see here, washes clothes all night and day.

(Pear Blossom enters and kneels. Two prop men bring her a wash tub. She washes invisible clothes, carefully wrings them out, and hangs them on an invisible clothes line.)

WING-WOO: Pear Blossom has a step-mother and step-sister, both of whom hate hard work, and hate most of all any house work.

(The stepmother and the stepsister enter, and address Pear Blossom.)

STEPMOTHER: Where is my handkerchief?

STEPSISTER: Why isn't my robe ready? I want to parade before the mirror and admire myself in it.

PEAR BLOSSOM: *(Replying sweetly.)* I am washing them now.

STEPMOTHER: Work is all you are good for, Little Pigling.

PEAR BLOSSOM: Please do not call me that terrible name. My name is Pear Blossom.

STEPMOTHER: Never mind what we call you, Little Pigling. You have your work to do. When you have finished the washing, there is the kitchen to put in order.

STEPSISTER: And the dusting.

STEPMOTHER: And the baking.

STEPSISTER: And the mending.

STEPMOTHER: And the polishing.

STEPSISTER: And the cleaning.

STEPMOTHER: And the cooking.

STEPSISTER: And the scrubbing.

STEPMOTHER: And when you're finished, close the door.

PEAR BLOSSOM: I understand.

STEPMOTHER: *(To the stepsister.)* Come, my beautiful child, you must rest, for in the morning we go to see the royal procession.

STEPSISTER: Little Pigling, be up early. I will need you to help me dress for the procession.

PEAR BLOSSOM: I will help you.

STEPMOTHER: *(To the Stepsister.)* In your new robe you will be the loveliest girl at the procession.

STEPSISTER: Thank you, Mother. You are kind to me.

PEAR BLOSSOM: May I have a new robe?

STEPSISTER: Don't be silly. Who would look at you?

STEPMOTHER: What a foolish Little Pigling you are. You in a new robe. Imagine! *(She laughs.)* You are lucky to get your sister's hand-me-downs.

STEPSISTER: Come, let's leave her and go to bed. I must rest so that I can be beautiful in the morning.

STEPMOTHER: Don't you dare go to bed until every instruction is obeyed, Little Pigling.

PEAR BLOSSOM: I won't. But please, oh please, call me Pear Blossom. My name is the only thing that I possess that is beautiful. *(Stepmother and stepsister laugh and exit. Pear Blossom sinks beside her bucket and weeps.)*

WING-WOO: As she was crying, Pear Blossom thought that if she finished all the work she had been instructed to perform, she too might go to the royal procession. She worked nearly the whole night through. She did everything that her mother asked. She did the washing. *(She pantomimes each action.)* She did the dusting. She did the baking. She did the mending. She did the polishing. She did the cleaning. She did the cooking. She did the scrubbing. And when she was finished, she closed the door, just as her mother said. And then she crept in the corner and went to sleep. *(The property men spread out a mat and Pear Blossom goes to sleep.)*

WING-WOO: But she hadn't long to wait until she heard the roosters crow. *(One of the property men crows in her ear.)* And then she felt the warm rays of the sun on her forehead. *(Another property man carries a paper cut-out sun with long yellow streamers on it; he dangles these in her face.)*

PEAR BLOSSOM: *(Stretching and yawning.)* I must get up and prepare the robes for stepmother and sister. *(The step-mother and sister enter wearing their new robes.)*

STEPSISTER: Pigling, help me with this sash. I can't get it straight.

STEPMOTHER: Fasten my kimono, Little Pigling.

PEAR BLOSSOM: May I ask your permission to speak . . .

STEPSISTER: Of course not, we are much too busy prettying ourselves to listen to your chatter, silly Pigling.

PEAR BLOSSOM: I only want to ask if I may go to the procession.

(Stepmother and sister laugh.)

STEPMOTHER: You silly child.

STEPSISTER: Ridiculous!

PEAR BLOSSOM: I worked nearly the whole night through so that I could see the royal procession. Please let me go.

STEPSISTER: The idea is ridiculous! What a peculiar Pigling you are. *(She roars with laughter.)*

STEPMOTHER: Very well, persistent Pigling, we'll let you go . . .

PEAR BLOSSOM: Oh, thank you, very much.

STEPMOTHER: I have not finished, Pigling. I was about to say you may go when . . .

PEAR BLOSSOM: When? What do you mean? May I not go now?

STEPMOTHER: You may go when you have husked all the rice in these three water jars. *(Prop men carry in large water jugs.)*

STEPSISTER: And don't miss a grain. *(She laughs.)*

PEAR BLOSSOM: One young girl cannot crack all this rice in a day . . .

STEPMOTHER: Yes, I think we realize that. *(She laughs again.)*

PEAR BLOSSOM: I should have known. You do not want me to go.

STEPMOTHER: Certainly you can't say that when I have given my permission only this minute.

STEPSISTER: A mirror, Little Pigling, so I may look at myself.

(Pear Blossom is handed a mirror by a property man. It is an empty square frame.)

STEPSISTER: *(Looking in mirror.)* How lovely I am.

STEPMOTHER: Indeed you are.

STEPSISTER: You always pay me such kind compliments, mother. Thank you.

STEPMOTHER: *(Pantomimes opening the door.)* Now let us go into the street. *(They go through the door.)* Oh, yes, Little Pigling, I forget. Before you go to the procession you must remove all these weeds.

PEAR BLOSSOM: *(Stepping through the door.)* But the garden is tended by stepsister.

STEPMOTHER: She cuts the tulips and poppies and lilies—that is all.

PEAR BLOSSOM: *(Sadly.)* Very well, I will remove the weeds after I have cracked and husked the rice.

(Stepmother and sister go off fluttering their fans and laughing.)

WING-WOO: Pear Blossom thought and thought how she might get all this work done, and still go to the procession. She was puzzled by the problem. And there was no answer. The work would take too long to finish. That was all there was to it. She tried not to cry. She took long deep swallows and even held her breath. But it did no good. She could no longer hold back those tears.

(Kneeling on a mat provided by a property man, Pear Blossom pantomimes crying. Another property man brings a small bowl filled with water and sprinkles a few drops on her cheeks.)

WING-WOO: It so happened that outside in a tree nearby sat several white doves who heard the conversation. They flew into the kitchen and fluttered around Pear Blossom. They wanted to cheer her up.

(During Wing-Woo's speech the birds have come through the door, and they dance around Pear Blossom.)

WING-WOO: And they knew a way they could help. Each bird took a jar of rice. *(The property men hand jars to birds, and they spread out the rice. The birds pantomime this and the following action.)* They took the rice and quickly cracked it.

PEAR BLOSSOM: *(Seeing the birds for the first time, she is at first alarmed.)* Pretty birds, you must not eat our rice. I wish I could give you some, but my stepmother holds me responsible for every grain. *(Then she realizes what they are doing.)* But you are not eating the rice. You are cracking and husking it. How did you know that I had to do this in order to go to the procession? You wonderful birds! ! ! *(In dance, the doves work faster and when they finish they hold up jars.)*

PEAR BLOSSOM: *(Excited and happy.)* You have done all my work for me! Now I will be able to go to the procession after all. Thank you. *(She pantomimes opening door and carefully closing it behind her and then stops suddenly.)* Oh, the weeds! I forgot all about the weeds! You can hardly get through them. *(She steps over the imaginary weeds.)* I will not be able to go after all.

WING-WOO: Once more little Pear Blossom was broken hearted. Once more she tried not to cry. Once more she had to cry just a little bit. *(This time the property man sprinkles one drop of water on her cheek.)*

WING-WOO: It so happened that in a field next to the garden, a big cow was grazing. And the cow heard Pear Blossom's plight and wanted to help her as best it could.

(The cow enters and comes to Pear Blossom.)

PEAR BLOSSOM: What are you doing here, kind Cow?

WING-WOO: The cow knew the easiest way to remove those weeds. And it went to work. *(The cow dances, eating the weeds.)*

PEAR BLOSSOM: I see. You are helping me just as the birds did. You are eating all the weeds. *(The cow nods and chews.)* How very kind! Now I can go to the procession, for all my work is finished.

WING-WOO: Pear Blossom hurried to the city. And then as she turned the next corner who did she meet but . . .

PEAR BLOSSOM: Stepmother, stepsister!

(The stepmother and the proud sister enter.)

STEPMOTHER: Pigling wretch! What are you doing here?

STEPSISTER: Go home this instant and do your work!

PEAR BLOSSOM: But my work is done.

STEPMOTHER: Every grain of rice?

PEAR BLOSSOM: Cracked and husked.

STEPMOTHER: Every weed?

PEAR BLOSSOM: The white doves who sit on our pear tree kindly cracked the rice, and the kind cow pulled up and ate the weeds.

STEPSISTER: Ridiculous!

PEAR BLOSSOM: You will see when you go home.

STEPMOTHER: Very well, if you are to stay here, do not walk with us. *(Noise and music off-stage.)*

PEAR BLOSSOM: *(Very excited.)* The procession is starting. I am to see it. I am.

(Enter the procession which includes a giant fish, a paper dragon, lanterns on poles. A tight-rope walker walks an imaginary rope which is a line on the stage floor. This procession may act out various tricks, stunts, dances, or acrobatics, accompanied by music.)

WING-WOO: At the end of the procession came Lin Yun, a rich young man, who was visiting in the city that day, and who for some time had been looking for a wife.

(Pear Blossom turns suddenly as the procession goes by and bumps into Lin Yun.)

PEAR BLOSSOM: I am very sorry. I was busy watching the procession, and I did not see you. *(She bows to him.)*

LIN YUN: *(He bows to her.)* What is your name?

PEAR BLOSSOM: My real name is Pear Blossom, but I am called Little Pigling.

LIN YUN: I will call you Pear Blossom.

PEAR BLOSSOM: Thank you. *(They continue to speak in pantomime.)* *(Stepmother and stepsister enter.)*

STEPMOTHER: *(Pointing at Pear Blossom.)* Look, that silly creature is talking to Lin Yun, the wealthiest man in all of China.

STEPSISTER: I have been looking everywhere for him all day. How did she find him?

STEPMOTHER: Let's shoo her away.

STEPSISTER: Make certain he notices me.

STEPMOTHER: This is my daughter. A lovely girl, isn't she?

LIN YUN: *(Still looking at Pear Blossom.)* Indeed she is.

STEPSISTER: Not that wretch. Me!

STEPMOTHER: Not Pigling. This is my daughter, Lin Yun. I know you are looking for a wife, and here is the perfect girl.

LIN YUN: *(Still looking at Pear Blossom.)* I quite agree.

STEPSISTER: Not her, me!

LIN YUN: I have found the girl I have long sought. Pear Blossom.

WING-WOO: The rich Lin Yun presented Pear Blossom—as she was called from then on—with a pair of beautiful red velvet slippers, which she wore on all special occasions, such as her wedding day. *(Lin Yun puts slippers on Pear Blossom's feet and leads her across the stage.)* And Lin Yun took her away from the life of drudgery she had known.

WING-WOO: And while Pear Blossom lived happily, her proud sister sat at home.

(The doves come in, followed by cow.)

STEPSISTER: Now listen, you dreadful doves, I am not going to tell you again, I want that rice cracked, so that I don't have to stay inside all day. So, do it. And you, you cowardly cow, remove those weeds. I have better things to do.

(The doves fold their wings and refuse to work. The cow sits down and ignores the stepsister.)

WING-WOO: And slowly the Proud Sister learned the lesson that she would never receive kindness unless she was kind herself. And this, honorable ladies and gentlemen, is the lesson of our simple story of Pear Blossom, who to this day keeps a picture of the doves and the cow on the walls of her house in honor of their kindness to her.

We thank you, honorable audience, for permitting us to present our play. We hope you took pleasure in it. Farewell. *(Wing-Woo, Pear Blossom, and Lin Yun bow to all sides and go out as a gong rings.)*

CURTAIN

PYRAMUS
AND
THISBE

by

WILLIAM SHAKESPEARE

the rehearsal scene from
A Midsummer Night's Dream

CHARACTERS

Peter Quince, director
Nick Bottom, the weaver
Francis Flute, the bellows-mender
Robin Starveling, the tailor
Tom Snout, the tinker
Snug, the joiner

TIME

Long Ago

SETTING

Elizabethan Athens

SCENE 1

(Enter Quince, Snug, Bottom, Flute, Snout, and Starveling, all comic rustics.)

QUINCE: Is all our company here?

BOTTOM: You were best to call them generally, man by man, according to the script.

QUINCE: Here is the scroll of every man's name, which is thought fit, through all Athens, to play in our interlude before the duke and duchess on his wedding-day at night.

BOTTOM: First, good Peter Quince, say what the play treats on; then read the names of the actors, and so grow to a point.

QUINCE: Marry, our play is, The most lamentable comedy, and most cruel death of Pyramus and Thisbe.

BOTTOM: A very good piece of work, I assure you, and merry. Now, good Peter Quince, call forth your actors by the scroll. Masters, spread yourselves.

QUINCE: Answer as I call you. Nick Bottom, the weaver.

BOTTOM: Ready. Name what part I am for, and proceed.

QUINCE: You, Nick Bottom, are set down for Pyramus.

BOTTOM: What is Pyramus? A lover, or a tyrant?

QUINCE: A lover, that kills himself most gallantly for love.

BOTTOM: That will ask some tears in the true performing of it; if I do it, let the audience look to their eyes; I will move storms, I will condole in some measure. Yet my chief humour is for a tyrant: I could play Ercles rarely.

The raging rocks
And shivering shocks
Of prison gates:
And Phibbus' car
Shall shine from far
And make and mar
The foolish Fates.

That was lofty! Now name the rest of the players.

QUINCE: Francis Flute, the bellows-mender.

FLUTE: Here, Peter Quince.

QUINCE: You must take Thisbe on you.

FLUTE: What is Thisbe? A wandering knight?

QUINCE: It is the lady that Pyramus must love.

FLUTE: Nay, faith, let not me play a woman; I have a beard coming.

QUINCE: That's all one: you may speak as small as you will.

BOTTOM: Let me play Thisbe, too. I'll speak in a monstrous little voice, "Thisbe, Thisbe." "Ah! Pyramus, my lover dear; thy Thisbe dear, and lady dear!"

QUINCE: No, no; you must play Pyramus; and, Flute, you Thisbe.

BOTTOM: Well, proceed.

QUINCE: Robin Starveling, the tailor.

STARVELING: Here, Peter Quince.

QUINCE: Robin Starveling, you must play Thisbe's mother. Tom Snout, the tinker.

SNOUT: Here, Peter Quince.

QUINCE: You, Pyramus' father; myself, Thisbe's father. Snug, the joiner, you, the lion's part; and, I hope, here's a play fitted.

SNUG: Have you the lion's part written? Pray you, if it be, give it me, for I am slow of study.

QUINCE: You may do it extempore, for it is nothing but roaring.

BOTTOM: Let me play the lion, too. I will roar, that I will do any man's heart good to hear me; I will roar, that I will make the duke say, "Let him roar again, let him roar again."

QUINCE: And you should do it too terribly, you would fright the duchess and the ladies, that they would shriek; and that were enough to hang us all.

ALL: That would hang us, every mother's son.

BOTTOM: I grant you friends, if that you should fright the ladies out of their wits, they would have no more discretion but to

hang us; but I will aggravate my voice so that I will roar you as gently as any sucking dove; I will roar you an 't were any nightingale.

QUINCE: You can play no part but Pyramus; for Pyramus is a sweet-faced man; a proper man, as one shall see in a summer's day; a most lovely, gentlemanlike man; therefore you must needs play Pyramus.

BOTTOM: Well, I will undertake it. But there are things in this comedy that will never please. First, Pyramus must draw a sword to kill himself, which the ladies cannot abide. How answer you that?

SNOUT: By'r lakin, a parlous fear.

STARVELING: I believe we must leave the killing out, when all is done.

BOTTOM: Not a whit: I have a device to make all well. Write me a prologue, and let the prologue seem to say, we will do no harm with our swords, and that Pyramus is not killed indeed; and for the more better assurance, tell them, that I, Pyramus, am not Pyramus, but Bottom the weaver: this will put them out of fear.

QUINCE: Well, we will have such a prologue.

SNOUT: Will not the ladies be afeard of the lion?

STARVELING: I fear it, I promise you.

BOTTOM: Masters, you ought to consider with yourselves: to bring in, God shield us! A lion among ladies, is a most dreadful thing; for there is not a more fearful wild-fowl than your lion living, and we ought to look to it.

SNOUT: Therefore, another prologue must tell he is not a lion.

BOTTOM: Nay, you must name his name, and he himself must speak, saying, "Ladies," or "Fair Ladies, I would wish you" or "I would request you," or "I would entreat you, not to fear, not to tremble: my life for yours. If you think I come hither as a lion, it were a pity of my life: no, I am no such thing: I am a man as other men are; and there indeed let him name his name, and tell them plainly he is Snug, the joiner.

QUINCE: Well, it shall be so. But there is two hard things: that is, to bring the moonlight into a chamber; for you know, Pyramus and Thisbe meet by moonlight.

BOTTOM: Ay, one must come in with a lanthorn and say he comes to disfigure, or to present, the person of Moonshine.

QUINCE: Then, there is another thing; for Pyramus and Thisbe, says the story, did talk through the chink of a wall.

SNUG: You can never bring in a wall. What say, Bottom?

BOTTOM: Some man or other must present some loam, about him, to signify wall; and let him hold his fingers thus, and through that cranny shall Pyramus and Thisbe whisper.

QUINCE: If that may be, then all is well. Here, masters, are your parts. *(Gives each his scroll.)* Pyramus, you begin when you have spoken your speech, enter into that brake; and so every one according to his cue. Speak, Pyramus. Thisbe, stand forth.

BOTTOM: *(Has difficulty in reading.)* Thisbe, the flowers of odious savours sweet—

QUINCE: Odours, odours.

BOTTOM:

—odours savours sweet:
So hath thy breath, my dearest Thisbe dear.
But hark, a voice! Stay thou but here awhile,
And by and by I will to thee appear. *(Exits.)*

FLUTE: Must I speak now?

QUINCE: Ay, marry, must you; for you must understand he goes but to see a noise that he heard, and is to come again.

FLUTE:

Most radiant Pyramus, glowing as a roaring fire,
As true as truest horse that yet would never tire,
I'll meet thee, Pyramus, at Ninny's tomb.

QUINCE: "Ninus' tomb," man. Why, you must not speak that yet; that you answer to Pyramus. You speak all your part at once, cues and all. Pyramus, enter: your cue is past; it is "never tire." Pyramus! *(They all call, "Bottom," Ad lib, confusion.)*

FLUTE: *(Over the noise.)* —As true as truest horse, that yet would never tire.

BOTTOM: *(Enters, speaking at same time.)* If I were fair, Thisbe, I were only thine.

QUINCE: Enough. Enough. *(Confusion stops.)* Masters, I am to entreat you, request you, and desire you, to learn your parts by tomorrow night, and we will meet here again by this oak. In the meantime I will draw a bill of properties, such as our play wants.

BOTTOM: Get your apparel together; every man look o'er his part. And, most dear actors, eat no onions nor garlic, for we are to utter sweet breath, so the ladies will say, it is a sweet comedy.

QUINCE: I pray, you, gentlemen, fail me not.

BOTTOM: We will meet; and here we may rehearse most obscenely and courageously. Take pains; be perfect; adieu.

QUINCE: At the duke's oak we meet.

BOTTOM: Enough; hold, or cut bow-strings. *(They exit.)*

SCENE 2

(Scene: The same. Enter Quince, Snug, Bottom, Flute, Snout, and Starveling carrying homemade costumes and simple props.)

BOTTOM: Are we all met?

QUINCE: Pat, pat; and here's a marvellous convenient place for our rehearsal. This green plot shall be our stage, this hawthorn-brake our tiring-house; and we will do it in action as we will do it before the duke.

BOTTOM: To your places, masters, to your places. *(All exit except Quince.)*

QUINCE:

The prologue is address'd. *(Speaks as Prologue.)*
If we offend, it is with our good will.
That you should think we come not to offend,
But with good will, we show our simple skill.

The actors are at hand; and, by their show,
You shall know all that you are like to know.

(Enter Pyramus and Thisbe, Wall, Moonshine, and Lion, as in dumb-show.)

Gentles, perchance you wonder at this show;
But wonder on, till truth make all things plain.
This man is Pyramus, if you would know;
This beauteous lady Thisbe is certain.
This man, with lime doth present wall,
That vile wall, which did these lovers sunder;
And through Wall's chink, poor souls, they are content
To whisper, at the which let no man wonder.
This man, with lanthorn, as it doth glow,
Presenteth Moonshine; for, if you will know,
By moonshine did these lovers, with blushing hue,
Did meet at Ninus' tomb, there, there to woo.
This grisly beast, which Lion hight by name,
The trusty Thisbe, coming first by night,
Did scare away, or rather did affright;
And, as she fled, her mantle she did fall,
Which Lion vile with bloody mouth did stain.
Anon comes Pyramus, sweet youth and tall,
And finds his trusty Thisbe's mantle slain:
Whereat with blade, with bloody blameful blade,
He bravely broach'd his boiling bloody breast;
And Thisbe, tarrying in mulberry shade,
His dagger drew and died. For all the rest,
Let Lion, Moonshine, Wall and lovers twain,
At large discourse, while here they do remain.

(Exit Prologue, Thisbe, Lion, and Moonshine.)

WALL:

In this same interlude it doth befall
That I, one Snout by name, present a wall;
And such a wall, as I would have you think,
That had in it a crannied hole or chink,
Through which the lovers, Pyramus and Thisbe,
Did whisper often very secretly. *(Holds up fingers.)*
And this the cranny is, right and sinister,
Through which the fearful lovers are to whisper.

PYRAMUS: *(Enters.)*

O grim-look'd night! O night with hue so black!
O night, which ever art when day is not!
O night! alack, alack, alack!
I fear my Thisbe's promise is forgot.
And thou, O wall! O sweet! O lovely wall!
That stand'st between her father's ground and mine;
Thou wall, O wall! O sweet and lovely wall!
Show me thy chink to blink through with mine eyne.
(Wall holds up his fingers.)
Thanks, courteous wall: Jove shield thee well for this!
But what see I? No Thisbe do I see.
O wicked wall! through whom I see no bliss;
Curs'd be thy stones for thus deceiving me!

THISBE: *(Enters.)*

O wall! full often hast thou heard my moans,
For parting my fair Pyramus and me:
My cherry lips have often kiss'd thy stones,
Thy stones with lime and hair knit up in thee.

PYRAMUS:

I see a voice: now will I to the chink,
To spy and I can hear my Thisbe's face. Thisbe!

THISBE: My love! thou art my love, I think.

PYRAMUS: Think what thou wilt, I am thy lover's grace; And, like Limander, am I trusty still.

THISBE: And I like Helen, till the Fates me kill.

PYRAMUS: Not Shafalus to Procrus was so true.

THISBE: As Shafalus to Procrus, I to you.

PYRAMUS: O! Kiss me through the hole of this vile wall.

THISBE: I kiss the wall's hole, not your lips at all.

PYRAMUS: Wilt thou at Ninny's tomb meet me straightaway?

THISBE: 'Tide life, 'tide death, I come without delay.

(Exit Thisbe and Pyramus.)

WALL:

Thus have I, Wall, my part discharged so;
And being done, thus Wall away doth go. *(Exits.)*

LION: *(Lion and Moonshine enter.)*

You ladies, you, whose gentle hearts do fear
The smallest monstrous mouse that creeps on floor,
May now perchance both quake and tremble here,
When lion rough in wildest rage doth roar.
Then know, that I, one Snug the joiner, am
A lion fell, nor else no lion's dam:
For, if I should as lion come in strife
Into this place, 't were pity on my life.

MOONSHINE:

This lanthorn doth the horned moon present;
Myself the man i' the moon do seem to be.
(Speaks as Snug.)
All that I have to say is, to tell you that the lanthorn
Is the moon; I, the man in the moon.

THISBE: *(Enters.)* This is old Ninny's tomb. Where is my love?

LION: OH! *(Lion roars. Thisbe runs off. Lion tears Thisbe's mantle, and exits.)*

PYRAMUS:

Sweet moon, I thank thee for thy sunny beams;
I thank thee, moon, for shining now so bright,
For, by thy gracious, golden, glittering gleams,
I trust to take of truest Thisbe sight.
But stay, O spite!
But mark, poor knight,
What dreadful dole is here?
Eyes, do you see?
How can it be?
O dainty duck! O dear!
Thy mantle good,
What! stain'd with blood!
Approach, ye Furies fell!
O Fates, come, come!
Cut thread and thrum;

Quail, crush, conclude, and quell!
O! wherefore, Nature, didst thou lions frame,
Since lion vile hath here deflower'd my dear?
Which is—no—no—which was the fairest dame,
That liv'd, that lov'd, that lik'd, that look'd with cheer.
Come, tears, confound;
Out sword, and wound
The pap of Pyramus:
Ay, the left pap,
Where heart doth hop: *(Stabs himself.)*
Thus die I, thus, thus, thus.
Now am I dead,
Now am I fled;
My soul is in the sky:
Tongue, lose thy light!
Moon, take thy flight! *(Moonshine exits.)*
Now die, die, die, die, die. *(Dies.)*

THISBE: *(Re-enters.)*
Asleep, my love?
What, dead, my dove?
O Pyramus, arise!
Speak, speak! Quite dumb?
Dead, dead! A tomb
Must cover thy sweet eyes.
These lily lips,
This cherry nose,
These yellow cowslip cheeks,
Are gone, are gone.
Lovers, make moan!
His eyes were green as leeks.
O Sisters, Three,
Come, come to me,
With hands as pale as milk;
Lay them in gore,
Since you have shore
With shears his thread of silk.
Tongue, not a word:
Come, trusty sword;

Come, blade, my breast inbrue: *(Stabs herself.)*
And farewell, friends; thus Thisbe ends:
Adieu, adieu, adieu. *(Dies.)*

PROLOGUE: Moonshine and Lion are left to bury the dead.

WALL: Ay, and Wall, too.

BOTTOM: *(Sits up.)* No, I assure you; the wall is down that parted their fathers. *(Dies again.)*

QUINCE: Now I will please the Duke with an epilogue.

BOTTOM: No. No epilogue, I pray you. Let us end the play, and please the duke, with a dance! *(All agree, "A dance, a dance!" All do a lively, country dance. They bow and exit.)*

CURTAIN

MR. HARE TAKES MR. LEOPARD FOR A RIDE

by

CAROL KORTY

from her play, **Plays From African Folktales**

MR. HARE TAKES MR. LEOPARD FOR A RIDE

CHARACTERS

Narrator
Mr. Hare
Mr. Leopard
Mrs. Leopard

SETTING

From the Hausa culture of Nigeria.

TIME

Long ago.

There are many trickster tales in West African folklore. Mr. Hare is a favorite figure in the Hausa culture of Niger and Nigeria. He is the granddaddy of our American Br'er Rabbit.

The hand and stage properties can be real or mimed.

NARRATOR: One day Mr. Hare was sitting out in front of his house.

MR. HARE: *(Sitting, twiddling his foot with a very nonchalant, ho-hum air.)*

Hey, ho, what do you know,
What will I do today, today?
What will I do today, I say;
Oh, what shall I do today?

(Mr. Leopard rushes by carrying something. It could be a bucket which he brings back filled or emptied on the return trip, or any other object to show he is taking care of business.)

MR. HARE: *(Leaps up, delighted.)* Good morning, Mr. Leopard! How are you?

MR. LEOPARD: Grrr . . . *(Throws a glance over his shoulder as he hurries off.)*

MR. HARE: Very nice friend! *(Calls after him.)* You can't even stop long enough to say, "Hello." I don't know why I'm surprised. The only time you are ever friendly to me is when you think you might be able to trick me and catch me for your next meal. Well, it hasn't worked yet. I'm too fast for you. *(Returns to sitting and twiddling.)* Hey, ho, what do you . . . *(Mr. Leopard hurries back again.)*

MR HARE: *(Leaping up.)* Hey! What do you know! Greetings, again, Mr. Leopard!

MR. LEOPARD: *(Charges across to exit without pausing to notice Mr. Hare.)* Grrr. . . .

MR. HARE: Right in front of my door he passes, and not even a nod! He knows I'm safe on my own territory, so he won't bother with me at all. Not even a nod. *(Calls after Mr. Leopard.)* That's not right! Just because you're big, you should not be rude. At least you can say, "Hello," even if you don't chase me. *(Mr. Leopard again rushes past, barely missing knocking over Mr. Hare.)*

MR. HARE: *(Brightly.)* Hello! *(Looks after him; realizes it's too late and shrugs, sitting down again.)*

Hey, ho, what do you know?
What will I do today . . .

Today! *(He jumps up.)* I know exactly what I'll do today. I'll do something to make that leopard notice me, *(Looking at audience.)* and I don't mean as something to eat! *(He hunches over and walks in a little circle with hands behind his back—or does a similar kind of activity to show he's scheming. He stops and continues to think aloud.)* If his house is that way *(Points to Mr. Leopard's first entrance.)* and he ran that way *(Points to Mr. Leopard's exit, then looks at audience.)*, it means he's not at home. *(He repeats the circling or his activity for thinking. Stops.)* I think I'll just take a little walk over to his house and leave a little message. *(Mr. Hare sets out with stylized walk or hopping sequence for long-distance running. Drum can accompany him, increasing in intensity as he progresses. Mr. Hare circles stage area, or does some other type of running, using entrances and exits to indicate that distance is being covered. He ends where Mrs. Leopard has come out to establish her house.)*

MR. HARE: Hello there, Mrs. Leopard.

MRS. LEOPARD: *(Very attentive and very polite.)* Greetings, Mr. Hare.

MR. HARE: How are you today?

MRS. LEOPARD: Fine, just fine, thank you. How are you?

MR. HARE: To tell you the truth, I'm not very well.

MRS. LEOPARD: *(Concerned.)* Oh, I'm sorry to hear that, Mr. Hare.

MR. HARE: Is Mr. Leopard home by any chance?

MRS. LEOPARD: No, he left this morning to go hunting.

MR. HARE: Oh, that's too bad. I needed to use him.

MRS. LEOPARD: Needed to use him? *(Not understanding.)* What do you mean by that?

MR. HARE: I'm not feeling well, and I want to go to the doctor. It's too far a walk for me feeling this poorly. I thought Mr. Leopard could give me a ride.

MRS. LEOPARD: *(More perplexed.)* What do you mean, "Give you a ride"?

MR. HARE: Well, I don't have a horse to ride, so I thought I would ride Mr. Leopard instead.

MRS. LEOPARD: *(Shocked.)* Ride Mr. Leopard! Are you crazy, you little rabbit?

MR. HARE: Hmmmmmmmm, no. I'm sure I could do it.

MRS. LEOPARD: *(Very worried.)* It's a good thing for you he isn't around to hear you say that. He'd eat you up in a minute for being so insolent.

MR. HARE: *(Reassuring.)* Oh, I doubt that. *(Very pointedly.)* Besides I know I could ride him, and I'll bet you I *will* ride before the day is over. You can tell him that for me, if you will.

MRS. LEOPARD: I just can't believe I'm hearing you right.

MR. HARE: *(Mimicking her voice.)* Oh, you're hearing me right. *(Mrs. Leopard looks at him, almost realizing he is mocking her. Mr. Hare stops the mimicking and continues in his own voice.)* Guess I'll go home again and lie down. Good-bye, Mrs. Leopard.

MRS. LEOPARD: Good-bye, Mr. Hare. *(Calling after him.)* And you'd better be more careful. *(Mr. Hare leaves slowly with his sick act until he is out of Mrs. Leopard's sight; then he skips merrily home in the reverse pattern of his trip to her house. Just before he reaches home, Mr. Leopard rushes past him and exits in the direction of his own house. Mr. Hare stops short with leg in mid-air.)*

MR. HARE: *(To audience.)* Leopards might be big, but they aren't very bright. *(Runs and stops short again.)* It's time they learned their lesson. *(Finishes trip home, ending with a jump in front of his house.)* I'd better get the bridle and whip ready for my ride. *(He gets stick and rope, or mimes getting them, and sits down to wait, pretending to be very unconcerned.)*

MR. LEOPARD: *(Rushing on in terrible anger.)* Mr. Hare! Mr. Hare!

MR. HARE: *(Jumping up bright and hoppity.)* Greetings, Mr. Leopard. How are you?

MR. LEOPARD: *(Confused.)* Ah . . . Greetings. *(Refocusing his anger.)* Mr. Hare . . .

MR. HARE: I saw you several times earlier. Sorry you didn't have time to say hello.

MR. LEOPARD: I was in a hurry. *(Angrily.)* Mr. Hare . . .

MR. HARE: How are you, by the way?

MR. LEOPARD: Fine. *(Exasperated, he grabs Mr. Hare and leans on him to stop his jumping around.)* Listen, Mr. Hare. My wife said you were by my house earlier and boasted you would ride me like a horse.

MR. HARE: *(Slipping out from his grip.)* Heavens, that's ridiculous, Mr. Leopard!

MR. LEOPARD: It's worse than ridiculous. It's insulting.

(Mr. Leopard paces up and down during this exchange, and Mr. Hare mimics him, falling in with the pacing with mock sympathy.)

MR. HARE: It is very insulting!

MR. LEOPARD: I'm absolutely furious.

MR. HARE: I would be too!

MR. LEOPARD: *(Stops.)* Wait, now you're the one who said that. *(Mr. Hare gives innocent shrug.)* My wife said so!

MR. HARE: Maybe your wife was mistaken.

MR. LEOPARD: *(Circling him and speaking slowly and deliberately.)* My wife told me very clearly that you told her to give me the message that you would ride me like a horse.

MR. HARE: There must be some mistake.

MR. LEOPARD: Now, wait a minute. *(Reflects.)* My wife wouldn't just make up a story like that. There is no mistake. *(To Mr. Hare with anger.)* And no one is going to make a fool out of me.

MR. HARE: Certainly not, Mr. Leopard.

MR. LEOPARD: *(Very sure of himself.)* I want to hear the two of you straighten this out. Come on home with me. *(He starts to leave, assuming Mr. Hare will follow.)* I'll ask my wife to repeat the message in front of you.

MR. HARE: *(Brightly.)* I'd really like to come with you, Mr. Leopard *(Changes instantly to sick act.)*, but I'm sick today. Didn't Mrs. Leopard tell you? I barely made it home myself.

MR. LEOPARD: *(Exasperated.)* Come on! You know I live nearby.

MR. HARE: *(Collapsing.)* That's true, but I'm feeling weaker every minute. I know I'd never be able to walk that far today.

MR. LEOPARD: *(Furious.)* I have been insulted today, and the matter is going to be settled today! Do you hear?

MR. HARE: *(Weakly.)* I don't see why it can't wait until I'm feeling stronger.

MR. LEOPARD: You're coming with me today, even if I have to carry you! *(Grabs his arm and pulls him to his feet.)*

MR. HARE: *(Weakly.)* All right, then. You'll have to carry me; I'm too weak to walk. *(He sinks down again.)*

MR. LEOPARD: *(Thoroughly exasperated and frustrated.)* Hurry up. Get on my back. *(Bends over.)*

MR. HARE: *(With a sparkle.)* If you insist! *(Jumps up and runs around to get ready to mount. Almost gives in to the temptation to kick Mr. Leopard in the rear while mounting but resists it; then decides to have a little more fun before getting on. Leans meekly on Mr. Leopard's back.)* I'm afraid I'll fall off your back while you're running. Do you mind if I get a little rope?

MR. LEOPARD: *(Considers and is unable to think of any objection.)* Nope.

MR. HARE: *(Gets rope and stops in front of Mr. Leopard, looking him in the eye.)* I'll just put this through your mouth so I'll have something to hang on to. *(Mr. Leopard nods, and Mr. Hare does the business of putting rope in Mr. Leopard's mouth. Again Mr. Hare starts to mount, is tempted to kick him, but thinks better of it; he leans on Mr. Leopard's back.)*

MR. HARE: Now I need a little stick.

MR. LEOPARD: *(Speaking through clenched teeth.)* What for?

MR. HARE: *(Directly to Mr. Leopard's face.)* To push aside the low branches so they won't knock me off your back while you're running.

MR. LEOPARD: *(Considers briefly.)* Okay. *(Mr. Hare gets stick.)*

MR. HARE: *(Runs around to mount.)* I'm ready now. *(He thinks of one more thing.)* Could you get a little lower? *(As Mr. Leopard continues to respond, Mr. Hare skips around with increasing delight at the situation.)* Lower, lower, lower, lower . . . *(Mr. Leopard looks around at him.)* . . . Ah, steady! *(With mock seriousness.)* Now let me get hold of the rope . . . and my stick . . . *(Jumps on Mr. Leopard's back.)* . . . We're off! *(They gallop to the Leopard house along the path that Mr. Hare previously ran. Drum can accompany this action.)*

MR. HARE: Faster, Mr. Leopard, faster. *(Using the stick.) (Mrs. Leopard comes out to establish the house.)*

MR. HARE: *(As they pull up in front of the house.)* Hello, there, Mrs. Leopard!

MR. LEOPARD: *(Very authoritatively.)* We just came by to check up on the boast that Mr. Hare would ride me like a horse. *(Mrs. Leopard looks alarmed as Mr. Leopard slowly straightens up. It almost dawns on Mr. Leopard what has happened. Mr. Hare slowly slides off his back and steps aside.)*

MR. HARE: Well, guess I'll be going now. I feel lots better. *(Starts moving off.)* Thanks for the ride.

MR. LEOPARD: Like a horse! *(Realization hits; he throws Mrs. Leopard a look and tears off, chasing Mr. Hare with a roar. Both exit in chase. Mrs. Leopard exits slowly shaking her head.)*

CURTAIN

GIANTS

by

SYD HOFF

is book **Giants and Other Plays for Kids**

GIANTS

CHARACTERS

Classroom of elementary school children.
The teacher.

SETTING

A classroom.

(Two children are standing on chairs or stools.)

FIRST CHILD: We're giants.

SECOND CHILD: Great big giants.

FIRST CHILD: We can see over trees and mountains.

SECOND CHILD: And tall buildings.

(Three more children enter and listen.)

FIRST CHILD: Hooray for us giants.

SECOND CHILD: We're not afraid of anybody.

TOGETHER: Hooray! Hooray!

THIRD CHILD: May we be giants, too?

FOURTH CHILD: May we?

FIFTH CHILD: *Please?*

FIRST CHILD: No, you're too small.

SECOND CHILD: You're too little.

FIRST CHILD: To be a giant, you must be big.

SECOND CHILD: Big like us.

THIRD CHILD: Then we'll get big.

FOURTH CHILD: Big like you.

FIFTH CHILD: Just you watch and see.

(They run off, return with chairs and stools, which they mount.)

THIRD CHILD: There! Now we're big.

FOURTH CHILD: Big like you.

FIFTH CHILD: Now we're giants too.

FIRST CHILD: Hooray for us giants.

SECOND CHILD: We're not afraid of anybody.

ALL: *Hooray! Hooray!*

(Footsteps are heard in the distance, getting louder and louder.)

FIRST CHILD: Shhhhhh! What's that?

SECOND CHILD: It sounds like footsteps.

THIRD CHILD: Coming closer and closer.

FOURTH CHILD: Maybe it's a giant.

FIFTH CHILD: A *real* giant!

FIRST CHILD: Ooh! What should we do?

SECOND CHILD: Let's make a run for it.

THIRD CHILD: Let's run before the giant sees us.

FOURTH CHILD: Before it's too late.

FIFTH CHILD: Before he eats us up!

FIRST CHILD: No, let's stay right here. Maybe the giant will think we're real giants too, and leave us alone.

FIRST CHILD: Shhhhhh! Here's the giant now.

(Enter the teacher or counselor.)

GIANT: *(Sniffing.)* Fee, fie, fo, fum! Yummy, yum, yum! I smell little children I can eat for my supper.

FIRST CHILD: We're not children, Giant.

SECOND CHILD: We're not children at all.

THIRD CHILD: We're giants.

FOURTH CHILD: Giants like you.

FIFTH CHILD: Just like you.

GIANT: Hmmmm . . . so I see. You're much too big to be children. Oh, well, if I can't eat my supper, I may as well go to sleep. That's what I always do on an empty stomach.

(The Giant falls asleep. He puts his face in his hands and closes his eyes.)

FIRST CHILD: The giant is asleep.

THIRD CHILD: Let's run away now.

FOURTH CHILD: Run for our lives.

FIFTH CHILD: Run while we can.

FIRST CHILD: No, no! The giant might awaken and catch us. I have a better idea. Listen.

(He covers his mouth as if whispering, and they lean forward as if to listen.)

SECOND CHILD: That's a good idea.

THIRD CHILD: A great idea.

FOURTH CHILD: Let's do it, quickly.

FIFTH CHILD: Before he awakens.

(They get down off their chairs and push them out of sight, then tiptoe back, forming a circle around the giant.)

FIRST: *(Whispering.)* You know what to say. *Now!*

ALL: Wake up, giant! Wake up! Look! Look! Look at us!

GIANT: *(Opening eyes.)* Wh-what is it?

FIRST CHILD: A terrible thing has happened to us.

SECOND CHILD: A giant shrinker came along and put a spell on us.

GIANT: A giant shrinker?

THIRD CHILD: Yes, he made us small.

FIFTH CHILD: But we're *still giants.*

GIANT: *(Scratching his head.)* Oh, what a terrible thing. Look at you! Why, you have shrunk to the size of children!

FIRST CHILD: The giant shrinker didn't notice you because you were asleep.

SECOND CHILD: But he may come back.

THIRD CHILD: You'd better get away fast.

FOURTH CHILD: Before he comes back.

FIFTH CHILD: Before he makes you shrink, too.

GIANT: Oh, yes! Yes! I'd better get away fast, before the giant shrinker returns. Thanks, thanks, all you giants, for saving me. *(He hurries off.)*

ALL: Hooray! Hooray! It worked! It worked! The giant is gone! We're saved! We're saved!

FIRST CHILD: It was fun being giants.

SECOND CHILD: But let's not be giants anymore.

THIRD CHILD: Let's be ourselves.

FIFTH CHILD: Just the way we are.

FIRST CHILD: I'm so hungry I could eat a giant.

SECOND CHILD: A giant ice cream cone.

THIRD CHILD: Or a giant hot dog.

FOURTH CHILD: Or a giant hamburger.

FIFTH CHILD: Hooray for giants!

FIRST CHILD: Hooray for us!

ALL: Hooray! Hooray!

CURTAIN

THE THREE LITTLE KITTENS

by

JUNE BARR

THE THREE LITTLE KITTENS

CHARACTERS

1st Little Kitten
2nd Little Kitten
3rd Little Kitten
Mother Cat

SETTING

Back yard.

(At Rise: Three Little Kittens come running through gate at stage left.)

1ST KITTEN: Oh, oh! We're three nice Kittens.

2ND KITTEN: But we've lost our mittens! *(All hold up hands for each other to see.)*

3RD KITTEN: I'm going to cry! Mee-ow, mee-ow!

2ND KITTEN: *I'm* going to cry! Mee-ow! mee-ow!

3RD KITTEN: Oh, me, oh, my! Mee-ow! mee-ow! *(Mother Cat comes out of door, onto porch.)*

MOTHER CAT: What is it, what's happened, my dear little Kittens? What makes you wail and cry?

1ST KITTEN: Oh, Mother dear, we sadly fear— *(Breaks into sobs.)* Mee-ow, mee-ow!

2ND KITTEN: That we have lost our mittens! *(All hold out hands.)*

MOTHER CAT: What! Lost your mittens? You naughty Kittens! Then you shall have no pie!

KITTENS: *(Wailing loudly.)* Mee-ow, mee-ow, mee-ow!

MOTHER CAT: *(Crossly, shaking finger at them.)* Unless you find those good warm mittens, then you shall have no pie! *(Goes in house and bangs door.)*

1ST KITTEN: Mee-ow, mee-ow! I want some pie!

2ND KITTEN: And so do I! Mee-ow, mee-ow!

3RD KITTEN: *(Stops crying.)* Let's be good Kittens! *(Others stop crying and look at him.)* We'll *find* our mittens!

1ST AND 2ND KITTENS: *(Joyfully.)* Then we can have some pie! *(All run off through gate at left. Mother Cat comes out with broom and carefully sweeps porch and steps, humming to herself. Kittens come running back through gate.)*

1ST KITTEN: *(Breathlessly.)* Oh, Mother dear—

2ND KITTEN: *(Holding up mittens.)* See here! See here!

3RD KITTEN: See! We have found our mittens! *(All begin to dance around crazily, waving mittens.)*

THREE KITTENS: *(Sing-song.)* We've found our mittens, we've found our mittens!

MOTHER CAT: *(Smiling.)* Well, put on your mittens, you silly Kittens!

KITTENS: *(Pulling mittens on hastily.)* And may we have some pie?

MOTHER CAT: *(Amused.)* Yes, yes! Now you may have some pie! *(She goes into house, and Kittens sit on steps like good little Kittens.)*

1ST KITTEN: Purr, purr! We'll have some pie!

2ND KITTEN: Purr, purr! We do love pie. *(Mother Cat comes from house with three plates with piece of pie on each, and hands them to Kittens. They set them on steps or else hold them on lap.)*

MOTHER CAT: There. You've been good Kittens, and found your mittens, so there's your piece of pie.

KITTENS: Oh, thank you, thank you, Mother dear, for we do love your pie! *(Mother Cat goes into house, and Kittens eat pie eagerly.)*

1ST KITTEN: *(Looking at mittens.)* Oh mee-ow! mee-ow! Look what I've done!

2ND KITTEN: *(Looking at his mittens.)* Oh, mee-ow! You're not the only one! *(3rd Kitten looks at his mittens, and all howl together.)*

MOTHER CAT: *(Appearing in doorway.)* What is it now?

1ST KITTEN: Oh, Mother dear—

2ND KITTEN: We greatly fear—

3RD KITTEN: That we have soiled our mittens!

MOTHER CAT: *(Gathering up their plates.)* What! Soiled your mittens! You naughty Kittens!

1ST KITTEN: We soiled them eating pie! *(All continue to wail. Mother Cat goes into house, reappears with pail of water. Takes tub from nail on side of house.)*

MOTHER CAT: Get up, get up, you naughty Kittens! *(All jump up and follow as she comes down steps and takes tub to center stage, where she pours water into it. She goes to porch and gets washboard and puts it in tub.)*
You'll have to wash those dirty mittens, or you'll get no more pie!

KITTENS: We will!

1ST KITTEN: I'm first! *(Puts mittens into tub and starts to scrub while Mother goes back into house with her pail.)*

3RD KITTEN: We'll wash them clean as any mittens you've ever seen! *(1st Kitten washes mittens briefly, wrings them out and goes to clothesline and hangs them up with pins from box.)*

2ND KITTEN: *(Putting mittens in tub.)* I'm next! I'm next! I love to scrub! Oh, rub-a-dub-dub!

ALL THREE: Rub-a-dub-dub! *(2nd Kitten finishes mittens and goes to hang them while 3rd Kitten puts his mittens in tub.)*

3RD KITTEN: We'll wash them all clean, and hang them to dry, and you'd never guess that we ate any pie! *(Finishes his and goes and hangs them up. All Three dance back and stand near steps.)*

ALL THREE: Oh, Mother dear, come here, come here! *(Mother Cat comes to door.)*

1ST KITTEN: We've washed our mittens!

ALL: We've washed our mittens!

MOTHER CAT: Washed your mittens! *(Coming down steps, she hugs them.)* You darling Kittens!

ALL: Purr, purr! Purr, purr!

MOTHER CAT: Hush! I smell a mouse close by! *(Starts looking around under steps and porch, with Kittens following.)*

1ST KITTEN: Hush, hush!

2ND KITTEN: *(Softly.)* Mee-ow, mee-ow!

ALL: We smell a mouse close by! Mee-ow, mee-ow, mee-ow! *(All are searching around porch and steps.)*

CURTAIN

CPSIA information can be obtained at www.ICGtesting.com
Printed in the USA
LVOW120958070912

297674LV00004B/1/P

9 780312 079734